"Mortician Quinn McFarland may work with the dead every day, but she's never been so close to murder. A blood sister oath with dangerous repercussions, a warning delivered with a dying breath, a journey into the dark underbelly of coastal Texas... Saralyn Richard's *Bad Blood Sisters* has suspense and surprises aplenty. A gripping story of a woman wrenched from the safety of her life, and her race to reclaim it."

—Tessa Wegert, author of *Death in the Family* and *The Dead Season*

"A delicious five-star mystery served with a side of nail-biting suspense and a dash of romance for dessert. Genre-smashing goodness!"

—Avanti Centrae, international bestselling author of the VanOps Thrillers

"You won't be able to put it down until the last twist is turned."

—Terry Shepherd, author of the Jessica Ramirez Thrillers

"After one delectable taste, you'll devour the rest of this cleverly plotted, neatly tied-up book in one sitting. Magnifique!"

—Laurie Buchanan, author of the Sean McPherson Novels

"An enticing story right from the get-go. Saralyn Richard has crafted one heck of a mystery. She effortlessly blends suspense with intrigue, turning up the heat as the story progresses. A well-plotted tale of what happens when a fifteen-year-old secret and pledge to keep quiet comes back to haunt Quinn McFarland. Put *Bad Blood Sisters* at the top of your must-read list!"

—Kathleen Kaska, author of the Sydney Lockhart Mysteries

"A perfect blend of wit, fun, and intrigue! *Bad Blood Sisters* is a must read.

—Debra H. Goldstein, award-winning author of the Sarah Blair Mysteries

"A tense, suspenseful novel about engaging characters. Will Quinn lose her life and a chance at happiness because of a fifteen-year-old secret?"

—Allison Brook, author of the Haunted Library Mysteries

Also by Saralyn Richard

A Murder of Principal

A Palette for Love and Murder

Murder in the One Percent

Naughty Nana

BAD BLOOD SISTERS

SARALYN RICHARD

Encircle Publications
Farmington, Maine, U.S.A.

Paperback ISBN 13: 978-1-64599-320-9
Hardcover ISBN 13: 978-1-64599-321-6
E-book ISBN 13: 978-1-64599-323-0
Kindle ISBN 13: 978-1-64599-324-7
Large Print Paperback ISBN 13: 978-1-64599-322-3

Cover design by Christopher Wait
Cover photographs © Getty Images

Published by:

Encircle Publications
PO Box 187
Farmington, ME 04938

info@encirclepub.com
http://encirclepub.com

For David and Karen—

This one's for you.

"The past is dead and buried. But I know now that buried things have a way of rising to the surface when one least expects them to."
—Dan Simmons, *Prayers to Broken Stones*

"Not everything buried is actually dead. For many, the past is alive."
—Louise Penny, *Bury Your Dead*

"There is no place for secrets in sisterhood."
—Erin Forbes, *Fire and Ice: The Kindred Woods*

"I love you with everything I am. For so long I wanted to be just like you. But I had to figure out that I am someone too, and now I can carry you, your heart with mine, everywhere I go."
—Ava Dellaira, *Love Letters to the Dead*

Chapter One

Quinn's family always joked about death, but that summer, death stopped being funny. For one thing, Quinn's older brother, Jack, was desperately ill with advanced juvenile diabetes and high blood pressure. The only thing that could save him was a kidney transplant. They'd been waiting since September, almost a year, and now he was at the top of the list, but still waiting. The hot, humid summer was the hardest time for Jack, and that summer had been the worst.

Preparing bodies in the family mortuary business required more physical exertion than Jack had been able to manage, so he'd moved from the "beauty parlor" to the "greeting parlor," mainly a desk job, and Quinn had picked up the slack.

Then, late on the evening of July 4, Quinn was watering the orchids she kept in a mini-greenhouse window above her kitchen sink, when her parents called. Jack had received the word they'd all been praying for—a kidney was available for transplant at the Texas Transplant Center at the local medical branch.

"You'll have to stick around and take care of whatever comes in," Quinn's father said, his voice grim. "I hope you're okay with that."

Quinn was more than okay. She wanted to be with the family, but they had rehearsed this event. She knew her role. When they'd discussed it, Jack, himself, had assigned her funeral home duty, ruffling her hair and murmuring, "Just so long as it's not *my* body you'll be preparing."

Too keyed up to go to bed now, Quinn threw on a T-shirt, shorts, and running shoes. Calvin, her West Highland terrier, perked his ears and leaped about, his tail wagging at the prospect of a late-night outing. Leash, dog, keys, and flashlight—Quinn thought of taking her cell phone along. Maybe talking to Josh, the guy she'd been dating for five months, would alleviate the tension she was feeling.

At the last minute, she decided to leave the cell phone at home. It was after ten-thirty, and Josh was on call at the hospital. He'd just started his fifth year of residency in general surgery. They had a date for the next night—hopefully, Quinn would have good news to share about Jack by then.

Quinn leashed the dog and locked the door behind her, taking off down the steps and into the thick, balmy night. The other houses on the block seemed darker and quieter than usual. The town's fireworks display was over now, but traces of gunpowder smells and occasional pops were enough to put Calvin on alert. Quinn had lived in this neighborhood for more than two years now, but, aside from the people on either side of her and the family across the street, she hadn't made friends. Calvin sniffed around, lifted his leg a few times, and stared at Quinn for direction.

"Want to go for a run?" she asked.

Hearing the "R-word," the little guy spun in a circle and sped down the block at a brisk trot. Quinn's longer legs matched the pace set by his shorter ones, and soon the pair were enveloped by the warm, moist air, the buzzing of insects, and the perfume of oleanders.

Halfway into the next block, Calvin pulled up short, ears high, like triangular antennae. Growls turned into yaps, and the dog yanked at his leash. Something beyond the bushes had captured his attention. It might've been another animal, a possum or a coyote, or even a squirrel. Or maybe something more sinister. There had been a rash of burglaries mentioned in the local news lately. Cold prickles lifted the hair on the back of her neck, and Quinn regretted having left her phone behind.

"Let's go home," she whispered, jerking the leash back. The little dog followed her cues, and the two of them retraced their steps, jogging up the wooden steps and entering the cool, quiet house. Calvin headed straight for the water dish, and Quinn went to the back of the house to wash her face and neck, and check for messages. Seeing none, she set the phone in the charger on the nightstand. She poured herself a glass of apricot-flavored fizzy water and took it into the bathroom with her. After taking a tepid shower and brushing her teeth, she donned her soft cotton nightshirt, turned out the lights, and climbed onto the queen-sized bed. Too warm to get under the covers, she lay on her back, eyes closed, imagining a sort-of prayer for her brother. Jack was still young, just 34, and she would soon be 30. Wasn't this too young to have to deal with kidney failure and organ transplants?

Not for the first time, Quinn considered how time seemed to speed by faster these days. If Jack's life, or even hers, were to end now, what imprint would each of them have left on the world? Neither of them married, no children, and except for working in death services, what had either of them accomplished?

Quinn had told her second-grade teacher she was going to be a doctor. Even at the age of seven, she'd wanted to work on the living side of things. What had changed her mind, she wondered now? How had all her aspirations evaporated into the salty Gulf Coast air?

Eyes closed, Quinn's thoughts drifted into the past, colorful threads of memories, leading her in a run along the beach. Her last thought before she fell into a troubled sleep was of the summer of '05. Now she remembered. That was how she'd gone off-course. That was the summer she'd been totally absorbed by Ana French.

Chapter Two

Something caused Calvin to jump off the bed and run to the window, howling like the diva at the end of an aria. Quinn startled awake and darted to the window. "Shhhh, Calvin." She rubbed her eyes and peered through the mini-blinds. A full moon lit the landscape, but nothing was there, just cracked slabs of sidewalk, patches of grass, and cars parked along the street. She thought again of the noise that had interrupted their walk last night. "Whatever you heard, baby, it's gone now. We can go back to sleep." The digits on the alarm clock said 2:37.

Quinn reached for her cell phone and looked for a text from her parents. Sure enough, one had come in about an hour before. Surgery went well. In recovery, then ICU. Planning to stay here till we can see him. Sleeping in waiting room. More later.

She exhaled, and a tightness in her chest uncurled. Jack might have a long recovery, but the first big hurdle was over. If she weren't so tired, she'd pour herself a celebratory drink. She couldn't wait to tell Josh. Maybe she should text him now. Then again, he might be in a middle-of-the-night surgery, or sleeping on a cot at the hospital. The good news could wait until morning.

As long as she was up, she trudged to the bathroom. She'd no sooner taken a sip of water than Calvin called her back to the window with a whimper and a bark. Again, she split the space between two slats and gazed out. This time something scraped against the plastic garbage can, out of her sight, around the corner. Maybe a squirrel or a possum? But would a squirrel be attracted to an empty garbage can? Pickup had just been today—or yesterday.

It wasn't like Calvin to be such a scaredy-cat, er—scaredy-dog. First on their walk, and now, in the middle of the night. Maybe she should pay more attention. Calvin was the smartest dog she'd ever owned, and he was totally protective of her.

Quinn bent to pick Calvin up, and he licked her face. "Wish you could tell me what you're smelling or hearing, buddy." Carrying the little guy, she made sure all the doors and windows were locked, and she set her rarely-used burglar alarm. Returning to bed, she checked her cell phone again, and lodged it next to her pillow. She climbed under the covers and rolled over on her side. Calvin circled around and nestled against her spine. Every muscle in her body screamed for sleep, but her mind was on high alert.

* * *

The next day arrived quickly. Quinn's cell phone, lying next to her head, chirped like a nest of hungry baby robins, the tone she had selected, because she thought it was cute. Now it annoyed her out of a restless sleep and reminded her about Jack.

Of course, it wasn't Jack, and it wasn't her parents either. It was the county morgue. "Cripes," she said, swiping her finger to take the call.

"Sorry to call this early," Sylvia's familiar raspy voice said.

"'S'okay," Quinn said, glancing at the time—6:35. "You need us to pick up a body?"

"Yah," the medical examiner replied, between what sounded like chomps of gum. "Worked through the night on this gal. Autopsy and lotsa toxicology. Released by next of kin to your place."

Quinn glanced at her hands, wondering if she'd be able to work all day and give herself a manicure before her date with Josh. "Female? What's her story? Did she come from the hospital?"

Calvin yawned and stretched on the bed, while Quinn waited for a response.

"In a roundabout way, *tch-tch*. Blunt head trauma. Taken to hospital, alive. Police case thereafter. Arrived here 'bout nine p.m. Now she's ready for your magic touch."

Quinn stopped herself from saying something flippant, like, "I'm a mortician, not a magician." Police cases were traditionally the most difficult to prepare, and she wasn't looking forward to working on the poor woman, especially with so few hours' sleep. Instead, she said, "Okay, I'll send our guys over to pick her up. What's the name of the deceased?"

Sylvia smacked her gum. She always chewed strongly-flavored gum during and after autopsies. She'd taught Quinn to do the same when embalming. It cleared the sinuses and signaled the brain to focus on something more pleasant. "Sorry. Trying to talk around a big glob of spearmint. Her name is Ana Renfroe."

Quinn's mouth went dry, and she almost dropped the phone. "W-what did you say?" she asked. She must have misheard. There was no way Sylvia had said Ana Renfroe.

"Ana R-E-N-F-R-O-E. *Tch-tch.* Just about your age—29. Ya know her?"

The intake of breath was sharp. "Yeah. I know her. And I know her next of kin, too. She used to be my best friend. Her name then was Ana French."

Chapter Three

"Quinn? Hey, Quinn? What kind of a name is that?" We were on the playground at recess, waiting our turn to dash into the double Dutch jump rope game. A sandy-haired girl, with braided pigtails and a voice like a foghorn, poked me with her index finger.

Caught off-guard, I couldn't think of an answer. Instead, I concentrated on the rhythmic slap-slap of the ropes on concrete.

"Did you hear me?" Ana shouted. "I asked you about your name."

Before I could respond, a shove from behind threw me squarely into the center of the jump rope game, almost knocking Cathy R down, and causing the white cotton ropes to pool around our ankles.

"Why'd you do that?" I yelled at the back of Ana's head. She was already skipping away, toward the school steps. "You ruined the game."

* * *

The memory caused Quinn's eyes to sting as she waited at the funeral home for Rory and Zeke to bring the body in. Unanswered questions and unnamed emotions were roiling in her mind, and a cold, sharp stone sat in her throat, motionless, no matter how many times she swallowed.

Ana, she thought. *Ana is dead.* She touched the spot where the silver friendship necklace in the shape of a half-heart used to sit. She hadn't worn it in over two decades, but right now it burned on her chest.

She wished she could talk to someone about this. Just uttering the words, *Ana is dead*, might alleviate the burden. But her parents were sleeping after a stressful night. Taking the responsibility of work off their shoulders was the best gift she could give them right now—she wouldn't do anything to negate that. Josh was probably sleeping, too. One of the unstated rules of their relationship was to let *him* contact *her* on days after being on call. And

Jack, who would understand her feelings most, since he was around during the Ana years, was in ICU, making friends with his new kidney.

Maybe some music would help. Quinn put a Lady Gaga song on her iPod and hummed along as she wiped down the stainless steel table in the prep room. She popped a piece of spearmint gum into her mouth and started chewing in time to the music. Visions of Ana pressed against her consciousness, but she pushed back. The next few hours would be hard enough.

Quinn had just turned on the ventilation system and assembled her supplies and equipment when the back door opened, and a blast of warm air gushed in. Ginger-haired Rory backed in, rolling the head end of the gurney. His cousin Zeke followed, bearing the foot end. The Angels, as her father called the pair, had worked for the family since they were in high school, maybe twenty years. They had both known Ana.

"Hey, Quinn," Rory shouted, pointing toward her iPod. "What d'ya hear about Jack?"

Quinn stuck her thumb up in an "all-systems-go" sign. "Last I heard he was graduating from recovery to ICU."

"High school football hero like him, still in good shape, he oughta do fine." Zeke kicked the door closed behind him and leaned his weight on the gurney. "You ready to roll, or you want us to put 'er on ice?"

Quinn turned off the music and put the earbuds in the pocket of her Looney Tunes smock. She patted the table and moved out of the way, so they could transfer the body. "Did you guys talk to Sylvia any?" she called out in an attempt to be heard over the thrumming of the ventilation hood. "She give you any special instructions?"

Zeke and Rory exchanged looks from one end of the gurney to the other, before Zeke replied, "You do know who this is, Quinn, don'cha?"

Quinn nodded, ignoring the flip of her stomach.

"I don't 'spect this'll be an easy one to work on. You two had too much history between ya." Zeke wiped his forehead.

"I'll be okay." Quinn grabbed a mask and hung it around her neck. "You can go ahead and put her on the table. Sooner I get started, the better." She chomped on her gum as punctuation.

Another exchange of looks, as they transferred the body to the clean table. "Maybe we'll stick around while you get started. Just in case you need our muscles, ya know," Zeke said. "Good looks and brains, you've got plenty enough. Guts, too."

Emotion welled up inside of Quinn, threatening to erupt at any moment. Touched by the guys' wanting to protect her, she nevertheless cringed inside. Without quite understanding the reason, she desired to be alone with Ana this one last time. She pasted a grin on her face. "Thanks for the offer, but I'm good. See?" She flexed a bicep. "I even ate my spinach today."

Rory grinned. "Okay, Popeye. But we'll be hanging around in front in case ya need us."

Left alone with the corpse, Quinn questioned her thinking. In the ten years she'd worked in the business, and another ten years she'd watched her mom preparing corpses, she had thought herself invulnerable to emotional reactions. But today her heart hammered against her rib cage as she opened the body bag. The face that awaited her, disfigured by violence, was still recognizable. The freckle on the neck, almost matching Quinn's own, made it a certainty. This was a person she'd known forever, once her best friend, then her worst enemy.

Chills prickled Quinn's arms and the back of her neck. Memories unspooled inside her brain.

"I double-dog-dare you," Ana sang, as she turned her eyelids inside out at the cafeteria table.

I was horrified at the ghoulish spectacle, but at the same time fascinated. "No way," I said. "What if your eyelids get stuck?"

"Don't be a wimp." With a brush of her hand, her lids returned to normal, and Ana let out a cackle. "It doesn't even hurt."

After school that day, we walked to Ana's house. "Wait here," Ana said, as we climbed the steps to the front porch.

When Ana returned, she had a needle in her hand. "Let's be blood sisters," she proclaimed. "Always together, through good times and bad."

Yes, I thought, honored to be chosen for the sacred ceremony. I held out my index finger to be pricked. Ana took charge, drawing blood from both of our fingers, mixing the two droplets together in a swirling pattern.

"Lick it," she said, demonstrating how. As I followed suit, she smiled and said, "Now we're sisters. Nothing can ever separate us as long as we live."

Now Quinn swallowed hard. Long ago, certain things had come between the blood sisters. Quinn had put distance between herself and Ana. It would take more fortitude than she'd expected to ignore the memories in order to do this job. Was it her imagination, or were there tears in Ana's eyes, too?

Quinn picked up her instruments. She could do this. She would do her best for Ana's sake. As she started to work, the thought occurred to her that living in a small town, nothing ever ended. Good things, bad things, new news, old news, all of it hovered over the landscape like a heavy, wet fog, ready to enfold her in its smothering embrace.

Why had Brad, presumably Ana's next of kin, chosen to send her body here? More importantly, who had done this to Ana, and why?

Chapter Four

Intent upon her work, and distracted by the music on her playlist, Quinn didn't notice when her father entered the room. He waved the *Daily News* in front of her to get her attention.

"Hi, Dad." She turned off the ventilation blower, removed her mask, and took out the earbuds, setting them on the counter behind her. "How's Jack?"

John McFarland's grin broke forth like fresh water from a dam. "That's what I came in to tell you. He's doing remarkably well. So far he's passed every benchmark with flying colors. Doctor says his youth is in his favor."

Quinn tore off the gloves and protective apron she wore over her smock and hugged her father. He smelled of aftershave and coffee. His arms restored her spirits better than an hour-long sermon, an extra-large Hershey bar, or a bottle of champagne.

When the embrace ended, Quinn's dad examined the work she'd done on Ana. "I'm so sorry you caught this job, baby. Hope it hasn't been too difficult for you. I know how close you and Ana used to be." He glanced at the pile of gum wrappers on the counter—two packs' worth.

For the first time, tears stung, and Quinn's throat thickened. "I guess it's harder than I thought it'd be. I've been trying not to think about the who, just about the what."

"That's wise. Remember how Mom used to pretend she was preparing a Thanksgiving turkey? We all have our coping strategies." He walked around the table, examining Ana from different angles. "Looks like she ran into bad luck or trouble or both, poor girl. I feel sorry for her family. Didn't she marry that guy you dated?"

Quinn walked to the other side of the room, not wanting her father to see the expression that must be on her face. *Yes*, she wanted to scream. *Ana married the only guy I ever loved.* Instead, she spit out the name, "Brad Renfroe." Surprised by the bitter taste of the name on her tongue, she turned back to her father. "Listen, Dad. I don't mind what I'm doing here for Ana, but I really don't want to come into contact with Brad. Can you or Mom do that?"

"No problem. I doubt he'll be hanging around much, though. The police will be keeping him pretty busy."

Quinn straightened and moved back to her dad. "The police?" The words reverberated in her ears.

"Sure." He opened the newspaper, revealing the headline on the local news page: GRISLY MURDER PUTS DAMPER ON JULY 4. Pointing to the article, he read, "Police are questioning the victim's spouse and relatives. Anyone with information related to this crime is encouraged to come forward."

The possibility of Brad being associated with Ana's murder swirled around in Quinn's mind like an out-of-control merry-go-round. Shootings, murders—these things didn't happen to people she knew. Out of nowhere, an image surfaced. Brad and Ana kissing in Quinn's own bedroom, the two of them pressed so tightly against the wall that they looked like one person. Not the sweet and tender kissing that she and Brad enjoyed. These two devoured each other. Quinn had ripped the friendship necklace and Brad's senior ring off and thrown them on the floor before running out of the house.

Her dad broke into her thoughts. "Something else." He turned to the obituary page. "Slow day for death notices—only three. One, a former resident who died in Virginia; one, a ninety-year-old; and Ana here. You know what that probably means?"

Quinn gazed at the page and then at her father's face, as she caught his meaning. "Omigod," she whispered. "Jack might have Ana's kidney."

Chapter Five

At a table for two with a view of the moon, bathing its glow over the Gulf of Mexico, Quinn twirled her wineglass. She had already had two glasses of Chardonnay and was contemplating a third. Leaving her unsettling day behind was a bigger challenge than she'd thought, despite the warm ambience of the restaurant and the exuberant, lop-sided grin of the handsome doctor across the table.

Josh reached for her hand and fixed her with an intense blue gaze. "Your hands are cold. What's going on tonight? Are you worried about your brother, or something else?"

Quinn squirmed, betrayed by the Reynaud's syndrome that restricted blood flow to her hands when she was stressed. Yes, she worried about Jack's recovery, but Ana's death and the flood of memories it released plagued her. She wasn't in the mood to share, but Josh had a way of reading her mind, something she hated about him. Still, his hand was strong and warm. She had a sudden urge to abandon dinner and go someplace where they could sit together in silence, enveloped by the salty ocean breeze.

"Quinn? It's called a date. We're supposed to communicate." Josh squeezed her hand.

The look on Josh's face, eyebrows furrowed and long lashes framing his narrowed lids, nearly broke her heart—so earnest. "I'm sorry. I'm not very good company tonight. Too much on my mind, I guess." Quinn withdrew her hand and rearranged her silverware. "Why don't you tell me about work? Were you involved with Jack's transplant?"

Josh drew a deep breath. "That's a bit of an unfair question, Quinn. You know I can't talk about patient business."

She couldn't help being a little peeved, although she respected Josh's ethics. "Even a little bit? I'm sure you would've wanted to participate in a transplant. They don't happen every day."

Josh shook his head. "All I can say is that I'm on a transplant team for this rotation. Please don't ask me anything more."

The waiter arrived with plates of fragrant hot fried shrimp and cold raw oysters. The aromas of tangy, freshly-cut lemons and spicy cocktail sauce piqued Quinn's appetite. She realized she had skipped lunch, and the wine was no substitute for food. She sat up straighter and decided to cut Josh some slack. What did it matter, really, whether he was there for Jack's surgery or not?

"Never mind about the transplant. I get it. Why don't we dig into this yummy meal? My stomach is howling." Quinn counted the shrimp, drew a line through the food and garnish on her plate, separating them in half, and began to demolish the first six.

Josh plucked an oyster from its half-shell with a cocktail fork and lifted it into his mouth, whole. All the while, he watched Quinn, his eyes crinkled as if from amusement. "That's what I like about you, Quinn. Whatever you do, you're all in." He took a second oyster and held it aloft with the curly-tined fork. "The way you're eating—it would make a great advertisement for the restaurant."

Heat rushed into Quinn's face, as she remembered a similar compliment from long ago. Brad used to call her The Gusto Girl, because of the way she attacked her food. "I guess I should be more lady-like. Maybe I missed that day of Manners 101."

"Not at all," Josh said. "I don't believe in curbing your enthusiasm when it comes to food. I like having a girlfriend who enjoys eating." He swiped at his mouth with his napkin. "Ready to switch?"

Quinn nodded and lifted her plate across the table in exchange for Josh's. "Hope you like the shrimp as much as I did." She squeezed lemon juice onto a plump, moist oyster and prepared to inhale it. "And when did I get promoted to girlfriend?"

"Oh, come on, Quinn. We've been together how many months now? Of course, you're my girlfriend. In fact, I was telling my parents about you when I talked to them last Sunday. They want to meet you."

Surprised at the turn of the conversation, and not too sure how she felt about it, she murmured, "Five."

"What?"

"We've been dating since January, five months, almost six." She washed the oyster down with the last swig of wine. The prospect of meeting Josh's parents both thrilled and frightened her. "What did you tell them about me?"

"Just that you're smart and pretty and funny. And you have the cutest dog ever."

Quinn laughed. She'd always been uncomfortable with compliments. "Calvin adores you, too, you know. Did you tell them what I do for a living?" Suddenly chilled by the air conditioning in the restaurant, she covered her bare shoulders with the fringed wrap, as she waited for an answer.

"Y-ye-es-s. What's wrong with working in a funeral home? Somebody's got to do it, and anyway, what you do is really similar to what I do. We've talked about that."

"We cut people and sew them up, but most people wouldn't see the similarity between a surgeon and a mortician. And I doubt your parents have been hoping you'll bring home a girl who makes her living off of dead people."

"Actually, my parents aren't judgmental. They're just glad I'm dating. When my younger brother got married last year, they gave me 'the talk.'"

"You mean the 'time to think about marriage and kids' talk? I get that, too."

"Yeah. Well, you know what a rat race my life has been, but hopefully after this year, I'll be able to settle down into a steady job with better hours. I hope we can have a more normal relationship, too. In the meantime, my parents want to meet you."

Quinn's mind twirled in a dizzying dance that had little to do with the wine she had drunk and everything to do with Josh's words. Even though he hadn't mentioned the "L" word, weren't they on the brink of that uncharted territory? Wasn't this what she'd been waiting for, stability, security, *love*?

For a moment, all thoughts of Jack, Ana's dead body, and Brad were swept away into a little black box, hidden in a corner of a closet in a remote house, somewhere far away. All Quinn could think about was the fact that Josh represented a second chance, too good to pass up. Maybe this was love. She wasn't sure in the same way as she'd been with Brad, and look how that had turned out. All she knew was love made her vulnerable—and scared.

She took Josh's hand in her own, cradling it and rubbing the palm with her thumb. "I'll be glad to meet your parents," she whispered.

"Great. They'll be here in two days."

Chapter Six

When Quinn returned home after her date with Josh, she realized she'd forgotten to arm her security system. Her living, breathing security system, however, was jumping and yipping as if he hadn't been outside for days. Quinn grabbed the leash from the inside front doorknob and hooked him up. Still, he held eye contact with her and barked.

"Okay, okay. What's got you so excited, Calvin? Did you miss Momma?" She led the dog onto the usual path, where Calvin did his usual business, but something wasn't usual, and Quinn couldn't put her finger on it. Maybe some kids in the neighborhood had been popping off left-over fireworks while she'd been out.

When they returned home, Quinn noticed the air in the house was warmer and more humid than usual. She wondered if the thermostat was on the fritz. Calvin followed his mistress into the kitchen for a treat, but instead of carrying it into the living room, as was his habit, he sat at Quinn's feet and whined, the biscuit between his paws.

Unnerved, Quinn chided herself for forgetting the alarm. She could be careless about things like that. Whatever had happened in her absence to ruffle Calvin worried her. She wished the little guy could talk.

Quinn hadn't checked her phone for hours, since putting it on airplane mode in the restaurant. She swiped it on and saw a text from her dad. Two things: Jack's in private room now. U can visit in a.m. Also, Brad Renfroe called the shop, asking for u. Said urgent. He asked for your phone number, but I told him no.

Quinn shivered. She hadn't spoken to Brad in almost fifteen years, but the old electricity she felt whenever he had called her, looked at her, or touched her had left its scars. Call it a spark, a flame, a magnetic field—whatever, it was primarily a curse. And now, with Ana dead—murdered—Quinn didn't know what to think.

It would be impossible to hide from Brad in this small town. His calling the funeral home was a logical first step, but did he know where she lived? Quinn recalled the late-night walk with Calvin two nights ago, and the noises outside her window. The idea that Brad might be stalking her filled her with a suffocating fear.

She sat at the kitchen table and re-read her father's text. Urgent? Was there really something urgent? Surely Brad wasn't making a play for her, now that Ana was dead. In high school, he'd never been without a girlfriend on his arm and another on deck. She had learned that the hard way. Another thing: why had Brad made arrangements for Ana's services with McFarland's? Was it calculated to give him access to Quinn, herself? And, of course, who killed Ana? The whole mess caused a vile acid to brew in her stomach and rise to her throat. She would really need to remember to arm the security system from now on.

Just when things with Josh were starting to become serious, and a butterfly of hope was fluttering in her heart, this had to happen. Quinn glanced at the clock on the stove—10:35. There was no way she'd be able to sleep unless she calmed herself. She picked up the kettle to make chamomile tea. While the kettle heated up, she examined the orchids in her kitchen window. A few would need repotting soon.

The *whe-ee-ee* of the kettle calmed her. She poured the boiling water into the ceramic teapot, where three fresh bags waited. She closed her eyes and inhaled the mild, sweet-smelling aroma. In the pantry a bin of chocolate-covered biscotti called her name. She chose one and sat down at the kitchen table.

She banished all unpleasant thoughts from her mind. She could deal with those later. Now she wanted to bask in the comfort of her night-time ritual and think of all the blessings in her life: her brother's new kidney, the lovely dinner-date she'd had with Josh, the prospect of meeting his parents—and all that might mean for the future. She sipped and chewed, repeating in her head, "I am a worthy person, and I deserve to be happy."

Refreshed, she was ready to head for bed. Calvin, meanwhile, had not eaten his treat. He still hovered about her heels, turning in circles. She walked past the bed, where Calvin would typically curl up for the night ahead of her. Entering the bathroom, she stopped short. The tiled floor was covered with broken glass. The only window in the room, near the commode, bore a hole in the center, surrounded by jagged glass.

The taste of biscotti rose in her throat. What a mess! Who had broken into her bathroom, and why? She flipped on the light and scooped Calvin into her arms. Setting him on the bedroom floor and telling him to stay in her 'I-mean-business' voice, she turned back to the bathroom. A dark, round object lay on the floor, near the baseboard under the sink. Still wearing her running shoes, she tiptoed to the sink, crunching glass as she stepped. She picked up the solid sphere, wrapped in paper and rubber bands.

Her hands shook as she removed the bands and unwrapped the paper, finding a golf ball at the center. She smoothed the sheet of lined notebook paper out on the countertop. Someone had printed in pencil: *Memories can hurt you. Don't talk, or you'll be next.*

Quinn dropped the note on the counter with a shriek. Her hands burned as if they'd touched a hot stovetop. She stepped backwards, careful not to slip on the glass shards, but bumping into Calvin, who yipped and circled her feet at the edge of the bathroom door. *So this is what you were trying to tell me.*

She reminded Calvin to stay, and dashed back into the kitchen, where she had left her cell phone on the counter. The time showed on its face as she picked it up: 10:57. Should she call Josh? Her dad? The police? While she decided, she ran back to close the door to the bedroom. She took the dog and the cell phone to the couch in the living room, and she punched 9-1-1 into the phone.

What could Josh or her father do for her that she couldn't do for herself? She was almost thirty years old, for heaven's sake, and she'd been working with dead bodies for more than a third of her life. She didn't scare that easily.

Still, she knew a threat when she saw one, and the image of Ana's bashed-in head rose to the surface. Calling the police was the smartest choice. Or was it?

Chapter Seven

Quinn nearly laughed out loud, despite the occasion, when she saw the police officer at her door. Taller and prettier than the last time she'd seen her, and, judging from the smile on her face, now minus the braces on her teeth, there stood DeJuan Hallom's little sister, Mary. Quinn's last memory of Mary was when she'd tried out for cheerleader in the high school gym. Strong and lithe, she had probably been every judge's first pick.

"Hey, Mary. When did you join the police force?"

"Sworn in last month. Working the night shift, so far. I really like it."

Quinn ushered the officer in, shaking her head at the idea of reporting a crime to her friend's little sister. Not that she harbored any biases against Mary. She was probably quite capable and energetic, and Calvin seemed to like her, the way he was sniffing and dancing around. She just made Quinn feel old.

Mary looked around. "You have a break-in tonight?"

"Yes, a broken window in the bathroom." She nodded her head toward the still-closed bedroom door. "Do you want something to eat or drink first?"

"No, thanks. I just had a cup of coffee right before you called in." She offered the back of her hand to Calvin before patting him on the head. "Why don't we check out the room, and then we can talk?"

Quinn picked up Calvin and led the way through the bedroom. Taking in the scene as if through the officer's eyes, Quinn recognized how neat the bedroom was, with the bed still made, the only light coming from the night light nearby. In contrast, the bathroom was a stage of chaos, with bright lights illuminating the thousands of pieces of glass.

"This exactly how you found it?" Officer Hallom asked, before entering the small room.

"Yeah." Quinn set Calvin down on the bed. "Well, except I opened the note that's sitting on the counter. I found it on the floor under the sink."

"You turn on the lights?"

"I must have. It was around 10:45 when I came in here and found this."

The officer read the note without touching it. "Anybody touch this besides you?"

"No. Nobody's been here, except Calvin and me."

"Do you notice anything missing? Any evidence someone came into the house?" When Quinn shook her head, Mary asked, "You didn't hear anything when this happened?"

"No. I was out to dinner. I didn't get home until after ten."

Officer Hallom faced the window and squatted to examine something. So far, she seemed quite professional. She pulled out her cell phone and snapped some photos. "I need to go outside for a few minutes. I want to check a few things. Be right back."

Quinn tidied up the kitchen while she waited. It was late, and she should have been exhausted, but adrenalin was pumping through her veins. She kept turning over in her mind, "Memories can hurt you." Which memories? She'd been mired in memories ever since Ana—"

"Knock, knock." Officer Hallom tapped on the front door frame. She wiped her feet on the welcome mat and entered the living room. "How well do you know your neighbors on this east side of the house?"

"Mr. and Mrs. Tartt? They're in their eighties, I think. They have a Scottish terrier named Duffy who barks a lot."

The officer showed a glimpse of orthodontic masterpiece. "I know. He treated me to a concert. An officer'll come back in the morning to interview his owners and see if they saw or heard anything."

She pointed to the sofa and asked, "Let's sit down and talk a little while."

Quinn nodded. Her eye was drawn to Mary's gun and holster, and she sat up straighter. This was no conversation with DeJuan's little sister.

"I only have a few questions." The officer removed a note pad and a pencil from her shirt pocket. "I'd like to narrow down the time frame when this might have happened. You said you were out—from when to when?"

"I left about 6:45 and got home about 10:15."

"Was anyone with you when you got home?"

"No. I was by myself. But Calvin was acting funny, and I knew something was off. I didn't discover the bathroom until a half hour or so later."

"Any idea who might have sent you that message?"

Quinn thought of Brad's call to the funeral home. Ana's death. Jack's kidney. None of it made much sense here on her sofa so late at night. "Not really."

"You sure? You sound like something is bothering you."

Quinn bit her bottom lip. "Well, you know I work at McFarland's Funeral Home?" Everyone in town knew that. "And yesterday we received the body of my old friend Ana French—Ana Renfroe, that is."

"I'm aware. You think Ms. Renfroe's death may be connected to this threat?"

"Not necessarily. It's just that last night Calvin got spooked on our walk in the neighborhood. Somebody might've been behind the bushes. And later we heard noises outside my bedroom window by the trash can."

"Was last night the first time anything like that happened?"

Quinn nodded. "First time I noticed, anyway."

"So you think someone may have been following you or trying to get your attention?" Hallom took a few notes. "How does this connect to Ana Renfroe, though?"

"I can't say for sure. It just seems like more than coincidence. And what else could the 'you'll be next' mean?"

The officer scooted back a little on the sofa. "Let's talk about the first part of the note. What do you suppose the note-writer meant about memories hurting you?"

Quinn shrugged. "I guess it's supposed to be a threat. That someone doesn't want me to talk about the past." For a few seconds, Quinn flashed to that first night when Ana had dragged her into the backyard behind Ana's house, where they had full view of a neighbor, through her bedroom window, dancing around the room without a stitch of clothes on. *What were we? Eleven? Twelve? Old enough to be giggly and curious, but unaware of what our spying might lead to.* Ana was always pulling Quinn into the next exciting adventure—*You have to come with me. We're blood sisters.*

The officer asked, "Is there anything in particular that comes to mind? Anything that would make someone afraid for you to reveal it?"

Quinn hesitated, and the officer's eyebrows rose, her eyes to probing into Quinn's. "I—I don't know. I'd have to think about it. I'm almost thirty. I've got a lot of memories to consider."

"Well, don't take too long to think. If we're gonna get to the bottom of who's threatening you, we need your help." Hallom put her notepad back in her pocket and pulled out a plastic bag. "I'm gonna take the note and the golf ball with me. I'll check for fingerprints. In the meantime, do you feel safe sleeping here tonight?"

"I was thinking I could board up the window with some plywood and nails

I have in the garage. I could zone out the window and put the alarm on. I should be okay."

"You have an alarm system?" Hallom asked. "Was it on tonight when the window was broken?"

Heat rushed into Quinn's face. "Uh, no. I forgot to set it before I went out. I won't make that mistake again."

"What happens when the alarm goes off? Who gets notified?"

Quinn had to think for a minute. The alarm had been installed before she bought the house. She'd paid the monthly fees, but she hadn't paid much attention to how it would work if she needed it. "I think the alarm goes directly to the alarm company, who notifies the police, but I'm not sure. I've never had an incident like this."

Officer Hallom pursed her lips and then drew them inward. "You think you could board up the window from the inside only, and then find another place to sleep tonight?"

"You don't think I'd be safe with the boarding and the alarm?"

"It's not that. That window's a crime scene. I'd like us to process the outside during daylight hours. Maybe we'll get lucky and find something. Meantime, I'd feel better if you weren't sleeping here."

"I hate to bother anybody at this time of night. But you're right. I might not sleep much, worrying that whoever did this might come back. It won't take me more than a couple of minutes to put up a barrier. Okay if I sweep up the glass, too?" The lateness of the hour was starting to sap her energy. "I guess I could take Calvin to the funeral home for the night. We've got a room downstairs with a cot in it. I wouldn't even have to wake up my parents."

"Don't sweep up the glass. This is considered a crime scene until the evidence techs clear it. Sounds like a good plan to sleep at the mortuary," Hallom said.

"Yeah," Quinn said with a grin. "And the people downstairs won't mind a bit. I couldn't possibly wake *them* up."

Chapter Eight

Well after midnight, Quinn settled into "God's anteroom," as the McFarlands jokingly referred to the room adjacent to the embalming room. Calvin sniffed around before joining Quinn on the camp bed and falling asleep. Quinn was so tired by then, her bones ached, and she couldn't get comfortable. It seemed like a week ago that she had worked on Ana, or dined with Josh. She petted Calvin, trying to soothe herself into sleep, but her mind wouldn't shut off.

At the heart of her worries was who killed Ana, and why? And who had gone so far as to break her window in order to threaten her into silence? Were these two crimes committed by the same person? Was Brad that person?

It had been almost fifteen years since she had been close to Ana, but prior to that, Quinn's whole identity had been wrapped around being Ana's best friend. *Inseparable*, is what everyone said in describing them, and the word fit. Quinn's parents had expressed concern at times, because if Ana wanted to go somewhere or do something, Quinn would pressure them to let her go along, and several times when they'd put their feet down, she'd sneaked out anyway. Her brother Jack used to tease her, too. His pet name for Ana was *Quinn's Twin*. When Quinn and Brad had started going out, Ana had been jealous. Brad had been jealous of Quinn's bond with Ana, too.

Quinn had found herself walking a tightrope between her boyfriend and her best friend, loving them both. She felt she was the luckiest girl in the world to have been chosen by the coolest girl and the handsomest boy in school. Of course, she hadn't stayed for long on that joyous mountain peak. It was less than a year into her relationship with Brad when Ana and Brad had hooked up and dumped her. The downward cliff had been steep and painful.

Worried by her lack of interest in food, school, or friends, her parents had sent her to her aunt's in North Carolina for spring break. When she came back, she'd started working after school in the funeral home. She'd been there ever since.

Now, with Ana's battered body in the next room, and Brad's attempt to contact her pressing into her thoughts, her heart raced down the same old tracks, but triple time. The comforter smelled vaguely of embalming fluid, or was it disinfectant? There was hardly room to turn over without clobbering Calvin. She climbed off the cot and staggered to the tiny powder room, where she filled her cupped hands with water and drank.

Tomorrow she would have to deal with her own bathroom. There she could clean up the damage with a broom and dustpan, but she couldn't sweep it out of her mind. In the end, around 2:00 a.m., the thought of her dinner with Josh, his wanting her to meet his parents, and the passionate goodnight kiss he had given her, put her over the edge into a deep, albeit restless, sleep.

* * *

Early the next morning, her dad opened the door and turned on the light. Calvin growled and jumped off the cot. "There you are!" he said in his booming voice. "I saw your car in the driveway. What's going on, princess?"

"Hi, Dad." Quinn sat up and rubbed her eyes and ran her tongue around her mouth, the dryness left by last night's wine. She still wore the jersey sundress she'd worn to dinner the night before. "Somebody broke the bathroom window at my house, so I needed a place to stay for the night."

Tall and solid, her father moved toward the cot, his heavy eyebrows coming together in a frown. "What? Why didn't you call me? I would've come over to help you."

Quinn rolled over and got up from the makeshift bed, pulling the comforter up and smoothing it out. "I know, but I called the police instead. They've filed a report and said they'd be back this morning to check it out in daylight. They thought I should spend the night elsewhere, so Calvin and I bunked in here. Glad we didn't wake you and Mom."

Her dad's eyes blazed, and, in the morning light coming in from the window, Quinn noticed several gray hairs at his temples. "Neither of us heard a thing on the second floor, but I wish you had woken us. Were you home when this happened, Quinn? Was anything stolen? I don't like this one bit."

Quinn moved in for a hug. "It's okay, Dad. I was out with Josh. Nothing stolen that I could see." She took a breath. She knew she had to tell him about the note, but she dreaded worrying him more.

Pulling back to stare into her face, he said, "Nothing taken? Then why would someone break in?"

Quinn swallowed, her mouth still dry. "There was a note. Actually, a threat."

Mr. McFarland paced furiously around the small space. "Threaten you? Why? What's this all about?" His face transformed from frowning to a piercing stare, to jaw-setting resolve. "Quinn, I hope this doesn't have anything to do with Ana Renfroe and that good-for-nothing husband of hers. I've been worried ever since he called for you yesterday."

Quinn avoided meeting her father's eyes. "I thought of that, Dad, but I can't imagine why Brad would want to threaten me. It's been so many years since I've spoken to him or Ana." She put on her shoes and hooked Calvin's leash onto his collar. "Anyway, I need to take the little guy outside. Then I want to visit Jack, and after, check in with the police, so I can get my broken window fixed. Okay with you if I take the morning off?"

"No problem, honey. But there is one thing more I want to say. Your mom and I never liked your association with Ana—or with Brad." He hesitated and paced several steps. "Neither of them was raised the way we tried to raise you. I know they meant a lot to you back then, but we always worried they would tarnish your reputation—our reputation—in this town." Touching her wrist, as if for emphasis, he said, "And you've done so much better for yourself without them. You've got a profession, a fine, upstanding boyfriend with good prospects. Whatever you do, I hope you'll stay as far away from Brad Renfroe as possible."

Her dad's lecture scorched the place in her heart that had been burned so many years before. Calvin's dancing around to go out was a convenient excuse to leave. Tugged by the locomotive at the end of the leash, she headed through the embalming room to the back door, where Ana's body had come in the day before. "Gotta go," she muttered.

Quinn's father followed her outside. "Something else. I'm going to call my friend, Marty Ramirez, Chief of Police. I don't like the idea of your being threatened. Marty will get on it right away."

Within seconds, Calvin had dragged Quinn to the nearest tree, so she shouted over her shoulder at her dad. "Not necessary. The officer who came out is Mary Hallom. Her brother DeJuan was in the Honor Society with me. She's taking care of it. She works nights, but she said she'd send someone out this morning."

"I'm sorry, Quinn. If it were just a bit of vandalism, I'd leave well enough alone, but a threatening note? I can't let someone's sister control the safety of my only daughter. Sometimes it's not what you know but who you know. And Marty owes me a few favors. I'm going to make sure this gets top priority."

Quinn had been afraid of that, even before she'd called the police last night. That was why she had wanted to handle the matter herself. Once her father got involved, who knew how far or how deep the investigation might go. In fact, it was this very same reason, years ago, that had driven her away from the police in another situation, that had bound her to Ana far more tightly than the blood sister ritual ever had.

Chapter Nine

Even though Jack had been moved to a private room, the protocols for caring for a transplant patient were strict, and visitors were limited, both in numbers and in time. Quinn figured the best time for her to visit would be early. She'd swung by her house to drop off Calvin and make sure the board in the bathroom window was still secure. She changed out of her slept-in sundress, now wrinkled and smelling like a mixture of perspiration and formaldehyde, then decided to shower in the guest bathroom. She didn't take the time to dry her dark, curly hair or put on makeup, though. Jack wouldn't notice, or, if he did, he wouldn't mind.

"Hey, good-lookin'," she said, through the toothy smile she had pasted on. Jack's face was swollen, his complexion a yellowish-white. Bruises lined both arms, from his fingers to the spots where his biceps disappeared into the too-large armholes of his hospital gown. Whatever her expectations had been, she hadn't counted on having her legs turn wobbly. She was used to seeing bodies in all kinds of conditions, but this was her big brother. Even with his illness, he had never seemed anything other than strong, smart, capable Jack. She grasped the rail of the hospital bed to steady herself, and leaned in for a kiss on the cheek.

"About time you came to visit," Jack said, his tone, at least, as playfully sarcastic as normal. "Hope you brought me a chocolate milkshake or two."

Chocolate milkshakes were code for consolation. The McFarland children had them after injuries, dental fillings, or difficult chores in the oppressive heat of the summer. Once Jack had been diagnosed with juvenile diabetes, milkshakes had become few and far between, and Quinn had called the hospital to make sure it was okay to bring one. "Matter of fact," Quinn said, turning to the chair where she had dumped her purse and a bag from Smoothie King, "just happen to have a carob smoothie with me." She removed the tall cup and straw from the bag and pierced the lid. "Breakfast of champions."

Jack closed his eyes as if in prayer before taking the first sip. "Mmmm. Heaven on earth."

While he enjoyed the smoothie, Quinn examined the tubes and beeping machines her brother was hooked up to, her initial queasiness replaced by curiosity. She toured the hospital room. This wing had just opened a few months ago, and the amenities fit more with a luxury hotel than a hospital. "All the comforts of home," she murmured, as she examined the contents of the mini-fridge.

"Ahhhh," Jack exclaimed, "that was great." He took a deep breath and exhaled. "I'm almost ready to get out of here and start living again."

Quinn understood. For the past couple of years, Jack had given up so much in the struggle to stay alive. He and his girlfriend had parted ways, and she had married and had twins. He'd given up bowling and taken up boating. He'd turned out to be a fine fisherman, but that didn't do much for his social life.

As if reading her mind, Jack said, "By the way, your Dr. Josh Brady and his entourage of docs have been checking on me the whole time I've been here. He's a great guy, clearly well-thought-of around here."

"He didn't tell me, but I'd hoped he would watch over your case. He really cares about you—apart and separate from me. I hope he's giving you the royal treatment."

A cloud passed over Jack's face, as if the burst of energy from the milkshake had dissipated, and the routine discomfort had returned, his voice diminished. "How're things at the Last Stop Shop?"

His pet name for the funeral home made her smile. Then Quinn thought about Ana's body, the broken window, and sleeping in the ante-room. She didn't want to bother Jack with any of these things. The least she could do was carry her end of the business and take as many concerns away from her brother as possible. "You know, death goes on."

"I'm going to let you rest," Quinn said, as she cleaned up the trash from the smoothie and blew her brother a kiss. Voices approached in the hallway and hovered outside the door. "Sounds like you're about to be poked and prodded some more."

Quinn started for the door, waving goodbye to Jack, just as the door was pushed open by the leader of a gaggle of white-coated doctors, male and female, tall and short, all fairly young-looking. In the center of the group, Josh looked away from the colleague he was listening to and into the eyes of Quinn.

Stunned for a second at this unexpected encounter, Quinn remembered she had no makeup on. Too late to run, she ran her fingers through her shiny curls and muttered something unintelligible, even to her own ears.

If she had turned fifteen shades of red, Josh didn't seem to notice, or to care, as his personal and professional lives collided. His eyes gleamed and the corners of his mouth turned up, as he winked at Quinn. His face was a package with a bow.

"Excuse me a moment," Josh said, as he stepped away from the group and cupped Quinn's elbow in his hand. "I'm going to have a word with the patient's sister." He walked Quinn to the elevator, where they stood for a long moment, gazing into each other's eyes.

"I didn't know I'd run into you," Quinn said.

As if absorbing her discomfort, Josh said, "You look gorgeous, as always. Wish we could go somewhere to be alone right now."

Quinn was warmed by the fact that Josh's expression matched exactly the way she felt, squishy inside. She'd settle for a broom closet just to be able to kiss him. But restraint had always been a part of their relationship. "Thanks for taking care of my brother." She touched the lapel of his lab coat. "He told me you've been checking on him."

"He's a good guy, a great patient. Glad to attend to him." As if reminding himself that the great patient awaited, he added, "Gotta go now. Talk to you later?"

Quinn pushed the elevator button, resigned to admiring Josh's backside as he dashed back down the hallway. When he turned into Jack's room, he waved, and she could have sworn he mouthed the words, *I love you.*

Chapter Ten

When Quinn arrived at home after visiting her brother, there were three police cars parked, one in her driveway and two on the street. *Daddy strikes again.* The seesaw of emotions inside her rushed at full tilt. On the one hand, she welcomed the police support. On the other, she dreaded what that support might lead to.

The sun bore down with the steady force of a celestial radiator, but an occasional breeze made it bearable. Three male police officers stood near her next-door neighbor, who, glistening with perspiration, pointed to her own upstairs window with one hand and played an aggressive tug-of-war with her dog's leash with the other.

A pang of regret for inconveniencing her elderly neighbor stabbed at Quinn, as she parked her car across the street. Quinn climbed out and strode toward the Tartts' yard, relieved not to see Chief Ramirez among the officers. She was certain, though, that the chief's authority was behind the swift service and attention. She had thought Mary Hallom's report to be sufficient, but her dad wouldn't leave it at that.

Quinn tried to catch the conversation as she approached the group, but Duffy's bullish bark drowned out the words, as he pulled in the direction of her boarded-up bathroom window with all the strength in his compact, burly body. His woofing was echoed by a sonata of Calvin's from inside.

"Hello, Quinn," Mrs. Tartt called out, and the blue-uniforms turned to stare. "I was just telling these officers that Duffy was barking louder than all the bagpipes of Scotland last night around nine-fifteen. I was helping the mister get situated in bed with his hot tea and honey." She pointed to the same second story window. "I looked from that window, and I could make out a dark figure right about there." She pointed to the patch of shade where grass wouldn't grow, about four feet from the exterior of Quinn's bathroom.

Quinn looked from one face to the next, not wanting to interrupt whatever questioning was in progress. Wouldn't it be amazing if Mrs. Tartt could identify the person who had threatened Quinn? She doubted it would be that easy.

The shortest of the male officers introduced himself and the other two officers to Quinn. "Are you Miss McFarland, the owner of this house?" When Quinn nodded, he said, "We're about to finish up talking to your neighbor here, and we'd like to interview you in a few minutes. Is that okay?"

"Sure," she replied, suppressing the urge to salute. Quinn took the hint. She wasn't needed here, and, besides, she wanted to get Calvin out for a walk before he strained his vocal cords barking at Duffy. She could use a few minutes to get her mind straight before talking with the officers. Her thoughts jumped around, and her stomach was knotted into a pretzel. Talking with Mary last night had been simple, but now, in the light of day, the prospect of a three-on-one interview set an acidic fountain flowing.

No need to worry, nothing to hide, she repeated to herself. Still, Ana's death had unnerved her in a way she never expected. In the years since she and Ana had parted ways, she had taught herself to forget. Now someone threatened to topple the insulating armor she wore. Was it Brad?

Quinn took Calvin for a spin around the block, returning to find two of the three officers getting into their squad cars and leaving. Relieved that only the short officer remained, standing on her stoop, she jogged to the steps, Calvin in tow. "Sorry to keep you waiting."

"No problem. The other guys had to take a call. Hope you don't mind. We can do this at the station if you'd prefer the company." Beads of sweat dotted the man's forehead, a few becoming rivulets down his face.

Maybe the officer was offering an alternative to a one-on-one interview out of kindness, but Quinn preferred being on her own turf. "C'mon in. Let me get you a cold drink." Quinn unlocked and opened the door. A blast of cool air enveloped her. She ushered the officer, whose nameplate said Sgt. Schmidt, into the living room, where she had sat with Mary a few hours earlier.

"Just some ice water'd be fine." Instead of sitting, he walked around the small room. "Mind if I take a look at the bathroom? Back here?" He pointed in the direction of the bedroom, visible across the hall.

"Go ahead. I haven't cleaned it up. I hope the evidence techs come soon. I'd like to get the window people here this afternoon."

Quinn met the officer in the bathroom with two tall glasses of water, the ice cubes clinking as she handed one over. He took a long, slow swallow, draining half the glass. "Thanks. I needed that." He glanced around the bathroom. "Anything missing? Any sign that the vandal entered the house?"

"No," Quinn said, having taken a drink of her own. "Just the note. Did you see it?"

"I did. How 'bout we sit down somewhere, so we can talk about that note?"

Quinn led the way back to the living room. Her throat constricted, so she took several small sips of water. She sat across from Sgt. Schmidt and stared at her hands. She wouldn't volunteer anything about the past, unless she had to.

"Ms. McFarland, who might've thrown that golf ball and note into your bathroom?"

"I was hoping *you'd* be able to tell *me*," Quinn said, still looking at her hands.

"You have any enemies? Boyfriends you've broken up with, people you've had run-ins with?"

Quinn couldn't help thinking about Ana and Brad. But that was so long ago. "Not really."

As if he were a mind-reader, Schmidt said, "How 'bout Ana and Brad Renfroe? Any relationship there? You're about the same age, grew up together here in town."

A quick intake of breath probably gave away her nervousness, but she couldn't control herself. "I used to know them both. But that was a long time ago."

"Ms. McFarland—"

"You can call me Quinn. I haven't spoken to either of the Renfroes in ages. Other than the fact that Ana's been killed, I don't see—"

"Okay, Quinn. The murder's exactly why I'm asking you about the Renfroes. Listen, we're trying to find out who's threatened you. Your neighbor saw a tall, broad-shouldered man outside your window. We're looking for evidence, analyzing the note, all the usual stuff. But Chief Ramirez wants this case to be priority, and the Renfroe murder, too. To do that, we need your help."

When Quinn spoke, her voice sounded tinny, pitiful to her own ears. "What do you want me to do?" Her heart was pounding a rhythmic, *take care, take care*. "How can I possibly help?"

The sergeant leaned forward, elbows on knees. "Y'see, we don't have that many murders in this town, so when someone is killed, and the next day someone who knows the victim is threatened, we can't dismiss this as a coincidence. We believe the two crimes are linked. We need your help to figure out how."

A chill caught Quinn, and she shivered. She thought she had moved on from Brad and Ana long ago, yet now she was apparently tied up in some dangerous situation with them, as though no time had passed at all. She didn't want this! Still, there was no use in playing games with the police. She had invited them into her home last night, and her father had cemented their role in protecting her. She took another sip of water. "Okay, I'll do my best to help."

Schmidt nodded and his lips drew into a half-smile, revealing pink gums. "Okay, you say you haven't spoken to the Renfroes in years. But surely you've crossed paths here in town. When was the last time you saw either of them?"

On safe ground for the moment, Quinn said, "I might have bought groceries or pumped gasoline at the same time here or there, and people are always trying to talk to me about Ana or Brad or both, but I assure you, I have avoided all contact with the Renfroes. We aren't friendly."

"What about in the past?"

Why did Quinn suspect Sgt. Schmidt was baiting her? That he knew already about her and Ana? Quinn needed another sip. The glass was only a third full. She'd better conserve the water for whatever was coming. "Ana was my BFF. We were together all the time when we were kids."

"And Mr. Renfroe?"

"Brad was my boyfriend."

Sergeant Schmidt's eyebrows shot up toward his balding pate. He waited for more, and when no more came, he asked, "So, what happened?"

Quinn shrugged. This part was easier to talk about than she'd expected. "The old love triangle. One day I found out my best friend and my boyfriend were a couple."

"I imagine that was hard for you." When she nodded, he said, "Hard to stay in the same small town, too. Who cut off contact?"

"I did, but I don't suppose that broke their hearts. If we did bump into each other, it was uncomfortable, to say the least."

"Have you had any contact with Mr. Renfroe since his wife died?"

Quinn thought about the call Brad had made to the funeral parlor, and the sounds outside her house and in her neighborhood. "Not really. Do you think Brad sent that note through my window?"

The officer's voice turned sharper, definitely less friendly. "Why do you say, 'Not really?' Has there been any contact between you and Mr. Renfroe?"

"My dad took a call from him. He didn't have my number and called McFarland's. I never talked to him, and my dad didn't give him my number."

Schmidt's eyes narrowed to slits. "When was this?"

Quinn's mind flew into a dizzy circle. Was it just yesterday? "So much has been happening. I'm not sure. I think it was yesterday."

Schmidt nodded slightly, folding his arms over his belly. "Can you think of a reason he would be calling you?"

Quinn was about out of water, as well as patience. She wanted to be alone. "I can't. Why don't you ask *him*?"

The sergeant's face reddened. "That's one of our problems, Ms.—Quinn. We are currently unable to locate Brad Renfroe."

Chapter Eleven

After the police had swung by to gather evidence, men from the glass company worked on replacing the broken glass. While they worked, Quinn dove into the back of her closet, looking for her high school scrapbook. Back then, she'd almost thrown it out several times, thinking she would never want to revisit memories that would only make her cry. Right now, she was glad she hadn't. Maybe examining the past would help her process the present.

There it was, on the top shelf in the corner, behind two shoeboxes labeled "strappy sandals." A stepstool enabled her to reach the corner of the scrapbook and wiggle it toward the front. As she brought it down, dust motes sprinkled her face and hair, while anticipation and dread whipped to a froth inside. Maybe this was a mistake, but too late to turn back now.

With a clingy Calvin on her heels, Quinn carried the thick volume to the kitchen table. She dusted it with a couple of bleach-wipes and tossed them in the trash. She washed her hands and face and put the tea kettle on before sitting down to open the scrapbook. Touching the lettering on the title page, she recalled how she'd stenciled the words. The artist in her had wanted the book to be beautiful and happy. She had been so idealistic then, so hopeful. "*The Life and Adventures of Quinn Lea McFarland, January, 2002 –*" written in perfect calligraphy. She had never entered an end date.

The tea kettle's whistle offered a reprieve. Going through the contents of the scrapbook would be difficult. She busied herself preparing a pot of Earl Grey, strong and full of caffeine. The steam and the metallic aroma invigorated her. She could do this.

Before sitting down with her tea, she checked on the glaziers, who were almost finished removing the broken glass. No, they didn't need anything. Quinn was impressed by the easy, efficient, and mostly silent way the two men worked together. They'd probably finish within the hour.

Back to the scrapbook, Quinn began turning pages. There were photographs, newspaper clippings, ticket stubs, notes passed during class, all of the usual souvenirs of a teenage girl's life. The newsprint was already yellowing, a fact that made her feel old.

Here were pictures of Quinn and Ana, washing cars for the Spanish Club fund-raiser, both looking so healthy and fit in their bathing suits. Ana's hair was pulled back in a ponytail, and her tan was already twice as hot as Quinn's. So was the way Ana filled out the top of her bikini. "When you got 'em, flaunt 'em," she loved to say. Quinn, on the other hand, in her tankini, looked like the all-American girl next door, Amy Adams to Ana's Carmen Electra.

As she turned a page, the silver half-heart necklace that she had worn every day for years slipped onto her lap and then to the floor. Quinn bent to pick it up, turning it over to see the engraving: BS/Ana/BF forever. She clasped the tarnished relic in her hand, remembering how wearing it had filled her with a sense of importance. She had belonged to someone. Before Brad, and long before Josh. She had belonged heart and soul to Ana, best friends, but not forever.

More pages with honor roll lists, perfect attendance and science project certificates, report cards. Quinn had been an excellent student with little effort. Her love of science had convinced her to become a doctor. Pretty soon Brad entered the scrapbook. Here was the picture of the two of them, both grinning and dressed in color-coordinated outfits, taken before they left for the first school dance they went to together. The pressed corsage was next to it, desiccated and brown. She recalled how he'd pretended to bite the orchid while they were dancing. Quinn touched the smile on her face in the picture. She had felt like a fairy-tale princess that night.

Louder sounds came from the bathroom. The workers were almost finished. She flipped through a few more pages, noting several pictures of her with Ana, her with Brad, and her with both. Ana had been Homecoming Queen their junior year, and Quinn, a duchess, on the arm of Duke Brad. That had been right before the break-up, when everything had come crashing down, changing Quinn's life forever. Even now, she felt the sucker punch in her gut, looking at her radiant face as she clung to Brad's arm. He and Ana had probably already found their mutual passion, and here she was, impervious to what was only two betraying steps away.

"Ms. Quinn, we're just about finished, if you wanta come take a look." The man with "Felix" on his shirt stood at the window, modeling how easily he could lift and shut the window. He demonstrated how smoothly the lock worked. "I 'magine you'll be wantin' to keep it locked from now on."

"You've done a very nice job," Quinn said. In addition to having a well-functioning window, she had a tidy bathroom. "Do you have an invoice for me? I'll get you a check."

"Nah, Clyde's gonna bill ya. You wanta come look at the outside, too?"

Not wanting to disappoint Felix, Quinn scooped up Calvin and carried him outside so she could examine the freshly puttied window. On the way, she glanced at Mrs. Tartt's upstairs window, wondering whom she had seen in Quinn's yard. The new glass was so shiny, it made the other windows seem dingy. Maybe she'd have time to clean them over the weekend—after Josh's parents left.

A few minutes later, the workmen departed. Quinn let Calvin romp around a little in the yard. She noticed many imprints of shoes in the dirt outside the window. If the note-thrower's prints had been there, they were covered over now. She returned to the kitchen to give Calvin a doggie treat and get ready for work. She started to put the scrapbook back in the closet, when she noticed several envelopes peeking out from the back cover. She knew what these were. She didn't want to touch them, much less read them. Written after a particular night neither of them would ever forget, Ana had sealed them with special red wax and stuck them inside a textbook in the locker they shared. In Ana's bold handwriting, she pleaded with Quinn never to tell a soul what they had experienced. It was a blood oath, and she, Quinn, had to take it.

Quinn should have destroyed the letters, even though they never mentioned specifics. Their mere presence in her scrapbook was testament to the solemnity of the promise she had sworn to keep. She wondered whether Ana had kept her end. Had she told Brad? Had she told anyone? Now that Ana was dead, Quinn might never know.

* * *

That afternoon, after the alarm company rewired the window, Quinn returned to work at the funeral home. It was a slow day, or as the family called it, a dead day. Quinn busied herself with inventorying supplies and rearranging things in the cabinets. There was always something to do. She kept thinking about what Sgt. Schmidt had said about Brad. How could he have been in town, arranging for Ana's body to come to McFarland's, trying to reach Quinn, and then suddenly absent? Had something happened to him, too? Or had he purposely fled to avoid police scrutiny in his wife's murder? Either way, these were things that happened to "other people," not to people she knew.

Without knowing what kind of life Brad and Ana had together, Quinn couldn't speculate on any of it. She wouldn't even try. She had her own life to think about. She wanted to make a good impression on Josh's parents, but she doubted that would happen if they knew everything about her. No one knew, except for Ana, and now Ana was gone.

She wiped the bottom of the storage cabinet under the sink with a vigor that came from too much thinking. The sticky residue yielded to her efforts. Moving on to the drawer where she stored many of her most-used tools, she stood to stretch her back and lunge in both directions.

The door to the "beauty salon" opened, and Quinn put down the cleaning rag. Her mother entered, her stance more regal than proprietary, her lips pursed as tightly as if she had sucked an unripe persimmon.

"Quinn, I hate to disturb you, dear." She floated into the room and gazed directly into her daughter's eyes. "I know you are busy, and you have quite enough on your schedule, but we have two *customers* in the front parlor who wish to speak with you." 'Customers' was her code word for those she considered to be lower-than-middle-class people. 'Clients' was the term she used for the wealthy.

But McFarland's advertising hook was personal service, so when a 'customer' *or* a 'client' asked for something, the McFarland family did their best to find a way to honor any request.

Quinn had a queasy feeling from her mother's demeanor. Why not just say outright who was asking for her? She put down her spray bottle and removed her rubber gloves. She rushed to the bathroom to wash her hands and check her appearance in the mirror. "Who's there, Mom? It isn't Brad Renfroe, is it?"

"No, not Brad. But you're close. It's Mr. and Mrs. French—Ana's parents. They came to discuss arrangements for the funeral, and they refused to leave without talking with you."

Chapter Twelve

Cynthia French, despite the red eyes and slumped shoulders, remained an attractive woman. Petite, with a better-than-decent figure, she wore a sundress that showed off her tan, and she smelled like apples and cinnamon. Sunglasses in a tortoise-shell frame were pushed up on her head, giving her an aged beach-blanket-movie-star look. Quinn's mother wouldn't be caught dead dressing like that, but Mrs. French didn't look half-bad. Except, she twisted a handkerchief in her hands, and she leaned into Mr. French like the Tower of Pisa.

Mr. French, about a foot taller and a good bit wider, had deep crevices in his cheeks and forehead. His eyes moved from side to side, as if he were looking for trouble, instead of having already found it. Handsome, in a craggy-faced sort of way, he had always been kind to Quinn, and he'd adored Ana. She was the Frenches' only child.

Quinn's heart stirred with sympathy for this bereaved couple, and the years of resentment toward Ana lifted. "I'm so, so sorry," Quinn said, as she moved into a three-way hug that seemed as natural as if she were standing in their kitchen instead of in her family's funeral parlor.

Mrs. French held onto Quinn for an extra-long time, and Quinn could feel the silent sobbing inside of the woman. "Why don't we sit?" Quinn said, taking her own seat in the plush wingback chair behind them. Mr. and Mrs. French perched on the adjacent love seat, holding hands. No one said anything for a few moments. What was there to say, really? Quinn felt their pain, but she had lost Ana a long time ago.

Quinn ran her hands back and forth on the arms of the chair. She tried to make her voice as gentle as possible. "My mother said you needed to talk to me."

Mr. French cleared his throat and looked at his wife. "Do you want to tell her, or should I?"

Quinn braced herself. She couldn't imagine what might come next. This felt like an episode of *Tales from the Crypt.*

Mrs. French took a deep breath and said, "I—I will." She played with the handkerchief, untwisting and retwisting it. When she began, her voice was barely audible. "The past year, Ana wasn't herself. She made excuses not to come over. It wasn't like her."

Quinn said, "You used to be so close."

"We still were close, but I knew there was something bothering her. She probably didn't want to worry us, but I worried anyway. I th-thought maybe she'd been trying to get p-pregnant and was having trouble. I'd had trouble, too, so I thought maybe she'd inherited that from me." After a pause and a deep breath, she went on. "Finally, over Memorial Day, she and Brad came over for a little backyard barbecue. They seemed tense with each other."

Quinn tried to picture Ana and Brad having marital problems, but the only image that came to mind was the one in her bedroom, clinging to each other as if they'd been Superglued.

"The next day I insisted that Ana go out for coffee with me. I told her *I* had something important to discuss with *her*. We sat at a back table at Three Brothers, and I brought up the topic of infertility. Turned out I was all wrong. Ana told me she hadn't been trying to get pregnant. In fact, she said she didn't want to burden her daddy and me, but she and Brad were having money problems."

Mrs. French made eye contact with her husband, and he squeezed her hand again. "I-I offered to help, but she thanked me and told me no. 'You and Daddy need your money. We'll figure something out,' she said." Mrs. French lapsed into another silence, apparently lost in her nightmare.

Quinn's hands turned cold, a sure sign of anxiety. She didn't know for sure where this was leading, but she knew the girl at the other half of her heart necklace, and "figure something out" was probably code for some desperate move. Was this what led to Ana's death? Not wanting to hear any more, she stood. "Can I get you some water?"

"Uh—n-no, thanks. Sorry I got lost for a minute. Anyway, Ana wouldn't talk about the money problems any more after that, and I didn't ask. But we never saw Ana and Brad together after Memorial Day, almost six weeks ago. And the last time I saw Ana, she came over to the house for dinner by herself." Mrs. French threw a look at her husband. "She was wearing heavier makeup than usual. The way the light shone on her face during dinner, I could tell she was covering up a bruise on the side of her forehead, near her eye."

Quinn's hands turned into icicles. Was Ana's mom suggesting Brad had abused her daughter? Quinn had known Brad almost as well as she'd known Ana, in some ways, better. Could he have become an abuser? A murderer? "This sounds like something you should be telling the police. I feel truly terrible for Ana, but why tell me?"

"That's just it," Mr. French broke in. "That night at the house, when we confronted Ana about the bruise—" His deep voice cracked, and he made eye contact with his wife.

"I'll answer, dear." It was endearing to see how the Frenches complemented each other. When one faltered, the other rallied. At least they had each other.

Mrs. French sat up and looked Quinn in the eye. "Ana wouldn't tell us how she got the bruise, even though we demanded to know. We kept after her. We told her we were worried that whatever happened might happen again, and worse, but she could be stubborn."

Stubborn and secretive, Quinn thought. She remembered so many scrapes and close calls she and Ana had experienced. How many times had Ana invoked the blood sister oath and demanded that Quinn tell no one whatever crazy thing they had done? The notes at the back of her scrapbook proved it.

"You still haven't answered my question," Quinn said, softening her tone. "Ana and I haven't been close for years. Why are you sharing this with me?"

"Because—at the end of the evening, after all our haranguing and cajoling, and she still wouldn't talk about how she got the bruise, she finally said one thing. 'If something bad happens to me, tell Quinn.' Ana sent us to you."

Chapter Thirteen

Astonishment rose in Quinn's chest and throat, like an unseen hand, squeezing her breath away. This was too much. Bad enough dressing Ana's dead body, seeing her like this after many years of loving her, then hating her. But the threatening note, the call from Brad, and now the eager looks in the sad eyes of Ana's parents? They expected something from her, something they could cling to at this devastating time.

She didn't know how to respond. More was required than good manners or courteous professional behavior. Those would have been easy to deliver. Things were happening too fast. Quinn needed time to process.

Praying her legs would support her body and all the swirling thoughts in her mind, as well, she stood and began pacing around the seating area, her sandals sinking into the plush new area rug. Two pairs of eyes followed her every move and expression.

"I don't know what to say," she said at last. "Ana and I haven't spoken. I-I didn't know anything about her problems with money or Brad or anything else. I wish I could be of help to you, but I have no idea why she mentioned me."

Mr. French stood, as well, his height posing an aspect of authority that hadn't been there before, when Quinn hugged him. "Don't you see, Quinn? Ana was giving us a clue. She knew she might be in danger, and she knew you would have knowledge about that danger. Whatever it is you know, we need to know it, too."

Ana's mother held out her hand, a request to be helped from the loveseat, and her husband obliged. He folded her small body under his arm and held her tightly against him. "Please, Quinn. I'm sure this has come as a shock to you, too, but if you think hard, I'll bet there is something that will come to mind."

Mr. French looked at Quinn with what might have passed for a smile, if his lips hadn't quivered. "We haven't told the police what Ana said—yet. We haven't told anybody. We wanted to come to you privately first."

Great, now I'm being pressured, possibly threatened, by the Frenches, too. Quinn turned away from the couple. She pressed two fingers against the stinging corners of her eyes. While she was contemplating what to say or not say, and how to end this conversation, Quinn heard the clicking of heels on the marble floor behind her. When she turned and saw her mother hurrying toward her, a surge of emotion burst through her. She forced herself not to let it show in her demeanor.

"I hate to break up this conversation, I really do. But we have some important business that you must tend to personally, dear. Your father is waiting for you in the back room." She turned to the Frenches with a smile. "Maybe I can help you?"

Quinn could have set her mother in a chair and carried her around town, so grateful was she to have an excuse to leave. "Of course, Mother." She turned to Ana's parents and considered whether to hug them again, but the vibes weren't there this time. "I apologize for having to leave you. I'll think about what we've talked about. And, again, my deepest condolences." With a slight bow, she fairly skipped toward the back room, leaving her mother with the inquisitors.

When she reached the back room, out of breath and her whole body shaking from tension, she flicked on the lights and blinked. Her father was nowhere to be seen. In fact, there was no one there, not even a "body without the some," as she liked to call a corpse. Her mother had conceived this ruse to interrupt the visit with Ana's parents. But why? Had she been eavesdropping and sensed that Quinn needed to escape? Quinn plopped into the ergonomic rolling chair she used for work, leaning her head back and closing her eyes.

She owed her mother big-time, but the relief would be short-lived. Her mother would, undoubtedly, subject her to a parental cross-examination about what the Frenches had wanted. Quinn had never been good at on-the-spot thinking. The reprieve provided by her mother would be temporary. She was going to have to answer to her mother, Ana's parents, and maybe even the police.

Her head was spinning with questions of her own, the same ones over again, like a scratched CD. Who had killed Ana and why? Who had sent the threatening note? What did Brad want from her? And a new one—why did Ana tell her parents to talk to Quinn?

As much as she wanted to separate herself from Ana and Brad, here she was, right in the middle of their worst tragedy. Quinn felt the foundation of the respectable life she had built for herself crumbling beneath her shaky legs. Josh's parents would soon be in town, eager to meet the intelligent young lady he'd been dating.

The problem was, as much as she didn't want to face it, she might actually know the answers to those recurring questions, at least the last one. Quinn had buried some secrets so deeply, she had almost forgotten them. She was going to have to think long and hard about what to do next.

She grabbed her car keys and her purse and slipped out through the back door.

Chapter Fourteen

The afternoon sun was still pouring heat over the town, without a cloud in the sky to mitigate it. The effect was oppressive, and, combined with Quinn's adrenalin-spiked metabolism, pushed her into an impulsive decision. She flipped the air conditioner switch to maximum fan and headed toward Josh's apartment at the east end of town.

She had only been inside a handful of times. Their relationship had been building slowly, partly because of the brutal schedule he kept, and partly because of Quinn's long-standing reluctance to trust anyone of the opposite sex. After Brad, anytime she had come close to being interested in another guy, bad memories had intervened.

When she'd accompanied Jack for his transplant interview, she'd been impressed by the gentleness of the resident asking the questions. Afterwards, he'd asked her to go for coffee sometime, and that had been the start of their relationship. Lots of coffees and lunches and dinners later, and she and Josh began to feel like a couple. Whenever they'd wanted privacy, they had gone to her house. There she felt more in control.

They had been dating for five-plus months now, and, although their physical relationship had been simmering for some time, neither of them had pushed for more intimacy. Never had they intruded on the other's time or space without prior notice. Still, the seed of impulsiveness had sprouted within Quinn, and she tingled with the need to see Josh, to be wrapped in the security of his arms. This was his afternoon off. He would work nights until Monday, and then his parents would be here. Her pulse throbbed in her ears as she approached his apartment. His car was outside, but that didn't mean he was at home—much of the time he walked to and from work.

Quinn parked her car and dashed up the steps to the second floor. She pounded on the blue weather-beaten door. She stopped to listen, and, hearing nothing, she pounded some more.

"I'm coming," she heard through the crack in the door frame. A few seconds later, she heard, "Who's there?"

"Quinn. I need to see you." A part of her was outside of her body, watching her actions and astounded by this reckless person, so out of character. Unsure whether she was seeking comfort, stability, affirmation, or something less wholesome, she recognized the rashness of her behavior. What would Josh think of *this* Quinn?

He opened the door, wearing a T-shirt and sweatpants, a towel around his neck. One side of his face had been shaved. The other was covered in tiny sand-colored bristles that glinted in the sunlight. His blue-gray eyes searched hers. "Quinn?"

"I know. I should have called first. Can I come in?"

He stepped aside, while Quinn strolled past him and perched on the sofa, maintaining eye contact all the while. He closed the door and locked it, rubbed his face with the towel, and sat down beside her. He draped his arm around her shoulders. "What's going on?"

The fragrances of toothpaste, shampoo, and shaving cream mingled. So ordinary, so refreshing. At that moment, Quinn had no use for words. She reached behind the neck of this clean, smart, stable, and kind man and pulled him to her for a kiss. After several seconds, he started to draw back, but she kissed him again, this time with unparalleled urgency.

When they came up for air, Josh touched Quinn's cheek. "I'm scratchy."

"I know. I like it." She slid down on the couch, pulling him with her. Of all the ambiguities and all the secrets in the world, there was one single truism. Josh was an amazing kisser, and right now, that was all Quinn wanted to think about. The weight of the world was on her shoulders, and she needed comfort. His heart was beating double-time against her, and an insistent throbbing of her own was pushing her forward with a wildness new to them both. *Come with me*, she said wordlessly, guiding his hand beneath her clothes, and running hers under the waistband of his sweat pants.

"Are you sure?" he asked, his voice a mere whisper.

Quinn nodded, and then she closed her eyes, yielding everything—joys and troubles, alike—to this perfect person, this perfect moment. She wondered whether she deserved it.

* * *

Afterwards, Josh played with the curly strands of hair around Quinn's face.

Was it her imagination, or were his eyes glistening with the same emotion she was feeling? "To what do I owe the honor of this very lovely afternoon surprise?" he asked.

Quinn expected the question, but she was in no mood to explain. "Shhh," she said. "I just want to hold you a little longer."

"I have to go to work," he said, his voice husky. He shifted his position, already moving away from her.

"I know." Quinn didn't want the moment to end, but the rash, unthinking person she had been when she arrived was already retreating, and she was being replaced by the usual level-headed realist. Except there was a difference. Once passion had been unleashed, there was no going back. Quinn gazed at Josh. She could still feel his skin on hers. The connection between them had changed, and with that change came more responsibility, more vulnerability.

"I have to finish shaving," he said. "Come with me?"

Quinn shook her head. She knew where chit-chat might lead, and she wanted to go home with at least some of her secrets intact. She stood and stretched, breathing in all that she'd just experienced. "I've got things to do, too." She wrapped her arms around his waist. "Let's talk tomorrow."

When she started the car, she looked at herself in the rearview mirror. She had no regrets. She felt calmer and more capable. Whatever was ahead, she could handle it. She had Josh in her corner, and that was no small thing.

Chapter Fifteen

The next day was Sunday, and Quinn woke up with the previous afternoon at Josh's on her mind. Why had they waited so long to have sex? If their first time had been that great, she couldn't wait to see how it was once they learned more about how to please each other. She regretted having left so abruptly, but Josh's schedule and her own worries had interrupted what might have been a perfect finish. Except for a quick exchange of texts, she hadn't even spoken to him since leaving his apartment.

That was what she had to live with as a doctor's girlfriend, and what she would have to live with as a doctor's wife, if they ever married. She refused to let the lack of an evening's phone call diminish the afterglow she was feeling.

When she arrived at work, there was a new delivery waiting for her. Old Mr. Murchison, who owned the Stop 'N' Shop across the street from the high school. He had died in his sleep at the age of 84. The family wanted a private viewing, followed by a closed-casket funeral. Nothing complicated or difficult, except that seeing his kind face in repose reminded Quinn of a time when Ana had shoplifted a sandwich and two Milky Ways from him, and Quinn had refused to eat the candy bar earmarked for her.

As she worked on the always-friendly merchant, she remembered having asked Ana at the time, "Why do you do these things? You know they're wrong."

Ana had tossed her sandy-blonde locks behind her shoulders and winked at her friend. "I like to see how much I can get away with. I must be invisible, 'cause I've never been caught."

A lump formed in Quinn's throat. Too late for apologies now, with both Ana and Mr. Murchison gone. At least Mr. Murchison had lived a fuller life and apparently met with a natural end. And if Ana's violent end had been payback for the wild and crazy things she had done when she was young—well, that seemed much too harsh.

As she rolled Mr. Murchison into the refrigerator and cleaned up her work station, her father entered the room, worry lines around his mouth and a squinty look in his eyes. "A phone call for you on line one. Sounds like that Brad Renfroe again."

"What? Tell him I'm not here, that I moved out of town." Quinn had no intention of speaking to Brad, now or ever. She turned off the vent and spit out her gum.

"I tried. Maybe it's not Brad, but whoever it is refused to identify himself. He said it's critical that he speak to you. For your own safety. He sounded pretty convincing—and pretty desperate." Her dad put his arm around Quinn's shoulders. "Maybe you should find out whatever he has to say."

Quinn removed her apron and washed her hands, trying to buy time. Given that the police were looking for Brad, he had taken a risk to contact her. He had cheated on her with Ana, and, if what the Frenches said was true, he had abused Ana—maybe killed her. Various reasons that he might want to talk to Quinn rolled through her mind, none of them particularly good. Still, "for your own safety" echoed in her mind, and tipped the balance. "Okay, I'll talk to him."

She strode toward the front of the building, where she shared an eight-by-ten-foot office with Jack, her father trotting along behind her.

"Do you want me to listen on the extension?" he asked.

"No, that's okay. I can handle this." Quinn closed the door and pushed the button to lock it. Line one of the utilitarian desk phone flashed red, and, as she picked up the receiver and went to push the button, she held her breath. She didn't know what she was getting herself into.

"This is Quinn," she said, lowering herself into the chair and leaning her elbows on the desk.

Heavy breathing, hard on the exhales, perhaps impatient. Then, "Is anyone else on the line?" Definitely, Brad. She'd know that voice anywhere, even though it had thickened and deepened. The way Brad said, "else," with the "s" slipping through a chipped front tooth, was distinctive.

"Just me." She hoped her father hadn't picked up the extension. "Who are you? What do you want?"

"Quinn, it's Brad. I've been trying to reach you for days. It's about Ana."

Despite the air conditioning, perspiration was colonizing on Quinn's forehead and upper lip. "Where are you, Brad? The police are looking for you. What have you done?"

"I didn't kill her. They can suspect me all they want, but I didn't do it. I found her—on the floor in the kitchen—and I called 9-1-1. She was badly beaten, but she was breathing—"

"If you didn't kill her, why did you run away? That makes you look ten times more suspicious." She had no idea whether Brad was telling the truth.

"Long story. I'm afraid whoever killed Ana meant to kill me. S-still wants to kill me. I've made some bad decisions." Brad paused, and Quinn thought she detected a "humpf." "Starting with when I did you dirty and took up with Ana."

"Ancient history," Quinn said. "What does any of this have to do with me?"

"I'm not sure, myself, but I felt obligated to tell you. You're the only Quinn I know, and *you* might be in danger." Brad's words tumbled out at the speed of light, and in a higher pitch than before.

"What? Brad, you aren't even making sense. Slow down and tell me what you mean."

"Sorry. I've got to run. Don't try to call me back. This is a burner phone, and I'm pitching it—"

"Brad. Don't hang up. You've got to tell me why you think I'm in danger."

"Right. When I found Ana, she was lying on her back, moaning. Her eyes were closed. One swollen shut. I kept telling her to talk to me—but I don't think she knew it was me." Brad's voice broke, and his anguish sounded real. "Anyway, she tried to say something, over and over again. I got the impression she was trying to scream the word. Maybe to save her soul."

Chills ran up and down Quinn's spine, and a salty, bitter fear filled her mouth. Her voice came out as a whisper. "What did she say?"

"That's why I called you. You need to be careful. The word she kept repeating was, 'Quinn'."

Chapter Sixteen

Quinn's father had been pacing back and forth past the windows outside of the little office the entire time Quinn was on the phone with Brad. When Brad hung up, the abruptness of the dial tone brought Quinn back to reality. Her staunch effort to divorce herself from Ana and Brad had come to naught. She was on the edge of involvement in the investigation of Ana's death, as sure as if she were standing on the edge of a dark pit with a vacuum ready to suck her in. Ana's parents, Brad, and even her own father, whose incipient questions were palpable, would tether her to the crime, no matter how much she wanted to run away. Furthermore, she ought to tell the police that she had heard from Brad.

Quinn braced herself for the conversation with her dad, and she opened the office door. "C'mon in, Dad. Take a load off, before you wear out the new rug." She pasted what she hoped was a charming grin on her face and pointed to the single guest chair.

Her father lowered his lanky frame onto the seat and threw one leg over the other. Morning coffee clung to his breath. His attempt at casualness didn't fool Quinn, though. "Was that Brad on the phone?" His voice was acidic.

"Yes, it was. I recognized his voice immediately." She might as well head off the questions she knew were coming. "He didn't say where he was, only that he had left town. He knows the police are looking for him."

"Of course, the police are looking for him. The victim's spouse is always a suspect. What does he want with *you*? You don't need to be involved in this mess." His hands clenched into fists, the knuckles white.

Quinn felt the same, but she needed time to sort out the information Brad had given her. How reliable was anything he'd said, and what did any of it mean? "I don't know exactly why he called me. He did warn me that I might be in danger. He also said he didn't kill Ana, but he thought the killer might have meant to come after him. Pretty confusing, but I need to tell Sgt. Schmidt."

"Forget about Schmidt. You should go right to the top." He slapped the desk. "Marty Ramirez needs to hear whatever that boy said to you. You don't want to be on the wrong side of this. That wouldn't be good for you or McFarland's. Brad might've killed his wife, and now he wants to drag you into it. You think he's the one who threatened you?"

Quinn scrambled mentally for a way to stop her father's runaway thoughts, particularly before he involved her mother. Joy McFarland would have a cow if her daughter were mixed up in some tawdry murder investigation. Quinn would handle the police her own way, but first, she needed to change the subject.

"Dad, that's a great idea. I'll go see Chief Ramirez right now. And maybe I'll stop by the hospital to visit Jack afterwards, if you don't need me here this afternoon. But before I go, I have some good news to share, something I know you and Mom will love to hear."

John McFarland let out a breath, and the worry lines morphed into an expectant smile. "What is it, kitten?"

"I know how much you and Mom love Josh, and he thinks the world of you, too. Josh's parents are coming to town, and they want to meet me. I'm going out to dinner with them at Number 13. This is a big step, don't you think?"

Quinn's father smiled with his whole face. "That's wonderful. I can't wait to tell your mother. She's had her heart set on Josh as a son-in-law ever since she met him."

Quinn smiled inside, a bit surprised, and maybe a little guilty at how easy it had been to distract her dad. She bet the excitement of progress in her relationship with Josh was enough to make him forget all about Brad's phone call. "Let's not get too far ahead of ourselves. It's just a meeting. Not a proposal."

"All the more reason to meet with Marty right away. This is serious. We can't have the taint of a murder clouding the first impression Josh's parents have of you."

Chapter Seventeen

Getting in to see Chief of Police Martin Ramirez turned out to be tougher than Quinn expected. When she'd pulled up to the Julius M. Brown Law Enforcement Facility, named after a much-loved sheriff, who happened to have been the husband of Quinn's erstwhile karate teacher, Quinn had almost changed her mind about reporting Brad's phone call.

She sat in the oppressively hot car for a minute and considered her options. What did she have to report, anyway, except that Brad was on the lam, using a burner phone—two facts they already knew. She had no intention of spilling the message Brad had given her, that Ana had spoken Quinn's name shortly before dying. Unless and until Quinn figured out the meaning of that, if it was even true, there was no need to offer such a clear connection between Ana's death and Quinn.

On the other hand, once she entered the police station and sat before its chief officer, how could she withhold any bit of information, especially if Ramirez asked her direct questions about what Brad had said. And he would. Quinn had known Chief Ramirez since she was a little girl, and he'd been a visiting policeman at her kindergarten class. Then there was the matter of the golf ball threat. Sgt. Schmidt had already told her that the police believed the threat to be linked to Ana's death.

Another aspect of living in a small town. Anything that touched one person, one family, undoubtedly touched another and another, until the whole town was wound tightly together like a ball of yarn. Apparently, she had been able to extricate herself only so long. She sighed and grabbed her sling bag. She'd do her civic duty and let the police worry about how the puzzle pieces fit together.

Only, when she entered the chilly police station, and stated why she was there to Ms. Frances, the clerk on duty, the plan started falling apart. "Oh, honey, you won't be able to see the chief this mornin'. He's been tied up in a meeting with bigwigs from the city council." She clucked her tongue against her bottom teeth, as if she were sorry to give bad news. "Why'n't cha talk to one a th' others on duty?"

"Is Mary Hallom on duty?" Quinn asked, hoping that somehow her hours had changed from night to day.

"Nah, she works nights. You know Mary? You two 'bout the same age?"

"I'm friends with her brother." Quinn turned to leave, thinking maybe she'd stop back by after visiting Jack at the hospital.

"Don't be leavin' now. Sgt. Schmidt is here, and he can see you straight away." Ms. Frances punched an intercom button to ring the sergeant's office.

Frustrated and trapped, Quinn ran a hand through her hair and rehearsed in her head what she would say. She would be strictly factual, and as brief as possible, doing her civic duty and getting out of there.

Sgt. Schmidt came out of his office to greet Quinn and walk her back to a cubicle, where he had a desk, two chairs, and a pile of folders about eight inches tall. The area smelled like day-old lunch meat, and Quinn saw a paper bag from Three Brothers stuffed in the trash can next to the desk. "What a coincidence. I was getting ready to drive over to the funeral home, see if you were there."

A stone lodged itself in Quinn's throat, but she swallowed it and sat in the chair Schmidt pointed to. "Why is that?" Maybe he had a lead on who had broken her window.

"Ladies first," Schmidt said, his lips curving upward and revealing a quarter-inch of gums. "What can I do for ya?"

"Yesterday you told me Brad Renfroe was missing. This morning he called McFarland's. Insisted on talking to me."

To Schmidt's credit, he didn't overreact. His eyebrows jumped to the top of his forehead, but he didn't interrupt.

"He said he was on a burner phone and about to dump it." Quinn knew she had to give him more, but the more she said, the more uncomfortable she would be, saying it. "I asked him why he ran, and he said something like, 'I didn't kill Ana. I'm afraid whoever did is after me, too.'" There, she said what she'd come to say. She was ready to leave. "And that's about it." She started to rise from the chair.

"Not so fast. You haven't told me nearly enough. Please sit." Schmidt opened his desk drawer and pulled out a pack of Juicy Fruit gum. "Want a piece?" When Quinn shook her head, he unwrapped a stick and folded it into thirds before popping it into his mouth and chewing. He leaned back in his chair, lacing his hands behind his head. "Why do you suppose Brad called you? Why not call the police, or his in-laws, or his supervisor at work?"

Why *had* Brad called her? To tell her Ana was thinking of her with her dying breath? To warn her of an unspecified danger? Quinn didn't know, but she didn't want to speculate with Sgt. Schmidt. That was for sure. "Maybe he thought I was a safe person to tell. Maybe he didn't want me to think that he'd killed Ana."

"Maybe there's something about your relationship with those two that you're not telling us." He opened a folder and jabbed an index finger at something on a page.

"I don't know what you mean, sergeant. I've been honest with you. I came in here to—"

"Yes. Yes, you did, and I thank you for that. But you haven't asked me why I was going to come see you this morning." His eyes bored into Quinn's, and she flinched, despite herself. She wouldn't give him the satisfaction of asking the question, though. She stared at the open folder instead.

"You see, we've been investigating Ms. Renfroe's murder, and your name seems to be coming up more than we expected, especially since you told us you haven't seen those two in a l-o-n-g while." Schmidt squinted at Quinn, as he drawled.

"Well, I was telling you the truth. You can ask anyone in town. No one has seen us together since we were teenagers." Quinn chewed the inside of her cheek. "Anyway, how has my name come up?"

"Well, let's say that we were going through the victim's things. We came across a necklace in the shape of half a heart. The back side was engraved: 'BS/Quinn/BF forever.' I think you might be the only Quinn in town, so I'm guessing that refers to you. Am I right?"

"Y-yes, and I have the other half of that necklace. But that's old news. We stopped being best friends a long, long time ago."

"You told me. You were dating Mr. Renfroe, and he started dating Mrs. Renfroe." Coming from the sergeant's mouth that way, the words stung. "So you split from both of them. But how come your address was on Ms. Renfroe's calendar for this month? Did you have plans to see her? And how come Ms. Renfroe's parents told us their daughter told them if anything happened to her, to contact you?"

So Ana's parents had spilled that. She couldn't really blame them. Perspiration popped out at Quinn's hairline, on her upper lip, and down her back. Did Schmidt suspect her of any wrongdoing? She tried to think of a way to answer his questions, but the truth was, she didn't know and didn't want to know.

"And now you tell me Mr. Renfroe's calling you. It seems mighty fishy. Are you sure you haven't hooked up with Mr. Renfroe again?"

That was the last straw. Quinn imagined herself morphing into a fiery dragon, beyond all control. She swished her tail and smoke poured out of her mouth. In reality, she stood up and leaned her fists against the top of Schmidt's desk. "You have a lot of nerve to talk to me that way. I've done nothing to deserve it, and I won't listen to your far-fetched insinuations. I came here in good faith, and this is how you treat me?" She stomped toward the exit, slapping the metal file cabinet as she passed. Before reaching the door, she turned back toward Schmidt. "Next thing you know, you'll be accusing me of killing Ana."

Schmidt shrugged and held his hands out. In a voice as soft as Quinn's was loud, he said, "Well, if you wanted her husband for yourself, you'd have to get her out of the way somehow."

Chapter Eighteen

Quinn was still steaming mad when she stormed into Jack's hospital room after leaving Sgt. Schmidt. She must've looked like a wild woman, too, because when she swung the door open and marched over to Jack's bedside, he held both hands up in surrender mode and screamed, "Help, help—it's the big bad wolf come to grandmother's house."

Quinn laughed, in spite of herself. Jack had a way of raising her spirits better than anyone else—except maybe Josh. "I look that bad, huh?" She leaned over the bed frame to kiss her brother on his freshly-shaved cheek. "I brought you a carob smoothie."

"Put 'er right there," he said, pointing to the center of his cart. "Mmm, I can taste it already." In two seconds' time, Jack had ripped the wrapping from the straw and sunk it into the tall paper cup. "Have a seat," he said, between slurps. "What's got you so worked up?"

"Oh, Jack. I don't want to bother you with my problems. You've got enough on your plate to rest and recover from your surgery."

"Hey, they didn't operate on my brain—or my ears. Now that I have a working kidney, I'm feeling much better. Plus, I'd be glad to have something else to think about besides anti-rejection drugs and blood pressure readings." He took a long swig and belched. "Lay it on me, sister o' mine."

Tears swam in Quinn's eyes, either from the joy of having her brother on the mend or the frustration of dealing with the police. She brushed them away with the back of her hand and took a deep breath. "So much has happened. I hardly know where to start. Okay—remember Ana French?"

"Quinn's twin? Sure. That's a name out of the past. What about her?"

"She's dead." Quinn paused to get her bearings. "Bludgeoned. The same day as your surgery. And then someone threw a note wrapped around a golf ball through my window, threatening me not to talk. And then Ana's husband Brad went missing, but he called me, and her parents came to see me at McFarland's. And Josh's parents are coming in and want to meet me. And—"

"Whoa, all that in just a few days? You *have* been busy." He took another swig from the cup.

"And that's not all. I went to tell the police that I had heard from Brad, and Sgt. Schmidt had the nerve to insinuate that I might have collaborated with Brad to kill Ana. That's where I was before I came here."

"You've got to be kidding me, sis. *You*? McFarland's doesn't need business *that* badly, do we?"

"This is nothing to joke about, Jack. They really might think I had something to do with Ana's death, even though I swore I haven't even seen or heard from Ana or Brad in years." Quinn started pacing around the small room, hands clenched at her sides.

"Okay, I'm sorry. I just can't figure why they'd think that about you. You don't have a killing bone in your body."

"Yeah, well, remember the heart necklace that Ana and I each wore half of? They found hers and saw my name on it. Then they saw my address on her calendar—why, I don't know. And Ana told her parents if anything happened to her, to ask me about it. They told that to the police."

Jack's brow crumpled as he took in each detail. "And Brad is calling you from wherever he disappeared to. It *does* sound bad."

"Thanks a heap." Quinn stopped at the side of Jack's bed and sat in the chair. "I hate to worry Dad with all this, but I probably need a lawyer. And heaven forbid Mom gets wind of it."

"Ain't that the truth? Mom would have a cow." Jack reached over to the molded plastic railing of his bed, where Quinn was resting her hand. "We'll get through this, sis. We always do." He patted a rhythm on her hand, as if to a familiar tune. "I must be missing something, though. Is there anything you might know—anything from the past—that might account for Ana's sudden interest in you?"

Quinn bit her lip. "Ana and I did a lot of stuff together. Some I'm not proud of. But that's all so far in the past. I don't see how—"

"You prob'ly need to think back over all that, even if it's painful. Sounds like you hold a key to understanding this case, and the police aren't going to leave you alone until you figure out what it is." Jack slurped the last of his smoothie and crushed the paper cup.

"Mr. and Mrs. French said Ana and Brad were having money problems, and that Ana had bruises the last time they saw her. That makes it sound like Brad was an abuser, like he may have hit her too hard and killed her." Shaking her head, she said, "But when he called, he insisted he hadn't killed her. He said he found her beaten up, and called 9-1-1."

"Did you ever know Brad to be a violent person? Did he ever hit you?"

Quinn looked her brother in the eye. "No and no. And as feisty as Ana was, I can't see her staying in a marriage where she was being abused, either."

"Well, I'm pretty positive you didn't kill Ana, and if Brad didn't kill her, who did? Whatever was going on in Ana's life before she died, she was thinking about you. Otherwise, why write your address on her calendar? Why tell her parents to talk to you?"

Quinn took a moment to consider a response. Once she crossed a bridge, she might not be able to return to safe ground. But how safe was that ground anyway? "Jack, have you ever made a pact to keep a secret?"

"Uh, probably, sometime in the past. Why? Are you keeping a secret of Ana's?"

"What if you knew something really terrible, and you took a blood oath not to tell? Would there ever be a circumstance where you might break that oath?"

Jack's face took on a mask of concern. "Are you feeling guilty for breaking a promise you made to Ana?"

"Not me. I've never told a soul. But I think maybe Ana broke the promise. And now I don't know what to do."

Chapter Nineteen

When Quinn left the hospital, it was a quarter to 2:00. The sun was high, and puffy clouds adorned the cornflower blue sky. Too pretty a day for the morose thoughts she was having. She needed to talk to her dad about hiring a lawyer, but Mom and Dad were running a funeral this afternoon. She should be there, helping to distribute memorial programs or directing people to sign the book. Maybe she was taking advantage of the time off, but she also didn't want to squander it. First, she swung by Shrimp 'n' Stuff to pick up a shrimp salad and a Diet Coke.

She drove to the public library and parked in a shady spot across the street. Rolling down her car windows to catch the cross-breeze, she opened the packet of plastic utensils, spread out the enclosed napkin over her blouse, and dug into the cool, tangy meal. She hadn't realized how hungry she was. She ate every bite of the salad and finished with the lettuce leaves that lined the container, washing it all down with the icy, sweet cola.

Refreshed, she rolled up the windows and exited the car, taking care to lock the door. She didn't think she was being followed, but since the break-in at the house, she was trying to be extra careful. She dashed up the outside stairs to the library, touching the sun-heated foot of the founder's bronze statue for luck, as she had done every time since she could reach it. As she pushed open the heavy door, Quinn's face and bare arms tingled from the chilly blast of air. She'd forgotten to bring a sweater.

She climbed the marble staircase to the fourth floor, where the history center resided. Quinn had been there before many times, particularly when she was researching information for high school and college papers. She had always loved the dry, papery smell of the room, the friendly service from the librarians. Today was the only Sunday of the month that the library was open, and only one other patron sat at a long table. The combination of the cool temperature and the thick silence reminded her of the time Ana had pushed her to cool off from the summer heat by crawling under the pier and beam structure of her house. Afraid of whatever critters might lurk there, Quinn had resisted, but Ana had led the way, undaunted by any adventure. The spot had turned out to be a comfortable secret hiding place, shady and serene.

The trick would be to find the information she was looking for, without raising suspicion with the librarian. The small-town gossip web was thick and strong, and she didn't need to give the police any more ammunition to suspect her of anything.

Quinn breezed past the stocky male librarian at the front of the room and sat down at the computer. She went to the *Daily News* archives and typed "local murders 2004" into the search bar. Pages of microfilm rolled up on the screen with the keyword, "murders," highlighted in yellow. There were only four hits: Salem Armstrong, Rodney Jackson, Sha'ronda Jackson, and Dawn Chrysler. She clicked on the last one and held her breath. A slew of articles from the time of the murder popped up, capped by two articles of more recent vintage. Quinn started from the bottom. The details of the case were spelled out as follows: Dawn Chrysler, 19, found strangled to death in her home in the 3200 block of Pelican Street on the evening of June 27, 2004. Neighbors questioned by police reported having seen a dark-colored Chevrolet Impala on the street at the time of the murder. The victim was employed at Palais Royal department store.

The top article, published in 2008, was a retrospective of five cold cases from the past decade. One new fact stood out in the Chrysler case: an unnamed witness had stepped forward with a movie on VHS tape dated 2003, believed to feature the victim. *Pornographic, no doub*t. Quinn's mind flashed to the many nude dancing scenes she and Ana had observed through the window. What had once seemed funny, and even tantalizing, now caused chills to climb up Quinn's spine.

"Where are her parents?" I asked Ana. "How come nobody's at home to stop her?"

"She just has a mother. She works nights, so Dawn can do whatever she wants."

"And this *is what she wants to do? Show off her body to the whole world?"*

The chirping of her cell phone reminded Quinn that she needed to get moving. It was Josh. She swiped to answer the phone and clicked on "print" on the computer. She would take a copy of the file home to review later.

"Hi, you busy?" Was it her imagination, or did his voice sound huskier than usual? Suddenly she wasn't cold anymore.

"At the library." She caught a dirty look from the librarian and lowered her voice. "How's it going?" She tried to keep the butterflies in her stomach from flying into her voice. This new stage of their relationship was thrilling and exciting, but why did she feel so vulnerable?

"Great. I just woke up and have to get to the hospital. Last night of the shift, and I'm off till Tuesday. Then I work days. Hey, what are you doing at the library?"

"Um, checking out some articles in the History Center. Nothing exciting." *Unless you're into old murders and new murders, that is.* "I've been thinking of you."

"Me, too. I wish you were here right now." The silence following this statement was loaded with innuendo. "But, hey, I wanted to remind you about my parents. We'll pick you up for dinner tomorrow night at seven-thirty. Okay?"

"Sure. Looking forward to it." Quinn remembered some of the things Josh had told her about his family. His father was a pharmacist, his mom a teacher. Having their older child become a doctor had been a dream come true. "I'll wear my new linen pant suit and patent leather stilettos. Does that sound okay?"

"Honey, you'll look great, no matter what you're wearing. And don't worry—they're going to love you. You know, I do." Quinn's heart leaped at the declaration, the term of endearment. Both were newer than the outfit she planned to wear, and they fit even better.

"Josh?" She started to return the favor, to say, "I love you, too," right here in the middle of the public library, but something held her back. There was a difference between loving a person and telling him so. The telling crossed a line, and you could never go back. Saying it was even more intimate than sex, and it made you less safe. That was a painful lesson Quinn had learned from Brad.

"Yes?" She could tell from the single syllable he had already moved away from the moment. She pictured him as she had left him yesterday, getting ready for work, half of his face shaved.

"Have a great night at work, and when you make rounds, tell my brother I said hello."

After she clicked off, she held the phone in her palm and caressed its face with her thumb. Her reverie was interrupted by the brisk approach of another librarian, a woman about her age with a pretty face and a noticeable baby bump. "Are these yours, Ms. McFarland?" she asked, holding a stack of about seven pages in the air between them.

Quinn flinched at the sound of her name. She had almost forgotten about having printed out the information about the murder. She'd had to use her library card in the machine. Maybe that hadn't been such a smart move. This wasn't a good time to have her name associated with any murder—even an old one.

Smiling and aiming for a casual tone, Quinn said, "Oh, yes. Thank you. I would have picked that up myself."

"So you have an interest in the Chrysler woman's murder from fifteen years ago?" the librarian asked, as she handed over the pages. "I find that quite interesting."

Panic struck Quinn's throat, and she tried not to gasp. "Why is that?"

The librarian stared at her a moment and said, "Hah. No one's been interested in that old case for more than a decade, and then two people in the past month."

Two people? The words reverberated in Quinn's brain. "Do you mind telling me who the other person was?" She held her breath.

"I'm sorry," the librarian said with a shake of her head. "Our library code of ethics will not allow us to disclose who researched what information here."

"Thanks, anyway," Quinn said, gathering her belongings to leave. Despite not having the answer to her question, she felt immensely comforted by the library's code of ethics.

Chapter Twenty

Much as she hated to, Quinn headed for McFarland's when she left the library. The afternoon funeral would be over with by now, and her parents would be in the back parlor, relaxing and enjoying a late afternoon cocktail. Maybe they would be too tired or too relaxed to ask her too many questions, but she doubted that, and, anyway, she needed her dad's help in finding an attorney.

After parking in the back alley, Quinn unlocked the back door into the treatment room. No matter how long the ventilation system had been on, or how long since the last "treatment," she always sneezed when she entered that room. The chemical residue and her nostrils were not best buddies.

She locked the door behind her and dropped her key fob on her rolling chair, as she headed for the parlor. Best case scenario, she'd get the name of the lawyer, thank her mom for bailing her out of the meeting with the Frenches, and be home to walk Calvin within the hour. Worst scenario—well, she didn't want to think about that.

As she approached the parlor, the whirring of a vacuum cleaner assaulted her ears. She checked her cell phone. Only 4:50. Typically Marlena didn't come in to clean until after 6:00.

Marlena switched off the vacuum and gave Quinn a flash of silver with orange and blue rubber bands. She was working after the school day and summers to pay for her braces and save for college. She and her family lived across the street from Quinn, and Quinn had gotten Marlena this gig. "Hi, Miss Quinn. How're you doing?" She wiped her hand on the legs of her blue jeans before extending for a handshake.

"Fine. Good to see you. A little early, isn't it? How's your family?" Quinn glanced past the girl for any sign of activity.

"Everyone's good. Thank you for asking. We're having a big dinner tonight for my cousin. She's visiting from Chicago. Your dad said it was okay for me to come early."

Quinn looked around again. "Speaking of Dad, do you know where he is?"

Nodding slightly and turning back to the vacuum cleaner, Marlena replied, "Yes. He and your mom left a few minutes ago. They said they were going to the hospital to visit your brother."

"Thanks." That made sense. They would probably visit with Jack, grab dinner at a restaurant near the hospital, and call it a day. When you lived in the same building where you worked, sometimes you had to get out. And working in death services could become oppressive. Nobody knew that better than Quinn. That was why she had moved to a home of her own as soon as she could afford one.

Quinn waved goodbye to Marlena and headed for her little office. She opened the door and turned on the light, taking in the smell of lemon furniture polish. She closed herself in to shut out the sounds of Marlena's work in progress. She was relieved, in a way, not to have to face her parents' inevitable questions, but the fact remained that she needed a lawyer, and the sooner the better. The librarian's remark about two people researching Dawn Chrysler's murder added another layer of urgency to Quinn's concerns. Was it coincidence, or had someone else linked the cold case to Ana's death? If the latter were true, Quinn could be in serious trouble.

One thing at a time. She picked up the landline to call her father. Hopefully the call would go through the hospital's telemetry. She braced herself for her dad's reaction when he heard she needed a lawyer.

Four rings, and Quinn almost disconnected, but her father picked up on the fifth. "Hi, kitten. Where are you?" He sounded like he was in a tunnel. Maybe he was walking between the parking lot and Jack's room.

"At the shop. Everything's dead—just Marlena and me right now." Quinn took a deep breath. "Did you see Jack? How is he?"

"Doing fine. They might let him go home soon. He's tolerating the anti-rejection drugs well." If his words weren't jubilant enough, the tone of voice sprinkled them with confetti. Of course, everyone was happy about Jack's new lease on life, but it made Quinn's reason for calling that much worse. She hated to ruin his good mood.

"Listen, Dad," she said, "I don't want to alarm you, but I think I need to consult with a criminal lawyer. Which one do you suggest?" There, she'd said it.

"A—what? A criminal lawyer? What for? This Ana mess?" Quinn could picture him holding his cell phone to one ear and pressing his other ear to help him hear better. She wondered where her mother was.

"It's kind of a long story. I went to see Chief Ramirez today and ended up seeing Sgt. Schmidt. He's got some idea that I might be hiding something about Ana's death, because Ana's calendar had my address on it, and Ana told her parents to contact me if anything happened to her."

"What? I can't believe that. What about your broken window and that letter? The police should be protecting you, not hassling you." Quinn could tell her dad's Irish was up now. "I'm going to call Marty Ramirez, myself."

Now Quinn could hear her mother in the background. "John? What's going on?" Her dad made a shushing noise, and she could picture him putting his arm around his wife's shoulder, hugging, as if he could quell this whole thing with a hug.

"Dad, please don't call Ramirez. Let me talk to a lawyer first. This is a complicated mess, and I need help sorting out the facts."

"You don't think you'll be arrested, do you?" The disbelief in her dad's voice stung. She'd always been Daddy's girl, and she hated to disappoint him.

"I don't think so, Dad, but I'd feel more confident. Who do you recommend?"

"What about David Becker? He's more than competent, and we can trust him to keep his mouth shut. Can this wait until the morning? I can call him—"

"I'd like to call him, myself," Quinn said. "We have him in the computer from his dad's funeral last year, don't we?" She wakened the computer at her desk and clicked on "clients." "It's not too late to call him at the office, is it?"

"Five-thirty. He should still be there." The connection was breaking up, but notes of puzzlement were layered onto the emotion in her dad's voice. "Your mom and I were going to grab a bite at Hearsay, but maybe we should come there instead."

"No, Dad. Please. You and Mom have a nice dinner, and I'll talk to you after I talk to Mr. Becker. I can handle this myself, and I don't want to disrupt your evening any more than I already have."

Murmuring in the background told her all she needed to know. She was going to have a lot of parental questions to answer. She couldn't worry about that right now. First, she needed to talk to Mr. Becker. Remembering the note wrapped around the golf ball, she shivered. *Don't talk, or you'll be next.* She needed to talk to a lawyer, but she wasn't sure exactly what she could say. She was, as her grandmother used to say, "Caught between the devil and the deep blue sea."

Chapter Twenty-one

Mr. Becker sounded as jolly and gregarious over the phone as Quinn remembered him. One wouldn't expect a person who defended criminals to present such a happy-go-lucky persona. Then again, she should be the last one to judge a person by his profession.

"How's that strapping brother of yours doing?" His voice boomed so loud, Marlena could probably hear it through the closed door and over the vacuum cleaner. "I heard he finally got a new kidney. Good for him."

Guess our town never heard of HIPAA. You can't even get an organ replacement without the whole world knowing. But then again, Jack's never kept his illness a secret. "Yes, sir. He's feeling so much better. He'll probably come home from the hospital soon."

"Glad to hear it. Glad to hear it." He paused for a moment and audibly gulped. Had Quinn interrupted his happy hour? "So, what can I do ya outta, young lady?"

Quinn took a deep breath and crossed her fingers for luck, the same way she and Ana used to start an uncomfortable conversation with someone of the older generation. "Well, I think I might need a lawyer, and I was wondering if—"

Something squeaked, and Quinn could picture the lawyer sitting up, leaning into the phone. "—Wait a minute. I'm a criminal defense attorney. You don't mean to tell me you've been arrested, do ya?"

"No, sir. It's sort of complicated. I met with Sgt. Schmidt at the police station today, and some of the things he was asking me—well, I'd feel a lot better if I could talk to you about them. In confidence, you know." Butterflies were dancing to the tune of her heartbeat.

"This have anything to do with the Renfroe murder?" Another sip and swallow. "Word around town's that they're looking for the husband."

"Yes, sir. They are. I mean—"

The attorney chuckled. "Well, far be it from us to say what the local police are doing, right? So, you want to come in for a chat. That's fine with me." The chair squeaked again, and fingers tapped on a keyboard. "I was just getting ready to head out. You think an arrest might be imminent?"

Quinn exhaled. By tomorrow she should be able to get her act together. "I sure hope not."

"How's about we meet here at my office tomorrow morning. Nine thirty?"

"That'll be great." Assuming no bodies came in between now and then, she was sure she could get the time off. The hard part would be getting her parents to stay behind and out of the picture. "Thanks so much."

"You're welcome, honey. Get a good night's sleep, now. Oh, one more thing, don't say another word to anyone about anything related to the case. If the police or anyone else questions you, tell them to talk to your lawyer."

After she hung up, Quinn held the receiver to her chest. Something about those two words, *your lawyer*, sent waves of warm comfort through her veins. Living in a small town had its good points. She had a lawyer to back her up, and she had yet to spend a single dime.

Sometime while she had been on the phone, the vacuum cleaner had ceased, and Marlena was nowhere to be seen. The place was quiet as a tomb. Quinn closed the office and headed to the prep room. She was looking forward to a quiet night at home with Calvin. In addition to getting ready for Josh's parents the next evening, she wanted to make an outline of exactly how much of her life she needed to share with the attorney. Before she did that, she would re-read those letters Ana had written to her after "the incident." She wanted every detail to be fresh in her mind.

Having a plan put some pep in her step, and Quinn found herself smiling as she bounced into the embalming room and picked up her key fob. She set the alarm and locked the back door.

She climbed into the Toyota and fastened her seat belt, tossing her sling bag onto the passenger seat. That's when she noticed the strip of notebook paper on the passenger seat. Picking it up with the tips of her thumb and forefinger, she held it up in the afternoon light to read two words, written in pencil: "Keep Quiet."

Chapter Twenty-two

This time, Quinn didn't call the police to report the hand-written note she found in her car. Instead, when she got home, she used a pair of tweezers to put it into a zippered sandwich bag. She would take it with her to the lawyer's office tomorrow morning.

Her brain was a minefield, and she was afraid to make a move for fear of stepping into the wrong place. Had she really been so careless as to leave her car unlocked? Or had she left the back door of the funeral home open, and the note-writer had entered and used her key fob to unlock the car? Either way, she needed to change her habits. Otherwise, she might as well wear a sign saying, "Come and get me."

She hated to let herself be paralyzed by fear, but, at the moment, she might be the target of Brad, the police, the note-writer, Ana's parents, or possibly a murderer. Even if some of these overlapped, Quinn was one very stressed-out person.

After she walked Calvin, looking over her shoulder and listening for unusual sounds along the way, she entered her house, locked the door, and checked all the other doors and windows. She set the alarm on "stay" mode and headed for the kitchen. While she washed her hands, she planned her evening. Dinner, shower, a final walk for the dog, and early to bed—but there were two other important tasks she wanted to accomplish, as well.

Quinn's stomach gurgled, reminding her that she hadn't eaten anything since the shrimp salad in the library parking lot. The refrigerator was mostly empty. She'd have to add a grocery run to her list of errands. Meanwhile, scrambled eggs with cheese and tomatoes and a side of buttered rye toast would suffice. Breakfast for dinner was good comfort food, too. Tomorrow night, if all went well, she'd be dining at the elegant steakhouse, Number 13, with Josh and his parents.

Once the food was ready, but before she plated it, Quinn went to her closet shelf to pull Ana's old letters from the back of the scrapbook. The letters had been written after "the incident," and while Quinn remembered the general content, she was fuzzy on the details. Maybe there would be some useful information in them. She could read them while she ate. Hopefully, they wouldn't make her lose her appetite.

The savory, cheesy smell of the eggs took center stage for several bites, before Quinn opened the four letters and laid them out on the table above her placemat in chronological order. Dawn's murder had been in June of 2004. The first note was written the following August, the first day of school, if Quinn remembered correctly. Ana's rounded penmanship, written in now-faded peacock blue ink, sent a pang of nostalgia through Quinn's heart. How many notes had they passed to each other over the years in school? Hundreds, at least.

> August 16 '04
>
> Dear Blood Sister,
>
> How's your first day back? I saw your curly head from the back in the hall after first period, but I couldn't get to you, and the bell was about to ring. Want to meet me at lunch at our usual table? Can you believe we're freshmen??? Awesome.
>
> Listen, I've been wanting to tell you something all summer, but no time was right. Either someone was with you, or we got interrupted. So here it is—I know everything's been hard on you. Me, too, but you've always been the sensitive one. Anyway, I'm proud of you for staying true to our pact. Never, ever tell, and it will all work out in the end.
>
> Love you bunches, sweet pea. See ya at lunch.
Your BS

Quinn remembered the time when Ana was her BFF, when their special lunch table was a school landmark, when a note from Ana was a treasure worth saving in a scrapbook. It *had* been a difficult summer. Quinn had suffered from nightmares, and even during the day, she had been moody and quiet. The happy memories and sad ones brought stinging tears.

Now Quinn pressed two fingers against the inner corners of her eyes and breathed deeply. Between having a meltdown or finishing her eggs while they were still warm, she preferred the latter. She shoveled another couple of bites in.

The other three notes were similar in tone and content. Specific details of "the incident" were never mentioned. There would be no need, as they were etched so firmly in her mind. It was a wonder they weren't as legible as the embroidered scarlet "A" on Hester Prynne's garment in the book they'd been assigned to read that year.

The final letter, written in December, 2004, said, "My Christmas wish is that I could turn back the clock. I wish some things had never happened. All my fault, but I can't change it now. Glad I can trust you, Curly Head. I know you'll never tell."

Within the next two years Brad and Quinn were a couple, and then they weren't, and there were no more notes after that. Quinn finished her dinner, washed the dishes, and returned the notes to the back of the scrapbook. Maybe they would come in handy later, if Quinn was forced to revisit "the incident" with the police.

Now Quinn found a legal pad and a pen. She started a list of items she needed to discuss with David Becker at tomorrow's meeting:

Noises outside of my house
Vandalism and first threatening note
Calls from Brad – Ana saying my name while dying
Visit from Ana's parents – Ana told them to contact me
My address on Ana's calendar this month
Second threatening note

Unless she had to, she didn't plan to talk about her visit to the library, the notes from Ana, or anything else related to "the incident." The same was true for her parents. She'd make sure the attorney would refrain from sharing information with them. *Attorney-client privilege notwithstanding, we live in a very small town.*

To head off a phone call with free opportunity to be inquisitive, Quinn texted her dad, asking if she could have the morning off to see Mr. Becker at nine-thirty. She added, "Going to bed. Talk to you tomorrow. XXOO."

Anticipation of tomorrow filled Quinn with both excitement and dread. No matter how it all unfolded, she was doing the right thing.

Chapter Twenty-three

Monday dawned with exquisite corals and lavenders, and a cooling northerly breeze. Josh and Mr. and Mrs. Brady couldn't have ordered better weather for their visit. When Quinn took Calvin out for his early morning trot, the neighborhood smelled of dewy sweet grass and wildflowers. Birds chirped, and, except for Anise, Marlena's mom across the street, who waved when she came out to pick up her newspaper, Quinn had the street to herself. At least it seemed that way.

Quinn had stopped assuming she was alone and safe, if not with the first threatening note, then definitely with the second. Calvin's typical scampering around without growling or barking was not enough to convince her these days. She kept him on a tight leash and kept her eyes moving from side to side. Occasionally she looked behind her, as well.

On the way home, she lengthened the leash and broke into a jog. A little morning exercise wouldn't hurt either one of them. Except, as she turned a corner, she saw an unfamiliar, tall jogger ahead of her. The man wore long pants and long sleeves, unusual for this time of year, even with today's breeze. He could have been anybody, yet Quinn's instincts caused her heart to rise into her throat. She slowed down and watched as the stranger maintained his pace. Probably nothing, but she couldn't dismiss the feeling of a close call.

When they returned home, Quinn unlocked the door and turned off the alarm, resetting it on stay mode. The air conditioning enveloped her in an embrace, and she headed for the kitchen to feed Calvin and grab a banana for herself. She checked her cell phone on the way, deleting a couple of calls from unrecognizable numbers.

Call me ASAP, her dad had texted at a few minutes past 8:00. Quinn's heart raced. Had something happened to Jack?

"Hey, sweetheart," her father said, as he answered her call. "No problem taking the morning off. Things are quiet right now, anyway..."

Quinn held her breath.

"In fact, I've told the answering service to take incoming calls, because Mom and I are going to Becker's office with you."

Vivid hot fireworks exploded in her brain, but a sharp intake of breath was Quinn's only external reaction. "Dad—"

"I know we're inviting ourselves, and you probably think you can handle this by yourself, but Mom and I have your best interests at heart. We only wish we had gone with you to the police station yesterday. I'd rather you hadn't talked to Sgt. Schmidt. I had already prepared Chief Ramirez about your situation."

Perhaps he was trying to keep the castigation out of his tone of voice, but Quinn heard it anyway. "So now, since I talked to Sgt. Schmidt, you don't trust me. Is that it?"

"No, no, honey. That's not it at all. Mom and I know that you're an intelligent and capable young woman. We just have more experience in these things than you do. We want to make sure David Becker understands who you are, what kind of background you come from, how much is at stake."

Quinn was pretty sure that was code for, "We don't want you to lose this chance for a good life, married to a surgeon." She should never have told them about Josh's parents. They had probably already started planning the wedding, and that caused Quinn's blood to boil. It had always been this way—she had never been enough for them the way she was. Especially her mother—she was always trying to make Quinn something more, something her mother could brag about.

Quinn paced around the small house, trying to find a way to quash her parents' interference. A trembling had started in her core, and she struggled to keep it out of her voice. "Listen, Dad. I appreciate all you and Mom do to support me. I really do—"

"I hear a *but* coming."

"—but I need to handle this myself. I'm almost thirty years old. By the time you were thirty, you were married with two kids, running a funeral home. You didn't need Grandma and Grandpa to smooth out the rough spots in your life." *You probably didn't have any rough spots, though, did you?* Glancing at the clock on her bed stand, she sped up her argument. "Tell Mom I appreciate your wanting to help, but I need you to trust me right now. I'm going to see the lawyer *you* recommended. I'm sure he'll give me good advice that you'll approve of. I'll come to the shop after I see Mr. Becker, and we can talk more. I've gotta go now."

A sputter and then silence came over the phone, and Quinn claimed victory. "I love you, Dad. Thanks for understanding." She disconnected before either of them could change positions. Now she would have to rush to shower and get ready for her meeting with David Becker.

She'd put on a good imitation of a confident, mature woman just now. She hoped she could maintain that bravado for the next few hours, at least. Showing her parents and the attorney that she was capable was important, but the real trick would be convincing herself.

Chapter Twenty-four

By the time Quinn drove to Becker's office, she was feeling quite proud of herself. Dressed in a navy cotton skirt, top, jacket, and heels, her uniform for funerals, she had her list and the bagged note found on the passenger seat of her car in her purse. Her checkbook was there, too, ready to pay a retainer for services. Having headed off her dad's involvement, she was ready, even eager, to listen to the attorney's advice about how to move forward. The sooner, the better.

Not wanting to be late, she parked the car across from the entrance and dashed inside with one minute to spare. When she entered the office, she ignored the faint smell of lavender and the sleek, shiny granite and glass reception desk, and she marched up to the matronly assistant whose glasses magnified her hazel eyes and gave her an owlish look.

"Quinn McFarland to see Mr. Becker."

The woman's face cracked into a polite smile. "Yes, Ms. McFarland. Mr. Becker is expecting you." She removed her glasses and gestured with her head, a slight nod to the right. Following the direction of the glance, Quinn turned toward the waiting room, and her stomach lurched. Sitting in two of the client chairs were her parents, also dressed in their funeral clothes.

No one else was in the waiting room, but Quinn wouldn't have cared if there were dozens. She stormed across the room with big strides. "What are you doing here? I told you not to come, and I meant it."

Quinn's mother's eyes widened in her typical surprised expression, but Quinn wasn't fooled. "Quinn, dear—"

"Oh, no. Don't, 'Quinn, dear,' me. This is a blatant disregard of my wishes." She looked at her father and said, "Dad, how *could* you?"

"Don't you see? We are here to help you. Why can't you understand that?" Her father stood and started to put his arm around her shoulder.

Now Quinn's insides were blazing, and her face was hot. Her hands shook as she brushed off her dad's gesture. "Why can't *you* understand *me*? Don't you think I have enough pressure with all that's going on? Now I have my own parents opposing me."

Joy McFarland raised her voice. "I don't see how—"

The woman at the reception desk rose and headed toward the family. At the same time, the door to the inner office opened, and Mr. Becker, himself, entered the room.

"What's going *on* here, people?" the attorney said, his voice reflecting a mixture of disbelief and consternation. He looked at his assistant, as if she were the only voice he could trust.

"I believe Ms. McFarland didn't know her parents—"

Quinn jumped in, not wanting anyone else to speak for her. "Mr. Becker, I asked my parents not to come here today. I'm an adult, and I am capable of speaking with you by myself."

The attorney tapped Quinn on the shoulder as if to say, "Let me handle this." He turned to her parents and stared at them with sympathy, smooth as if he had done this a million times before. "John, Joy, I know how you must feel. We all want to protect our children, even long after they've grown up. But the truth is, I can't have you sit in on the meeting with your daughter and me.

"I'm sure you've heard of attorney-client privilege." He paused to scratch his head. "That protects the client, because no one can be forced to testify in court to anything that is divulged in conversation with the attorney. If you, or anyone else, except my assistant Ethel here, who is considered an extension of me, comes into the room, that waives the privilege, putting Quinn at risk, and, frankly, you, too."

Quinn's parents stared at the lawyer, perhaps in disbelief, but probably stunned that they weren't going to get their way. "W-well, all we wanted to do was support our daughter," her mother said. "We certainly didn't mean to create a scene."

Quinn glowered at her mother. Creating scenes had been a specialty of her mother's, and this was specifically why Quinn hadn't wanted her parents here. Well, at least in part.

"No problem," Becker continued. "In addition, I'm going to instruct Quinn not to repeat a single word about what we discuss to anyone, and that includes you. Nothing personal, but, at this point in time, we need to keep a lid on the ol' soup pot."

The heat in Quinn's belly had started to cool, and her view of David

Becker now topped the charts. The man had guts, along with a great sense of professionalism. Somewhat vindicated, Quinn turned to her dad. "I know you care about me, both of you, and I appreciate that. After I meet with Mr. Becker, I'll come in to work. Okay?"

Staring at the floor, as if the upheaval had cut a crevasse between his daughter and himself, her father replied, "That will be fine, sweetheart. Zeke and Rory just brought in another body as we left to come here." He put his arm around his wife and squeezed her shoulder. "Let's leave these two to their meeting."

As they exited the building, Quinn turned to Mr. Becker and said, "Thank you so much. I apologize for all the unpleasantness."

"No need to apologize, young lady. You aren't the first person in this town to have parents coming in here, and you won't be the last. Try not to be upset with your folks. In the end, they came here because they love you. Now let's get down to business, shall we?"

Chapter Twenty-five

Quinn felt a lot better about talking to Mr. Becker, now that he'd explained attorney-client privilege to her parents. Still, her emotions and memories were jamming in her head, and the result was a head-banger's cacophony of sound. She wanted to unburden herself of the anger, fear, jealousy, and guilt, but she had lived with them so long, she didn't know who she was without them. And Becker was an attorney, not a psychiatrist. She should probably stick with the facts.

She walked past a whirring machine as she took a seat in his office. She wondered whether it was there to remove odors or to muffle privileged conversations.

"So, what brings you here today?" The attorney sat across from her, pen in hand. His folksy demeanor was fading fast. He was all business now.

Swallowing hard, Quinn said, "As I told you over the phone, this has to do with the murder of Ana Renfroe. I met with Sgt. Schmidt at the police station yesterday, and the questions he asked made me think I may be a suspect."

Becker leaned back in his chair and gave Quinn an appraising look. "Did he ask you where you were at the time of the murder?"

"Not in so many words. He asked me when was the last time I'd seen either of the Renfroes, Ana or Brad. I told him I had intentionally avoided them for the past fifteen years."

"And why was that?"

"The old love triangle—my boyfriend hooked up with my best friend. They got married. I went to work in the family business. End of a sad story."

The attorney tapped his pen against the edge of his desk. "So where *were* you at the time of the murder?"

Quinn thought back to the night before Ana's body was brought in. "That was the night my brother Jack was called into the transplant center. It was July 4. I was at home. I'd watched the parade from the porch of the funeral home that morning, worked on a body that afternoon. I came home late—around 6:30 or 7:00. I fixed dinner, ran a load of laundry. After the fireworks display, I took my dog for a run. Pretty typical night." She drew in a deep breath.

"Can anyone corroborate your whereabouts, if need be?" The attorney's eyebrows were drawn so close together, like dark valances on a drapery rod. Quinn felt sorry for anyone having to oppose those eyebrows in court.

"Probably not. My parents were with Jack at the hospital. My boyfriend is a fifth-year surgical resident, so I don't see him that often and didn't that night. My neighbors might have seen me walking the dog, but I do that every night, so they might not have paid much attention."

Becker tapped his pen again, apparently considering his next question. "What reason or reasons would the police have to suspect you in Ana Renfroe's death, allowin' that you haven't seen her in so long?"

Quinn took a deep breath. "Sgt. Schmidt mentioned a couple of things when I met with him at the station. First of all, let *me* ask *you* a question. Do you know what it means to be blood sisters?"

"Some kind of secret sorority?"

"Yes, but only two people. Actually, drawing blood and mixing it together. Taking an oath. Till death do us part, sort of." Quinn almost choked on the irony. "Anyway, Ana and I were blood sisters. We kept each other's secrets. When we were in high school, we both wore necklaces, each in the shape of half a heart, engraved with the initials B.S. and the other's first name on it."

The attorney nodded.

"So when the police searched Ana's house after she was killed, they found her half heart with my name on the back."

"So, assumin' Ana didn't know another person named Quinn, that establishes you were friends long ago. Not incriminatin', in my book."

"There's more. Apparently Ana, or someone, had written my address on a desk calendar open to the month of July. It was in Ana's house."

The attorney made a brief note. "Okay, anythin' else?"

"Unfortunately, yes. Ana told her parents, who told the police, that if anything bad happened to her, to 'ask Quinn'."

The eyebrows drew in tightly at that, and Becker rose and started to pace behind his desk. "Do you know why Ana would say that to her parents?"

"No." Quinn swallowed hard. "And there's something else. Ana's husband Brad, who's disappeared, called me at the funeral home a couple of times. When I finally spoke to him, he told me about finding her in the house with her head bashed in, but still alive. He told me she was saying my name."

"Did he tell that to the police?"

"I-I don't think so. To my knowledge, the police haven't interviewed Brad. He's currently MIA."

Becker sat on the corner of his desk. "Is there anythin' else to tell me, related to Ana's death or the time since her death?"

Quinn opened her handbag and pulled out the plastic bag with the note. She set it on her lap, impressed that Becker wasn't rushing her. "You probably should know that I've been threatened twice. The first time at my house. A note wrapped around a golf ball, thrown through my bathroom window. I filed a police report, and they have the note."

"What'd it say?" Now he was back in his chair, writing.

The words were burnished upon Quinn's brain. "Memories can hurt you. Don't talk or you'll be next." Even now, the words sent a shiver down her spine. "Before you ask me who could've written that, here's the second note. I found it on the front passenger seat of my car yesterday afternoon." She handed over the bag with the note. The printed words, "Keep Quiet," showed as she handed it over. "I knew I was coming here today, and you told me not to talk to the police without you being present, so I bagged the note and brought it here instead of reporting it."

"You did right. If I represent you, *I* will deliver this to the police station."

"*If* you represent me?" Quinn's stomach squeezed in protest. "I *definitely* want you to represent me." Not until that very moment had Quinn realized how much.

The attorney tapped his pen and said, "No worries. I would like to represent you. Let's just get these preliminaries out of the way first." He continued by asking several logistical questions about the second note, who had access to Quinn's car, whether it had been locked, and why someone would go to such lengths to warn her to keep quiet.

Quinn answered as best she could without going into too much detail. Specific memories were, as she had promised herself, off limits.

Becker shifted in his chair and asked if Quinn would like some coffee, apparently not finished with the interview.

"No, thanks. I'm a tea drinker."

"I can have Ethel bring tea. How 'bout it?"

"I'd better not. But you go ahead, if you'd like."

The attorney rose and headed for the door. "Let's take a short break. Be right back."

Whether he needed a bathroom break, or truly craved coffee, Quinn didn't mind. This gave her a chance to circle the room and decompress a little. As she passed behind Becker's chair, she glanced at his notes. The last thing he'd written was what looked like a heading in block letters: THE PAST. Quinn shuddered at what was coming next.

She returned to her chair and checked her phone for texts. Josh had sent one a few minutes earlier. Mom and Dad here. Can't wait to introduce them to you. Save your appetite. xo.

Quinn loved it that he said, "them to you," instead of, "you to them." As for appetite, she wondered if he meant for food. She must have been smiling when Becker returned, carrying a mug of steaming coffee.

He returned the smile, as he sat at his desk and drank. "Let's shift gears," he said. Quinn knew what was coming. "I think we need to talk about the past, your relationships with Ana and Brad."

Was it the strong coffee smell or the turn of subject that caused nausea to rise in Quinn's throat? She tamped it down with a couple of deep breaths. "I told you, Ana and I were very close. Inseparable, really. When I started dating Brad, there was a little tension. Sometimes I had to choose one over the other. But Ana had a few boyfriends, too."

The attorney asked several questions about how and when the relationships had begun, and Quinn rolled off the answers with little or no emotional impact, although she dreaded what would follow.

Becker tapped his pen. "How exactly did the relationship end?"

Quinn's stomach lurched. "It was a Saturday. The three of us were at my house, trying to decide where to go that night. I wanted to go to a movie, *National Treasure*. Brad and Ana wanted to go to the beach. I should've suspected something, that they had ganged up on me, but I didn't. I left the room for some reason, and when I came back, they were—they were all entangled."

"Kissin'?"

"Yes, but much more than that. Ana never did anything in any ordinary way. She had an—intensity—about her." Quinn shook her head, trying to dislodge the memory. "Anyway, that was it. Ana and Brad declared themselves a couple, and I was left on the sidelines, bereft of both. It wasn't an easy time, but I made it through."

Becker cleared his throat. "Let's move on, shall we? Is there anythin' else about your relationship with Ana or Brad that could possibly become relevant to Ana's murder case?"

Quinn's thoughts leaped to the many nights she and Ana had watched Dawn, parading naked around her house, with the lights on and draperies open. Curious young girls playing at voyeurism, unaware of the consequences. Dawn's murder. Ana's murder. *Memories can hurt you. Don't tell, or you'll be next.*

"No, nothing that I haven't already told you."

Becker's eyebrows rose, and he turned his head as if to hear better. "Are you sure? Y'know, a criminal defense attorney hears a lot of stories, and my radar tells me you're holdin' back. Let me remind you again of attorney-client privilege, young lady."

Panic flew around inside Quinn's body, like a caged bird, desperate to get out. She had lived with this panic for so long. The feeling had wrapped itself around her organs and become a part of her. What she and Ana had seen and done was etched into her heart, though she had never told a soul about it. Despite the attorney-client privilege and her growing trust in Becker, himself, she wasn't ready.

"I can't talk about it. Not yet, maybe not ever."

Becker frowned, his eyebrows throwing shadows over his face. "You put me in an indelicate position. I need to know all the facts if I'm to represent you. On the other hand, you haven't been charged, yet."

He took a clean sheet of paper from a desk drawer and started writing. After a minute or so, he drew two horizontal lines at the bottom of the page and signed his name under one of them. He turned the page around and set his pen down in front of Quinn. "I'll make a deal with you, young lady. You don't have to tell me now, but if and when you become a suspect or are arrested, you'll have to tell me everything you know, or I'll withdraw from representing you. Is that clear?"

Quinn nodded, relieved.

Becker nodded back, the corners of his mouth hinting at a smile. "Okay, then read and sign."

Quinn's eyes roamed across the words, "refused to answer all of this attorney's questions," "at such time as the client becomes a suspect or is charged..." She signed her name to the document. Conflicting emotions battled inside of her. She understood Becker's concerns. She had no intention of doing anything to cause him to withdraw from representing her. At the same time, she hoped she wasn't signing her life away—literally.

Chapter Twenty-six

After leaving the attorney's office, Quinn had gone into work to prepare a body, and now she was back at home, getting ready to go out with Josh. When her cell phone rang, she was tempted to ignore the call, but when she saw Jack's name flashing, she picked up immediately. Jack was one of the few whose calls she would never dodge.

"Hey, Sis. How're things going? You have a minute?" Jack's voice was growing stronger each time Quinn heard him. She put down the flat iron she was using to tame her curls.

"Sure."

"Two things. First, we got so involved with talking about Ana and Brad this morning, I never commented on your news about meeting Josh's parents. Way to go, sister."

"Oh, thanks. Let's not make too much out of this, please. I'm anxious enough without the whole family putting pressure on me." She drew an angled line on her cheekbone with the rouge stick and feathered it into a natural-looking glow. "It's starting to make me feel inadequate, like I'm nobody without Josh."

"C'mon now, you know that's not me. I adore you *just the way you are.*" The phrase taken from "Mr. Rogers' Neighborhood" had been an inside joke between the two of them since childhood. "I'm guilty, though, of hoping you and Josh get married eventually. Remember, I'm the one who introduced you."

"True enough. When you get out of the hospital, I'll pay you a matchmaker's fee." She brushed her hair on one side, and then switched the phone to her other ear.

"No need. Just name your first-born after me."

Quinn loved bantering with her brother, but the waning light from the newly-installed window reminded her that she really needed to finish getting ready and let Calvin out. Running short of time would make her even more nervous. "You said there were two things."

Jack's voice dropped a register. "Yeah. Wanted to alert you that Mom and Dad are miffed. They stopped by after leaving the lawyer's office. I could tell they were anxious about Ana's murder."

"Not surprising. I expected Mom to pump me for information when I was at the shop this afternoon. She hates not being in control."

"Agreed. Did she?"

"Nope, not Dad either. In fact, I didn't see either one of them. I went in, did the body, and ducked out. Anyway, I can't. The last thing Becker said to me when I was leaving his office was, 'No discussing this case with anyone, including your parents'."

"Well, don't worry. *I* won't press you for information, and I won't breathe a word of anything you've ever told me about Ana or Brad. Whatever you're going through, I'm completely on your side."

Quinn fought back tears. She couldn't afford the time to redo her makeup. "What did I ever do to deserve such a loyal brother? How can I ever repay you?" Her brother was recovering from a life-threatening disease, and all she had done was take him smoothies.

"Are you kidding? Have you forgotten all the times you bailed *me* out with Mom and Dad? Let's face it—they haven't been the easiest parents, and *working there*? There are times, if it weren't for you, I would've marched out and headed for who-knows-where."

Quinn's thoughts rushed to the time last year when Jack's fiancée had dumped him, basically because of his illness. Their parents had tried to interfere. Quinn had persuaded them not to harass Shelley's parents, to let the relationship end naturally. Now that Jack had a new kidney, she hoped he would find another woman to love him. He deserved that.

Quinn wanted to talk longer, but now there was no time to spare. "I've gotta run, Jack. Thanks for everything. I'll come by tomorrow." Although she'd disconnected, her tender feelings for her brother continued. Jack had been her sidekick, her confidante, her defender. Ana may have been her blood sister based on a silly juvenile ceremony, but Jack was the real deal. He was truly her blood brother.

Chapter Twenty-seven

When Josh arrived at the door to pick Quinn up for dinner, it was all she could do not to melt into his arms. He'd had a haircut, his British-something cologne was firing up her hormones, but, most of all, the look in his eyes reflected a new passion. Ambrosia made of desire, confidence, possession, and a bit of reverence. Quinn was thrilled, but also scared. The flip side of loving Josh was the fear of losing him.

He kissed her with a dizzying fervor. If it weren't for his parents meeting them at the restaurant, she would have suggested a cozy evening at home.

"You look spectacular," he said, his voice breathy and low.

"You like my outfit?" She turned from side to side, like a model on a runway. She had selected this pant suit for its stylish, yet tailored look. Her shoes, though, were drop-dead sexy. She'd bought them on sale at the end of last summer, and she'd only worn them once.

"Outfit's great, but I like what's in it better." He tucked a strand of her hair behind her ear. "What'd you do to your hair?" He seemed in no hurry.

"Flat-ironed. I thought your parents might like sleek better than curly. Want to come in for a few minutes?" Calvin seconded the motion by jumping up and resting forepaws on Josh's leg.

Josh picked up the Westie and nuzzled his face. "I think we'd better go. Wouldn't be polite to keep Mom and Dad waiting, especially on a 'first date.'"

"Okay." Quinn picked up her handbag, told Calvin she'd be home soon, and set the alarm on the way out.

As he drove to the restaurant, Josh wore a Cheshire-cat grin. He glanced at Quinn every so often and patted her knee. "You look mighty happy," she said. "Aren't you even a little bit nervous?"

He stopped at a red light and gazed into her eyes. "Nope. Not even an infinitesimal amount. And you don't need to be, either." He took her hand and squeezed it. When the light turned green, he said, "You shouldn't worry about things like your hair, either. My parents aren't that petty."

"Oh, come on. Maybe they don't judge a book by its cover, but I'm sure they'd notice if their only son's girlfriend had messy hair. First impressions matter." She pulled down the visor to check herself in the mirror one last time.

"They already know how you look, and they think you're beautiful. I showed them that selfie we took at Saltwater Grill. Just relax and be yourself."

"And you're sure they don't mind what I do for a living?" Quinn had been afraid to ask for a long time. In her mind, that could be a deal-breaker.

"I told you before. The fact that you work on dead bodies doesn't bother them any more than it bothers me. They even commented, when I told them, that your profession wasn't that different from mine." He made the last left turn before the restaurant. "Look, Quinn, my parents are so delighted that I'm finally serious about a woman. They've waited a long time for me to find someone. You'd probably have to have three heads and five arms for them not to love you. All they want is for me to settle down with someone of fine moral character—exactly like you."

The lurching of Quinn's stomach had nothing to do with the near-miss of a car backing out of a parking spot and almost colliding with Josh's front bumper. Fine moral character might be a relative concept. She hadn't told Josh anything about Ana or the threatening notes, but the time might be coming soon when she'd have to. No telling when he might find out in this small town, and it would be better, she thought, for him to hear about it from her.

As they parked and walked into the restaurant, hand-in-hand, Quinn asked, "What should I call your parents?"

"Hm, never thought about that. Their first names are Michael and Elise, but I don't know how they'll want you to call them. Let's just play it by ear."

Easy for you to say. Quinn's stomach was wedged into her throat at this point. Josh held the heavy glass door open for her, and she said a quick prayer. What to call the Bradys was only one of the things she worried about.

* * *

A smart-looking couple at the bar walked toward Josh and Quinn, drinks in hand. Quinn would have picked them out anyway. Josh had Mr. Brady's tall, lanky shape and sandy-colored hair, Mrs. Brady's thick-lashed gray eyes and full lips.

"Mom and Dad, this is *Quinn.*" The emphasis he put on her name made Quinn's heart soar.

"So nice to meet you, Mr. and Mrs. Brady. Josh has told me so many wonderful things about you." Quinn shook hands with each of them. Their hands were almost as cold as hers.

"Call us Mike and Elise," Josh's father said, his voice a good deal warmer than his hand. He turned to tell the hostess that they were ready to be seated.

The restaurant was posh and homey at the same time, with comfortable chairs on rollers and ambient lighting. There was enough conversation in the room to make it seem festive, but not so much as to drown out one's thinking. And the aromas of fresh-baked bread and charcoal-grilled steaks were heavenly. Once they were ensconced at a table overlooking the bay, with drinks ordered for Quinn and Josh, the getting-to-know-you conversation began.

Elise took the lead. "Josh tells us you have a West Highland terrier. Aren't they the sweetest dogs? I had one growing up. Cammy was her name. She never left my side. Lived to be 16."

Quinn could talk about Calvin all evening. "Sixteen is a ripe old age, though I'm sure it was hard to lose her. My Calvin is four. Still has a lot of puppy in him. He adores Josh."

Josh beamed and gave Quinn a quick wink. "And the feeling is mutual. I miss having a dog of my own, but with my schedule it wouldn't be fair. Besides, dogs aren't allowed in the apartment. Calvin helps me get my doggie fix."

Turning to Mike, Quinn asked, "Do you have dogs at home?"

"Yes, indeed. We have a menagerie—all rescues. Elise volunteers at the local shelter, and she's so soft-hearted. When she meets a dog that nobody else wants, she can't let them euthanize it. She brings it home."

"How many dogs do you have, then?" Quinn couldn't imagine walking multiple dogs, but she couldn't help being impressed by Elise's generosity toward animals.

Elise answered, "Currently we have seven. Rusty is nearly blind, and Cleo has a bad leg, but the other five are healthy and spry. They keep us on our toes."

The canine talk continued for another few minutes, and then the waiter came to distribute menus and recite the evening specials. The discussion turned to food, another topic Quinn was comfortable with.

Mike donned a pair of burgundy-colored readers that matched his tie.

"The steaks look great—pricey, but if the quality merits it, I don't mind paying for a steak dinner. What do you think, son? You've had steak here before?"

"The bone-in veal chop's my favorite. The bone gives the meat additional flavor as it cooks. But I'm going to order the filet. The other steaks are enough for two meals, and I'm not that hungry."

"What do you recommend, Quinn?" Elise asked. Quinn wondered whether Josh's mom had a hearty appetite like her own, or whether she was one of the eat-like-a-bird ladies. Quinn could recommend several things from the lighter side of the menu.

Jumping to the rescue before Quinn could decide, Josh interjected, "Quinn is the kind of woman who eats when she's in a restaurant, like you, Mom. That was one of the first things that attracted me to her."

Beginning to relax, Quinn recommended the kale and quinoa salad, the six-ounce filet topped with crabmeat, and the creamed spinach with mushrooms. She and Elise ordered identical meals. Josh had told her to be herself, and he'd been right. Everyone seemed congenial and in a good mood.

While they ate, the Bradys talked about their plans for the next couple of days of their stay. "We hope we have the chance to see you again, Quinn. I can see why Josh is so fond of you."

After the plates were cleared, and coffee, tea, and dessert were served, a woman sitting across the room rose from her table and made a beeline for Quinn. "Excuse me for interrupting."

"Oh, hi, Anise," Quinn replied. "This is my neighbor, Anise Castellanos. My friend, Josh Brady, and his parents, Mike and Elise." Everyone nodded at one another and smiled, and there were a few seconds of awkward silence.

"Nice to meet you." Anise smoothed her already-smooth skirt. "Well, seeing you here reminded me of something. I took in a package for you the other day. The FedEx guy left it on the porch, but I've had porch pirates steal from me. I planned to let Marlena bring it to you that afternoon, but I had houseguests from Chicago, and it slipped my mind. I'm so sorry. I'll bring it over later tonight or tomorrow."

Quinn couldn't recall having ordered anything lately, and she wasn't expecting any packages. A finger of dread tickled her brain. She had a feeling this wasn't an ordinary package. "Well, thank you. I'll come by later to pick it up."

Anise continued, as though Quinn hadn't spoken. "Not sure, but I think it was the day before all those police officers were in your yard. Friday, maybe? I meant to come check on you. Ms. Tartt told me you had a terrible break-in."

Quinn's delicious steak dinner sat like an immovable rock in her stomach. She could have crawled into a hole and covered herself with dirt. Josh's dad's eyes widened, and he stared at his wife, who had set down her coffee cup with a loud clink. Josh looked at Quinn with questioning eyes.

Realizing her mistake in not cutting off Anise at the pass, Quinn tried to end the conversation before things got worse. "Thanks for stopping by. It was lovely to see you."

Apparently getting the hint at last, Anise took a step backward, gave a small bow, and said, "Good night, then. A pleasure to meet you." And she was off, leaving a table full of suspicious looks in her wake.

Chapter Twenty-eight

The ride home from the restaurant was quiet. Before Anise's revelation, Quinn had sensed the Bradys' acceptance and approval, but now, she wasn't sure. 'Police' and 'break-in' could be easily explained, except for the fact that Quinn hadn't even mentioned the incident to Josh, and he would wonder why not. Josh looked straight ahead, his jaw tight.

Quinn couldn't stand the tension. "I loved meeting your parents. They really seem like great people." *Surely a little thing like police in my yard wouldn't cause them to dislike me.*

Josh pulled the car onto a side street and parked in a school parking lot. He turned off the headlights but kept the motor running. "You want to tell me about the police in your yard?"

Quinn unfastened her seat belt and turned to face him. "I was afraid that would upset you. I was going to tell you about it, but I didn't have a chance."

"Well, tell me now. I'm listening." Quinn wanted to touch his face, or at least his hand, but the expression he wore was remote, almost clinical. He wanted the simple truth, uncomplicated by feelings. She would give him the truth. Maybe not the whole truth, but the truth.

"It was nothing, really. Somebody threw an object and broke my bathroom window, so I had to replace the window. You know how connected my dad is to the police. Instead of one officer, three came out."

"Why didn't you tell me about it? If we're going to be a couple, we should tell each other things like this." The word "if" snagged a piece of Quinn's heart. She thought they already were a couple.

"You were on call. I handled it. I met with the police, filed a report, cleaned up the mess, had the glass people out. It was over and done. No big deal."

"What day did that happen?" The streetlight at the corner of the parking lot illuminated Josh's face as he stared through the windshield. His expression was unreadable.

So much had happened since Ana's death. The days seemed to roll together. After thinking a minute, Quinn replied, "The break-in happened while you and I were out to dinner Friday night. When I got home, I walked Calvin. I didn't find the broken glass until I headed to the bathroom to get ready for bed."

"Why didn't you call me then? I would've come right over. I would've helped you."

"It just didn't seem necessary. Or important."

"What did the police think? Was it a random act of vandalism, or something more?"

"No sign of entry, nothing taken, if that's what you mean."

Josh gripped the steering wheel. "I still don't know why you didn't tell me about this. You came to my house the next day and made love to me, for gosh sakes, and I had to hear about this, days later, from a neighbor? It makes me feel—I don't know—upset that you would neglect to tell me."

Somewhere a stray cat meowed, and Quinn winced. There was so much more she hadn't told him. "Listen, Josh. Remember when we were at Gaido's, and I asked you if you had participated in Jack's surgery?"

"That's different. That's a matter of professional ethics, not an event in my personal life." Even in the dark, his face glowed red.

"Still, I had to accept that there are things in your life that you can't share with me. We can be together without telling each other every single detail of every single day, can't we?"

Josh didn't reply for so long that Quinn wondered whether he had heard the question. He gazed straight ahead, and his jaw was working. Quinn stared at the dark playground. The empty swings and roundabout made her feel even sadder.

"Listen, Quinn. I love you. I've looked a long time before finding someone like you. You're pretty and smart and fun to be with, and just quirky enough to keep things interesting. There aren't many women who understand the crazy demands of a surgeon, but you've got similar demands in your work. I love your independence—"

"But?" Quinn held her breath.

"But I always feel you're holding back on me, like you can't trust me or something." The wavering of his voice and the accuracy of his perceptions stung Quinn like an arrow. She reached for his hand and held it tight.

"I love you, too." Her voice was a whisper. They sat in silence for a while, seconds, maybe minutes, the whine of an ambulance adding a somber backdrop. No one had ever expressed such raw emotion to her before, such love. She wanted to be worthy of Josh, and she wanted to tell the truth.

It would feel like being cleansed by a cool, fresh waterfall to be able to unload her burden. Her shoulders were tired, and Josh was a person she could depend on—she knew that. But things had become so twisted since Ana's death. Not only had she vowed silence years ago, but now she had promised her attorney not to discuss anything with anyone. Attorney-client privilege most assuredly would not apply to boyfriends. Dragging a brilliant, hard-working, and morally upright person like Josh into this sordid business would truly be selfish on her part.

"You're right, Josh. I've had trust issues in the past. I guess that's how I became so independent, as you say. I've waited a long time, too, and our relationship is important to me. Maybe it's a good thing that Anise brought this up about the police. If she hadn't, I wouldn't have known how you felt. Now we have something to work on to make things better." She took his hand to her lips and kissed it gently. "I'm going to try to do better to share what's going on in my life. I mean that."

As Josh wrapped his arm around her shoulder and drew her in for one of his most amazing kisses ever, Quinn swore to herself that her pledge to Josh, of all the pledges she'd made, was the most sacred. She'd do everything she could to keep it.

Chapter Twenty-nine

The next morning, there were two texts on Quinn's phone. The first was from Jack. Woohoo! I get to go home today.

Thrilled for her brother, Quinn hit reply. You rock. Be over later with smoothies. She marveled at Jack's ability to recover from transplant surgery in such a short time. But that was Jack—he was nothing if not resilient.

The second text was from her father. Two bodies waiting at the shop. Mr. and Mrs. Stovall, car accident last night. Had the ambulance she'd heard from the school parking lot been on its way to these next customers? She knew the Stovalls. They owned a café on the east end of town. She hated jobs like this. Not only did they require long, delicate handiwork on her part, but preparing for and hosting double funerals was emotionally difficult, with the grief multiplied for the mourners. It would be a long and busy day.

Quinn threw on a pair of shorts and a halter top to take Calvin out for his morning run. When she got back, she found Anise standing at the doorstep, ringing the bell. She held a cardboard box in one hand. Calvin ran ahead, yapping his displeasure at anyone disturbing his territory, but he calmed down when Anise stooped to pet him behind the ears.

"I know you're up early, and I wanted to get this to you while it was on my mind. Sorry not to have delivered it sooner."

"That's okay. Appreciate your holding it for me." Quinn took the package and turned it over in her hands. The return address was 2501 Main Street, the address of McFarland's Funeral Home. More importantly, Quinn recognized the handwriting. She'd know those curly letters anywhere—they were Ana's.

"No problem. See you later," Anise said, and she darted back to her own house. Quinn stood on her porch, staring at the package. Lightweight, the contents slid when she shook it. *One mystery solved*, she thought. *Now I know why Ana had my address written on her calendar. She had most likely looked it up and written it down so she could send me this package.* But every question answered raised two more. What was inside the package, and why had Ana sent it?

The first was easily answered. Quinn took Calvin into the kitchen for a treat, and she pulled the kitchen shears out to cut open the wrapping tape. The box had no label, but Quinn recognized it from the local department store. Inside, wrapped in a single sheet of tissue paper, were two videotapes. Two X-rated movie cassettes with artistic drawings, rather than photographs, of a cowboy copulating with a long-haired woman in various poses, on the front and back. The titles were *Southern Lass Gets What She Deserves* and *Ride Me, Cowboy*. The lower right-hand corner of each tape had the words, "Distributed by Gulf Coast Adult Entertainment," and a year, 2003 and 2004, respectively.

Leaving the package on the counter, while she got cleaned up and dressed in scrubs for the day, she thought about all of it—Ana, Brad, even Dawn.

Quinn had an inkling why Ana would send her porn tapes, but before she could be sure, she would have to view the tapes. Who in the world still had a VHS player? Even if she found someone, how could she explain why she needed to use it?

A few things were starting to fall into place. For example, Ana had told her parents if anything happened to her to go to Quinn. When the Frenches asked Quinn why, she'd had no idea. Now that she had the tapes, *if* the tapes showed what Quinn suspected, she would hold in her hands the reason. The same would be true for why Ana repeated Quinn's name to Brad as she was dying.

Quinn wrapped the videotapes in the tissue paper and returned them to the plain box. She folded the outer wrapper and put it in the box, too. She had a long day's work ahead of her, with two bodies to prepare. The sooner she got started, the sooner she would be able to search for a VHS player. Meanwhile, she put the box of tapes in the trunk of her car, underneath the carpet, with the spare tire. She checked to see if anybody was watching, but the street was quiet.

Remembering her promise to Josh, she sent him a quick text. Hope you and your parents have a great day. Jack is going home (you probably already know)! <3 you.

The sun inched its way over the Gulf as Quinn drove to work with the car windows down. The temperature was already in the eighties, but the wind created by the moving car gave the illusion of coolness. The salty tang in the air and the screeching of the seagulls filled her with a sense of normalcy, something she craved right now. If she could get to the bottom of this Ana business, maybe she'd have a chance at a happy life with Josh. There was still another nagging problem, though—the threats. Someone desperately wanted her to keep quiet. And the more she learned, the harder that was going to be.

Chapter Thirty

When she got to work, Mr. and Mrs. Stovall were waiting, 'ever so patiently,' as she and Jack used to say. This summer none of the standard quips had quite the same amusement factor as before. Maybe that was a function of growing older, or maybe it was all the stress in her life. Ana's death had cast everything in a different light.

Quinn put on her apron, popped the spearmint gum into her mouth, and began working. The loud humming of the ventilation system and the iTunes from her ear buds allowed her father to sneak up on her. She hadn't spoken to him face-to-face since they had been in Becker's office.

"Hi, Dad," she said, as she washed her hands and removed an ear bud. "How're things with you and Mom?"

"That's what I came in to talk to you about. Mom and I are doing okay. We're elated that Jack is going home today. Your mother has already gone to the hospital to help. But we've been talking over what happened in David Becker's office." Quinn held her breath. She hoped he wasn't going to suggest she change attorneys.

He took a deep breath. "After much discussion, we think Becker was right not to include us in your meeting. We only want what is best for you, but we realize that you're an adult now, and you're perfectly capable of handling yourself." He made eye contact, and Quinn could swear his eyes were glistening. Hearing these words caused her own eyes to well up, as well. "It's hard for us not to think of you as our little girl. But we understand your need to be independent in this."

Quinn appreciated how difficult it must have been for her parents. Her mom, especially, had probably had a sleepless night. She felt good to have one less thing hanging over her head, but until she could resolve this whole mess, this seemed like a pyrrhic victory, at best. "Thanks, Dad. Means a lot to me. And thank Mom, too."

She gestured toward the table, where her work was just getting started. "Guess I'd better get back to work." Her dad nodded and left her to her gum and her music.

The routine of loosening rigor—flex, bend, rotate, massage—gave her a rhythmic backdrop for thinking. She needed to locate a VHS player. Her original thought was to return to the library. She was pretty sure they had one in the back of the history center. But she wasn't sure how private that area would be, and if the tapes matched their covers, she might attract too much attention, watching porn in a public setting.

The best course, she thought, would be to return to Mr. Becker's office. He could probably set her up with a VHS player, and he would know what to do with the tapes. If and when the police learned that Ana had mailed the tapes to her, she would need his advice and support. She might as well involve him now, rather than waiting. If he could see her this afternoon, that would be perfect. Afterwards, she would pick up dinner and some smoothies and take them to Jack's house to celebrate his homecoming.

Quinn chewed almost four packs of gum and worked straight through lunch. Mr. Becker had told her to stop by the office at four. Yes, he had an old VCR, and the office would likely be quiet at that time of day.

As soon as she finished Mrs. Stovall, Quinn washed up and changed into one of the spare outfits she kept in the closet. The yellow jeans and sequined T-shirt weren't exactly go-to-the-lawyer's-office attire, but they would have to do.

* * *

Ethel's reception desk was clear of paper, and the assistant was on her way out as Quinn walked in. "You can go on in. Mr. Becker's expecting you." The after-hours smell of paper and computer toner gave Quinn a sense of security, as if everything in this office were properly arranged.

The lights had been dimmed, probably by timer, and the effect was soothing. The office was a stark and welcome contrast to Quinn's workplace. She tiptoed toward Mr. Becker's closed office door and put her ear next to it. Fragments of what must have been a phone conversation filtered through the crack. "Ain't that the truth…? Yes, indeed… keep me posted, will ya?" Once she couldn't hear any more, Quinn knocked on the door.

"Come on in," the voice boomed, and then a squeak, as Becker rose to greet her. "Sit right down." He pointed to the upholstered chair in front of his desk. "What have we here?"

The question was rhetorical, since Quinn had told him over the phone about the videotapes. She laid the package on the edge of Becker's desk. She couldn't have been more tense if she were placing a bomb there. "Thanks for seeing me on such short notice. I came as soon as I could."

"No problem. As I said earlier, late afternoon is a quiet time here in the office. So, let's see what you got." He leaned forward and stared as Quinn removed the box from the envelope and opened it.

"Here's the outside envelope." Quinn unfolded the FedEx wrapper and laid it in front of Becker. "The handwriting on the label is Ana's. I have samples at home that match exactly. I don't know what name she gave to FedEx, but the return address is McFarland's. Guess she figured it would get to me either way."

"Hmm. If I remember correctly, Ms. Renfroe was killed on July 4." He made a note on his yellow legal pad. "Now when was this package delivered?"

"*I* didn't receive it until this morning. My neighbor, Anise Castellanos, saw FedEx deliver it on Friday afternoon. She knew I wouldn't be home for a while, and she'd had a package stolen from her porch, so she said she picked it up for safekeeping. She meant to give it to me that same day, but she forgot."

"So, between Friday afternoon and this morning, Tuesday, the package was in the sole custody of Ms. Castellanos?"

"I believe so. Ana must have taken it to FedEx the day before she was killed." The image of Ana planning the details and sending the tapes, in hopes that Quinn would know what to do with them, gave Quinn a cold, sharp pain in her gut, as if an icicle had pinned her to the client's chair.

"Once your neighbor handed the package to you, this morning, what did you do with it? Just so you know, I need to know details to determine your exposure with regard to handling the contents. There are several criminal matters involved here, and my job is to make sure you can't be seen as mishandling or withholding evidence."

"I understand. That's why I came here as soon as I could. I opened the package, looked at the covers on the two tapes, and put the whole package, including the envelope, in the trunk of my car, until I could bring it here."

Becker picked up one of the tapes, perused the cover, front and back, and put it back, repeating the process with the other tape. "These look like pornographic movies."

Quinn nodded. "Until we look at them, we won't know whether the tapes match the covers."

"I assume you aren't an actor in either of these two movies, and you didn't play any part in producin' or distributin' either of them." The piercing look, eyebrows notwithstanding, could have flustered anyone with the slightest ration of guilt, but not Quinn.

"Hah. If you look at the distribution dates on the back covers, 2003 and 2004, I was only thirteen and fourteen years old."

"So?" The eyebrows merged. "The question remains valid. I absolutely need to know if there is anything in these tapes, or any tapes like these, that might be incriminating to my client."

Quinn shook her head, thankful that in this one situation, she could answer on the clean side of things. She'd heard stories of girls and women who were trapped in sex trafficking and prostitution, and she couldn't imagine the trauma and danger they must endure. She had a hunch that Dawn was one of them, and, if so, having watched her dance, naked, all those years ago, made Quinn's face burn with shame and fear.

"Do you have any ideas why Ana Renfroe, a person you say you haven't spoken to in years, would send you these tapes, assuming she did so?"

Quinn had been thinking about that very question, all day long, even while she was working. After hours of rumination, she was no closer to an answer that she wanted to put into words, but those serious eyebrows were boring holes through her skull and demanding an answer. "I—I'm not sure. Maybe after I view them, I'll have a better idea."

The attorney put his pen down and drew a deep breath. As he exhaled, Quinn thought of a whale's blowhole. "May I remind you that I have a signed statement by you regarding your cooperation and collaboration with me, if I am to represent you in this matter? I realize that statement refers to such a time as when you may be suspected of or charged with a crime. However, the fact that you may be in possession of pornographic videotapes sent to you by a murder victim in the days before her death, and the fact that other such crimes—Brad's disappearance, and the break-in at your house—put you squarely in the center of the police department's radar—"

"I'm not trying to avoid answering your question." Quinn looked at her hands.

"You're not?"

"No, I'm trying to figure out the answer, myself. That's why I asked if you had an old video player. If I could see the tapes, I think I might find some answers—for you *and* for me."

For the first time since she'd sat down, Quinn saw the hint of a smile playing on the lawyer's lips and crinkling his eyes. He rose from his chair and slapped the desk with his palm. "Okay, then. Let's go to the movies."

He led Quinn into a bookcase-lined conference room, where a VCR machine was already hooked up to a TV. Quinn's experience with watching porno movies was limited to one time when she walked in on Jack and his friends when her parents were out for the evening. The thought of being alone in a quiet office with a man the age of her grandfather, watching a Southern lass 'get what she deserves', should have had her insides in turmoil. Oddly enough, though, the circumstances took away the anxiety and left her feeling quite clinical—almost as if she were dissecting a corpse.

As the attorney pulled the first tape from its sleeve, a small sticky note fell out. "What's this?" He turned the yellow rectangle over and handed it to Quinn. There was nothing on it, except for the two letters, *ID*. "Do you know what this means?" he asked.

A wave of nausea struck Quinn, but she struggled to keep her voice steady, as she handed the note back to Becker. "No idea."

Becker queued up the tape. Before he pushed the "play" button, he handed Quinn a notepad and a pen, identical to the one in front of his own chair. "We need to watch the two tapes in their entirety. They're each about eighty minutes long. Feel free to jot down comments or questions as we go along. I can also stop and rewind, if need be."

The volume was set on low, which was fine with Quinn. She was much more interested in the visual aspects. The movie was in black and white, and the quality was grainy. She'd forgotten how much better today's CDs and DVDs were in general, but it was obvious that whoever Gulf Coast Adult Entertainment was, they hadn't put a lot of money or technology into this movie.

There was nudity from the get-go. The young Southern lass spent the opening scenes cavorting around with a variety of men, everyone in skimpy clothes with holes in particular parts, so the viewer had access to boobs and butts and genitals. While her voluptuous body parts were on grand display, her face was hidden from the camera, but it was obvious from her body and her movements that she was young. She had long, dark tresses which she used artfully to cover and expose herself at will, or at least according to the script.

"Recognize anyone or anyplace?" Becker asked, his voice even.

Quinn shook her head but kept her eyes on the screen. Approximately an hour into the tape, a masked man came into the scene, wearing only a neckerchief, a leather vest, and boots with spurs, and carrying a lasso. Apparently, he was the punisher, ready to give the lass what she deserved. What followed was rough sex that included authentic-looking scratching, biting, cutting, and bruising. Quinn shuddered from the violence, remembering from her research how common this type of abuse occurred in the industry. The scene had been shot from the back of the man's head, so all she could observe of him was dark hair and ears that protruded at an unusual angle, a trait that Quinn had seen before.

Not until the final scene, as Southern Lass was clinging to Masked Man as if he were Prince Charming, was Quinn able to see the actress's face, and even then, she couldn't be absolutely certain. Sixteen years had passed, and memories had faded, but Quinn concluded that the Southern lass could have been Dawn.

While Becker rewound the tape and set up the second one, Quinn sat with her eyes shut, trying to conjure the images of Dawn, dancing provocatively inside the house behind the Frenches', with clothes off and curtains open for anyone, even two giggly young girls, to see.

When she opened her eyes, Quinn began writing on her notepad, listing similarities between the actress and the young girl she and Ana had watched. When she finished, there were five items on the list: long, straight dark hair; medium height; narrow waist; rounded buttocks; large, firm breasts. Estimated age? Maybe eighteen. Probably half the girls in town would fit that description. Still, the only thing that made sense was if the actress was Dawn.

"Ready for the next one?" Becker asked. If he were viewing these tapes as anything but potential evidence in criminal matters, his voice and facial expression didn't show it.

She gestured to roll the tape, and she fixed her vision on the images before her. The plots of these movies, she was learning, were flimsy excuses for people to run around naked, or in revealing costumes, acting naughty in one of a half dozen different ways. There was no real story to speak of, just intercourse with repeated grunts and groans for accompaniment.

Quinn concentrated on the female, this time dressed in white leather pants and vest with studs. High heels, no shirt. Same long, dark hair. Same body type. This time the girl had more lines to speak, and the voice was tinny and unnaturally high, not the voice of a mature woman. Dawn was only nineteen in 2004.

The girl on the screen was dancing, throwing her head back and thrusting her shoulders and hips in a languorous manner, not unlike the way Dawn had performed those nights in her house. If this was, indeed, Dawn on the tapes, had she been practicing for her role in these movies?

The viewer had the impression that there was another person in the room, perhaps a man for whom the dancer was performing. The fact that she sashayed close to the camera and whispered invitations to join her gave the impression that she was reaching out to the viewer, as well. The more she watched, the more convinced Quinn was that this was Dawn, and, knowing the ending of Dawn's personal story made this viewing both eerie and gripping.

Quinn shivered, though the temperature in the room was comfortable. She slid her eyes to observe Becker. He was tapping his pen against the table, as if he were listening to testimony in a courtroom, instead of watching a sexual seduction. He glanced at his watch and murmured, "About fifteen more minutes."

By now, Quinn was bored with the dancing. She kept watching, but allowed her thoughts to roam to Ana. If the young actress in the tapes was Dawn, and Quinn was fairly certain it was, then Ana had sent the tapes to Quinn because she expected Quinn to recognize and remember having watched her. She knew Quinn would remember "the incident" and the vow they had made to each other never to tell.

Why, though, did Ana have the tapes to begin with? Were she and Brad into watching porn, and coincidentally, they happened on these tapes with Dawn in them? Or had Ana searched for and found them with a specific purpose in mind?

While Quinn was thinking, the dancer on the screen had intensified her moves, and she was reaching her arms toward the camera, begging someone to dance with her. Now a tall, muscled man in cowboy attire stepped into the picture, groaning, and pulling the dancer into a tight embrace. Quinn's heart beat faster. Was this the same man who'd been wearing a mask in the previous film? She thought so, but now she could see his face, his large hands, and the ears that stood out from his head. Tingly chills ran up and down Quinn's body, while perspiration dotted her forehead and upper lip. She sucked in air and fought an impulse to run from the room and never return.

"What? What is it?" Becker asked, hitting the pause button on the old machine. He rushed to the cooler in the corner of the room and drew a cup of cold water to hand to Quinn.

She emptied the cup in two swallows, grateful for the few moments to gather her thoughts. She would be required to answer the lawyer's questions, and she wasn't at all ready.

"Thank you for the water. How much is left on the tape, do you think?"

"About eight minutes."

"Let's watch the end, and then we'll talk," Quinn replied. She quelled the shakiness inside enough to get herself a second cup of water.

Becker punched "play," and the movie moved toward its inevitable conclusion, with wild and rough sex abounding. Quinn had seen more than enough, however. She used the time to compose her thoughts.

She knew now why Ana had sent her the tapes, and why Ana had told her parents to talk to Quinn. She even knew why Ana had murmured Quinn's name as she was dying. She didn't, by any means, have all the pieces to the puzzle, but this last scene of the second video opened the door.

She would have to explain things to Mr. Becker, clinging to attorney-client privilege with all her might. She was about to break her promise to Ana, but maybe that's what Ana wanted her to do. Sending the tapes probably equated to giving Quinn permission to talk. Trying to calm herself, Quinn imagined how pure and fresh she would feel after telling the attorney her secret. She could trust him. She could do this.

Not until the final images and credits played on the screen did Quinn think about the words on the note, wrapped around a golf ball, and thrown into her house—"Don't talk, or you'll be next."

Chapter Thirty-one

The clock on the dashboard said 7:00, later than Quinn had planned to stay at the lawyer's office. Now she had to hustle to pick up the dinner and smoothies she had promised to take to Jack's. Physically, she was on to the next thing, but emotionally, she was still sitting at Becker's conference table, watching the credits of *Ride Me, Cowboy*, looking for information that would identify the actors or the producers of the film.

The two main actors were listed as DeeDee Young and Keith Underwood. Neither name rang a bell, probably stage names. Becker had pressed her with questions. When she had been tentative in responding, he gently reminded her of the document she had signed. So she'd told him—all about how she and Ana had watched Dawn's nude dancing.

That hadn't been enough. Becker had kept on with the questions, each one tearing down the protective wall Quinn had built around her memories, brick by brick. *Memories can hurt you.* Finally, Quinn broke down and told her attorney about "the incident," the event she had sworn never to share with anyone. All the tissues and glasses of water offered did nothing to ease the telling, and her eyes still burned from the tears.

When she had finished, Becker rose and walked around the table. "You've done the right thing to share this with me. I know it was difficult, but you really had no choice. Given what you've told me, I'm afraid I have to turn these over to the police on your behalf. Not to do so would be unethical and dangerous."

In her imagination, icy hands grabbed Quinn by the throat. *Don't tell, or you'll be next.* "Do you have to tell them what I've told you?"

Becker shook his head. "I'm under no obligation to explain anything to them, but I have to give them the tapes. There's a record of their being sent to you, and withholding evidence in a crime is a serious offense." He paced around the table. "They may want to question you once they see the tapes.

They'll want to know more about your connection to Ana and to Dawn. That will be fine, as long as I am with you. Let me remind you. you are to talk to no one about any of this without my being present."

Now, as Quinn paid for the baked ziti and chicken mozzarella at Mario's, a painful hammer was pounding behind her eyes. Having skipped lunch, her stomach was in full protest. Between the pressure to talk and the pressure not to talk, she felt like a ragdoll, a pawn in someone else's chess game. To add to the tension, she wasn't even certain about how things fit together. She'd have to organize her thoughts later.

The drive-up line at Smoothie King was four cars deep. Other people might have chosen something bubbly and alcoholic for a toast, but Jack hadn't been able to drink alcohol for the past three years, so carob smoothies were the celebratory drink of choice. She used the time to check for texts, and, seeing one from Josh, she perked up for the first time all day.

Out to dinner with my parents. They'd like to have breakfast with us tomorrow before they get on the road. My schedule permits. Does yours?

She guessed Mr. and Mrs. Brady hadn't been as put off by Anise's mention of the police as Quinn had thought. Maybe she worried too much, but, then again, there seemed to be so much to worry about. She texted back. What time? Quinn's parents wouldn't mind if she came in late, as long as there wasn't a last-minute rush. Besides, they would be only too happy to excuse her from duty to be with Josh and his parents.

Early—8-ish? Pancake House by the hospital? I have to be at work at 9, and they have a five-hour drive. BTW, they think you're great! I do, too!

Not a lot of words, but enough to create a warm, soft ball of comfort to grow in Quinn's heart. She allowed herself this bit of happiness after a long and difficult day. She had passed the audition. She hoped she would be able to play the part. Her feelings for Josh were intensifying, and she didn't want to do anything to screw up this relationship. She texted back, On way to Jack's. Give parents my best. Yes to tomorrow at 8. Text you when I get home. <3

Quinn pulled up to the drive-up window and shouted, "Two large carob smoothies." She pictured the look of ecstasy on Jack's face when she showed up with his favorite foods. His coming home from the hospital was major cause for celebration, and she intended to put all thoughts of Dawn and Ana aside, so she could be in the moment with her brother.

In fact, she'd start her own celebration a few minutes early. She took a long, slow slurp of her cool, thick chocolatey smoothie and savored it.

Whatever happened with the police and the videotapes, at least for now, Quinn's tastebuds and stomach were happy.

Chapter Thirty-two

As Quinn pulled into her brother's driveway and got out of the car, she saw Mary Hallom in uniform, striding toward the driveway next door. Wondering what was going on over there, but having no intention of asking, Quinn waved a hand and called out, "Hey, Mary."

The young officer stopped in mid-stride, held a hand up to shade her eyes, and crossed over the two front yards to meet Quinn in the middle. "Hi, there. What are you doing?"

"Bringing dinner to my brother. He's just home from the hospital today." Quinn shifted the bags of food from one hand to the other. *I could ask you the same thing, but I won't.*

"You're kidding me. Your brother lives here? I had no idea." Mary turned to inspect Jack's house, as if viewing it in a whole new light. "Jack, right?"

"Yeah. I think I mentioned him to you the other night. He just had a kidney transplant."

"Well, whaddya know? Jack McFarland is my next-door neighbor." She grinned as if she'd won the lottery. "Didn't he win a lot of football trophies a few years ahead of us in school?"

Quinn started to acknowledge Mary's excellent memory, when the front door opened, and the former football star himself appeared at the door, dressed in navy sweat pants and a turquoise polo shirt that showed off his broad shoulders, looking healthier and happier than Quinn had seen him in years. No doubt, he had been coming out to grouse at Quinn for being so late with dinner, but when he saw Mary standing there, he turned on his best Joy-McFarland-manners.

"We-ell," he said, drawling out the syllable for what seemed like two minutes. "Guess my sister's keeping better company these days." If he was put off by the fact that Mary was wearing a police uniform, he didn't show it a bit. He extended his right hand, saying, "Jack McFarland."

Mary gripped his hand and shook, her face lit up like a July firecracker. "A pleasure to meet you," she said. "I moved in two days ago." She pointed to her house.

"You remember my friend from high school, DeJuan Hallom? Mary's his little sister." Quinn had the feeling neither person was paying attention to her at this point, the way they were looking at each other.

Mary broke the eye contact first. "Gotta run. Working nights, and I can't be late. See ya 'round." She headed to her car with the grace and agility of Simone Biles on the balance beam, while Jack looked after her, apparently all thoughts of his late dinner forgotten.

"Shall we go inside?" Quinn asked, moving toward the door. "Dinner's getting cold, smoothies getting warm." Jack followed, still turning back toward the street, as if to see whether Mary would return.

"Okay, let's eat," Jack said. He had set the table with silverware and napkins. A half-eaten bowl of fruit and two day-old floral arrangements sat on the kitchen counter next to the table. "I'm starving."

"Hold on. I've got to microwave the food from Mario's." Quinn pulled out the generous-sized containers and took over the kitchen. "Here's your smoothie. I've already drunk out of mine."

Jack sat at the table, allowing Quinn to wait on him, while he slurped his smoothie. "What took you so long at the lawyer's office?"

It was an innocent enough question, but Quinn's stomach lurched anyway. Jack was trustworthy, but Becker had stressed the importance of not discussing anything about the case with anyone. If she had been tempted to exclude Jack from the no-talk list *before* he had met his new next-door neighbor, she certainly couldn't exclude him now. "You know, filling out forms, stuff like that. Becker is really thorough, likes to talk a lot, and I couldn't cut him off. Sorry I'm so late."

"No problem, sister. I'm so happy to be back in my house and feeling better. A little delay of food can't bring me down." He opened the top of the smoothie and stirred it with the straw. "Anyway, I have some interesting news to share with you tonight."

The tone of his voice, halfway between ominous and elated, caused Quinn to look up from the plates, where she was spooning the now-hot Italian food. "What?"

"Just before I left the hospital, Ms. Stacey from the transplant center came in to talk to me. I had signed papers months ago, stating that I would be receptive if the family of the kidney donor wished to contact me. Ms.

Stacey said that the donor's next of kin had agreed to make contact, and asked if I'd be willing to set up a date for us to get together."

Chills took over Quinn's body from head to toe. Somehow, she knew what was coming. She carried the food to the table and sat down opposite her brother. "So, who is it? Whose kidney do you have?"

Jack set his cup down and looked his sister in the eye. "It's either an amazing coincidence, or karma—whatever you want to call it. My new kidney came from Ana."

Chapter Thirty-three

By the time Quinn cleaned up after the meal at Jack's and came home, it was after 10:00. Calvin's excited yaps and exuberant leaping about made her feel guilty. Despite the doggie door she had installed when she moved in, the little guy craved exercise, and nothing made him happier than running with his mistress.

Quinn didn't have the heart to deny him, although she was dead-tired, and she had so much on her mind. Also, although her pup was loyal and protective of her, running at night—with a threat hanging over her head—didn't have the same appeal as it used to. And if she were attacked, a Westie wasn't exactly a Rottweiler.

"Okay, okay. I'm happy to see you, too." She picked up the pooch and let him bathe her face with doggie-kisses, while she hooked his leash and changed into her running shoes. Setting the alarm and locking the door on her way out, she took off down the street, glancing from side to side as she ran.

The air was thick with humidity and the sweet smells of summer—oleander, crape myrtle, and cut grass—and it didn't take long for perspiration to drench her clothes and her hair. She welcomed that, along with the chirping of insects and muffled barking of dogs from inside their houses. Running gave her a high, better than Chardonnay or carob smoothies, or almost anything. She suppressed a laugh as she thought of being at Josh's apartment last week. *Not better than* that.

Still, she couldn't imagine life without running. It was her way of staying healthy and clearing her head. As she ran, the tension of threatening notes and pornographic tapes melted away and splattered on the pavement like so many droplets of sweat. Right now, all she cared about were her legs, her lungs, and her little dog, pushing forward into the July night.

Once she cooled down and entered the house, she gave Calvin fresh water and food, and she headed for the bathroom, peeling off articles of clothing and casting them aside along the way. The shower was heavenly. She lathered herself with citrus-smelling soap and shampoo, and planned what she would wear to breakfast with Josh and his parents the next day.

After the shower, she sat cross-legged on the center of her bed, her hair wrapped in a towel-turban, texting Josh. Home from Jack's. Did you know his kidney came from my friend Ana? No, don't answer. You probably did the procurement.

Smile. (A non-admission admission.)

Case closed. Hope your parents have had a good visit.

Yes. Highlight—meeting you.

Flattery is good for the soul. Or what's that saying?

Smile. Flattery will get you everywhere, I think.

I think I'm already there.

* * *

Later, after Quinn laid out the mauve cowl-neck top and a white polished cotton skirt that Josh said showed off her legs, Quinn climbed into bed and pulled the covers up under her arms. This was the signal for Calvin to curl up alongside her waist and lay his chin on her hip. One hand petted the dog, while her mind reviewed the events of the day.

With so much going on in her life, she would have to sort out the significance of everything, but right now, she was content to have a wonderful boyfriend, a healthier brother, a comfortable bed, and a warm, furry companion to ease her into sleep.

Once asleep, though, she dreamed she was on a hot, brightly-lit stage. A tall, dark man, half-dressed and with protruding ears, was coming after her. She screamed at the top of her lungs, the same word, over and over. The screaming woke her up, and she found herself twisted in the covers, the dog on the other side of the bed, staring at her with ears perked. The dream started to evaporate, but she closed her eyes, trying to grab its smoky trail. What was it she had been screaming? She was pretty sure the word was, "Ana."

Chapter Thirty-four

When Quinn breezed into the sweet-smelling pancake house the next morning, Josh and his parents were already sitting at a table by the window. As she approached, Elise was pointing at her and laughing. It wasn't until she reached the table that she understood why. Elise stood up and showed her own skirt and top. They were wearing the exact same outfit.

Before they even said good morning, the two women high-fived and said in unison, "J.Jill." Breakfast was off to a great start. Everyone ordered coffee and tea and some version of pancakes and sides, and while they waited for the meal, they chatted about what the Bradys had done the past few days, and what they planned to do when they returned home.

"I know it's a long way off," Elise said, "but Mike and I would like you to come with Josh for Thanksgiving this year. That's my favorite holiday to cook for, and we usually have a few family members at our house."

Quinn glanced at Josh. His whole-faced grin and surreptitious wink on his face said he wasn't surprised. Quinn felt like a princess being welcomed to the kingdom. "I-I'd love to." She tried to banish thoughts of being unworthy and luxuriate in the warmth of this family's opening its arms to her.

Josh's dad piped in, "The two of you will have to coordinate your wardrobes before November." And everyone had a good laugh.

After Mike paid the check, they all stood to say goodbye. Josh and Quinn would go to work, and the Bradys would leave for home, directly from the restaurant. Instead of shaking hands, as they had Monday night, both of the Bradys opened their arms for hugs, to Josh, and to Quinn. Afterward, Josh put his arm around Quinn's shoulder and pulled her in for a kiss, right there in front of the whole world, including his parents. It was practically an engagement.

On the way to McFarland's, Quinn stopped to buy a ten-pack of spearmint gum and a box of small dog biscuits for Calvin. Just before she reached the pet food aisle, she was stopped by an acquaintance of her mother's, Mrs. Nash. Not even 9:00 a.m., and the lady was dressed at least to the fives, including makeup and jewelry.

She poked Quinn's forearm with her bony, manicured hand. "Quinn, dear. How nice to run into you. I've wanted to tell you how sorry I am about your friend, Ana French—or Renfroe, that is. Didn't you two used to be inseparable?" Without waiting for an answer, she went on. "I feel so sorry for Ana's parents. Nice people. Of course, no one deserves to go through such heartache." She held a hand to her bosom. "Poor child. She never had a chance at a decent life after she married that Brad Renfroe."

Hearing Brad's name, even in this context, still caused a punch to Quinn's stomach. How many times she had envied Ana and the life she was having with Brad. "What do you mean by that, Mrs. Nash?"

"You don't know?" The woman patted her heart again. "Brad was a looker, I'll give him that, but he never made an honest living for himself or his wife. All kinds of rumors about drugs, gambling, what have you. Probably killed poor Ana, too, bless her soul. Even if he didn't bash her head in, he put her in harm's way by the way he conducted himself. Why I tell you—"

Quinn had heard enough. "—need to buy a couple of items and get to work right away. Nice to see you, Mrs. Nash." She waved and turned into aisle seven.

As she sprinted away, she could hear the woman calling after her. "Best thing your parents ever did, breaking you and that scumball apart."

In the ten minutes it took Quinn to drive from the grocery store to the funeral home, she thought about what Mrs. Nash had said. If Brad had really been involved in illegal activities, wouldn't he have been arrested? Wouldn't she have heard about that, even though she had shunned all contact? On the other hand, Brad had said during his phone call that he thought whoever killed Ana had meant to kill him. Maybe Ana's murder was the result of a drug deal gone bad.

But, if that were the case, why would somebody be threatening Quinn? Quinn needed time to think. So much was happening all at once, and her days were full. She needed to research Gulf Coast Adult Entertainment. She couldn't help thinking Ana's murder was connected to Dawn's. Knowing she was probably being watched, even now, she'd have to find a way to investigate without attracting suspicion. She needed time, but she had the feeling time was running short.

She parked in her usual spot and entered through the back door, cringing at that first smell of chemicals. She'd no sooner closed and locked the door behind her and tossed her fob on the rolling chair, when her mother came rushing into the chilly room.

"Oh, *there* you are, darling. I was looking for you. Sergeant Schmidt and another officer are in the front parlor, waiting for you. They said they have a few questions to ask."

Quinn must have blanched, because her mother came running to her side. "What is it, sweetheart? Are you okay?"

Taking a few steps backward to the rolling chair and picking up the fob, Quinn sat down, thinking. "I'm okay, Mom, but we need to call Mr. Becker. He told me not to say a word to the police without his being present."

"Oh, dear." Joy ran her hand through her coiffed hair. "You don't think they're here to arrest you, do you? Surely it wouldn't hurt to find out what they want—"

But Quinn was already speed dialing David Becker's office. She had no intention of talking to the police without legal support.

Chapter Thirty-five

"Law Office, may I help you?" Ethel's "telephone voice" was courteous and professional, without being warm.

"Good morning, Ethel," Quinn said, trying to keep calm. "This is Quinn McFarland. Please tell me Mr. Becker is in the office. I need to speak with him right away."

"Oh, hello, Quinn. Let me connect you." Quinn appreciated the smile in the assistant's voice, now that she knew who was calling. More importantly, within ten seconds Mr. Becker was on the line.

"'Mornin'. How can I help you today?"

Quinn glanced at her mother, who appeared to be frozen, hands cupping the sides of her face. She didn't want to reveal too much in front of her. "I'm at the funeral home, in the back room. Sgt. Schmidt and another officer are out front, asking to speak to me. They told my mother they had a few questions for me."

"This is to be expected. That's why I cautioned you not to speak to them without my being present." He paused for a few seconds, and Quinn thought she could hear him swallow. Probably his morning coffee. "Well, well, well. Is this your cell phone you're calling me from?"

"Yes, sir. Would you rather I called you from the land line?"

"No, no, I'm just thinking. Actually, yes. Is there an extension of the land line phone, so that you could be on one phone, and the sergeant could be on another?"

"Sure."

"And is there someone with you, who could direct the sergeant to the extension, so that you would not have to speak directly to him?"

"Y-es-sss. My mother is here with me."

"Okay, call me back from the land line, and I'll instruct you from there."

Quinn did as told, and held on while Joy McFarland summoned Sgt.

Schmidt to the extension in the front office. While Quinn waited, she practiced yoga breathing. Otherwise, she was afraid the panic brewing in her belly might cause her to scream.

After what seemed like an hour, Schmidt came onto the line, his voice snippy. "Schmidt here. I don't know what's going on. I came to check something out with Ms. McFarland. I don't have a lot of time to waste."

Nonplussed, Mr. Becker said, "Schmidt, David Becker. I've got Ms. McFarland on the extension, so she can hear everything we say. First, will you please give me your full name, title, and badge number? I want to verify whom I'm speaking with for the record."

Schmidt grumbled, but complied. "What d'ya have to say, Mr. Becker? I've got a murder to solve, and time's a-wasting."

"I'll be brief, then. Two things—first, I've instructed my client not to speak to anyone, including the police, about the Ana Renfroe murder, unless I am present. If you have questions to ask her, I will be happy to set up a meeting in my office, so we can hear your questions."

"Yeah? What's the other thing?" Schmidt asked.

"Secondly, I am in possession of some materials that may be relevant to your murder investigation. I would like to bring them to you at the station this morning."

Schmidt's voice rose several decibels. "Well, whaddya know? Can you tell me what this is about?"

"No. You'll see when I deliver the package to you. I can be there within the hour."

Schmidt appeared to consider. "How 'bout you come on over to the funeral home with the materials now? That way we can kill two birds with one stone."

Becker was obviously not going to be manipulated. "Let me put it this way, Sergeant. I'm going to deliver the materials to the police station this morning. If you don't wish to meet with me, I'll hand them over to Chief Ramirez."

"Ahhhh," Schmidt replied in a cross between a cry and a belch. "That won't be necessary. I'll meet you at the station in an hour. Will you bring your client with you? I don't need to tell you how important it is that I speak with her today. We've got some new information."

Refusing to be baited, Becker repeated himself. "If you want to speak with my client, you'll have to make an appointment to come to my office. We will meet with you, but I won't promise that my client will answer your questions."

Quinn was relieved to have a strong advocate to handle her side of things. As the two men batted about potential times for an afternoon meeting, she wondered what new information the police had. Whatever it was, she hoped it had nothing whatsoever to do with her.

Chapter Thirty-six

After the policemen left, Quinn's mother sat down with her in the "beauty parlor." The day was just getting started, and already Quinn's neck was tight and her stomach was at odds with the rest of her body. Having her mom stare at her with squinty, shiny eyes wasn't helping.

"Thanks for taking dinner to Jack's last night. I know you've got a lot going on, and that was very sweet."

Quinn had a feeling the compliment would be a prelude to lots of questions—about Josh and about Ana. "No problem. So happy Jack is feeling better. He looks great." *So great, in fact, that his new neighbor practically couldn't take her eyes off him.* "So, Mom, what's on tap for today?"

"That's what I wanted to talk to you about. We've got the Stovall funeral at 10:30. Can you do the cemetery? I hate for your dad to stand outside in the heat." Quinn nodded. She didn't mind the heat, and she was happy to take cemetery duty. "Also, the Frenches are coming in to arrange for Ana's funeral this afternoon at three. The funeral's been on hold, waiting for Brad to surface, but, apparently, something's changed, and they want to move forward. I'm guessing you don't want to meet with them. Am I right?"

Quinn thought of the tapes Ana had sent her and the comments Mrs. Nash had made about Ana in the grocery store. She actually wouldn't mind talking to Mr. and Mrs. French, but she knew Becker wouldn't approve. In fact, he'd probably fire her as a client. She shook her head. "Not a good idea." She stood and started checking the contents of cabinets, more as something to do than out of need. "Anyway, I've got a meeting with Mr. Becker at 3:30."

The worried expression returned to her mother's eyes. "I sure hope he's helping you. It's not easy for your dad and me, having the police show up looking for our daughter." She twisted her hands in her lap. "You know, we'd do anything to help you. You wouldn't need to ask twice."

Quinn hugged her mother. "I know that. But the best way you can help me right now is to trust in Mr. Becker's advice." The clock on the wall said 9:45. "Hey, it's a quarter to ten, and we've got a 10:30 funeral. We'd better get crackin'."

Her mother startled and turned to check the clock for herself. "Oh, dear. I guess I'll ask you about Josh's parents later, then."

Quinn smiled to herself. She knew she wouldn't get off that easily.

* * *

Whoever decided that black was the color to wear at funerals must not have lived on the Gulf Coast. Dressed in her funeral attire, Quinn made sure as many family members and elderly as possible were seated under the tent, but she had the full benefit of the brutal sun and high humidity. She was used to the climate, and most of the time it didn't bother her, but today her head and face were dripping wet, and she was sure her hair had puffed into a single ball of frizz.

While Reverend Hoskins intoned prayers for the recently departed, Quinn allowed her thoughts to wander. This morning's visit from the police had raised her level of concern. She couldn't believe how suddenly she had been drawn back into her connection with Ana. She felt like a wingless fly, caught in a vortex, unable to escape.

Ana had been her blood sister, and now Ana's kidney was keeping Quinn's brother alive. She would have to be devoid of all feeling not to have recognized the debt of gratitude she owed to Ana. Also, Ana had trusted Quinn enough to send her the tapes. Now it was up to Quinn to understand that gesture and to do something, take some action. She didn't think turning them over to the police would be enough, but, given the feeling that someone was watching her every move, that might be the best she could do for now.

She wanted to return to the library and research the Gulf Coast Adult Entertainment Company. An internet search from her home computer hadn't yielded a thing. She needed to know more about those movies that Dawn made. And, most of all, she wanted to find out more about the tall man with the protruding ears.

As she directed the pallbearers down the narrow pathway toward the final resting places for Mr. and Mrs. Stovall, she noticed a man at the edge of the cemetery staring at her. She shivered in the hot air and crossed her arms in a protective stance. It was starting to sink in that, no matter where she was, she wasn't safe.

Chapter Thirty-seven

After the funeral, Quinn drove toward McFarland's with the air conditioning going full blast. Her stomach was begging for food, so she pulled into Burger King's drive-up and ordered a grilled chicken sandwich and onion rings. She had a cooler with left-over ice-cold water, chilling in her trunk.

Of all the fast-food restaurants, Burger King was her favorite. When the clerk handed her the hot, salty-smelling bag of food, her mouth watered. She took a bite out of the sandwich before she pulled away from the drive-up window. As she drove the short distance to the funeral home, she stuffed an onion ring into her mouth, as well.

Before she turned off Main Street into the cross street leading to the entrance, she noticed a dark gray car in her rearview mirror, two cars behind her and going well below the speed limit. Was she being followed? She hated the feeling that something sinister might happen every time she went anywhere. The unmarked car didn't make the turn behind her, but it did appear to slow down at the intersection.

Not wanting to spoil her lunch, she shook off worries about the police and gray cars, and unlocked the back door at work. She plopped her lunch sack and her sling bag onto the counter and went back for the cooler. That was when she saw the car turn into the street behind her and slow down. Putting on her best I'm-ignoring-you posture, she picked up the cooler and carried it into the building, kicking the door shut behind her. It was bad enough that she would have to face the police in two hours at the lawyer's office. Right now, she intended to enjoy her food.

No sooner had she sat down and taken another bite, though, than her father peeked his head in the door. "I *thought* I heard you come in. How'd the cemetery go?"

Swallowing her food before answering, she replied, "Hotter than the hinges. Sad, too. Mr. and Mrs. Stovall were such nice people. Hard for the family to lose them both at the same time."

"Sometimes that happens. Fortunately, rarely." Her dad walked in and sat down in the chair inhabited by his wife earlier. "Listen, Mr. Becker called while you were gone. Said he tried your cell phone, but it went straight to voicemail."

"Did you tell him I turn off my phone during funerals?"

"Yes. He'd already figured that out. Anyway, he wants you to call him right away. Said it's very important that he talk to you as soon as possible."

The onion ring in her mouth turned to ashes. "Okay, Dad. Thanks for the message. Now, if you'll excuse me—"

John McFarland held both hands up as if Quinn were holding a gun on him. "Okay, okay. I'm leaving, but I do want to talk to you later about Josh."

Quinn winked at her father and motioned for him to shut the door on the way out. Talking about Josh would have to wait. Right now, her stomach was holding her brain captive, and it wasn't from the lunch.

Ethel answered and put Quinn through quickly. "Hi, there," Becker said in his usual booming voice. "Sorry to change plans at late notice. Can you meet here at my office at 2:30 instead of 3:30 today?"

Quinn looked at the clock. It was already past one. "I think so. What's up?"

"Well, I took the tapes to Sergeant Schmidt this mornin', right after our phone conversation. I got him to tell me a little about why he wants to talk to you. He was goin' to spend the next couple of hours watchin' the tapes, if he could find a working VCR." He chuckled. "I offered to let him come here and use ours. Anyway, I need an hour to prepare you for the questions I believe he's gonna ask."

"Okay. I'll be there at 2:30. I think I should tell you, though. I think the cops might be following me. It's making me jittery. Do you think they might arrest me?"

"Nah, at least not at this time. I think they're on a fishing expedition. But I told Schmidt in no uncertain terms that he would have one shot at questioning you. We aren't going to be setting up meetings like this every time they come up with a new line of questioning."

"I imagine he didn't like that. Can lawyers talk to police like that?"

"Yes, indeed. Unless he's ready to charge you with a crime, there're a lot of things we can say and do. And we will. I'm not having your valuable time wasted at the sergeant's whim—or mine either."

"Thanks for protecting me," Quinn said, thinking again how lucky she was to have an experienced attorney representing her.

"You bet. That's what you're paying me for." He chuckled again. "Can't wait to see what's on Schmidt's playlist. See you at 2:30."

Quinn threw away the rest of her lunch and put away the various items Rory and Zeke had brought back in the empty hearses. At least she wouldn't have to worry about running into Ana's parents at the funeral home. She changed into a clean pant suit and tried to do something with her wayward hair. She wished she had time to run home and shower, but these days, wishes were a luxury she simply couldn't afford.

Chapter Thirty-eight

Quinn arrived at her attorney's office at the stroke of 2:30. Ethel ushered her into Becker's office without preliminaries, as if there were not a second to waste. Though impressed with the efficiency, the importance the office was placing on this pre-conference kicked Quinn's tension level into high gear. Her hands were so cold, she sat on them.

"Make yourself comfortable. We'll get right down to business." Seeing the way Quinn was sitting, Becker gave a quizzical look. "What's the matter?"

"What?" Quinn looked where he was staring at her lap. "Oh, trying to warm my hands."

Becker summoned Ethel to get Quinn a cup of hot tea. "Let's begin, shall we?" A legal pad was in front of him, and he was tapping the edge of his desk with his pen. "When I delivered the tapes to Sergeant Schmidt, we engaged in a little do-si-do typical of attorneys and police officers. He was trying to get information from me, and I was trying to get information from him.

"Of course, the fact that I was bringin' him the tapes, and the note you found in your car, that he never would have had otherwise, earned points for our side. I explained to him how I came to be in possession of them, what the chain of custody had been, ostensibly from Ana, to your neighbor, to you, and to me. I told him that we had watched the films in their entirety."

Ethel knocked on the door with a large cup of hot tea, sugar, lemon, and a stirrer on a small tray. She set it down on the desk in front of Quinn, and, before Quinn could thank her properly, turned on her heel and left, closing the door behind her. Quinn wrapped her hands around the hot cup and breathed in the metallic aroma of the Earl Grey. The warmth and the caffeine would both do her good.

"Did you tell him about Dawn?" she asked, holding her breath for the answer.

"No, and I don't intend to. It's not my job to provide answers to unasked questions. My job, as I've told you, is to assess your exposure and judge how best to protect your interests." He looked at the clock on his desk. "Anyway, as I handed over the tapes, I cajoled Schmidt to gimme an idea of what he wants to talk to you about. He'd hinted that he had new information, and I pushed him to share. All in good faith, ya know."

Becker's eyebrows merged, and he gave her a piercing look. "Before I go any further, let me ask you. Were you aware that your brother received his transplanted kidney from Ana Renfroe?"

Whatever Quinn expected, it wasn't this. When she nodded, Becker asked, "When did you *first* learn that your brother's new kidney would come from or had come from Ana Renfroe?"

Perplexed by the line of questioning, and the question itself, Quinn replied, "Jack told me last night. Jack, himself, didn't find out who the donor was until yesterday. I guess they wait to make sure the surgery is a success before they allow communication between donor families and recipients."

The eyebrows didn't let up, so Quinn braced herself. She still couldn't see a connection between Jack's kidney and any of this.

"Is it true that you are dating a fifth-year surgical resident on the transplant team?"

Quinn put down the tea and crossed her arms in front of her. "Josh? What on earth?" Icy prickles made the fine hairs on her forearms and at the back of her neck stick up.

"What is the full name of the young man you are dating?"

"Josh. Josh Brady. Please don't tell me the police are interested in talking to Josh." Quinn had a fleeting image of Josh's parents, so proud of all he had accomplished. Quinn hated to drag him into a murder case.

"Before I answer that, I must know. Did Josh ever tell you anything about Ana's kidney being a match for Jack?"

"No, of course not. Josh can't—won't—tell me anything at all about his work. He's bound by medical ethics, and he takes that very seriously."

"Have you and Josh ever had a conversation about the fact that Ana's kidney was a match for Jack?"

Quinn thought about the text messages she and Josh had exchanged the night before. She pulled her cell phone from her bag and punched up the recent message string. "This is the one and only 'conversation' we've had about it. You can see it was last night, and Josh didn't really answer my question." She handed the phone over to Becker to examine. "What does Jack's new kidney have to do with any of this?"

Becker turned the clock on his desk to face Quinn. 3:11. Schmidt would be there in nineteen minutes. "Can you get Josh on the phone for me right now? It's important."

"I—I don't know. He's at work, and a lot of times he has his cell phone turned off." Quinn wasn't sure where this was headed, but she really didn't want to involve Josh if she could help it.

"Please try. I need to clear something up right away, and Josh is the only person who can do that."

Quinn called Josh and waited for the connection to go through. At least the call didn't go straight to voicemail. Now to get past the hospital's telemetry. After a brief delay, the phone rang, and after several rings, Josh answered. "Can I call you back later? In a meeting."

Quinn's voice was unsteady. "I-I'm so sorry, but this c-can't wait. Can you step out of the meeting for a minute to talk to my lawyer?"

"Your lawyer? What's going on?" She could hear him excusing himself and moving with the phone. "Okay, I'm out in the hallway."

Quinn handed the phone to Becker, tension forming a vise on her forehead.

Becker took the phone. "Is this Josh Brady, fifth-year surgical resident at the medical branch?" He looked at his notes. "This is David Becker. I am an attorney, representin' Quinn McFarland. I promise not to keep you long."

Becker nodded at whatever Josh said. "The questions I'm about to ask you may be related to a police investigation, and, in fact, you may receive a visit from the police, if you haven't already, to ask these same or similar questions. Because of this, I'm sure you know answerin' them is within the ethical parameters of the medical profession."

Another nod. "Well, then, were you involved with the kidney transplant process from Ana Renfroe to Jack McFarland?" Josh's answer was obviously more than a simple yes or no.

"I see," Becker said. "Now, at any time did you discuss any of the particulars related to this transplant with Quinn McFarland?" Quinn was certain Josh was giving a resounding no, adding that he never talked about his work outside of the medical community.

"Okay, one last question, and this is important. At what point did you realize that Ana Renfroe's kidney was a match for Jack McFarland?"

It was starting to dawn on Quinn how Jack's kidney might be connected. She covered her eyes with her hands. Josh was giving a rather lengthy explanation to Becker, and Quinn's mind was flashing like a strobe light, as she put two and two together.

Becker thanked Josh for his time and disconnected. "That's all I needed to know. We're in the clear."

"Omigod," Quinn said, afraid to put her thoughts into words. "The police suspect I killed Ana so Jack could get her kidney?" Her voice rose with each syllable. "That's absurd."

"People have been killed for lesser motives, I'm afraid. Still, your boyfriend's ethics and the fact that no one tested Ana's kidney for matching until after she was brought to the hospital in a comatose state makes that whole line of thinking impossible. You would have had to know about the match well before you committed murder."

"So, I'm officially a suspect, as far as the police are concerned." Quinn thought of the many times she had envisioned killing Ana. Brad, too. The woman scorned is a perfect scapegoat.

"Let's say you're a person of interest." Becker pointed to the clock and said, "However, the phone call with Josh, here, has given us very strong ammunition for this meeting. In the nick of time, too." The clock said 3:28.

Just then the phone rang. After Ethel answered, she put the call through, saying, "Sergeant Schmidt."

"That sonofa—" Becker punched the button and answered the call. "Yes, she's here. Yes. Yes, I understand. Okay, I'll tell my client." He hung up the phone and looked at Quinn, eyebrows and all. "Schmidt's canceling the meeting. Says it's taken them longer than expected to watch the movies, and he can't get over here this afternoon."

"Strange, don't you think?" Quinn asked.

"Not really. Probably an intentional zinger at me. You see, I told him this morning, when I delivered the tapes, that he would only have one chance to interview you, so he'd better get all his questions ready before 3:30."

"He probably didn't like being bossed around, then?"

"Exactly. He's waited until the last minute to back out on us, just to make sure we are both inconvenienced. That's all right, though. Our talk with Josh was quite productive. That will take the salt out of his shaker."

Quinn exhaled. Regardless of the reason, she was glad to escape the meeting with Schmidt. "So the new information Schmidt was referring to was the fact that Jack has Ana's kidney?"

"Uh, yes—but there's something else, as well. Brad Renfroe has finally turned up—way down at the west end of the island. Unfortunately, he's dead."

Chapter Thirty-nine

Brad's death hadn't been as shocking as Ana's. When he'd called Quinn at the funeral home, his voice had the timbre of desperation, a tightness unlike the way he had ever sounded before. Quinn tried to remember his exact words—something about him being the intended target, instead of Ana. Then, again, if he had been abusing Ana, and the abuse went too far, maybe he had been covering for himself by inventing a third-party killer. The Frenches had said that Ana was bruised the last times they saw her.

Quinn sat in her car outside of Becker's office, her nerves strung like a too-tight cello. How did she get into such a mess, when all she wanted was a normal life? What had she done to deserve being thrown into a double murder investigation—make that a triple, if you counted Dawn? To be threatened? To be followed? *Brad had thought I was in danger. I should have made him explain.* It was all too much. Even though she had separated herself from Brad and Ana, hell-bent on cutting them out of her future, she would never be able to cut them out of her past. Her blood sister, her first love.

She owed Josh an explanation. If she had told him what was going on bit-by-bit, as things were unfolding, she might have had an easier time. Now the complications had multiplied, and she would still have to sort out which details to share and which fell into the restrictions set by Becker and her own heart. The words "person of interest" echoed in her mind and set a bitter taste in her mouth.

Since it was almost four o'clock, and maybe time for a hospital shift change, she texted Josh. Can you come over for dinner tonight? We can talk.

She closed her eyes, trying to recall what was in her pantry and refrigerator. Maybe she should stop at the grocery store on the way home, but that didn't give her time to walk the dog and shower and change clothes.

A return text pinged. Good idea. I'll pick up barbecue. 6 ok? Off at 4, but on call.

Perfect. Leave it to Josh to keep things simple, food-wise. Quinn wished she could say the same for the conversation part. They'd almost had an argument before about her keeping information from him, and she'd promised to do better. What might happen if she failed to keep her promise? Tonight would be another challenge in what appeared to be an endless string of trials.

* * *

By six o'clock, Quinn had walked Calvin, taken a shower, blown her hair dry, put on fresh makeup, and dressed in a pair of white linen shorts and a robin's egg blue, off-the-shoulder top. She set the table and included wine glasses. A bottle of Chardonnay was chilling in the ice bucket on the counter, and a bottle of Merlot stood ready, in case Josh would rather have red with beef. A frozen cherry pie baking in the oven emitted a heavenly aroma.

The preparations took Quinn's mind away from being a murder suspect and put her in a happier mood than she'd been in for days. She found herself humming and dancing around the kitchen. Even Calvin seemed to sense that a special evening was in the making.

Josh rang the doorbell promptly at six, and, when Quinn opened the door, he brought the tangy barbecue smells into the house with him. The fact that they'd just seen each other at breakfast did nothing to lessen the fervor with which they stared at each other for what seemed like a full minute. Then Josh set the bags of food down on a console table and took Quinn into his arms for a long, slow kiss.

"Nice shirt," he said, when he finally came up for air. He ran his fingers along the neckline, revealing more shoulder.

Quinn buzzed with a dizzying pleasure that had nothing to do with barbecue or cherry pie or Chardonnay. She reached both hands around Josh's neck and pulled him in for another kiss. By mutual consent, dinner was pushed back in favor of a different type of appetizer.

Afterwards, Josh opened the white wine and played with Calvin, while Quinn reheated the barbecue in the microwave. Once they were seated and ready to eat, Josh raised his wineglass. "To the woman in my life who makes an ordinary day extraordinary."

They clinked glasses and drank. "Thank you," Quinn murmured, mentally giving Josh points for not pushing her toward the inevitable conversation. "As much as I love dining in a great restaurant, there's something special about just the two of us in the privacy of home."

"Agree. We should do this more often." His lop-sided grin caused her heart to flip.

"Which part?"

His eyes met hers. "All of it." Was that a pink tinge rising from Josh's neck to his cheeks? *How did I ever get so lucky to find this adorable man? I hope I don't blow it.*

Quinn took a fork full of the spicy beef. "Yum. Glad you thought of barbecue. This is delicious. Did your parents get home okay?"

"Yes. They texted me around one. They told me again how much they enjoyed meeting you. They love it that you're so down-to-earth." Josh used his bread to scoop potato salad onto his fork. "I think the matching outfits sealed the deal."

"I enjoyed meeting them, too. Fun to see where you come from, biologically speaking. Thanks for fitting me into your visit with them. I know that was precious time."

Josh put down his fork and reached across the table for Quinn's hand. "Okay. Enough polite conversation. Let's talk about this business with the lawyer." His jaw clenched, and Quinn was reminded of the conversation they had after Anise mentioned the police. She had promised to be more forthcoming, and she would do her best. She took a deep breath and let it go slowly.

"Mr. Becker is representing my interests in a matter related to the death of Ana Renfroe."

Josh nodded. "The woman whose kidney Jack has."

"Yes, and my former best friend. We grew up together, knew each other very well."

"I never heard you mention her."

"That's because I stopped speaking to her when we were still in high school. It's all a very long story, not terribly interesting." Quinn stood and began clearing the table, buying time to think of how far she should go.

"Please sit down. I'll help you clean up later. Right now you have my full attention, and I want yours."

"So," Quinn reached for Josh's hand and patted it, "Ana was murdered, and the police are investigating. I've been forbidden to discuss any details of the case or my connection to it—even with my parents. Becker explained that any conversation I have with anyone, except for him, can be used as testimony in court. Our conversation right now is not considered 'privileged,' for example. So my silence is a protection for you, as well as for me."

"You're talking as if the police suspect you of murdering Ana. That's totally crazy. What reason would you have to kill her?"

The barbecue dinner was burning like a lump of coal in Quinn's stomach. "Think about the questions Mr. Becker asked you today."

"About the kidney transplant? He wanted to know when the match was made between Ana's kidney and Jack."

Quinn nodded, but didn't comment.

"Oh, my God. They were thinking you could have known about the match and killed Ana for her kidney! Why didn't I put that together sooner?" Josh's mouth formed a thin line, and he looked down at the table. "So now—now that I made it clear that the match wasn't made until Ana came to the hospital, that we kept her alive until we could get Jack prepped for surgery—now you should be completely in the clear."

The hopeful look in his eyes broke her heart. "Not exactly. I wish I could tell you more, but right now, all I can say is that there are other things that connect me with Ana's death." With that, Quinn put her head in her hands and began to cry.

Chapter Forty

The next morning, when Quinn arrived at work, everything seemed quiet. She hung up two clean outfits to replace the ones she had worn in the last few days and wandered into the front office.

"Hey, sis," an unexpected voice greeted her.

She bridged the few feet between them to give Jack a hug. "Hey, what are you doing at work? Aren't you supposed to be at home all this week, recuperating?"

"Yeah, well. I got super-bored, and asked Dad to bring me here for a few hours. I'm not allowed to drive yet."

Quinn had to admit, staying home for a week, doing nothing, held no appeal for her, either, and Jack looked really good. "You look rarin' to go, and I'm sure Dad is happy to have your help." She looked at the open folder on the desk in front of him. The tab said, Arrangements for Ana Renfroe.

"That's right. The Frenches were coming in to plan Ana's funeral yesterday. When's it set for?"

He tapped the folder with his pen. "Pending."

"Pending? Ana's been dead one week today. What's the holdup?"

Jack stood in the small space and put his arm around Quinn's shoulder. "Not sure whether you know. Brad Renfroe's dead, too. Found on the west end, shot in the back of the head."

Quinn nodded and fought tears. "It's okay," she said. "I'm sorry Brad's been killed, but I'm not emotionally involved."

"You sure?" he said, handing her a tissue. "Even though you didn't end up together, Brad spent a lot of time over here, and he was a big part of your life."

Quinn dabbed at her eyes and threw the tissue in the wastebasket. "So what does Brad's death have to do with Ana's funeral? Or are we looking at a double header?"

"Exactly. Brad's parents are dead, and his family's out of town, so the Frenches volunteered to take care of both at the same time. Ana's ready to go, but Brad's being autopsied. Once he gets here, Dad will do the beauty parlor treatment. I'd do it, but it's against doctor's orders for another five weeks."

"I can do it," Quinn replied. "I told you I'm not emotionally involved." Despite the bravado, Quinn swallowed hard to make the lump go down her throat. "Nice of the Frenches. Double the cost, and they're not exactly wealthy. Not to mention the added grief."

"Yeah, I think Dad cut them a deal. Anyway, don't be a martyr. Let Dad do the duty on this one." Jack closed the folder, as if that was the last of that topic. "Anyway, there's something else I want to talk to you about privately. Want to close the door?"

"Sure." Without making noise, Quinn shut the door and sat across from Jack. "What's on your mind?" It wasn't unusual for Jack to confide in her, but, these days, a bid for privacy drove her apprehension level sky-high.

"You know I'm attracted to Mary Hallom, right? The police officer who moved in next door?" Jack's voice was almost giddy, a tone Quinn hadn't heard from him since he was a kid. That, and the ear-to-ear smile on his face, caused Quinn to laugh, despite the circumstances.

"Why, Jack McFarland, have you fallen in love?"

"Shh. I don't want Mom or Dad to hear. It can't be love. I really just met her, but she is such a fine-looking woman, and that voice of hers—strong, silky, sexy—well, let's just say, I'm kind of mesmerized." He pushed the folder back and forth on the desk. "I think she's interested in me, too. Doesn't seem to bother her that I've been cut from stem to stern. She gives me that sideways glance with those long, curly eyelashes."

"Shall I get out the smelling salts we use for funerals? You're swooning." Quinn laughed. It was good to hear her brother talking about a member of the opposite sex. It had been at least a year since his girlfriend broke up with him, and Quinn had thought he might never recover.

"I know it's only been two days since we met, but she's stopped by to say hello on her way in or out, and I really dig her."

"Hey, want to tell me how you really feel about her?" Quinn didn't want to cut him off, but she needed to get to work, and it was only a matter of time before one or both parents found them holed up in the office and started asking questions.

"Okay, let me get to the point. When Mary came over yesterday, she took a glass of iced tea from me and sat down to visit for about a half hour. I thought it was because she was interested in getting to know me better, but all she seemed to want to talk about was you."

"Me?" Icy chills grabbed Quinn by the throat and held her. "What about me?"

"Not sure. She was fishing to see what I know about you and Ana and Brad, though. She tried to act casual, like she remembered the three of you from high school, but I was pretty sure she was looking for something that might relate to Ana's death, or Brad's."

Quinn sat on her hands to warm them and to keep from revealing the quivering inside. *Person of interest* was echoing in her brain. again "Can you remember exactly what she asked you?"

Jack scratched his head. "She knew that I had Ana's kidney. That totally surprised me. She wondered whether you'd been in touch with the Renfroes recently, whether you or I knew Ana would be a donor match for me. She knew about you and Josh, but asked if you ever talked about your old relationship with Brad. Some of her questions didn't make a lot of sense to me, but I definitely sensed that she was on a mission—like someone at the PD sent her to talk to me."

Quinn really liked Mary, and she hated to think she might be using Jack to get information about her. "I'm sure you handled her well. Did it upset you that your conversation with her was all about me?"

Jack gave the old quarterback-in-the-end-zone grin. "Not at all. She might've come over to ask about you, but she stayed to visit with me."

Quinn pulled her hands out from under her. "What does that mean, pray tell?"

"Let's just say, when she left, she kissed me goodbye."

"Hmm," Quinn said, "You don't waste any time, do you?"

"Hey, at my age, and after all I've been through, you might say this is my Hail Mary pass."

Relieved that the subject had changed from questions about murders, Quinn shook her head at the football metaphor. "I hope it works out for you." She wondered how their parents would feel about Jack's being involved in an inter-racial romance, but that was a subject for another day. She started for the door.

"Oh, I almost forgot," Jack said, and Quinn turned back. "Why do you think Mary asked me about Dawn Chrysler?"

Chapter Forty-one

Quinn hated not answering her brother's question about Dawn. She had shrugged and invented an excuse to leave. His question had, though, provided Quinn with important information. The police had obviously watched the videos and either recognized the actress or found out through research that she was Dawn. Mary was trying to find out what connection Quinn or Ana had to the cold case from 2004.

The good news was, thanks to Mr. Becker's actions to protect her, the police received the information without having it come directly from Quinn. The bad news was that whoever was threatening her not to talk might not see it that way. With Ana and Brad out of the way, could she be next? She had to find out who was threatening her. She couldn't rely on the police to find out for her. Even Mary Hallom probably regarded her as "a person of interest" now.

It was a dead day at the funeral home—no new corpses, no scheduled visitations. The coffee smell led Quinn into the luncheon room, where she knew she'd find her father, sitting around, drinking from a paper cup and gossiping with his cronies. She recognized each of them, both by name and by occupation. Mr. Peterson, the florist; Mr. Clemensen, the newspaper editor; Reverend Hoskins—all were connected to the business in some way, and Quinn had known them since she was little.

"Look who's here," one called, as she entered the room. "My, what a lovely young lady." Quinn barely registered the compliment. Her mind was on other things. She mumbled a thank you, just to be polite, but she walked over to her dad and put a hand on his shoulder.

"Can I talk to you for a second in the hallway?" The family never mentioned business matters, even unimportant ones, in front of others.

"Sure, sweetheart." John McFarland excused himself and led his daughter out into the hall. "Did you see Jack? We're so delighted he feels well enough to come in for a little while." When they were a good fifty feet from the lunchroom, he said, "What's going on?"

"Since things are quiet, I'd like to take some time off, maybe the rest of the day. I've got a whole list of errands to run and things to catch up on. Do you mind?"

Her dad tilted his head and gave her a piercing look. "You haven't had any more scares, have you?"

"No, Dad. Nothing like that." *Not unless you count the note in my car and the sense that I'm being followed.* "I've just fallen behind on a lot of the everyday things, and I can use the dead time to catch up." Quinn didn't like misleading her father, but if she told him the whole truth, she'd have Chief Ramirez and the entire police force to contend with.

"Fine by me. I still want to hear about Josh's parents, though. What were they like?" Quinn suppressed a chuckle. She knew this was a topic her parents wouldn't forget to interrogate her about.

"Super nice people. You and Mom would really like them." At least this was the absolute truth. "I'll tell you all about them when we get a chance, maybe later today." She stood on tiptoes and kissed her father on the cheek. Times like this, she appreciated having a benevolent boss.

* * *

On the way back to the library, Quinn stopped at the drugstore to buy a spiral notebook, an inexpensive ball point pen, and a package of sticky notes. She threw a couple of protein bars onto the counter, too. She had a feeling this next bit of research might take a long time.

When she arrived in the history center, the stool and podium where the male librarian had sat before was vacant. In fact, it appeared that Quinn had the chilly room all to herself, a prospect favorable to her mission. She sat at the computer she had used last time and inserted her library card, wishing she didn't have to do this—she'd be leaving tracks of her research, but there was no alternative.

Within a minute, the pregnant librarian appeared at her side. "Hello, Ms. McFarland. Welcome back to the history center. How may I help you today?"

While the woman knew Quinn's name, the reverse was not the case. "I'm sorry. I didn't get your name the last time I was here. I'm Quinn McFarland."

"Lauren Anderson. It's always nice to have repeated visits from our patrons. It means you value our services." She held one hand on her belly and leaned on the desk with the other.

"Thank you. Looks like the library is quiet this morning." She looked toward the empty podium and stool.

"Oh, Dustin is on vacation this week. Unless we have walk-ins, you and I'll have the room to ourselves." She straightened out a stack of note paper and container of golf pencils on the table. "I'll be at the desk in the back over there if you need me."

Grateful for at least the illusion of privacy, Quinn set up her materials and took a deep breath. She was about to educate herself about a subject she knew almost nothing about—the porn industry. First, she searched in the library system database for Gulf Coast Adult Entertainment. Immediately, a message came up, saying, "Access to this site has been blocked according to company policy." Figuring the word "adult" triggered the filter, Quinn tried Gulf Coast Entertainment. That brought up information about a party business that appeared to have nothing whatever to do with sex videos.

Next, she tried sex trafficking. This yielded pages of content, way more than Quinn could read, even if she had weeks. She skimmed one op-ed piece which touted the vast profits of the industry, in the hundreds of billions of dollars per year, and the diversity of products available, from movies to clothing to sex toys. An article entitled, "The Dark Side of the Adult Film Industry," caught her eye, and she read about how actresses in porn movies are typically abused during the filming, that the sex portrayed is overly aggressive and brutal, and often causes lasting or permanent damage. Poor Dawn. She may have imagined that she was a glamorous dancer, an up-and-coming actress, and maybe she needed the money, but ending up dead at nineteen years old—it was a real tragedy.

Quinn realized how sheltered she had been when it came to sex. Her exposure through health classes and the Catholic Church had been clinical and moralistic, and somehow, through discussions with Ana and other girls, she'd cobbled together a personal paradigm that linked sex to love and commitment. The adult entertainment business was apparently a whole different world.

Quinn was not there to judge. She also could see that, unless she narrowed her searches, she could become bogged down in each of these articles, without making progress on her mission—to learn more about the tapes Ana had sent her. She typed in the title, "Ride Me, Cowboy," and found more than ten pages of listings for erotic books, movies, and songs by that name. Fewer for "Southern Lass Gets What She Deserves," but apparently Dawn hadn't cornered the market with either of the titles.

Next, she tried searching for Dawn's stage name, DeeDee Young. There were six of them on Facebook, even more on Instagram, Twitter, and Pinterest. None of them looked like Dawn, though. Not surprising, since Facebook didn't start until 2004, when Dawn had died.

At this point, Quinn had only taken about a page and a half of notes, mostly generalities. The person she was most interested in learning more about was Keith Underwood, the man with the big ears. A search of the name came up with dozens of people, some famous, some dead. None seemed to be the "person of interest" for Quinn. *Oh, well,* she shrugged mentally. *That probably wasn't his real name, anyway.*

By now, lunch time had come and gone, and Quinn considered sneaking a bite or two of protein bar from her purse. On the other hand, reading about how a select group of mostly men took advantage of mostly young females, desperate for money, had mostly stripped her of her appetite for food.

The information was out there. She knew she could find what she was looking for, if only she had the right keywords. She searched in the library files for "sex offenders in Texas, 2004 to present." This gave her a slew of listings of names and offenses, but, without photographs of the offenders, she couldn't tell one case from another. Still, she read and took notes on a few that mentioned assault and battery. There was no way she could compete with the police in researching bad guys. Their databases were better, they knew what to look for, and their computers weren't filtered. Anyway, her goal was not to catch a criminal, but to arm herself with information that might keep *her* safe from harm.

Finally, she tried a Google search for "male clubs and bars, local." Yelp handed her the top ten places, according to reviews, and she took copious notes on each. "A crusty dive," "not worth the cover," "women are too ordinary," the reviews weren't raving, even at the top ten places, but Quinn took down the addresses and a few salient facts about each place listed.

At this point, her notebook was a third full of scribblings and sticky notes to organize them by topic. An idea was beginning to germinate in her mind about what to do next, but, for now, she was satisfied that her time had been well-spent. Quinn erased the history of her searches, even though a good IT person could resurrect them from the firewall. She restarted the computer, stood and stretched, and piled her materials and sling bag into a stack in the crook of her arm.

Quinn waved goodbye to Lauren, who appeared to be talking on the telephone and jotting down information. The sky was black in the east as Quinn left the history center and the building and walked into the natural sauna that was a part of her island paradise. Thunderstorms had been predicted, but she decided to head toward The Spot for a hamburger, anyway. Maybe she could eat and go home before the heavens opened up. Her mouth watered at the image of the thick and juicy beef, topped by fresh condiments and vegetables. Maybe she'd splurge and have some spicy French fries and a chocolate milkshake, too.

Quinn's cell phone rang as she pulled into the gravel parking lot of the restaurant. Her growling stomach told her to ignore the call, but her suspicious instincts told her not to. *Uh-oh*, she thought, when she saw the caller ID. *It's Becker.*

Chapter Forty-two

A protein bar was no substitute for a meal from The Spot, but Becker had insisted that Quinn come to the office right away. Meanwhile, the storm front had moved closer, and lightning flashed in the not-too-distant east. The police wanted to meet at 2:00, and Becker needed to prep her. The Toyota's clock said 1:15—not much time, even with skipping lunch.

Truthfully, even though she wolfed down the first protein bar while she was driving, and she'd ripped open the wrapper on the second, her stomach wasn't providing a warm welcome for the food. The prospect of talking to Sergeant Schmidt again, with his cynical tone of voice and those exposed gums caused her insides to tighten.

The first splashes of rain hit just as Quinn pulled into the parking space at Becker's office. Having no umbrella, she grabbed her bag, jumped out of the car, locked it with her fob, and dashed into the lobby of the building.

When she reached the lavender-scented office, Ethel speed-glided her in, just as before. Becker rose and motioned her into what she was starting to think of as "her" chair. "Want some tea?"

Quinn nodded, and Ethel left to fill the offer. Quinn sat on her hands, more to keep them from engaging in nervous behaviors than from cold, although the office thermostat could be turned up several notches and she'd be happy—well, more comfortable.

Becker leaned forward and peered at Quinn, his eyebrows having merged into a single salt-and-pepper shrub. "I'm sure you're somewhat anxious about this meeting. You'd be a fool otherwise. But I want you to remember this—the police are just as anxious as you are. Interviews like this are like a game of chicken. The last time Schmidt questioned you, you didn't have an attorney present. This time you can count on me to guide you through it. I want you to maintain as calm and confident a demeanor as possible."

"I-I'll try. But it's getting harder and harder not to feel like a captured butterfly, pinned to a board."

"I understand, and that's why I want you to pay attention to what I have to say now. Schmidt is going to ask you some fairly specific questions related to the tapes, the notes, Ana, Brad, and probably Dawn. It's important that you give truthful answers to his questions, unless I object for a particular reason. Not to cooperate with the police in a murder investigation, when you have pertinent information that might help to solve the murder, is a crime."

"But what about the threats against me if I tell?"

"Fear of harm does not excuse you from answerin' the questions, although I may steer some of the more difficult questions to another time and to the grand jury. Today, you need to listen carefully to what's being asked and answer only that. No additional information."

"Wh-what if he asks me about 'the incident'? Do I have to answer that?"

Before Becker could respond, Ethel knocked on the door. She brought two large cups of tea this time, along with the set-ups. As she set them down in front of Quinn, she winked. "Extra strength, in case you need it."

As soon as Ethel closed the door behind her, Becker said, in the gentlest tone, "You understand that at some point you will have to reveal everything that you know—about Ana, Brad, and Dawn. Whether that point is today in the office, or a few days from now before the grand jury, you can't withhold that information forever. How and when you tell it, however, will depend on criteria that we control to a certain extent. Let me be the judge of that."

Becker rose and began walking a track around his desk and Quinn's chair, hands intertwined behind his back. "One more thing. Schmidt may try to rattle you, thinking he can get more information from you if you're upset and not thinking clearly." He stopped pacing and sat on the corner of his desk. "When I talked to him earlier, he dropped a hint that they're still considering the transplant motive. With Brad dead, they've lost their chief suspect."

"So they don't believe that I didn't know Ana was a match for Jack?"

"I don't know if they do or they don't, but don't be surprised if they suggest that they suspect Josh. Whether they actually suspect him or not, they know that will get a rise out of you."

Heat rushed into Quinn's face, and she wanted to slam a fist against the desk. "This is absurd. Josh is in the business of saving lives—not taking them."

"You see? Your face is redder than a July tomato, and your voice just rose by several decibels. That's what I don't want you to do. Don't fall for their bait."

Quinn sweetened her tea and took several small sips. Once again, she was grateful to have Becker's wisdom. "Okay," she said. "I think I'm ready."

"That's good," Becker replied, pointing to the clock on the desk. "Tee time's in two minutes."

Chapter Forty-three

Quinn ran to the bathroom before the confrontation with Sergeant Schmidt. There, she practiced a yoga posture and stabilizing exercise she had learned in a karate class a few years ago. On the way out, she finger-combed her dark curls and mouthed into the mirror, "Bring it on, Schmidt. I'm ready for you."

When she returned to the office, a somewhat-drenched Schmidt was shaking hands with Becker, as civilized as two boxers before a highly contested match. Schmidt had started to sit in Quinn's chair, but Becker stopped him. "That's my client's chair. Please sit over here."

Quinn caught the irritated look on the policeman's face. He might have muttered, "Holy Mary—" before he saw her and pasted an unconvincing smile on his face. He didn't bother to shake hands with her, which was perfectly fine. She didn't like being in the same zip code with him.

A loud boom of thunder caused everyone to jump, and Quinn stared out the window. Summer squalls weren't that rare here on the coast, but this one seemed darker and heavier than usual. It was a good time to be inside, except Quinn wished she were anywhere but here.

Once everyone was seated, Becker played host. "We're meeting at the request of Sergeant Schmidt and the police department, who are investigating the murder of Ana Renfroe. As you know, Quinn, the police would like to ask you some questions. They have assured me that you are not a suspect at this time, and I have assured them that they will have our full cooperation within the necessary limits. One of those limits is that this meeting is not to be recorded on any device."

Quinn nodded and resisted the impulse to sit on her hands. Reminding herself that the police were probably anxious, too, she breathed normally and willed the corners of her mouth to turn up, at least a little.

Schmidt wiggled his bottom from side-to-side in the chair, as if to settle in more comfortably, but it put Quinn in the mind of a recalcitrant donkey. She wished he would start talking, so he could finish. "Yes, well, we have viewed the two media tapes Mr. Becker brought to our office. We watched them in their entirety." His mouth stretched into an odd expression, again revealing too much of his gums. "My first questions have to do with these tapes." He cleared his throat. "Please review for me how and when you received the tapes."

Quinn glanced at Becker, who gave a slight nod. She explained how her neighbor, Anise, had taken the package from Quinn's porch and forgotten to give it to her until after she ran into her Monday night.

"Were there any notes inside the package or any identifying marks that led you to believe the package came from Ana Renfroe?"

"You have the entire package," Quinn replied, looking at Becker to confirm. "There was no note, only the sticky note that says ID. The only way I knew where it came from was the handwriting, which was clearly Ana's."

"Mr. Becker told me you have other samples of Ana's handwriting to compare this to. Is that correct?" Quinn nodded. "Why would Ana Renfroe mail you two old pornographic movies?"

Becker interrupted. "My client cannot answer that question. You are askin' her to speculate on the motives of a woman whom my client hasn't spoken to in fifteen years. She would have no idea."

Schmidt didn't skip a beat. "What did you think when you opened the package and saw these two tapes?"

Quinn looked out the window at sheets of rain. "I couldn't imagine why Ana would be sending me two old movies."

"Two old *pornographic* movies," Schmidt said. "Had you or Ana ever participated in the making of erotic movies, either individually or together?"

Schmidt's tone of voice sent chills up and down Quinn's spine, but she answered with a forced calmness. "I can't speak for Ana, but I never did, and I have no knowledge that Ana did, either."

Becker interrupted. "You must have noted, Sergeant, that the two films were made in 2003 and 2004. At that time, Ana and Quinn were only thirteen and fourteen years old."

Schmidt went on as if Becker hadn't spoken. "You viewed the two movies in their entirety. Is that correct?"

Quinn nodded. She felt dirty, sitting here, talking about sex tapes with the policeman, even though she hadn't felt that way watching them with Becker.

"Did you recognize anyone in either of the two tapes?" Schmidt fixed her with a piercing look, one that made her stomach flip. She stole a look at Becker, who blinked.

"I can't be positively certain, but I think the actress in both movies is Dawn Chrysler." Quinn bit off the syllables of Dawn's name, as if she were speaking to a person hard of hearing. There, she had answered the question, but she wouldn't offer anything more.

"Dawn Chrysler was murdered in 2004. Were you aware of that?"

Quinn nodded. She only wished she weren't aware of Dawn's murder.

"Yes, indeed," Schmidt said, rocking back a little in his chair. "Dawn's murder remains unsolved to this day." He leaned forward and stared into Quinn's eyes. "How did you know Dawn Chrysler?"

Quinn tried to swallow, but a boulder was clogging her throat. "Dawn was Ana's neighbor. Her house was right across the back alley from the Frenches. I spent a lot of time at Ana's, hanging out in the neighborhood."

"Really?" Schmidt replied. "Dawn was about seven years older than you and Ana. With that age difference, you wouldn't have had much contact in the normal course of things. Please explain to me how you would recognize someone that much older on the basis of her living in your friend's neighborhood."

Quinn gulped, hoping it wasn't audible. Becker's admonition that withholding answers would be tantamount to a crime rang in her head. "Dawn had a habit of dancing in the nude at night with her curtains open. Ana had seen her and showed me. We were little girls, amused and intrigued. We watched her many times."

Schmidt sat back, apparently pleased, judging by the too-wide smile on his face. "Did you recognize anyone else in the movies?"

Quinn's body tensed, and her throat constricted. Quinn hoped the policeman didn't notice a change in her demeanor. "I-I'm really not sure. I think I might have seen the 'cowboy' before, but I don't know who he is."

"What makes you think you might have seen him before? Would it help to review the tape? I happen to have brought the two tapes with me." Schmidt pointed to the VCR on the counter.

"I-I don't think that's necessary. I'm pretty sure the same man was in both tapes. I recognized him, especially from the back, by the ears." The storm was easing up outside, but, inside, her pulse was thrashing. Quinn had a momentary yearning for Ana. If Ana were here, this would be so much easier.

Schmidt's lips formed a tight line. "Let's change subjects for a moment.

You're aware, I'm sure, that Brad Renfroe has been found dead since we last talked in my office. Were you in communication with Brad after that phone call to you before he went missing?"

Quinn bit her lip. It was still hard to believe Brad was dead. "No." She started to expand on her answer, to say that there would be no reason for Brad to call her again, that she still didn't fully understand why he had called her to begin with. But Becker had said not to offer anything more than the answers to Schmidt's questions.

"Do you have any theories as to who might have wanted Brad dead?"

Becker intervened. "Now wait a minute, Sergeant. You told me you were coming to interview my client about Ana Renfroe's murder. So far, you've asked questions about everything else but Ana Renfroe. Surely you don't think my client has knowledge about all of your open cases."

If he felt chastised, Schmidt didn't show it. He just plowed on into the next question. "As you well know, your brother, Jack McFarland, received a transplanted kidney from the deceased, Ana Renfroe. It's well-known around town that Jack was waiting for a kidney for a long time. In fact, if he didn't receive a kidney soon, he might die. Is that right?"

Quinn sipped the now-cold tea and braced herself for what would come next, insinuations that she would have killed to get a new kidney for her brother. Or that Josh would. "Yes."

"If you, or someone close to you, knew that Ana was a match for Jack, that might've provided a mighty compelling motive to murder Ana, wouldn't it?" The gum-showing sneer on his face caused Quinn to flinch, despite every effort not to.

Becker interrupted, his scowling eyebrows jutting out further than ever. "Listen here, Schmidt. You go way too far—this whole line of questioning is far afield of what we understood to be your purpose here. Are you here to arrest my client? To accuse her of murdering a woman she hadn't even laid eyes on in fifteen years? If so, where is your warrant? If not, I strongly suggest you ask only informational questions about the murder of Ana Renfroe."

Schmidt's sneer intensified. "Sorry if my questions disturb your sensibilities, but this police department has three unsolved murders on our plate. In a town this size, that's huge, but we are doing our best to solve them all, even the one from 2004. Now it's not my fault if each one of these cases somehow involves your client. We believe that she has information we need, and we are determined to get that information."

Quinn took several small sips of tea as she listened to the back-and-forth between policeman and lawyer, a tennis match between King Kong and Godzilla. What was most clear through it all was that she was in the center of a serious and tragic maze with no clear path out. And, apparently, she had dragged Josh into it, as well.

"What other questions do you have, Schmidt?" Becker poured himself a glass of water from a small pitcher on his credenza and held an empty glass up to offer one to the policeman.

"No water. Thanks. I want to go back to the tapes that Ana purportedly sent you." He pointed a finger at Quinn. "I can't help thinking there's a reason Ana wanted you to have the tapes. Ana told her parents, if something happened to her, talk to Quinn. Well, something *did* happen to her. So there's something about these tapes that figures into Ana's murder, and maybe Brad's, too."

Becker tapped his pen against his desk. "What's your question, Schmidt?"

"Two questions." Schmidt inhaled, as if he were about to dive off a cliff into a deep, cold river. "First, Quinn, you must have been thinking about these same things—why Ana would send you the pornographic movies featuring her neighbor, why she would send her parents to you, if your relationship with her was long over. I asked you before what you thought when you opened the package from Ana. Now I'm asking you what you think now—after viewing the tapes and having some time to think about them."

"What I think," she said, her voice hoarse and muted, "what I think is that Ana was trying to warn me." At that moment all the emotion, pent-up for years, broke forth like gushing waters through a breached dam. Half of Quinn's life had been spent loving Ana French, and half hating her. Maybe Ana sending the tapes had been an olive branch, a way of saying she was sorry for betraying their friendship. Maybe she sent the tapes, because she knew Quinn was the only person who would understand their significance. And that understanding could put Quinn in danger. Quinn had held up without showing emotion until now, but the thought of Ana's final message overwhelmed her with loss, grief, and a helplessness that frightened her with its intensity. She covered her face with her hands and sobbed.

"Shall we give you some time to pull yourself together?" Becker asked, as he pushed a box of tissues within Quinn's reach.

"N-no, I'll be all right."

The tears must have had an effect on Schmidt, too, because when he spoke, his voice was softer. "Okay, I'll make this quick. Given that you've had two hand-written notes, both threatening you not to talk, and you feel Ana was trying to warn you, it stands to reason that there is something relevant on these tapes. And I can't help thinking it ties in with Dawn Chrysler's murder. So what I want to know is, were you present at the time and place of Dawn's murder? And did you, in fact, witness Dawn's murder?"

"*Those* are questions, I'm afraid, that I am instructing my client not to answer." Becker stood and walked to the window, where afternoon shadows were gathering outside. "If she did witness a murder—even though she was, what, fourteen years old at the time?—failing to come forward could be considered a crime."

"Come on, Becker. We've got three murders to deal with. We aren't interested in going after a juvey for withholding evidence fifteen years ago."

"That may or may not be true," Becker said, as he returned to his desk, but didn't sit down. "But if you want to question my client about Dawn's murder, we can discuss an immunity agreement with the DA, and you can bring her before the grand jury." He leaned both hands on his desk and peered through his eyebrows at the policeman. "Are those all of your questions?"

Schmidt hoisted himself from his chair and trudged toward the door, the package with the tapes tucked under his arm. When he reached the door, he straightened his posture, turned back and said, "That will be all for now. Thank you for your cooperation."

Once Schmidt had left and closed the door behind him, Becker chuckled and said, "Well, that didn't turn out so bad."

Quinn blew her nose and wiped the wells under her eyes, where she was sure there were mascara tracks. "I'm glad you think so. I thought it was awful."

Chapter Forty-four

After leaving Becker's office, Quinn headed for home, her mind grinding through the many problems weighing on it. The sky had cleared completely. If not for puddles and wet pavement, a person might have thought there hadn't been any rain at all. As she passed the Kroger, Quinn swerved into the parking lot. Her appetite was returning, and the cupboard was bare, but, more importantly, she was hatching an idea that involved a proper dinner.

Within fifteen minutes, she had purchased chicken breasts, mushrooms, red pepper, sugar snap peas, teriyaki sauce, and quick-cooking brown rice. Stir frying was one of her specialties, and right now her mouth was watering for some fresh, savory food. When she pulled into her driveway, she texted Josh. Did u mean what u said last nite about doing this more often?

He was on a daytime rotation and should be getting off in time for dinner. Without waiting for an answer, she hoisted the grocery bags out of the trunk and took them into the house, disarming the alarm on the way. Calvin greeted her with his usual doggy-dance, so she put the chicken in the refrigerator, leashed him up, and took him around the block.

While Calvin ran through the still-damp grass, sniffing every bush in sight, Quinn checked her emails and texts, and waited to hear back from Josh. If he didn't respond soon, she would go ahead and start cooking for two. The worst that could happen would be delicious left-overs. Maybe she'd take some to Jack's.

As soon as she got home, she put the other groceries away and ransacked the pantry for a snack. Her day at the library and then at Becker's office had left her depleted. She found a half-eaten package of dried cranberries and dug into it on her way to the shower. While the hot-as-she-could-stand-it water nipped at her skin, Quinn imagined it washing away all her troubles and draining them away. A good soaping and shampooing later, she emerged from the shower, invigorated.

Here she was, in the worst situation of her life, being threatened, badgered, and suspected, and yet she had never felt so alive and purposeful. It was as if "the incident," along with the betrayal by Ana and Brad, had set her into a cocoon state, where nothing much mattered. Now her brain and heart were fully engaged in everything. Ana's death had set her on this course, and she was determined to see it through to its best possible outcome.

Josh's text had come in while she was showering. What do u have in mind? On call, but can be there at 7.

It was already 6:45, and Quinn wasn't even dressed. Make that 7:30. Chicken stir fry and a surprise. Come hungry. Throwing the phone down on the bed, Quinn dried off, selected a clean pair of shorts and top from her closet shelves, and started in on blowing her hair dry. A bit of makeup later, and she headed for the kitchen, where she washed and sliced the chicken breasts and vegetables.

By the time Josh rang the doorbell, the house was filled with the sweet, pungent smell of teriyaki sauce, and the rice was fluffy and perfect. Quinn opened the door to three dozen long-stemmed pink roses, brandished by the handsome and well-scrubbed doctor. He folded her into his arms, holding the roses aloft. How tempting it was to put dinner on hold and celebrate being together in the same way as last night, but Quinn had other plans.

After returning a few long kisses, she pulled back and looked Josh in the eyes. "How about we eat dinner now? Don't know about you, but I missed lunch, and I'm starving."

Was that disappointment in his voice? He said, "Okay, sure. Dinner smells wonderful." He followed her into the kitchen. "Where should I put these flowers?"

"Oh, forgive me for not thanking you. They are gorgeous and smell divine." She pulled a large vase from the pantry and filled it with water, while Josh picked up Calvin's squeaky toy and tossed it. "What's the occasion?" Quinn asked.

Josh's mouth turned up, giving lie to his sad tone of voice. "I'm wounded that you don't know. It's our six-month anniversary." He washed his hands and dried them with a dish towel. "How can I help with dinner?"

"You can open the wine, and let's have a toast. Has it really been six months?"

"Almost to the minute. Does it seem longer or shorter to you?" He removed the cork and sniffed. "Mmm, this chardonnay has a nice bouquet." He poured the wine into two glasses and handed one to Quinn, who was stirring the chicken and the sauce in the wok.

"Seems just right."

"What? The wine?"

"No, the amount of time we've been together. Still short enough to be new and exciting. Long enough to feel like I really know you." She clinked her glass against Josh's. "Here's to many more great times together."

Josh sat at the table and sipped his wine, while Quinn finished the stir fry. "There's something I need to share with you."

The tone of voice caused Quinn's stomach to clench. Whatever was coming, it wasn't going to be roses or chardonnay. "Okay?"

"I had a visit at work this morning from a police officer, Tom Porter. He said he's investigating the death of Ana Renfroe. He had my statement about not knowing that Ana was a match for Jack until she arrived at the hospital in a coma, but he wanted to follow up. Seemed like he didn't believe me."

"Oh, no. I'm so sorry I dragged you into this mess. They still think that you—"

"—may have had something to do with Ana's death in order to get her kidney for Jack. Fact is, though, that transplants are way more complicated than that."

Quinn spooned servings of brown rice topped with stir-fried chicken onto two plates and set them on the table. "Can you explain it to me while we eat, or isn't this good dinner table conversation?"

"Nothing would ruin my appetite for your stir-fry. This smells delicious." He blew on the first forkful and then took it into his mouth. "Mmm, so good. You could have a second career as a chef."

Quinn started eating, too, shoveling the food in, in fact. "So what did Officer Porter want to know?'

"Well, I explained to him about the National Kidney Registry, how they are the main source for screening for compatible kidneys, particularly when the donor is living." He took another bite. "Porter wanted to know why you hadn't volunteered to donate a kidney to your brother. Wouldn't siblings be the best matches?"

Quinn swallowed her last bite. This topic gave her a bitter aftertaste, and she set down her fork. "Did you tell him I offered a kidney to Jack?"

"Yes, and I explained that even though you are siblings, you and Jack have gender difference and blood type difference, different antibodies, so your compatibility match power isn't promising. Jack had risen to the top of the NKR list, so it was just a matter of time before a living donor would turn up for him, but when Ana came in, we tested her blood and antigens and found them to be highly compatible. Plus, her height and weight were greater than yours."

"How come the gender difference didn't matter with Ana's kidney?"

"It did, in a way. It kept her from being a perfect match, but the other factors overrode the gender difference. More importantly, Ana had signed a donor card, and her family supported her decision. She was being kept alive on life support until we found matching donees for her various organs. The fact that Jack's need and her geographic availability crossed in terms of place and time made it a perfect decision to perform the procurement and transplant surgeries."

Quinn took up her fork again. "Well, I hope that settled the matter once and for all, and the police can leave you alone."

"One can only hope. Porter claimed he was just on a fact-finding mission, but he had that I'm-in-control-here attitude that was quite unsettling." Josh took his last bite and washed it down with wine.

Quinn reached across the table for his hand and stroked it with her thumb, the wine and dinner having relaxed her. "I regret bringing you into this whole thing. If you weren't dating me, the police wouldn't care a whit about how and why Jack got Ana's kidney." She stood and began clearing the table. "Want the last bit of wine?"

"Sure. This was a good bottle. And no problem about the police. I don't have anything to hide, and I'm sure you don't either." Josh drained his wineglass and moved to the sink. "How 'bout I wash, you dry?"

"Deal." Whether it was the wine, or the roses, the full stomach, or having a partner to share cleaning up the kitchen with, Quinn was enjoying the inner warmth of the moment.

While Josh filled the sink with detergent and water, he touched a few of the orchids in the window on either side of him. "These are amazing. You must give them a lot of care for them to bloom like this. My mom's tried to grow orchids many times, and they never re-bloom."

"One of my projects. When you work with dead people, coming home to something alive and growing is a pleasure."

"Hey," Josh said, as he handed a dinner plate over to be dried. "You said you had a surprise. What is it?"

"Oh, yeah. Almost forgot." Quinn put away the plate and set the dish towel on the drain board. She took Josh by both hands and gazed into his eyes. "How would you like to do something different tonight?"

Josh tilted his head, a sparkle in his eyes that could've been from wine or lust or both.

"How would you like to accompany me to a gentleman's strip club?"

Chapter Forty-five

Quinn laughed as the shock registered on Josh's face. His gray eyes stared at hers, one eyebrow cocked. "A strip club? You're kidding me, right?"

"Actually, not." Suddenly the idea of walking into a bar with naked women swarming all over her boyfriend didn't seem like fun, but it was too late now. "But I have an ulterior motive."

"Can't imagine, but tell me."

Maybe he's starting to wonder whether I'm introduce-to-parents material, after all. "It's getting late. Why don't I tell you in the car?"

"Okay, I'll drive." Did he seem a little too eager? Quinn picked up her list of club names and addresses and her sling bag, and followed him out, securing her house behind her.

The daytime breeze had disappeared, and the humidity clung to Quinn's bare arms and legs like an extra layer of moist skin. She was sure her hair had frizzed, as well, but she had more important things on her mind.

The dashboard on Josh's Acura was lit up like a slot machine, and Quinn had the thought that this whole adventure might be a gamble. "Let's head toward the causeway. They put these clubs away from schools and churches and hospitals and mortuaries."

The radio was playing "Survivor" by Destiny's Child, but Josh snapped it off. "You want to tell me what this is all about?" He was smiling, but his sideways glance spoke volumes. "Guessing we aren't going solely for the show."

Quinn swallowed some air. "This has to do with Ana's death. I can't go into detail, because our conversations aren't privileged." A tiny part of her ego high-fived her for explaining this way. Becker would be proud of her, too.

Huffing a little, Josh said, "You know you could trust me to be discreet. I keep lots of people's business private every day."

"I know, but this is different. Anything I tell you can be used against me in court. It's just better if you don't know certain things—at least, while this case is open." Quinn patted his knee and then left her hand there. "Believe me, I wish I *could* tell you everything."

Josh covered Quinn's hand on his thigh and squeezed. "Well, can you tell me what we're looking for, or am I just supposed to play the role of a guy taking his love to a peep show? You know what goes on in these places, right?"

"Turn right onto that feeder road. That's it, the Heartbeat Cabaret." Quinn dug into her handbag for her ID and money for the cover charge. "Cover's on me, since this is my idea. And what we're looking for is a man—tall, dark-haired, with ears that stick out. Maybe the manager or owner."

Josh parked next to a light pole that illuminated his car, as if it were a theater stage. "Okay, boss. You lead, you pay. I'm along for the ride—and to protect you."

Their feet crunched on the gravel as they approached the old wood-frame house that had been converted to a business. The face of the building had been painted in pinks and purples, shadowy abstract shapes. Pulsating music bathed their ears and left no doubt about what awaited them inside.

A sign on the door said, "No one under the age of 21 will be admitted. No firearms. No drugs. No photography. Cover charge—$10, applied to bar bill. Press button to enter." Josh and Quinn exchanged glances, and he pushed the button. A loud click could be heard over the music, and Josh turned the doorknob and pushed.

The world inside was dim, loud. A fog machine created atmosphere, such as it was. The temperature in the room wasn't much different from that in the parking lot. Quinn peered beyond the bald-headed guy at the door, but a tall Chinese screen blocked her view of the room where the action was.

"You gotta pay to look, lady," the bouncer said, the smell of liquor-tinged halitosis punctuating his greeting.

Quinn shoved a twenty-dollar bill and her ID at the man and turned her head in the opposite direction.

"Go on over to the bar," he said, snatching the bills and stuffing them into a cigar box. "First drink's on the house."

As they walked around the screen, Quinn gazed at Josh and held her hands to her ears. "Want a drink?"

"Sure. It's already paid for." They walked over to the bar, where a female bartender, wearing nothing but a low-cut rhinestone-studded apron, filled their order for two gin-and-tonics.

Past the bar there was a half-wall that reminded Quinn of the bowling alley, and, three steps up, a stage lit with colored lights where the pins would be. Tiny tables were set up against the half-wall, and people could sit on chairs or padded benches. The dim lights and the fog prevented her from seeing well, but no more than a few tables were occupied, and all the customers appeared to be men, sitting alone.

There were plenty of women in the large room, though. A cocktail waitress, wearing the same uniform as the bartender, but showing more flesh because she was out in the open, strolled from table to table, taking orders. Two dancers on stage were completely nude, except for glittery body paint around their nipples, money belts around their waists, and tiny G-strings. A third dancer was giving a lap dance to a guy in a corner.

Quinn shivered, despite the room being warm. In her shorts and top, she had more clothes on than any other woman in the room. She and Josh took seats on a banquette as far away from a speaker as possible. As she observed the dancing women, she couldn't help thinking of Dawn. Had Dawn, as a teenager, known what she was getting into, using her body like these dancers?

The women in this cabaret were tired-looking. The fog didn't completely hide their battle scars—wrinkles, sagginess, a tooth missing—but, most of all, a weariness in the eyes, as if life's troubles couldn't be solved by dancing. Quinn studied Josh's face as he glommed onto the dancer who was doing splits on the stage. She couldn't imagine what he was thinking. Was it a mistake to bring him here?

The lap dancer, having finished her job in the back corner, ascended the three steps to the stage and began gyrating to the music. One of the other dancers descended and undulated toward Josh, her expression seductive. Ignoring Quinn, she purred, "You're cute. How about a nice, long lap dance? I promise you'll love it." She leaned both arms on the table and gave Josh a view of full, though overripe, breasts.

Josh glanced at Quinn and shook his head. He took a sip of his drink.

The woman appeared to see Quinn sitting there for the first time. "She won't mind, will ya? Maybe she'll learn a few tricks to practice with ya later."

"No, thanks." Josh turned toward Quinn and put his arm around her shoulder.

The woman took the hint and moved on to the next customer. Not for the first time, Quinn was grateful to earn a decent living at her family shop. Even if the services she performed might give someone else the creeps, she'd never had to consider selling her body to support herself.

After finishing their drinks and watching two semi-athletic pole dances,

Quinn excused herself to go to the restroom. She nosed around the entire facility *en route* both ways, and, seeing no sign of the person she was looking for, she returned to Josh.

"Any luck?" he asked. He fidgeted as if he were itching to leave.

"Maybe I can ask one of the dancers. Give me a minute."

In the time that had elapsed while Quinn was in the restroom, the dancers had rotated positions, so there was a new lap dancer strutting around the room. Quinn marched over and asked to have a word with her. As she leaned closer, she smelled a mixture of perspiration, perfume, and tobacco on the dancer's breath.

"Sure." She pointed to an unoccupied corner of the room. "Let's go over there where it's quieter."

The corner was, indeed, quieter. Quinn looked across the room at Josh, who was slouching on the banquette with an elbow on the table and his head in his hand. She whispered to the lap dancer, "Is the club manager on duty tonight?"

The woman hugged herself, bunching her breasts together like two dirigibles. "You ain't complainin' 'bout anything, I hope. Nobody here means no harm." Could that be fear in her voice?

"No, nothing like that. I have a business-related question. That's all."

"Okay, then." She nodded her head toward the front door. "That's him over there. You met 'im when you came in."

"Thanks so much." Quinn slipped a folded bill into the woman's money belt. "You take care now." Quinn returned to Josh and gave him the new information.

"That guy at the door sure doesn't fit your description. Can we leave now?"

Although she was somewhat gratified that Josh had seemed impervious to the dancers and the scuzzy milieu, she couldn't abandon the mission yet. "I hate to mention this, but there are four other gentlemen's clubs in the area."

Josh groaned. "I hate to be a party pooper, but I've got an early day tomorrow."

It was almost eleven, and their mission, for tonight, at least, was accomplished. "Okay, let's hit the road."

When they got into Josh's car and headed back to Quinn's house, she said, "Well, that wasn't too bad. Can we try a different club tomorrow night?"

"Not my favorite way to spend time with you, but, knowing you, you won't give up until you've found the person you're looking for." She nodded and patted his thigh. "And, for sure," he added, "I don't want you going to these places without me."

"Thank you, Josh. And now, if you come in the house with me, I'm inspired to try out a little lap dancing."

Chapter Forty-six

The next morning Quinn arrived at the prep room promptly at nine, sneezing as she crossed the threshold. The room was clean and quiet, but there was a sheet of white computer paper taped onto the metal table with the words, "Come upstairs when you get in. We need to talk."

The banana and yogurt she had eaten for breakfast lodged in her stomach, as if waiting for assurances to continue digesting. This wasn't the first time her parents had left a note like this, but normally they kept work separate from home. Even growing up in the upstairs, months would go by between visits to the downstairs for any reason, except to access the staircase or elevator. Now that she had a place of her own, Quinn rarely spent time in her parents' living quarters, unless it was a family dinner or a holiday. If her parents needed to talk to her while she was at work, they usually came down to her area.

Considering their hyper-curiosity about everything in her life, as well as Mr. Becker's admonition against sharing anything with them, she dreaded whatever conversation they had in mind, but there was no avoiding it. This was one of those times that it was a detriment to work in the family business.

Quinn mentally ticked off items on the list of what she didn't want to discuss with them as she climbed the stairs. A carpeted hallway led to an alcove, where an exterior doorway, flanked by planters of artificial geraniums, had been installed ages ago. Quinn rang the doorbell like the reluctant guest that she was.

Seconds went by before she heard her dad's voice as he approached the door. "Hello, kitten." His mentholated shaving cream smell reminded her of the times when he would come into her bedroom to wake her up for school. He was dressed in khakis and a green polo shirt. A non-funeral morning, then.

"You wanted to see me?" Quinn held up the note, and stepped inside, as her father motioned her in.

"How about giving your ol' dad a good morning hug, Miss Grouchy Face?"

Quinn folded herself into the frame made by her father's tall stature and long arms. In her childhood, she remembered being the safest and happiest wrapped in his hugs, but that was a long time ago. She pulled away and dropped the note and her sling bag on the console table in the entry hall.

"Sorry if I seem grouchy. Up late last night and didn't sleep well." She looked beyond him into the vast family room, where panels of early sunshine were bathing the modern furniture with light. "Where's Mom?"

"In the kitchen. Making French toast for the three of us."

French toast had always been Quinn's favorite breakfast. Her mother prepared it with egg bread, stuffed with cream cheese and raspberry jam. "I wish I'd known. I ate breakfast at home."

She followed the heavenly aromas of cinnamon and vanilla through the family room to the kitchen/breakfast room.

The table was set with orange and red placemats and napkins, white china, a pitcher of orange juice, and a bouquet of zinnias from the back garden. *All this for a breakfast for three? Something must be up.* "Morning, Mom." Quinn breezed around the kitchen island to give her mother an air-kiss. "How can I help?"

"Hello, dear. We're almost ready to eat. Go ahead and sit down." She pulled the platter of golden French toast from the warming oven and added two more pieces to it before carrying it over to the table. "C'mon, John. Breakfast will get cold."

Quinn unfolded her napkin and set it in her lap. Her father sat across from her and started pouring orange juice into the glasses. "Quinn ate earlier, but I'll bet she can't pass up today's specialty of the house. Right, Quinn?"

"I'll have a little piece. What's the occasion, anyway?" *Why do I feel like the proverbial fly in a spider's web?* She tried not to swoon over the first bite of French toast.

Her parents exchanged glances, and her mother took a sip of juice before speaking. "We've been so wrapped up in Jack's surgery lately, and we know you've been carrying a lot of the load for the business. We wanted to show our appreciation."

"Okay," Quinn said, between bites. "Glad to help." She was certain more was coming, but this wasn't her show. "Okay if I make myself some tea?" Without waiting for permission, she took her coffee cup to the instant hot water faucet at the sink.

"Oh, I think we're out of tea bags. How about some coffee instead?" Her mother rummaged through the cabinet, looking for tea. "I'm so sorry. I know you prefer tea."

"That's all right," Quinn said, carrying a cup of hot water to the table instead. "I'm fine with this."

Joy McFarland was not one to let things go. She opened drawers, canisters, cabinets, even the refrigerator. Finally, she found a single tea bag tucked behind a bag of sugar in the pantry. "*Voila*—here's one." She brandished it to the table and set it down by Quinn's cup.

"Thanks, Mom." Quinn unwrapped the tea bag and dunked it into her boiling water, slightly annoyed that her mother would go to such great lengths to fix her favorite breakfast, but forget that she preferred tea to coffee. Oh, well. Better to be grateful for the French toast than grumpy over the tea. Anyway, the underlying motive for this delicious repast was yet to be announced.

Once she sipped a respectable amount of tea, and unable to take the suspense any longer, Quinn started cleaning up the dishes. "Thanks for the treat. Guess I'll head down to the prep room and get to work now."

"Uh, wait," her father said, his hand pushing hers down onto the table. "Why don't you tell us about Josh's parents first? We haven't had a chance to hear how your dinner with them went."

"Well, I told you they are very nice people. We had dinner and breakfast together while they were in town. They're like Josh, salt-of-the-earth people. Easy to talk to. They invited me for Thanksgiving."

"Did they ask about us? When will we have a chance to meet them?" Quinn's mother was probably making a guest list for a dinner party to introduce the Bradys to her friends and family.

Quinn smiled to herself. Josh's mom would most likely fit in with any crowd, while her own mother might not. "They did mention that they are looking forward to meeting you, but let's not get ahead of ourselves, please."

"I assume Josh has told them what our business is."

It was easy to see where Quinn's own insecurities about being a mortician came from. "Yes, they don't seem to have a problem with it." She sipped her tea. "Really, it's not like we're bank robbers or something."

"Don't be sarcastic, Quinn. We're only trying to look out for you. You and Jack have both had your share of heartbreak. We want to do all we can to make sure that doesn't happen again." John McFarland looked out the window.

Quinn held back the question of what they would've done if Josh's parents hadn't liked her occupation. Despite their meddling, her parents meant well.

"No worries. Josh and his parents are fine with what we do. I think they respect the fact that I come from a good family and have a good profession." She folded her napkin, set it on the table, and picked up the dishes to take them to the sink.

"There's something else we need to talk about," her father said. "A not-so-pleasant topic, I'm afraid."

Quinn kept moving toward the sink. She hoped they weren't going to quiz her about Ana's murder. She scraped the plates of crumbs and turned on the hot water.

"Come on back and sit down," her mother said. "I'll take care of those later."

Reluctantly, Quinn returned to the table. "Look, if this is about—"

"No, not about Ana. At least not directly." Quinn gave her father what she hoped was a piercing look, and he held his hands up, surrender style. "It's about Brad."

Quinn's mother looked away. Her hands fidgeted with the place mat. She had never liked Brad, even when Quinn was besotted with him.

Even though Quinn had washed her hands of Brad long ago, and despite the fact that he was dead, the mention of his name still caused Quinn's stomach to flip. "What about him?"

"His body's on ice downstairs. Shot in the back of the head with a .22. Either a professional hit or made to look like one."

"Jack told me the Frenches are taking responsibility for the body and are payinbg for a double funeral with Ana's. But why all the drama? I'm not emotionally involved with Brad or Ana anymore. I prepared Ana's body, and I'll do the same for Brad. In fact, I'll get started now."

Joy McFarland gripped her daughter's wrist and held it. "No, Quinn. You won't."

Quinn looked from her father's face to her mother's. What was going on?

"Listen, kitten. The police have been nosing around town, asking a lot of questions of people we know. You know how people talk, and it's come back to us from more than one source. Questions about you and Ana, you and Brad, you and firearms. They even asked Father Frank how often you come to church."

Quinn's heart was racing, and icy prickles made her think she might pass out. Even after the meetings with Mr. Becker and turning over the tapes to Sergeant Schmidt, she was still being pegged as a murderer? Surely this was a nightmare, and she would wake up soon.

Her mother wet a cloth napkin and handed it to Quinn, motioning to put it on her forehead. "Dad and I think it's best if you have nothing to do with Brad's body, the funeral, any of it. In fact, we think you should go on a vacation for a while. Until things settle down here. We can manage."

"*What?* There couldn't be a worse time for me to leave town. Jack can't help, and you two can't manage all the embalming by yourselves anymore. You've forgotten how physically demanding it is. Especially the double funeral—whenever it is—those never go smoothly, even when all four of us are working." Quinn put her head in her hands. She needed to think. Her parents' fears for her were only half of the picture. She was just beginning to understand what Ana had been going through, why Brad had called to warn her.

Quinn's father took one of her hands in his. "We've contacted Aunt Virginia, and she says you can stay with her for a month or so. Hopefully things will have blown over by then, and the police will be on to the real perpetrators—"

An intense heat poured itself into Quinn's face, and she threw the wet napkin on the table. "You contacted Aunt Virginia without talking to me? I'm not a child anymore, in case you haven't noticed. I'm almost thirty years old. I'll be the one to decide these things, not you." She stood and clenched her fists. "Besides, did you ever think that running away might make me look guilty?"

Her mother was trying to calm her, to get her to sit down, but all Quinn could think of was the ball of anger, frustration, and even fear, rolling around inside of her. As furious as she was, a little voice in her head was reminding her that she was lucky to have parents who loved and looked out for her. "I'll tell you what. I'll discuss this with Mr. Becker and see what he says." She headed for the foyer. When she arrived at the outside door, she turned to yell over her shoulder. "Maybe it's best if I don't work on Brad. If you think the two of you can handle that, I'll take today off."

Hustling down the hall after her, her father murmured agreement.

Quinn had swiped her sling bag from the console table and opened the exterior door, when she remembered her manners. "Oh, and thanks for the great breakfast."

Chapter Forty-seven

When she marched out of her parents' house, Quinn's emotions had formed into a cold, tight knot, but hot rays of the sun on her face caused the knot to loosen. How rare to have a whole day off with nowhere she had to be! If she hadn't been weighed down by so many troubles, she was sure she would've flown around town like the happiest bird on the coast.

As it was, she needed to touch base with Mr. Becker, and a major grocery run would be time well-spent before her date with Josh. Those were the things her *mind* was leaning toward. Her *heart* was telling her to go to Jack's. While some women ran to their girlfriends with every problem or confidence, Quinn—maybe because of having been burned so badly by Ana—trusted her brother the most. Not that she was going to tell him everything, but when it came to Mom and Dad, nobody understood like Jack.

On the way to Jack's house, the low gasoline indicator flashed on. Quinn detoured to the gas station, and while she filled up her tank, she called Becker's office. When Ethel answered, Quinn exchanged pleasantries before asking for the attorney.

"I'm sorry, but he's in court this morning. Can I give him a message?"

Quinn considered leaving a detailed message and decided against it. "Sure. Will you have him call me on my cell phone when he gets in?"

The gas nozzle popped off at the same time as she disconnected from Ethel. Quinn took her receipt and resumed the route to Jack's house. She'd do the grocery shopping afterward. That way she could pick up whatever Jack needed, as well.

As she pulled into Jack's driveway, some instinct told Quinn to call before ringing the doorbell. She and Jack never had stood on ceremony when visiting each other before, but the fact that he was recovering from major surgery gave her reason. Never did she expect, though, that her brother would be entertaining company—especially not the beautiful, but sleepy-voiced Mary Hallom.

Mary answered Jack's cell phone after several rings. "Hey, Quinn. How you doin'?"

"Who *is* this?" Quinn asked, her tone of voice more incredulous than she intended.

Mary yawned into the phone. "Sorry. It's Mary from next door. I stopped by to check on your brother when I finished my shift."

"Where's Jack?" Quinn's imagination ran wild as she considered what she might be interrupting.

"He's in the bathroom. Takes him a little longer than usual since his surgery. Want me to have him call you when he gets out?"

"Actually, I'm in the driveway. Ask him if it's okay if I come in." As weird as she felt, asking permission from an acquaintance to visit her own brother, Quinn imagined how she might feel if Jack walked into her house without notice, especially now that she and Josh were spending more time together there. She was glad she had called.

Jack's voice piped up in the background. "Who's on the phone?"

"Your sister. She's outside."

"Tell her to come on in." Whatever misgivings Quinn was having disappeared when she heard his jolly, booming voice. She put away her phone and sauntered to the front door, shaking her head at how fast the relationship between Jack and Mary was developing.

Mary met her at the door, rubbing her eyes and holding the screen door open. She was wearing her full uniform, including the gun, but minus the hat. "Come on in."

"Sorry to interrupt your visit," Quinn said, looking around and finally seeing her brother seated at the dining room table. He was removing what looked like an egg white sandwich and a smoothie from a Smoothie King bag. A twinge struck her at the thought that Mary had most likely brought breakfast.

"That's okay. I've gotta get some sleep now anyway." Mary picked up her hat and made for the door, but turned back, when Jack called out to her.

"Hey, don't leave before I've thanked you properly for this amazing feast." He hurried past Quinn to embrace Mary. "You're an angel for taking such good care of me." And then, as if Quinn weren't in the room at all, he gave the policewoman a long, slow, movie-star kiss.

When they came up for air, Mary mumbled something like, "Wish I didn't have to go." She waved goodbye and exited. Through the front window, Quinn could see her walking across the yard, a bounce in her step.

"Well, *that* was interesting," Quinn said, winking at her brother. "Looks like I've been replaced as chief smoothie provider."

"Don't feel bad, little sis. She asked me what she could bring, and I told her. Apparently, she likes taking care of me." He showed every tooth in his head with a happy grin. "Anyway, you deserve a break now and then." He ran his hand through Quinn's curls. "Sit down and keep me company while I eat. Do you want half?"

"Oh, no. I just came from Mom's. She fixed French toast."

"Uh-oh. French toast is only for special occasions, or sad ones. Why did you need cheering up?"

"Seems Mom and Dad are worried because people around town are talking about me."

"You and Josh?"

"No—nothing would make them happier than if the topic were my romantic inclinations. They say the rumor mill has it that I had something to do with Ana's murder—maybe Brad's, too." She shrugged. "They don't want me to work on Brad's body or the double funeral. In fact, they want me to go stay with Aunt Virginia. Do you believe that?"

Quinn expected her brother to laugh out loud, but instead, he put down his sandwich and stared into her eyes in a way that chilled her insides. "Don't tell me *you* think I'm a killer, too, now."

He looked away. "No, it's not that. You aren't any more a killer than Sister Karolina at the church, but that won't stop the town gossips, and you know it. If it makes you feel any better, Mary has been actively chasing a narcotics ring. She didn't say, but I think that's somehow aligned with Brad's murder. Just putting two and two together."

"Narcotics? You mean Brad may have been using, or dealing?" Quinn couldn't imagine that of the old Brad, the high school Brad, who had such high ambitions and better-than-average grades. But the recent Brad, who thought his wife had been killed by people who were after him? Maybe.

"Mary did tell me Brad was killed by two shots to the back of the head. That's typical of a drug killing. Quick, clean, anonymous."

Quinn cringed at the image. These were the sordid crimes movies were made of, not things that happened to people she knew, people she had once loved. "I'm still getting used to you and Mary as a couple. Does it bother you that she works in such dangerous situations?"

Jack guffawed. "Who are we to question what anyone chooses to do for a career? Some would say we have the worst job in the world."

"That's true, but probably the worst thing that could happen to us is having a corpse scare us to death by sitting up. Police work involves a different level of risk."

"Also true, but Mary is passionate about doing something with her life to help social justice. Did you know she and Dejuan had a grandfather who was a cop? Growing up, they heard many stories about their granddaddy's experiences, the community awards he received. Mary says it's in her blood."

"Gotta respect that. Seems like she's passionate about you, too—"

The chirping of Quinn's cell phone caused her to jump, even though she was expecting a return call from Becker. Caller ID confirmed it, so Quinn muttered a quick, "I've gotta take this outside," and she dashed for the front door.

She sat on the top step of the cement porch stoop, phone-to-ear. Becker's voice was friendly and calming. Whatever he ended up costing her, he was worth it. "The reason I called you has to do with my parents. They claim word's around town that I'm the chief suspect, maybe in both Brad's and Ana's deaths. They want me to stop working at McFarland's and to go live with my aunt in North Carolina. I told them I'd discuss their proposition with you."

Becker said something that sounded like, "Hnh," which Quinn interpreted as an expression of surprise. Or maybe he was thinking about a response that might satisfy her parents' concerns and her own needs. She held her breath, waiting.

"Well, let me say that I don't believe you've told me anything about your involvement with Brad or Ana to make you a chief suspect. Nor have the police indicated to me that an arrest is imminent. Assuming you've told me everything, I don't see anything pointing to your being arrested and charged with any crime."

Quinn exhaled.

"That said, I've lived in this town all my life, and I know how the rumor mill operates. I think the saying, 'Where there's smoke, there's fire,' started here."

"So what do you advise me to do?" Quinn squeezed the phone tightly against her ear and clenched her other hand.

"You have to do what you think is best. Probably not a bad idea to stay away from the funeral home until after the funeral. You don't want to herd the pigs into the sty any more than normal. If your parents can manage without you for the next several days, okay. As for leaving town—"

"I told them that might make it worse for me because it would look like I'm running away."

Becker chuckled. "You've been watching too many movies. No one has told you not to leave the city or county, so you are not being watched that carefully. How do you feel about leaving town? Have you received any more threatening notes?"

"No more notes. I've been careful about locking doors and setting alarms. I don't see a need to leave town. I can step back from preparing Brad's body and helping with the funeral, but I worry about my parents being able to carry on all the work of McFarland's without me. Jack is still recuperating from surgery, you know."

"Yes, and that's mighty thoughtful of you. You might add that your boyfriend is here in town, as well."

It was Quinn's turn to chuckle. "Yes, there's that." She was warming to the lawyer's suggestions. They provided a concession to her parents and one to her, as well. "Thanks so much for your advice. I'm going to stay here in town, then."

"My pleasure. Call me if you need anything else, and I'll keep you posted if I hear anything to share."

Quinn disconnected and went back into Jack's. She was starting to feel a lot better about her day off, and she didn't want to waste another minute. She had a lot to do before her date with Josh tonight.

Chapter Forty-eight

After talking with Becker, Quinn returned to Jack's kitchen, where the two of them made a grocery list. Quinn had thought *her* cupboard bare, but Jack's empty refrigerator and pantry made hers look full.

She spent the next hour at Kroger, filling every inch of her cart with essentials. The store was crowded with tourists, many of whom rented houses on the west end of the island. Quinn didn't mind waiting in the checkout line with them. She wasn't in her usual rush today, and being surrounded by strangers was better than being on guard all the time.

After she checked out, she drove back to Jack's to deliver his groceries. Her heart thumped when she turned off the two-lane street where Kroger is, and a dark gray car followed her. She could swear it was the same car she'd spotted outside of the back entrance to McFarland's, maybe a Lincoln. As much bravado as she'd shown to Becker over the phone earlier, staying in town had its scary aspects, and this was one of them.

Instead of driving directly to Jack's, Quinn gripped the steering wheel, turning this way and that, trying to lose the tail. Originally, she'd thought it might be an unmarked police car. Now she thought the police might be too busy chasing narcotics rings to follow her from the grocery store. If not the police, perhaps her other nemesis, the writer of the threatening notes, was after her. If she was right, he was also the tall guy with the big ears who had gone by Keith Underwood in the VHS tapes Ana had sent.

Gray Car turned three times, but at the fourth turn, he kept going straight. *Okay, you made your statement. I know you're watching.* Quinn willed her heart back to normal and backtracked to Jack's, hoping the yogurt bars hadn't melted during the detour.

Quinn carried in Jack's groceries and started to put them away, over protests from her brother that he could do that himself. "Not yet, Mr. Self-Sufficient. A certain chief resident told me you weren't supposed to lift anything over five pounds for at least two weeks." She moved quickly, since her own groceries were baking in the hot car.

"Well, at least let me pay you. You don't have to buy my groceries." He walked toward the bedroom, as if to get his wallet.

"Absolutely not. I want your new girlfriend to know she's not the only one who looks out for your nutrition." She tossed a loaf of bread in the freezer.

Jack returned to the kitchen and tapped Quinn on the back, as she put the vegetables in the hydrator drawer. "You aren't really jealous of Mary, are you, Sis?"

She turned around with a scowl on her face, and then broke into a grin. "Of course not. I'm grateful to you for introducing me to Josh. I hope Mary will make you happy, too."

"So far she's batting .1000. I'm the luckiest guy in the world. I've got a new kidney, a new girl, and a top-notch sister. What more can a guy ask for?"

* * *

After Quinn put away her own groceries, she made a tuna fish sandwich and a glass of iced tea and took them out on the back porch. Last summer she had installed a ceiling fan under the overhang, so between that and a bit of Gulf breeze, she was comfortable. She ate, played fetch with Calvin, and reviewed her situation.

If her parents were right, she was facing imminent arrest by the police for one or two murders. If her attorney were right, she was safe from the police, but possibly facing danger from the person in the gray car. If her brother were right, Brad's death was a drug hit. If that could be proven, she'd be off the hook, at least when it came to Brad.

Quinn tried to imagine a scenario in which Brad would be killed by drug lords. As far as she knew, Brad hadn't sold, or even used, drugs in high school. The most they had done together was sit on the beach drinking Bacardi and Cokes a few times. Ana had started smoking weed in high school, after "the incident." She'd tried to get Quinn high, too, but when Quinn resisted, she'd backed off. Maybe she figured she'd gotten Quinn into enough trouble already. Or maybe she'd already fallen for Brad and was easing off of their blood-sister relationship.

Some of the kids in their class had gotten involved in dealing drugs, and their lives had been ruined. A couple of the guys had already been to prison, and Quinn had embalmed one, Rodney Black, last winter. Brad had known someone was after him—that's why he went on the lam. All of this pointed to probable heavy drug involvement on Brad's part. Maybe he owed money and couldn't pay.

But what about Ana? If money were a problem for Brad, it would have been for her, too. The Frenches had intimated that Ana was unhappy with Brad, that she may have been abused, even. Whether she was trying to raise money to leave Brad or to help him, she wouldn't have had many options. Her parents weren't wealthy, and, as far as Quinn knew, Ana had never held a job that paid well. Maybe she'd been desperate enough to consider working in the adult entertainment industry, like Dawn. The thought sent shivers through Quinn's body, and she hugged herself.

Whatever Ana had done or not done in the weeks before her death, Quinn was certain her former friend had caught the attention of the so-called Keith Underwood. Otherwise, why would she have sent the tapes? And who else could it be, besides the former porn actor, who was warning Quinn not to tell what she remembered?

As frightening as this was, to be threatened and followed and suspected of murder, there was a certain satisfaction in thinking through all this and arriving at some clarity. No other living person had the pieces to the puzzle that she had. Knowing that made her feel important and intelligent. The problem was, it also made her feel endangered.

* * *

Having tired of chasing after his tennis ball, Calvin had come to curl up by Quinn on the porch, but after a few seconds of peaceful quiet, his ears perked up, and he howled. A few seconds later, the front doorbell rang, and Quinn gathered the remains of her lunch and headed through the back door toward the front, with Calvin barking at her heels.

Grateful for the peephole, she recognized Mrs. Tartt from next door. She was holding a red-plaid leash with Duffy at the other end, barking his head off.

Quinn opened the door, as the two dogs faced off in a barking match, each determined to win. "Hello, Mrs. Tartt. Would you like to come in?"

The older woman wore a printed house dress with snaps down the front, and Quinn could see the tops of her knee-high stockings. "That's all right. I've got the Duffer and wouldn't want to make a mess. I just wanted to tell you—I rang the doorbell last night around ten-thirty, but nobody answered."

"I'm sorry. I was out. Didn't get back until around eleven. What's up?"

"Duffy started barking around nine-thirty. I'd just given Mr. Tartt his night-time pills, and we were trying to watch *Everybody Loves Raymond*, but Duffy wouldn't hush up. I looked outside the bedroom window over toward your house, and, sure enough, there was a man over by the same window as before. Looked like the same man, too. Tall, slim."

Quinn's blood ran cold. "Wh-what was he doing?"

"Couldn't see much of anything, just his shape. He must've heard Duffy, though. Probably your dog, too. He straightened up and ran away."

"How long was he here?"

"Judging by the barking, maybe a coupla three minutes. Maybe he woulda stayed longer if it hadna been for the dogs."

"Could you tell what he was wearing?"

The woman shook her head. "Too dark to tell. Dark pants and shirt, maybe a mask. All's I know is I couldn't tell much about him. I thought of calling the police, but Mr. Tartt tol' me to mind my own business. So I waited till he went to sleep, and I came over to tell you. Only you warn't at home."

Quinn shuddered. She'd been at the Heartbeat Cabaret with Josh. What if she had been at home? What if she'd been alone in the house, or out jogging with Calvin? Had the tall man come back to kill her, as, presumably, he had Ana?

"Did you happen to see an unusual car parked out in front? A dark-colored Lincoln, perhaps?"

"Funny you should ask. After I watched from my bedroom window, I ran to the front to see what might be happening on the street. Everything was quiet, no unusual cars, but I saw the man leave the window." She pointed toward the west. "He trotted off thataway. About a minute later I saw a dark sedan drive down the street in the opposite direction. Maybe it was him."

Quinn stuck her head out and looked up and down the street, as if someone were watching her right now. "Thanks for letting me know, Mrs. Tartt. I'm glad Duffy has such good ears."

The woman smiled, revealing an empty space where her upper teeth should be. "That's what neighbors are for. You'd do the same for me, I'm sure."

"Yes, ma'am, I sure would."

The old woman took her dog back into the house next door, as Quinn watched, hugging herself tightly against the shivers that had taken hold. There wasn't time before Josh arrived for dinner to make another police report, and, besides, what would she say? They would have to interview poor

Mrs. Tartt and get the dogs all riled up again. Nothing bad had happened, so she doubted the police would be that interested.

Quinn left Calvin in the house and strode over to the area outside of her bathroom window. The ground had dried out from the thunderstorm the day before, but, apparently, it had still been damp when the tall man had been there. There were one full and two partial footprints in the dirt surrounding the bushes. Whoever he was, he had big feet. Quinn pulled her cell phone from the pocket of her jeans. She snapped several pictures of the prints from different angles. She examined the window for fingerprints, but wasn't surprised to find none visible. The man probably had been wearing gloves. There were no signs of jimmying the window, either. Had he intended to enter the house and been scared away by the dogs' barking?

Next Quinn looked around on the ground and in the bushes. Had he dropped something? Nothing that she could see on the ground, but there was something hanging from one of the branches of the pittosporum hedge. It looked like a cluster of black nylon threads, about four inches long.

Quinn knew better than to touch the threads. She ran back into the house to retrieve a zippered plastic bag and her kitchen shears. When she returned, she opened the bag as wide as it would go, then snipped the entire branch of the shrub off, so branch and threads fell into the bag. She sealed the bag and went back inside.

Becker didn't want her talking to the police on her own. Should she call Becker? It was already after four, and he was probably leaving for the day. Tomorrow morning she could take the pictures of the footprints and the branch with the thread to Becker's office and go from there.

Josh was due for dinner at seven, and she had a lot to do to get ready. As upsetting as it was to know that she was being stalked, Quinn knew she was on the right track with her plan to learn more about the person who was threatening her. For a moment she asked herself what Ana would do in her shoes. The answer came swiftly. Ana had never backed down from a plan, and Quinn wasn't going to, either.

Chapter Forty-nine

With only a few hours to get ready for the evening with Josh, Quinn put thoughts of tall men with big ears and big feet aside and attacked more domestic issues. The orchids needed to be watered, the sheets needed to be changed, the skirt steak needed to be marinated, and the house needed to be dusted and vacuumed. Quinn plugged her ear buds in as she accomplished her tasks, moving in rhythm with the snappy music.

There was something satisfying about cleaning house: the smell and texture of clean sheets, smoothed on without a wrinkle, the sheen of the dining room table after a coating of lemony polish. Before Josh, Quinn had kept things clean, but she hadn't cared so much about the finer points of housekeeping. Now that she was entertaining company, she wanted everything to be perfect. Maybe she could convince Josh to spend the night.

After dinner tonight, they were going to a more upscale gentlemen's club, Heaven's Door. Quinn had never pictured herself in such places, but, after researching all the local spots, she was becoming a bit of an expert. While she wouldn't choose to go there on her own, she was learning a lot about the business aspect. Most of it made her happy to be an embalmer. At least she and her family treated their employees and customers, living or dead, with the utmost respect.

Once the house was company-ready, Quinn jumped into the shower. While the hot needles of water invigorated her skin, her mind turned over the risk she was taking to chase after the person who was, ostensibly, chasing her. The more she thought about it, the more convinced she was that Big Ears would be associated with a club like Heaven's Door, rather than the Heartbeat Cabaret, where they'd been last night. Was she smart to put herself into the kind of environment that had gotten Dawn killed, and probably Ana, too? How would things change if her stalker saw her on *his* turf? He would recognize her more easily than she, him.

Maybe she should disguise herself. She could snoop around more easily if she looked less like the fresh-faced Quinn McFarland and more like Mata Hari. The thought of donning a costume and make-up made her giggle, something she hadn't done in a long time. She had no idea how Josh would react, but it could be a lot of fun.

As she climbed out of the shower and toweled off, Quinn thought of the supplies she had on hand. Once she had played Guinevere in a high school production of *Camelot*. A blonde straight-haired wig had been part of the costume. What had she done with it? She put on her terry cloth robe and tied the sash. Then she padded over to her closet. The wig had been in a blue-and-gold shoe box at one point. Her eyes scanned the shelves above the clothing rack, then the stacks of boxes on the floor under the hanging clothes. Yes, there was the box, in the back corner on the floor.

She pulled the wig out and sniffed it. Not too bad, considering the hairpiece had been hidden away for umpteen years. She brushed her wet hair away from her face and tried it on. The bob hairdo was a bit out of style, but she thought she could get away with it. Setting it down on the counter, she went to the kitchen to work on dinner. Her own hair could air-dry, while she baked potatoes and cut vegetables for grilling with the steak.

All the while, she speculated about how Josh would react to her disguise. A six-month relationship wasn't exactly long-term. Quinn hated that she was dragging Josh away from the stable, respected atmosphere of the hospital into who-knows-what kind of debauchery. What would Mike and Elise Brady think of her if they knew? It was one thing to compromise Quinn's own safety, but Josh had nothing to do with Dawn or Ana or Brad, and it wasn't fair to subject him to these risks.

On the other hand, what had Jack said to her about becoming involved with a policewoman? Mary felt police work was in her blood, something she was born to do. And if Jack cared for Mary, which he obviously did, he accepted the risks. Mary's work was part of the package.

The comparison was skewed, because Quinn hadn't chosen to be the center of a triple murder situation. Her livelihood didn't depend on it, and, hopefully, someday, she would emerge from these circumstances with her life intact. But right now, there was no easy way to extricate herself from the trap that she'd fallen into years ago, when she and Ana had giggled over Dawn's nude dancing. She was doing the best she could to stay one step ahead of danger. If it weren't for Josh, she probably would have flipped out by now. So far, he'd been a good sport and a good sounding board. She hoped her plans for tonight didn't push him too far.

Tomorrow she'd take the footprint photos and nylon thread to Mr. Becker's office. Maybe they would give the police something more to go on. Ana had been dead for more than a week, but, to Quinn, the tension build-up felt like years in the making. She was tired of being in a pressure cooker with no escape valve. It was time to shift the pressure to the person who deserved it—starting tonight.

Chapter Fifty

When Quinn opened the door to greet Josh, he did a double-take and looked around, as if to make sure he was at the right house. Evidently the straight blonde hair, heavy make-up, large hoop earrings, low-cut top and slit skirt had done the trick of disguising Quinn's appearance.

"What the hell?" Josh stepped into the house and closed the door behind him, a furrowed brow barely concealing the squinty disapproval in his eyes. "You didn't tell me this was a costume party, Quinn."

Quinn had never heard such a strident tone of voice coming from Josh's mouth, and it caused her to freeze in her tracks. "Aren't you going to kiss me?"

"I—I'm not sure. Maybe you'd better tell me what's going on first." He bent to pet Calvin, who was leaping around him. Otherwise, the set of his lips and the lack of eye contact made Quinn want to run into the bathroom and ditch the disguise.

Instead, she took him by the hand and led him to the sofa. "It's a costume. That's all. The wig's from a high school play. The rest is me, trying to be creative." She looked at her hands. She had painted her fingernails a shiny dark purple. "I guess you don't like it."

"I guess not. Maybe that makes me shallow, but it's hard to see your beautiful self through all that garbage. More importantly, why on earth would you do this to yourself?"

Quinn bristled. "I didn't do anything to myself. It's not like a tattoo or body piercings. I didn't do anything I can't undo. I'm still me."

Crossing his forearms over his chest, he said. "Okay, but why the outfit? Don't tell me it's the latest style in strip club attire." He bit off the last four syllables, as if desiring to spit them out.

"Well, I can certainly take the hint. If you don't want to go with me to Heaven's Door tonight, that's okay. I didn't know you minded so much."

Josh took a deep breath, seeming to notice the aromas of steak, potatoes, and vegetables for the first time, but not commenting. "Look, it's not my favorite thing. Maybe at a bachelor party or hanging out with a bunch of rowdy guys, but when I'm with you, I want to be looking at you, not some mostly naked bimbo who wants to give me a lap dance in front of you. If that makes me a prude, so be it."

Quinn fought against tears. How had she miscalculated Josh's feelings? "I'm sorry you feel that way. I—I didn't know." She shoved her hands under her thighs. "You don't have to come with me anymore then."

Josh scowled, and he blinked. "Look, I said I'd go with you, and I will. B-but, you're asking an awful lot of me to go places where I'm uncomfortable, and not telling me why we're there, or why—"

"—or why I'm dressed in a disguise that you don't like." Quinn attempted a quivery smile. "I'm not hiding things from you because I want to. You know this all has to do with Ana's death. The costume is obvious—I don't want to be recognized. I didn't think you'd mind so much. I thought it might be fun for you to take 'a different Quinn' out tonight."

"I don't need a different Quinn. The real Quinn is the one I'm in love with—or I *think* I'm in love with." Josh put his face into his hands. "If it's so dangerous for you to be recognized at these clubs, then why are you going there? Why don't you let the police do their job?"

The *think I'm in love with* was sticking in Quinn's craw. She jumped up and started pacing in the small room. If Josh was doubting their relationship, then so was she. Her emotional self was ready to kick him out of her house and out of her life right this minute. Her rational self urged her to tamp that Irish temper. It had taken her years to find someone she could love and trust. Who knows if she would ever have another chance?

"Look," Josh said. "It's not really the strip club, *or* the costume that's upsetting me most. It's the fact that you can't trust me. I know what your lawyer said, but if you're innocent, and I believe you are, then I don't see why you're worried about my testifying against you." He ran his fingers through his hair. "And if we can't trust each other at this point, then—"

"—Okay, okay." She drew in a long breath and sat down again. "There are things I know that the police don't. They don't trust me, and I can't help them until I learn one more thing. I've come so far already, and I have a feeling I'm getting very close." She scooted back against the sofa cushions and raised her chin. "I agree with you about trust, though. I *do* trust you, Josh, and I'll prove it. Back in 2004—"

"Quinn, I—I don't want you to say any more." He stood and put his hands on her shoulders.

"What? I thought—" Now she was really confused. Was she going insane?

"You've said enough to show me that you *do* trust me. Now I need to show you that I trust you. I can wait to hear the whole story, now that I know you weren't deliberately hiding something from me."

"So I passed the test?"

"Yeah, something like that." Josh's lop-sided grin lit up all of the neurons in Quinn's brain, sending warm vibes to every part of her body.

"So can I have a kiss now?"

"Take off that wig, and I'll do even better than that."

* * *

After they messed up the clean sheets, Quinn and Josh ate dinner and split a bottle of Merlot. They talked about the hospital, Josh's parents, Jack and Mary—everything but the evening's plans to go to Heaven's Door.

Finally, Quinn began clearing the dishes, and Josh rushed over to the sink and turned on the hot water. "Let me do my job, please."

"Okay. It's getting late, and I still want to go to the club tonight." She picked up the dish towel to dry. "I can go by myself, if you'd rather not."

It was hard to read Josh's expression. Was it that of a puppy who'd been taken off his leash? Or was he disappointed that she'd suggest such a thing?

He soaped and rinsed the vegetable platter and handed it over to be dried. "Let's be clear. I don't want you going to these places alone. Whatever you're looking for, I hope you find it soon, but in the meantime, I'll be by your side."

Quinn finished drying the platter and spread the wet dish towel on the counter to dry. Then she stood on tiptoes to plant a heartfelt kiss on Josh's cheek. "Good deal. Thanks for being my partner in crime."

"Let's hope not," Josh replied. "I'll settle for plain ol' partner."

Chapter Fifty-one

Heaven's Door was a bigger, fancier, and more populated venue than Heartbeat Cabaret. Located across the causeway, the club attracted a more urban clientele. Quinn gripped Josh's forearm as they entered the cool, dark entryway. The music was loud, sultry and pounding at the same time, nothing Quinn was familiar with, even though her iPod list was eclectic.

Inside the front door was a metal detector, then a counter with a cash register. A well-groomed man with a goatee and black-framed glasses looked up at them and smiled. "Welcome to Heaven's Door. Have you been with us before?"

Josh shook his head. He pulled his wallet out and held it on the counter.

"Friday's Couples Night. Two dollars off the cover for each of you. Come before eight next time, and you get two free appetizers, too. So that'll be ten apiece."

Josh set a twenty-dollar bill on the counter, and the man tore off two neon green wristbands, which he fixed to each of their wrists. Free to enter, Quinn and Josh moved into the main area, walking slowly and looking around.

A clean-cut guy in a business suit ambled toward them, as if he happened to be walking by. "Welcome to Heaven's Door. Please make yourselves at home." He gestured toward the expansive arena—if it weren't for the music and the odors of smoke and alcohol, Quinn would have thought she'd entered an upscale supper club.

"Is my wig on straight?" Quinn asked Josh, as they stepped further into the cavernous building. The disco lights shot stripes of purple and green on Josh's face, then pivoted to highlight the action on the large stage in the center of the main room.

"You look fine, Blondie. Where do you want to sit?" There were bench seats against the wall, and, closer to the stage, plush leather-like rolling chairs on the floor.

Quinn peered through the smoke and lights to see three more stages, two large bars, two buffet tables, a pool table, and what looked to be a string of semi-private areas near the back on both sides of the main room. The printed carpeting throughout had a celestial theme—dark background with stars, moons, clouds, and golden harps. People were scattered about in every area.

"Let's go past the buffet tables toward the back. Maybe it'll be a little quieter there." It was easy to tell who the club personnel were, as opposed to the patrons. There were several bouncers, like the guy who'd greeted them, all wearing suits. Cocktail waitresses and bartenders wore Alpine-looking uniforms that could have fit in at any beer garden restaurant. The patrons, on the other hand, wore flip-flops and casual clothes. Josh, in his khakis and polo shirt, and she, in her plunging neckline and slit-skirt, fit right in.

Quinn counted the dancers on the four stages, as she walked toward the furthest stage on the left. There were a total of five, in various stages of undress. Another five or so mostly-naked women walked around or sat down next to members of the audience, apparently schmoozing them for drinks.

As Josh and Quinn seated themselves on a bench behind a tiny cocktail table, the song ended, and the dancers rotated to the next stage without a break, except to put their discarded garments back on. Quinn guessed, if they sat there long enough, they would be treated to shows by the full complement of dancers. Their stage, unlike the others, had two poles on it.

While they were becoming acclimated to the sights, sounds, and smells, a willowy, but busty, girl in her early twenties whisked past them, flicking the tails of a fur-trimmed see-through jacket. She ascended the stage and introduced herself as Skye Blue. The music started up at a high volume, and the lights pulsed with the rhythm.

Quinn couldn't help thinking of Dawn, and every other young girl whose desires for fame, fortune, or fun had landed her on a stage in this industry. Skye may have been tired or thirsty, or in need of a potty break, but her job required her to fulfill other people's pleasures, not her own.

An Alpine waitress appeared at their table and took their drink orders. While they waited for the drinks to come, Skye danced her heart out, bending forward and backward to give ample views of different body parts. Josh squeezed Quinn's hand.

"Look at that staircase." Quinn pointed toward the back of the stage, where a balustrade and a dozen steps were visible. "It leads up to that gallery." The second floor appeared to have three or four separate doorways into rooms, similar to the floor plan of a Hampton Inn. "I'll bet those are private rooms where patrons can access more expensive services. What do you think?"

As they watched, a woman wearing a short, silk bathrobe emerged from one of the doors, her hair disheveled. Josh's mouth formed the thin line Quinn was getting used to as an expression of disapproval. He said, "Tell me again what we are looking for."

Quinn looked around before answering. The cocktail waitress was back, sidling up to their table and unloading two gin and tonics onto napkins printed with art deco letters of HD. Josh paid cash and included a better-than-decent tip. Pangs of guilt flooded Quinn's gut. Not only was she dragging Josh to places he didn't enjoy, but he was paying for the privilege, and the prices here were exorbitant. "I'll pay you back," she whispered, after the waitress left.

"Don't worry about it." He clinked his glass against hers. "Here's to you, Blondie."

Quinn sipped her drink. "Is it me, or are these drinks watered down?"

"Not you. Less booze, more profit. All these employees can't be cheap, you know." He glanced at Skye who had slinked over to one of the poles, ramping up her dance number. Quinn could swear she was looking right at Josh, who seemed impervious.

"You asked what we're looking for. Not a what, a who. A tall, lanky man with big feet and big ears that stick out."

"*Otopostasis*? The ears protrude more than two centimeters?"

"Is that what it's called? Yes. The ears are noticeable."

"What else? Does this guy have any other distinguishing features I can diagnose for you? How old is he? What color hair does he have?"

"Let's see. He must be around forty or fifty. I'm not sure about the hair—maybe black or brown, straight." Quinn looked around, hoping to see the object of her search. "I think he might be the owner or manager."

Skye's second dance had come to an end, and she slid down the pole and picked up her clothes from the stage floor, slinging them over her arm. Wearing nothing but a tiny blue thong, she descended the three steps into the audience. Without an apparent thought about her nakedness, she sauntered over to Josh and sat next to him, swinging a bare leg over the other. Since this was the last stage in the room, maybe Skye's tour of duty included visiting with patrons for this set. "What brings you two cuties here tonight? Buy me a drink?" she asked, looking only at Josh.

"Sure." He motioned for the cocktail waitress, who took an order for a gin and tonic for Skye. "We're shopping for a venue for our bachelor and bachelorette parties," Josh replied, not skipping a beat. "Do you do those here?" Quinn giggled inside at Josh's ingenuity and smoothness. A tiny wish flickered inside her that the cover story were true.

"Sure, we get those all the time. My favorite. Nobody appreciates us girls more than a groom and his buddies. Bachelorettes, not so much." She glanced at Quinn as if she were invisible.

Skye's drink arrived, and she downed half of it in one swallow. "You want male dancers, we can get them, but that's not our typical."

"If we wanted to schedule a party here, who would we talk to?" Quinn hated nothing more than to be ignored.

Skye leaned over Josh, placing an elbow on the table and giving Josh an up-close view of her too-firm breasts. She smelled like perspiration and cheap cologne. "Blackie's the one to talk to. He's the manager." She looked around, as if to identify him on the floor. "Ain't seen him yet tonight, but he's around, for sure."

"Is he Black?" Josh asked.

"No, honey. He's white as you and me. Calls himself Blackie 'cause he wears all black. You know, like Johnny Cash?"

Quinn was delighted with the topic of conversation, if not with the converser. "What's his real name?"

The stripper showed light gray teeth in a patronizing smile. "None of us have 'real names' here. Blackie's what he goes by. That's all I know." She straightened and looked Josh in the eye. "Anyway, how about a sample lap dance? You can try me out before you book the party."

Quinn held her breath. She trusted that Josh would decline the offer, but she had to admit, Skye was the most attractive of all the dancers she'd seen at both clubs, and the thought of her moving around on Josh's lap sent stabs of jealousy through her.

"No, thanks," Josh replied. "Thanks for the information about the party, though." He slipped a folded bill onto Skye's fur-trimmed jacket.

At that moment, the stage lights came on full blast. A new dancer took the stage in front of them, and the speakers pumped out a high-energy tune. Skye thanked Josh for the drink and walked over to another patron, her bare behind glowing yellow and orange in the rotating disco lights.

Quinn returned to her own drink and thought about what Skye had said. "That was brilliant, about the bachelor party."

"First thing that came to mind."

"Would you really want to have a bachelor party here?"

"Don't you think that's putting the cart before the horse a bit?"

Before Quinn could come up with a cogent response, the slamming of a door from the upper level overshadowed the loud music and drew her eyes upward. A tall man wearing a black shirt and pants stormed out of one of the rooms and ran down the stairs in front of them.

"Blackie, I presume."

Quinn stared as the man rushed past them, obviously preoccupied. He was the right height and build as the actor in the tapes with Dawn. His feet looked big, too. He had dark hair, conventionally styled. As he strode past in the glare of the stage lights, Quinn gazed at the back of his head, and her heart sank. "That guy doesn't have oto—whatever."

"That's where you're wrong, Blondie." Josh wore a smile that lit up their area better than the disco lights. "Aren't you glad you're dating a surgeon? That guy's had otoplasty to fix his protruding ears. I'd recognize those scars anywhere."

Chapter Fifty-two

After a fitful night's sleep, Quinn staggered out of bed Saturday morning. Josh hadn't spent the night. He had an early morning surgery at the hospital, and, by the time they left Heaven's Door, it had been almost midnight. By then, they were both tired and smelly from the smoke. They'd made plans to go out to a nice restaurant the next night, tonight.

Despite being exhausted, Quinn couldn't turn off thoughts of the footprints outside her window, the interaction with Skye Blue, and especially the sighting of Blackie, the man with the ear surgery. She was growing closer to understanding how everything fit together.

Through the blinds of her bedroom window came strips of summer sunshine and glimpses of flitting birds. The forecast had predicted a hot and sunny day, a less-than-perfect day for a double funeral. Quinn had mixed feelings about skipping out on attending the ceremony for Ana and Brad. Despite the years since they had been close, the emotional attachments to her best friend and her first love remained strong, like dying branches that still clung to the tree. On the other hand, she was relieved not to have to worry about curious looks or uncomfortable questions from people in attendance, including the police.

Besides, she had a full agenda of things to do before her dinner date with Josh. Top on the list was dealing with the evidence she'd collected from outside her window yesterday. Too wiped out to take Calvin for a run, she let him out through the back door and put the tea kettle on in the kitchen.

Throwing her terry cloth robe on over her nightshirt, Quinn opened the front door and picked up the *Daily News* from the porch. The headline was, "Drug Bust at Heartbeat Cabaret." Skimming the article, Quinn let Calvin in and gave him a treat. She couldn't believe what she was reading. She and Josh had been there the night before the bust. If they had gone to Heaven's

Door first, they would've been right there when the police raided the smaller venue.

"Police arrested two employees of the adult entertainment venue on suspicion of distributing and selling narcotics." She wondered whether the bald-headed guy at the door was one of the suspects, and whether Mary was one of the officers who made the arrests. Jack had said she was working on a narcotics case. More importantly, was this tied to Brad's death in any way?

Between drugs and sex, threats and murder, Quinn's head was spinning. She made herself a cup of tea and peeled a banana. The article mentioned that local police had been cooperating with officers and FBI agents all along the Gulf Coast on a string of crimes, ranging from extortion to narcotics to murder. The word, "murder," sent waves of chills through Quinn's body. How had she ever gotten involved with such things? And when would they ever end?

The clock on the stove said nine-eleven. Would Becker be in his office so early on a Saturday morning? There was only one way to find out. She speed-dialed his number and waited through a couple of rings, counting. Almost hanging up after the third, she was pleasantly surprised to hear the lawyer's voice at the other end.

"Becker here. How may I help you?" His tone was as weary as Quinn felt. Maybe he, too, had had a sleepless night.

"Oh—Mr. Becker. I'm so glad you answered. I didn't know whether you'd be working today. This is Quinn."

"Just walked in as the phone was ringing. What can I do for you, Quinn?"

"Can I stop by? I've got some new evidence to turn over to you." She was already walking toward the bedroom to lay out her clothes.

"Sure. What's the evidence, though?"

"Pictures of footprints and some nylon threads from a bush outside my window. A neighbor saw a man there again."

Becker's voice sounded stronger, and she pictured him sitting up straight, his eyebrows furrowed. "When was this?"

"Thursday night."

"Thursday night? This is Saturday. Why didn't you call sooner? Did you call the police to report it?" Now he sounded like her father on the French toast morning.

"You told me not to talk to the police without you, remember?" Quinn hated to be on the wrong side of Becker or his advice. She was only doing what she thought he'd told her to do.

"Yes, well—that was about the investigation into Ana's death. This is something different. Anyway, come on in, and we'll talk when you get here. I'll be here till noon."

"Coming right now." Quinn disconnected and rushed through her hygiene routine. Tired or not, her Saturday was off and running.

* * *

Becker's office had a different ambience on the weekend. No light shone over the desk where Ethel usually sat. No lavender smells, no whirring machine, no phones ringing. The gray-haired attorney wore slacks and a sport shirt and a kindly smile that lit up his hazel eyes. "Didn't mean to fuss at you earlier. I *did* tell you not to talk to the police without me." He stretched out a hand. "So let's see this here evidence."

Quinn pulled the zippered plastic from her sling bag and handed it over. "These threads were stuck to the bushes outside of my bathroom window. And these," she grabbed her cell phone to click on the photos of the footprints, "are the footprints his shoes made in the mud. Remember, we had heavy rain on Thursday morning?"

He set the bag on the desk and grasped the phone, looking over his reading glasses at the first photo. He swiped to the next two photos, and then looked up. "You say a neighbor saw this person at your window?"

"Yes, Mrs. Tartt from next door. She thought he was the same one she saw the last time." Quinn fidgeted in her chair. "I think he's been following me around town."

Becker's demeanor changed, and he gave her a piercing look. "Where else have you seen him?"

"Maybe in the neighborhood. A dark gray Lincoln's been following me, too. I've seen it outside of the funeral home."

Eyebrows raised. "License plate?"

Quinn shook her head. "If it happens again, I'll try to get a photo with my phone."

Becker stood and stared down at her, a giant talking to a ladybug. "Let me make something clear. When I told you not to talk to the police without my being there, that was strictly related to the murder case. You shouldn't be afraid to call the police when you or your property is being threatened. Email me these photos, and I'll turn them in with the black threads, but the police aren't going to be very happy that you didn't call them as soon as you found out about the trespasser. They want to gather their own evidence, and, coming in this late, they might question the chain of custody. Hell, they might even believe you concocted this evidence to throw them off something you were doing Thursday night."

Quinn looked at her hands. "I—I thought I was being helpful." She pulled a tissue from the box on his desk. "I wish I could make all of this go away."

Becker returned to his chair and softened his voice. "I'm sorry if I was harsh. Dealing with the police can be tricky, and you're lucky not to have had much experience with that. What concerns me most right now is this guy who's following you. I know you didn't want to go stay with your aunt, but is there any place else you can stay for a while? I don't like the idea of your being so easy for this guy to find."

Quinn's heart fell. She hated to give up her independence or privacy, and what about Calvin? "I guess I could ask my parents, or my boyfriend, or my brother—" She walked over to the window and gazed at the cars driving by, birds flying, and an airplane in the distance. Everyone, it seemed, was free, except her.

"There's something else I probably should tell you," she said, her voice a bare whisper. She turned back toward Becker's desk and sat in the client chair.

Leaning both elbows on the desk, Becker turned an ear toward his client. "I'm listening."

"I might be close to finding out who's behind all of it—Dawn, Ana, me—maybe even Brad. Heaven help me!"

Chapter Fifty-three

When David Becker heard Quinn's admission that she had been investigating the murders, he smacked his desk with both palms. "What on earth are you talking about?" Quinn might have heard him even if she had been at home in her kitchen.

"I've done some research, and I think I've found the man who was in the tapes with Dawn, the actor named Keith Underwood. Not his real name, of course."

Becker's eyebrows framed the fire in his eyes. "You mean to tell me you've been investigatin' on your own? I don't believe it." He jumped up and paced around the room. "Quinn, this is very dangerous. You could get yourself killed."

Heat rose into Quinn's face, and she lost control. Words began pouring out faster than her brain could filter them. "Don't you understand? I've been in danger ever since Ana was killed. My home was broken into. I was threatened more than once not to tell anyone what I know. I was warned by Ana and Brad. My car was invaded."

She stopped to take a breath. "It seems like years that I've been stalked. And what have the police done to *help* me? All they've done is turn things around so I'm a suspect, instead of a victim." Hot coals were burning in her stomach now, pushing her on. "If I'm ever going to have a normal life, I've got to be my own detective, my own advocate. I can't count on anyone else to solve my problems—even you."

Becker's hooded eyes glowed, and he sat heavily on the corner of his desk, inches from Quinn. "Okay, okay. Let's step back and look at this calmly. I understand your motivation. It's true—you're caught in a bad spot, and you're under a lot of pressure. I'm sorry you think you can't count on me to solve your problems, but right now, I'm the best you've got. If I'm gonna help you, I need to know exactly what you've been researching and what you've found out." He returned to his desk and picked up a pen.

Quinn told him everything—from the newspaper articles she'd found at the library's history center to the evenings at Heartbeat Cabaret and Heaven's Door, and the lawyer took notes. "Once I received the tapes from Ana, I was locked into searching for 'Keith Underwood.' What other reason could Ana have had for sending me the tapes? When you and I watched the movies, I never got a really good look at Keith Underwood's face, but I remembered he had protruding ears. I remembered that from Dawn's house, too. So I was looking for a tall, lanky man with protruding ears."

Becker tapped his pen against his desk. "And you think this Blackie is the guy?"

"Yes. Although he doesn't have protruding ears now."

"I'm not following. I thought that was your single characteristic to look for."

"It is. But if you were a murderer, and you had a distinctive feature like that, wouldn't you do something to hide it? Blackie has had otoplasty—surgery to pin his ears back."

"How can you tell that?"

"I couldn't, but my boyfriend Josh was with me at the strip club. He's a surgeon, and he noticed the scars."

"Amazing." Becker asked questions about Blackie and about Heaven's Door, taking notes as Quinn answered.

"It all makes sense to me. Blackie, or whoever he is, remained in the adult entertainment business, where he could hide in plain sight. Nobody uses a real name. It's a nocturnal business, easy to hide behind costumes, darkened rooms, fantasy-seekers who are happy to stay anonymous." As she spoke, many of the random thoughts she'd been having coalesced into theory. "We know he stayed in the area, because he and Ana connected somehow, and he's the one who's been threatening me."

"Hard to stay anonymous in this small town. But you think he lives on the mainland. So you think he killed Dawn, and he killed Ana? Fifteen years apart?"

Quinn nodded.

"But what evidence do you have?" Becker's lips compressed and disappeared as he ruminated over Quinn's explanation.

"That's the problem. I'm still putting together some scenarios in my head, but, except for the tapes, the notes, and the things I brought in today, there isn't any. That's why he's gotten away with murder for so many years. And I still don't even know who he is."

Becker managed a smile, accompanied by a grandfatherly twinkle in his eyes. "Quinn, you are quite an impressive one-woman police force. You really are—brave and smart and stubborn as hell—in a good way, of course. But I can't emphasize enough that you've got a target on your back now. I strongly recommend that we turn all of this information over to the police and let *them* get the evidence to reel in this scumbag."

"If I do that, I'll be doing exactly what I've been threatened not to do."

Becker chuckled. "Those threats haven't kept you from conducting a thorough and effective investigation on your own, have they? And I know you don't want to go on this way. With your permission, I'll involve Sergeant Schmidt at this juncture. I'll call and ask him to meet with us here. I advise you to find another place to live, as well."

Quinn sat on her hands and thought before responding. There was no surprise in Becker's advice. The logical side of Quinn's brain had always known the police would be better equipped to handle a murder case, and the truth was, she didn't feel safe in her own house, even with the alarm system on. Her emotional side, however, was full of resentment for Sergeant Schmidt and his innuendos about her having a motive to kill Ana.

"Okay, I'll find someplace else to live temporarily. And I'm okay with turning the information over to the police, but only under one condition."

Becker's eyebrows danced over his piercing gaze. "What would that be?"

"I won't meet with the police unless Officer Mary Hallom is present."

Chapter Fifty-four

Quinn drove home from Becker's office, mulling over the limited options for a place to stay. The cot in the funeral home was okay for an occasional night, but she needed a place with a bathroom and a kitchen. Her parents' home upstairs was spacious enough—in fact, the bedroom she'd occupied growing up was still available and comfortable, but Quinn was uncomfortable involving her parents any more than necessary. Staying there would give them way too much opportunity to question and advise her, neither of which she wanted.

Josh's apartment was tiny and didn't allow dogs, so, as much as she would love to live with him for a while, that wasn't a practical option. As close as they were becoming, she wasn't ready to invite herself to move in with him. It was bad enough that she'd been dragging him to strip clubs.

The only realistic option was to ask Jack if she and Calvin could stay in his guest room. While not ideal, at least she could make herself useful in cooking and cleaning and doing laundry for her brother while he recovered, and if she felt unsafe, there was a police officer living right next door. The more she thought about it, the more she warmed to the idea, although she doubted either Josh or Jack would be thrilled with the arrangement.

"—a major inconvenience, but it's just temporary." The cell phone connection broke up as she pulled into her driveway. Frustrated, Quinn redialed her brother's number. When he answered, she continued, "Hopefully, I can move back home in a few days' time."

"*Mi casa es su casa*, little sis. You know that."

Quinn's eyes filled with tears. At times she'd taken for granted having a big brother like Jack. This past year his health had been so precarious. How would she ever have coped with losing him? "Okay, I'm going to pack up now. Calvin and I will be on your doorstep in an hour or so."

Breaking the news to Josh would be dicey. No matter what spin she put on it, the reason behind the move was unsavory and even ominous. She could text him now, something light and jokey, or she could wait until they were face-to-face, so he could grill her.

Before she could get out of the car, the cell phone chirped in her hand—her father. "Hi, Dad. I was just getting ready to call you. How did the funeral go yesterday?"

"We got through it. The Frenches asked for you, and we missed you, but Zeke and Rory did good. A three-hanky affair. A couple of dozen attendees, at least two policemen in plain clothes. All in all, glad you weren't here."

As a person who had lived with death all her life, Quinn rarely choked up over a funeral. But thinking of Brad and Ana, both murdered, emotion welled up inside Quinn's chest and rose to her throat. Here she was, embroiled in this sinister drama, her own life perhaps in jeopardy. Escaping the funeral hadn't allowed her to escape her fear.

Keeping her voice light, she asked, "Anybody on deck in the prep room today? I can swing by if you need me." As she spoke, she scanned what she could see through the back window of her car. Maybe she'd better go inside and lock the doors behind her.

"No, everything's quiet. How are things going with you? Mom and I have been concerned."

"Just a second. I'm getting out of the car and going into the house." Phone-to-ear, she managed the logistics and let Calvin out into the backyard. She sat on the stoop and watched while he sniffed and peed. "Everything's fine. I'm moving in with Jack for a few days, though. Wanted you to know in case you were looking for me."

"What? Is Jack all right?" Her father's voice had flipped from concerned to panicked.

"He's fine, he's fine." Quinn debated pretending that the move would be in Jack's best interests instead of hers, but she landed on the side of honesty. "I told Mr. Becker about your idea of my going to Aunt Virginia's. He agreed it might be best for me to live somewhere else for a few days. So Jack's taking me in." Hopefully, framing the concept as her parents' idea would make the actuality more palatable.

"Okay, then." Relief flooded his voice, and Quinn could picture his grin. "We'd rather you were out of town, but I suppose Jack's house is better than yours."

"Yeah, I'm planning to help him out with cooking and laundry. Whatever he needs. Listen, I'm gonna get moving. If you or Mom need anything, let me know." As they said goodbye, another surge of emotion rose into her throat. As annoying as her parents could be at times, she did love them, and if something should happen to her—well, she didn't even want to think about that now.

* * *

While Quinn was lugging her suitcase and a duffel bag filled with Calvin's food and equipment into Jack's, her phone *dinged*. Maybe that was Josh—the timing was right for his lunch break, although it was only a little after eleven. Once she set everything down in the guest room, she plopped onto the futon, cross-legged, and checked.

Dinner at my place at 7? My parents want to FaceTime us. They got a new dog.

Quinn had been thinking about asking Jack if she could cook dinner there for Jack and Josh, and Mary, too, but this might be better. She still had a lot to do, and Becker could call any minute to summon her to a meeting with the police. Eight dogs? She couldn't imagine. She texted back, Dinner yes. Bring dessert?

While she waited for Josh's response, the phone chirped. It was Becker. Quinn squeezed her eyes shut as she swiped the phone to answer.

"Hate to bother you, but can you make a three o'clock meeting in my office with the police? Tried to get them to come earlier, but that was the earliest they could get Mary Hallom."

Quinn appreciated Becker's efficiency, as well as his lack of complaint for having to work on his day off. She needed to unpack and make a quick trip to the library before that, but the request was more than reasonable. "I'll be there. Thanks."

As she disconnected and returned to Josh's text, a pleasurable warmth washed over every part of her body. His reply was—Only dessert I'll ever need is you.

Chapter Fifty-five

Quinn was unused to having to explain where she was going and when, so it felt strange, having just arrived at Jack's, to drop off Calvin, and rush off so soon. "I wanted at least to fix lunch for you, but I've got an important errand to run at the library, and a meeting at the lawyer's office. Here are Calvin's treats if he goes outside while I'm gone."

"No worries. I've got a big container of gazpacho that Mary brought over last night before she went to work. Enough for you, too, if you want some." Calvin had curled up at Jack's feet and barely looked up as Quinn prepared to leave. So much for adjusting to his new surroundings.

"Sounds delicious, but no thanks. Oh, I'm having dinner at Josh's at seven, also." She unpacked a thermal lunch bag containing six low-fat yogurts and made room for them on the inside of the refrigerator door.

Jack chuckled. "Too bad you don't have more to do today. Thanks for stopping by."

"I'm sorry if I'm being a rude houseguest." Maybe she should have gone to her parents' after all.

"Only teasing. I don't expect you to babysit me. Oh, by the way, I'm meeting with Ana's parents tomorrow at one at the Transplant Center, if you want to come along. You know them better, and you're so much better at these things than I am."

"Maybe I will. It still gives me chills to think that Ana's kidney is saving your life. Who would have ever thought things would turn out like this?" She picked up an afghan from the sofa and folded it. "I'm feeling a little guilty about missing the funeral. If I go with you tomorrow, I can extend my condolences again." She thought for a few seconds and then said, "Okay, count me in."

Her brother's broad show of teeth was enough to erase any doubts she had about facing the Frenches. "And thanks again for housing Calvin and me.

We'll try not to get in your way too much."

"Nonsense. Feel free to come and go as you please. In fact, take the key in the top lock there. The alarm code is my birth month and day."

Quinn pulled the key out of the lock and fastened it to the key ring in her purse. "I probably won't get back until after five." She patted Calvin, gave Jack a peck on the cheek, and marched out of the door. She congratulated herself on everything accomplished so far, and it was only a little after noon.

When she walked into the library's history center, Dustin was back at his station near the door. He nodded at Quinn, but another patron walked over to ask him a question, so Quinn was able to slip past him. She really wanted to see Lauren Anderson. Quinn circled the room, peering through the glass wall in the back, but no Lauren. Maybe she had Saturdays off.

Disappointed, Quinn sat at the same station as last time and inserted her library card into the computer. She accessed the archives of the *Daily News*, but now there were new keywords to use: Heaven's Door, Blackie, and otoplasty. The last was a throwaway. She didn't expect to find anything specific or new, but it was worth a try.

Heaven's Door had several hits, dating back to 1997. She started flipping through screens with news items from the past—some lawsuits, some health inspection ratings, but nothing specific about personnel. She wondered whether Blackie had been there since the beginning. She wished she had a real name for him.

As she added the word, "manager," to the browser, she looked up. Lauren was entering the room from the back. She was carrying a stack of books, balancing them on her belly. Quinn jumped up to help the librarian take the books to a table. "Should you be carrying so many heavy books right now?"

The woman blushed. "They *were* heavier than I expected. Thanks for the help." She neatened the pile of books. "It's Quinn, right?"

Quinn was glad the woman had remembered her. She smiled and twirled a lock of her hair around her index finger. "That's right. I was here last Sunday, and you helped me research a murder case—"

"—Yes, the Chrysler case. I remember. So you're back again?" She tapped the stack of books with her thumbs.

Quinn inhaled and mentally crossed her fingers. "I'm hoping you can help me. I'm in need of one bit of information."

The librarian's lips pursed, and her eyes sought Quinn's. "Of course. That's what I'm here for."

Quinn looked behind her to see if Dustin or anyone else was listening.

"Well, last time I was here, you told me someone else had researched Dawn's murder recently."

Lauren's expression of sympathy froze. "Yes, but—"

"—I know, you don't reveal names, and I wouldn't ask if it weren't that my life may be in danger, but I need to know. Can you at least tell me if it was a man or woman? Was it a man?"

The librarian stood stock still, and the scent of deodorant mixed with perspiration emanated from her. Her head shifted a few millimeters, which Quinn understood to be no.

"Was it Ana Renfroe?" Seeing the librarian's flinch, Quinn made her case as best she could. It was now or never. "You see, Ana and I were best friends, and she sent me a package just before she died. It's a long story, but I'm pretty sure Ana's research here in the history center played a part in it."

Lauren's internal debate showed on her face, as she winced and blinked. "I—I don't—"

"I'll tell you what," Quinn said, looking around and behind her again and keeping her voice low. "If it was Ana, cross your arms."

The librarian frowned, her eyes roving the room. After a long thirty seconds, she crossed her arms. She whispered, "Good luck," and turned toward the back room she had come from.

I thought so. Quinn closed out the open files on her computer and shut it down. Things were starting to come together in her mind about the weeks before Ana's death. Knowing that Ana had researched Dawn's death didn't exactly make her happy, but it did provide a significant piece of the puzzle. Now she was a bit more prepared for the three o'clock meeting at Mr. Becker's office.

A gurgling stomach reminded Quinn that she should fortify herself with something to eat before the meeting. She would have just enough time to stop in at Mario's, and she had a craving for a large, gooey slice of their four seasons pizza.

As she stepped outside of the sliding glass doors of the library, she sprinted across the street to where she'd parked her car between a tree and a large brown panel truck. She held out her key fob, and, hearing the click, opened the car door.

Before she could climb in, a woman with a blonde ponytail and huge breasts appeared at her side and grabbed her above the elbow. "Remember me?" She chomped a spearmint-smelling wad of gum as she spoke. Red-rimmed eyes stared at Quinn's with an intensity inappropriate to the setting—a warm summer day outside of the library.

Quinn stared back. The woman looked familiar in the sense of being someone Quinn had met recently, but her appearance was different in some way. Of course. This was the stripper from Heartbeat Cabaret, with clothes and without makeup, the one who had offered to give Josh a lap dance.

"Y-yes, I think so." Quinn tried, but couldn't, shake off the woman's grip on her arm. Something about the woman's expression kicked Quinn's instincts into cautionary mode.

"You and yer boyfriend visited with me at the strip club the other night. I was one of the dancers?" Without the makeup and the skimpy clothes, the woman looked like an ordinary person who was down on her luck. Maybe she wanted a handout. "You asked me some questions, so, seein' you out here like this, I thought you might be interested in what I have in my truck here."

Quinn had no intention of looking at whatever this woman had to show her. "I'm sorry. I've got an appointment I'm late for. Maybe another time." She shook her arm again, but the woman wouldn't let go.

"I'm afraid I must insist." The stripper's grip was bruising, and she all-but-dragged Quinn over to the back of the van in the next parking space. "Sorry," the woman whispered, as a deep growling voice and a rough shove with a cold, hard object altered her plans. "Don't scream, or I'll shoot."

Chapter Fifty-six

Shocked, Quinn dropped her sling bag, and she considered abandoning it and making a run for it, but the woman's iron grip on her arm had been replaced by the man's even tighter one, not to mention what was probably a gun in her ribs.

The library was only about a hundred feet away, but there were no patrons in sight. There wasn't a soul around to hear, even if she tried making a scuffle. She had no doubt that if she ran, she'd be shot.

Her chances were better if she could calm her rapid breathing and talk her way out. Her body was tense, every muscle singing a screeching tune that only she could hear. She couldn't get a look at the person holding her, but his body odor hung in the humid air around her, causing her to cough.

Quinn struggled to breathe, willing herself to relax against the weapon and the stranger who held it. "You want my purse? Go ahead and take it." She bent her knees as if to pick up the bag from the shell-and-gravel surface where it lay. Her mind raced over the items inside—her cell phone, her keys, the key to Jack's house.

A jab in the ribs convinced her that what she was feeling was indeed the barrel of a gun. "Don't move. I'll pick up the purse. Get in the van." The man was short, maybe a few inches taller than Quinn's five feet six, certainly not Blackie, who was over six feet. He scooped up Quinn's sling bag as he pushed her toward the rear of the panel truck next to her Toyota. She caught a glimpse of his face. Except for dark sunglasses, he wore nothing to conceal his features. Not a good sign, according to what Quinn had read and seen in movies. If the plan were to kill her, it wouldn't matter if she saw what he or the stripper looked like. She was pretty sure he was the "manager" of Heartbeat Cabaret, the one who had sat at the entrance.

He opened the back cargo doors of the truck. Quinn tried to get a good look at the license plate and the make and model of the truck, but she only had a split second before he shoved her rear end, motioning her into the vehicle. Plastic ties and a mouth gag lay ready on the truck's floor. Panic seized Quinn's body, and she thought she might have to pee. This couldn't be happening to her—it must be a nightmare. Is that what Ana had thought, too?

Quinn found her voice. She dreaded being gagged. "What's this about? Where are you taking me?" As she spoke, she twisted her body in the direction of her assailant and dug her bare big toe into the gravel, making as big a hole as possible. If she hadn't been wearing sandals, she might've tried kicking.

"Find out soon enough. Easier if you cooperate. Now get in." He pushed again, forward and upward. Quinn had no choice but to climb into the back compartment of the truck, but as she did so, she dug her toe in and dragged it one last time, thinking of the breadcrumbs in Hansel and Gretel.

Quinn wished she knew the name of the stripper, who stood behind the man with the gun, looking uncomfortable. "Listen, Mister, Miss, I promise I'll be quiet if you don't gag me. I have asthma, and the gag might trigger an attack." She looked around the van's back compartment for a tool, something to use as a weapon. Nothing. "In fact, you don't need to tie me, either. I'll go peacefully." A noxious odor caused her stomach to heave, urine or feces or both. Who or what had spent a miserable time in this compartment before her?

"Not how this goes down." He pushed her further into the truck to make room for himself and closed the doors behind him. The stripper had disappeared, probably moving to the front passenger seat. The combination of heat, darkness, and nasty smells, as well as the pounding of Quinn's heart, created a dizzying sickness within her.

"Now, hands together." He put down the gun and picked up a cable tie to bind her wrists, and Quinn considered grabbing the pistol and pulling off a shot. What would she have to lose if it didn't work? As if reading her mind, the assailant moved the gun out of reach.

Yelling wouldn't help. Unless someone had suddenly appeared outside the truck, the nearest person was inside the library. Quinn lay still while he strapped her wrists and ankles and tightened the ties, but her thoughts were roiling. Who was this guy, and what was he going to do with her? Was he somehow connected to Blackie? How did he know she was at the library? She tried one last stab at conversation, as he picked up the gag. "Why are you doing this?"

His voice was gravelly. "No more questions." The gag filled her mouth with a dry thickness, all the way to her throat, and she thought she'd pass out from lack of air. She coughed, tried to swallow, but even that was hard to do, and the binding was so tight. A headache began pounding on both sides above her ears, and tears filled her eyes.

Her captor jumped out of the truck and closed the back doors. Quinn fought against the scream in her throat. Her nose worked fine. She needed to calm down and think. She'd read once about a tied-and-bound woman who'd kicked the rear lights out from inside a car's trunk, and the person driving behind the vehicle called the police. She tried to find a way to do the same, but, even if she could position herself correctly, her bound and sandalled feet wouldn't be effective.

Use your brain, instead. The truck was moving now, out of the parking lot, and turning onto one of the side streets by the library entrance. The windows back there had been covered over, but Quinn was familiar enough with the streets to be able to guess their location if she paid attention to the speed of the vehicle and how long it went without turning. Guessing they were on Main Street, heading toward the causeway, she started counting seconds.

After stopping for a couple of traffic lights and reaching 1000 seconds, she stopped counting. She could be more productive thinking of other things. How soon would she be missed? It had been a few minutes after one-thirty when she left the library. Although it seemed like hours since she'd been bound and gagged, it had probably only been minutes. No one was expecting her anywhere until the three o'clock meeting at Becker's office. But that was only a little over an hour away, and the police would be there, including Mary Hallom. She had never missed or been late to a meeting with Becker, so she was certain he would jump on looking for her right away.

He'd probably call her parents, Josh, and her brother. She was supposed to have dinner at Josh's and talk to his parents online. Had she told any of them where she was going? She vaguely recalled having told Jack she was going to the library. A check there would reveal her card's activity in the history center, and Lauren would be able to confirm her having been there. Actually, Lauren knew a lot about what Quinn had been researching. And her car was in the parking lot, and her toe marks in the gravel. Maybe the library's security cameras reached that far, too.

The traces she'd left behind encouraged her and gave her hope. If she could manage to stay alive long enough, maybe all the smart people in her life would be able to follow the breadcrumbs and save her. She closed her eyes and said a fervent prayer in her head. As she got to the "amen," the truck sped up. Now maybe they were leaving the island.

Chapter Fifty-seven

If Quinn had ever had a bumpier ride, she couldn't remember it. Between the hot, fetid air in the back, the tightness of the plastic around her wrists and ankles, the pressure of the gag in her mouth, and the frequent lurching of the truck, she felt bruised and battered, inside and out.

Keeping track of where they were going by the traffic sounds and movements on the road, Quinn noted the incline of the causeway and the decline about two minutes later. She pictured the exits on the other side of the causeway, each leading to a familiar coastal town. The further they went away from home, the heavier her heart became. Maybe she was being taken to a kill spot and left in a ditch somewhere on the mainland.

She thought of Calvin, his pointy little ears and wagging tail. At least he'd be well taken care of at Jack's. The thought of never seeing Josh again was too painful to bear. If she got out of this alive, she would never leave his side.

A bout of nausea pushed these thoughts aside. She needed to focus on breathing, on ignoring the gag. Her sanity and even her life depended on it. The rhythm of the tires on the pavement, the metallic banging of the van as it moved over bumps—these helped Quinn to concentrate on the here and now. Whatever she heard or felt might help her survive.

About ten or twelve minutes into the ride, the truck pulled up an incline and drew to a stop. The driver spoke to the stripper in a hushed, gravelly voice, and Quinn strained to hear. "Three Whoppers, three fries, three chocolate shakes. And hurry." *A Burger King.* Some of the fast-food restaurants were built up as protection against flooding. That would account for the incline. Quinn's stomach clenched and growled, despite being tied up in knots of fear. Maybe Gravel-voice was planning to feed her. That would be a good sign.

A few minutes later, the woman returned, and the truck took off down the incline. The faint aroma of greasy, salty French fries caused Quinn's saliva to flow against the gag. She couldn't remember the last time she'd eaten anything, and, by now, it must be almost three o'clock. The police would be gathering at Becker's office, waiting for her to arrive. Quinn was so glad she had insisted on Mary Hallom's being present at that meeting. When Quinn didn't show, Mary would call Jack. She convinced herself that help would come quickly. But what if they couldn't find her?

She banished that thought and concentrated on other questions. Why was she being kidnapped? Were her captors connected to Blackie? What were they planning to do with her? And, most importantly, what could she do to foil their plans?

In the next minute, the truck made a left turn and slowed to a roll and then a stop. Her attention was riveted by the whirring of an electric garage door, and her stomach seized with a new fear. Where was she, and what would happen next?

The truck moved forward several feet and stopped. The garage door whirred again, louder this time. They'd arrived at whatever destination, away from scrutiny or help. The little coastal towns north of the causeway were sparsely populated, and homes were far apart. She pictured herself like one of the Russian dolls she had played with as a child, a body within a container, within a container. The gag and the plastic ties were cutting into her skin. If she lay still, now that the truck wasn't moving, she could minimize the discomfort. *Breathe, Quinn. Keep your wits about you.*

The van was still now. Footsteps and a creaky door were the only sounds. Quinn's stomach tensed, and a quivering took over her insides. Would she be left in the truck to die? Or did Gravel-voice have something even more sinister planned for her?

A whoosh of gasoline-smelling air accompanied the opening of the back of the truck. Gravel-voice's rough hands pulled at her middle, as if she were a rolled-up carpet, and he were the installer. "C'mon, roll over." At the edge of the truck, Quinn lay face-up, her hands tied at her midriff, her gagged face turned away from her captor. If she didn't stare at him, maybe he would treat her better.

"Gonna undo your feet. Don't get any ideas about running. There's nowheres you can go from here. Understand?"

Quinn nodded. Between the gag and the hot garage, she wondered if she'd have the strength to run anyway. Right now, just getting enough oxygen was a challenge.

Quinn knew all about cable ties. Caskets delivered to McFarland's came wrapped and strapped with tight plastic ties. She shivered at the association.

Once her feet were released, she flexed them at the ankles to get the blood flow going. The tight straps bit against her wrists, even as Gravel-voice grabbed her by the shoulder and elbow and hurried her to stand.

Not being able to use her voice or hands kept her off-balance and somewhat disoriented, but she was determined to stay alive. She surveyed the garage, as her captor pushed her toward the door to the inside. The truck took up more than half the space. She saw nothing noteworthy, except for a large box of yard bags, opened. No lawn mower, bicycles, gardening tools, or brooms—nothing to suggest a family lived here.

The inside didn't offer much either. The air was cooler compared to the back of the truck or the garage, but the air conditioning thermostat must have been set at eighty degrees or so. Dark draperies covered every window, allowing only cracks of daylight here or there. A battered-looking table and four chairs were the only furniture. Except for the bag of Burger King, sitting on the ledge between the kitchen and eating area, there was so sign of food or meal preparation anywhere. In fact, there was an empty space where the refrigerator should be. Wherever they were, this house was not being lived in.

Quinn breathed in the stale air, wishing she could brush the perspiration from her forehead or fan herself. She was so uncomfortable, she could have screamed, but the gag prevented her from moving her tongue, and she was probably better off not being able to show her terror. For the first time since she'd left the library, she thought, *What would Ana do?* And a clear image came to mind of Ana, posture erect, eyes clear, unafraid.

Ana had faced every challenge with bravery and a spirited, positive attitude. If Ana could do that, so could she. Quinn lifted her head, pretending she was a queen at a parade.

"Keep walking," Gravel-voice said, shoving her from behind. "Turn right at the end of the hallway." When she made it to the open door of the last room on the right, her heart sank. Her prison awaited.

Chapter Fifty-eight

The blonde stripper stood inside the eight-by-twelve-foot room, hugging herself and shifting her weight from one foot to another. She made Quinn think of a weather-beaten Barbie doll. Her body partially blocked Quinn's view of a twin bed, set in the middle of the room, with a heavy oak headboard and footboard. Next to the center of the bed was a portable potty.

"Move it," Gravel-voice said, as he pushed Quinn toward the bed. Barbie jumped and moved over, too, revealing the heavy chains and hardware at each end of the bed. It didn't take a rocket scientist to figure out these contraptions were meant for Quinn. Her heart leaped into her throat, and she felt like throwing up, even though she hadn't eaten all day.

Gravel-voice motioned to Barbie to come closer. "Take off her pants." Quinn flinched and moved her bound hands, trying to pull away from the man's strong grip. "C'mon, hurry. Can't wait all day."

Barbie averted her face from Quinn's. She unfastened the button and zipper of Quinn's jeans, and pulled down pants and panties in one motion. Barbie nudged Quinn to sit down. The stripper removed the pants at the ankles, folded them neatly, and placed them on the floor out of reach.

Quinn was mortified. Was she about to be raped? She was accustomed to viewing naked bodies, and she had seen plenty of Barbie's body that night at the strip club, but *being* the naked body was totally different, and she felt so vulnerable. If the gag hadn't been in place, she would have screamed until her lungs ran dry.

"Lie down." Gravel-voice specialized in issuing orders. Quinn tried to control the shaking inside. She had no choice but to comply, her present fear second only to her fear of the future.

The bed was hard. The mattress was shallow. How many others had been forced to lie here, fearing for their lives? Quinn could only assume that she was here because of the chain of events set in motion by Ana's death. No, by Dawn's death. Was she about to end up the same way?

She wanted to kick and writhe, to resist being imprisoned or raped, or both, but what was the point? She had been physically powerless since that first moment in the library parking lot. The room was warm and stuffy. The windows in the room were apparently closed and probably locked, out of reach, anyway.

"Undo her wrists." Barbie released the plastic ties with a practiced skill. She had done this before. As she removed them, she grazed Quinn's forearm with her little finger, perhaps a gesture of sympathy. Maybe Barbie had once worn these bonds, been chained to this bed. Maybe she knew what was in store for Quinn.

Gravel-voice fastened the metal cuffs to Quinn's wrists and ankles with robot-like efficiency. Beads of sweat popped up on his forehead and rolled down the sides of his face, but his sunglasses blocked Quinn's perception of any feelings he might have. A faint tobacco smell mingled with his body odor. Maybe the rasp in his voice had come from cigarettes.

Quinn took in as many details as she could, hoping she could piece together the scenario that had put her in this situation, and a scenario to get her out. The metal of her bonds was cool and unyielding, but the chains were long enough to provide for some movement—enough to reach the port-a-potty. Once she was fastened to the heavy chains, her captor put his face into Quinn's. "I'm gonna take off the gag now. But there's no point in screaming. There's nobody here but us chickens, and two of us are about to leave. You can wear yourself out screaming, but I guarantee you, no one will hear. There's no other house close by."

Quinn nodded. Apparently, rape wasn't imminent, but the thought of being left alone, chained to a bed, where no one could hear her, filled her with a new fear. What if there were a fire? How long would she be left alone? As he removed the gag, she coughed. Her mouth was dry, and her throat was sore. Finally able to talk, she asked, "What's going to happen to me?" Her voice came out puny and weak.

Gravel-voice shrugged and headed for the door. He beckoned to Barbie. "C'mon. We've gotta get ready for work." Without as much as a backward glance, he stomped out of the room, his task here apparently completed.

Quinn's heart sank, and her stomach hurt from hunger, anxiety, or both. Barbie followed, the swishing of her ponytail belying her grim manner. Definitely, not a happy camper. Quinn wished she could have a minute alone with the woman, especially now, without the gag. As she considered what she would say if given the opportunity, Barbie walked back in, carrying the grease-stained bag from Burger King.

Quinn sat up on her elbows. Her initial modesty about being naked took a back seat to more important worries. She waited until the woman came closer, and, when she spoke, her voice was a mere whisper. "What are they going to do with me?"

"Don't know," she whispered back, and then, louder, "Here's something in case you get hungry." She set the sack of food on the bed next to Quinn, leaning over to speak into her ear. "Blackie wants to talk to you. That's all I know."

The woman left, and a minute later a door slammed, the garage door whirred open and then closed, and Quinn was left in a deathly quiet house located who-knew-where. By now the three o'clock meeting at Becker's office would have convened, and, hopefully, the police had initiated a search. Whether they thought of her as a kidnapping victim or as a fleeing suspect, she didn't care. She just prayed they would find her.

Chapter Fifty-nine

Quinn's thoughts whirled in her head, as she adjusted to the new reality, being chained to a bed in an abandoned house. She tested the chains, one-by-one, and then arms together and legs together, hoping for, but not expecting, a weak link. Moving her limbs required effort, as the hardware weighed at least five pounds on each limb. There was a bit of good news, though. The chains were long enough to allow Quinn to sit, stand, and reach the portable toilet. That, she supposed, was the reason Barbie had removed her pants.

The headache that had started in the van had multiplied in intensity, and Quinn's stomach was screaming for nourishment. A cold Whopper, cold French fries, and a tepid milkshake might soothe her and allow her to think more clearly.

She gobbled and slurped, barely tasting the meal, hoping it wouldn't be her last. A wad of napkins filled the bottom of the bag. She used one to wipe her face and hands, saving the rest. They might come in handy.

After eating, she stood and stretched, surprised to feel a little better. She used the toilet and wiped herself with a napkin. Not being able to flush, she tried to ignore her smelly and dirty surroundings. What she wouldn't give for a shower. Or enough links in the chain to enable her to reach the closest window. Her bed had a thin mattress, a fitted sheet, and a pancake-like pillow, but no top sheet or blanket. The corpses at McFarland's had better accommodations.

Surely this set-up hadn't been designed solely for her. She'd heard about sex-trafficking, about how coastal towns were drop-off places for girls coming into or going out of the country. Had this hideout been used for girls in transit? She banged against the scarred bed frame, using arms and legs, trying to use the power of the chains to knock it apart. Nothing budged, and all she accomplished was injuring her wrists and ankles.

How long would she be here in this stifling bedroom, and what was the point? Why hadn't Gravel-voice killed her? He'd had every chance to do so. Barbie had said Blackie was coming. What was the connection was between Blackie and her two captors? Maybe Blackie owned both the Heartbeat Cabaret and Heaven's Door, and Gravel-voice and Barbie worked for him. That would make sense.

Soon it would be Saturday evening. Those three would work until the wee hours of the morning, most likely. Quinn imagined the police were looking for her by now. Maybe Jack had told them she was at the library, and they had found her car. Maybe they had contacted Josh, who'd told them about the two strip clubs. Becker would have turned over the photo of the footprints and the nylon fabric from outside of her house. Everybody had a piece of information, but nobody had it all. Whatever trail Quinn had left, she was powerless to add to it now. She had to hope and pray they had enough to lead them to this dreary place, before it was too late.

With all the windows covered, very little light came into the bedroom, and what did seep in through cracks in the draperies was waning. Soon she would be completely in the dark, alone, chained, and half-naked. Refusing to look at the negatives, she made up her mind that this was the perfect opportunity to think and plan, without distractions.

Blackie wanted to talk to her. That meant she had something of value, something he wanted badly enough to have her kidnapped, but not killed. Whatever it was, she needed to discover and use it as a bargaining chip.

Oh, who was she kidding? She was in no position to bargain, tied to a bed in some remote location. Whatever she knew, she had to milk it for everything it was worth, to delay telling it until the police found her. Otherwise, what motivation would Blackie have for keeping her alive?

What could she possibly know that Blackie wouldn't know? If he'd killed Dawn, he would know that. He would probably know, too, all that she and Ana had witnessed. Old news. He'd gotten away with murder, so what had brought him to the surface now?

Had he killed Ana? And Brad? If so, why? She wished she could summon Ana's spirit to help her figure out what Blackie wanted from her. The VCR tapes were a big clue, but, aside from helping her to identify Blackie's ears, she couldn't figure out how they gave her any special knowledge.

She wished she had ignored Ana's insistence to keep secret the fact they'd witnessed Dawn's murder. According to Becker, it had been a crime to do so, even though they were juveniles at the time. If they had gone to the police back in 2004, Blackie, or whoever he was in real life, may have been prosecuted, convicted, and maybe even executed. And she wouldn't be in this position now.

Quinn should've refused to go along with Ana. Of course, Quinn had never had a backbone when it came to Ana. They were blood sisters, and, according to Ana, that meant Quinn had to follow along with whatever Ana suggested. Ana had had nerves of steel, and the confidence to go along with them. The tag-along role had suited Quinn so well that she'd never questioned, just complied.

The big question was *why*. Why did Ana swear her to secrecy? Those notes in her scrapbook documented the fact, but didn't address the reason. Had Quinn never asked Ana the simple question of why?

Quinn drilled into her memory of "the incident." So much of it she had repressed, intentionally refusing to process what she had seen and done. Whatever Blackie wanted from her had to relate in some way to what had happened that night. As if she were pushing through a thick, wet fog, she forced herself to revisit the night of June 27, fifteen years ago.

Chapter Sixty

The morning of Dawn's murder, teenaged Quinn had helped her parents with a funeral. One of the food servers from the school cafeteria had died, and Quinn handed out programs. She'd been sad, because the woman had always greeted her with a wink and a smile. She would miss her.

After the burial, the McFarlands stopped at a restaurant for lunch. When they got home, there was a message on the answering machine from Ana, inviting Quinn to spend the night at the Frenches'. It was a Sunday night in June, and since there was no school the next day, and as a reward for Quinn's having helped out, her parents let her go.

Mrs. French had made a huge spaghetti casserole, garlic bread, and green salad, and they'd all eaten at the sturdy wooden table in the kitchen. Anyone who had ever been a guest in their home had autographed the table, and Quinn had carved her name in block letters with a Swiss army knife years before.

After dinner, they had make-your-own-sundaes with three flavors of ice cream and all the toppings. Ana and Quinn had done the dishes, and Mr. and Mrs. French had gone into the living room to watch *60 Minutes.*

The girls went to Ana's room, where they listened to the top songs by Britney Spears, Usher, and Jessica Simpson. The tunes led to dancing, and dancing led to thoughts of Dawn, whom they'd watched dancing on many evenings.

By nine o'clock, Ana's parents were watching a movie on TV. They didn't comment when Ana and Quinn slipped past them through the kitchen and out the back door.

Now, all these years later, and chained to a bed, awaiting who-knows-what, Quinn marveled at the vividness of so many details from that night, especially from before "the incident." A multi-sensory snapshot of that evening flashed in her brain—the inky sky, the chirping crickets, the earthy geranium smell from the back garden.

Dawn's house had backed onto the same alley as Ana's. The fig tree on the side of Ana's garage was in full bloom, the sugary globes of fruit giving off aromatic hints of what it would offer in the coming weeks. At that time of year, the fig tree provided a perfect spot for snooping on Dawn's nude dancing. The girls could fit in a curved, thick branch, camouflaged by the broad leaves.

As soon as they nestled into their lookout perch and focused on Dawn's open windows, with the thin, parted curtains and the pulsating music beyond, the show began. Bright lights turned the view of the bedroom into a stage, their seats into a dark outdoor theater. Dawn wore a sarong around her waist, and her hair was wrapped in a towel, but everything from her neck to her belly-button was exposed and glistening in the light. As she swayed and bumped to the music, the sarong came loose and dropped to the floor. She didn't bother to pick it up. Instead, she removed the towel from her head, releasing a cascade of long, wet tresses. Dawn continued to flit around the room, flinging her arms.

Doesn't she even care that someone might be watching? Quinn couldn't imagine being that uninhibited, that lost in music and movement. Dawn's eyes were closed, and her lips were pressed together into a half-smile, as if the pleasure she felt had come from a guilty source. She was lost in the dance, sexy, but in a natural, uncalculated way.

"Do you think she's turned on?" Ana whispered.

"I dunno. How would you tell?"

Only five or ten minutes passed before Dawn left the room. When she came back, still naked, the tall man with the big ears followed her into the room. They might have been arguing. Their voices could be heard over the music, but the words were indistinguishable.

In the past, Ana and Quinn had watched that same man dance with Dawn, moving his hands over her body. The scenes had filled Quinn's head with tantalizing ideas and her body with shivery sensations. Was this what men and women did together? Was this love, or something else?

Once they had watched while Dawn took the man's shirt off, but soon after, the couple had disappeared from view. That night, on June 27, 2004, the man had kept his clothes on, and both he and Dawn were visible through the open curtains. Now, as Quinn tried to reconstruct the scene from the dark and dank room where she was imprisoned, the sharp detail grew fuzzy.

Dawn had stopped dancing, stopped smiling. She was shouting and flailing her arms. There was no mistaking this for love. The two were arguing, and the body language intensified. Time passed—a minute or ten—and Big Ears raised his voice so loud that Quinn had covered her ears. He was screaming, repeating the word, "money," in a nasty, sarcastic tone. Quinn glanced at Ana, always considering things through her blood sister's perspective. Was she as horrified?

Ana seemed calmer, but her eyes were glued to the scene, as if it were a late-night movie on a night she couldn't sleep.

When the shouting escalated to physical violence, panic thrummed in Quinn's veins, and she wanted to run. She grabbed Ana's arm and shook it. "Let's get out of here," she whispered.

"No." Ana shook off her friend's grip. "We need to see this."

What happened in the subsequent minutes was a blur. Vague impressions of quick, hard movements, loud screams, then abrupt silence. A limp body sprawled on the bed. A scurrying about. Was he cleaning up fingerprints? Quinn took quick, shallow breaths, and she must have covered her eyes at times. At some point Ana had scooted closer and put her arms around Quinn, either to protect her or to keep her in place. Perspiration rolled down both of their faces, and the aroma of figs was replaced by the odor of horror.

"Omigod, omigod." Quinn murmured. "I think she's dead. He killed her."

"Sh." Ana held her even tighter. "It's gonna be okay. Just be still a little longer."

Quinn closed her eyes, hoping to escape and obliterate the images from across the alley. Maybe when she opened her eyes, this would all be a bad dream. Quinn had no idea how or when Big Ears disappeared, but the next thing she remembered, Ana was shaking her. "C'mon. We've got to see something."

Quinn had already seen too much, and all she wanted to do was curl up into a ball and sob. But Ana was pulling her by the hand, speaking in hushed tones as she took her into the alley. "Did you see something fall when that guy ran down the alley? Let's see if we can find it."

Quinn had no recollection of much of anything, except that she had witnessed a violent crime. She was shaking all over, amazed that Ana seemed so much in control. But that was Ana—fearless and bold, as always.

Ana dragged her to the alley, beneath the windows of Dawn's room. The dancing music was still playing, with no one there to turn it down or turn it off. The alley was paved with rocks and shells, uneven, with weeds growing through in spots. Their feet, clad in flip flops, made shuffling noises as they moved, but it didn't take long to find the object Ana was searching for.

"Look, here it is." Ana picked up a shiny gold bracelet, with thick links, broken at the clasp. Ambient light from a streetlamp at the end of the alley and the too-bright rays emanating from Dawn's bedroom caused the man's ID bracelet to gleam as it hung from Ana's fingers. "This fell as the man ran down the alley." She turned it over in the light, looking at whatever was engraved.

Quinn's voice was hoarse, as if she'd been screaming her heart out. "It looks like real gold. What does it say?"

If Ana answered her, Quinn couldn't remember. Ana had already gripped the ID bracelet in her fist. "We need to get rid of this. Put it where no one will find it."

Quinn wanted to ask why. Wouldn't the bracelet be regarded as evidence? But Ana had already run into her garage, and Quinn followed in her wake.

Ana picked up a gardening shovel and a pair of dirty gloves. "C'mon, we've got to bury this."

Quinn tagged along, as Ana found a spot she liked behind the geraniums, to the east of the back steps of the Frenches' house. "You hold this and keep watch while I dig." Ana worked quickly, making a hole about a foot and a half deep, below where her mother might plant annuals. The soil was soft and wet, and each shovel-full released a stronger earthy smell into the night air. A single-bulb porch light aided the mission, and Quinn held the ID bracelet as though it were an unexploded bomb. When the hole was deep enough to suit Ana, she dropped the bracelet in, and Ana covered it with dirt. For good measure, she dug up a geranium and planted it over the hole.

By this time Ana was dripping with perspiration, and Quinn wasn't far behind. Ana put away the shovel and gloves, and the two girls sneaked in through the back door and into Ana's bedroom. They took turns showering in the adjacent bathroom. The Frenches were still sitting in the living room with the TV blaring.

Later, when they were lying in the twin beds with a nightstand in between, Ana said to Quinn, "We can't ever tell anyone what we saw tonight. We have to keep it a secret until the day we die."

So used to having Ana run the show, Quinn didn't ask why. She just assumed that Ana had good reason, and at that point, she was depleted of thought or emotion, possibly in shock.

"Promise me you won't ever tell. A blood-sister oath."

Quinn was already trying to forget it, and her eyelids felt like bricks, closing her off from all the ugly things in the world. "Okay, I promise."

Fifteen years, and Quinn had kept her promise, except for what she had told Becker. Now she realized it was a promise she never should have made. She'd made a lot of mistakes, and so had Ana. She just hoped the mistakes wouldn't turn out to be fatal.

Chapter Sixty-one

Quinn didn't know how long she had remained chained to the heavy, thin-mattressed bed in the dark and musty house. Other than the sound of a passing train outside, everything was utterly quiet. She had used the portable toilet a few times, and the meal she had eaten no longer filled her up, so it might be close to midnight. Adrenaline and a strong instinct to think her way out of this situation had kept her keyed up, but now she was having a hard time keeping her eyes open.

Maybe it wouldn't hurt to take a little nap. She pictured the various people in her life—Josh, her parents, Jack, Becker, Mary Hallom—even Sergeant Schmidt, and her neighbors, Mrs. Tartt and Anise, worrying about her, searching for her. She said a prayer that they would find her and save her before it was too late. She didn't want to end up like Ana and Brad.

If only she could use telepathy to get Ana's parents to dig up the flower bed behind their house. Try as she might, she couldn't remember the name on the gold ID bracelet, but she was sure that if she could, she would know Blackie's real name. If they found the bracelet, it would lead them to their daughter's killer—Quinn was sure of it.

Quinn closed her eyes and tried to picture the shiny gold bracelet. The name engraved on the front took up most of the space. It was a six- or seven-letter name, something unusual. She squeezed her eyes tight, but nothing came to her. She tried thinking of something else—Jack's having Ana's kidney. Wouldn't it be great if some of Ana's energy and knowledge had been transferred with it?

Grasping at straws—that's what Quinn's mom called it when Quinn went off on a tangent like that. But straws may be all she had available, so Quinn allowed herself to drift from one thought to another, and finally to drift into an uneasy and uncomfortable sleep.

When the overhead light snapped on, Quinn startled and uttered a sound halfway between a groan and a roar. She squeezed her eyes tight, only daring to open one at a time. When she did, a giant of a man, fiftyish, dressed in all black, was standing over her, holding a gun in one hand and a pizza box in the other. He reeked of cigarettes and stale beer, enough to overpower any pizza aromas. Not in any hurry, he stared at Quinn, as if she were a jigsaw puzzle to be solved.

Without thinking, she lifted her chained hands to cover her naked genitals.

"Don't bother. I see so much p-us-sy every day, I don't need to look at yours." His voice was of the same resonance and pitch as that of the actor in the porn tapes, Keith Underwood. Plus, he said the word "pussy" as if it had three syllables. If Quinn had ever doubted that Blackie and the porn actor were one and the same, she now knew for sure.

"Why bother to point a gun at me, then? I'm obviously not going anywhere."

"Oh, so you're a smart-aleck, too. We don't get too many like you coming through here. Mostly all the girls are too scared to do anything but cry." He set the gun down behind the bed, out of Quinn's view.

"My parents always told me I was one in a million." Quinn didn't know where this sarcastic tone was coming from. Her instincts were guiding her, for whatever good they might do. "Anyway, I knew I wasn't the first to wear this jewelry."

"Hah, not by a long shot. Why don't you sit up? I brought you a pizza." He set the pizza box down at the foot of the bed and busied himself by taking the bowl of the portable toilet out of the room.

Quinn sat up and scooted backward, so her back was flush against the cool wooden head board. She fit easily between the sturdy brackets that held the arm chains. A toilet flushed in a nearby room, and Quinn composed herself for whatever might come next.

Blackie trudged back into the room and replaced the toilet bowl. He closed the lid and sat, sighing. "Why aren't you eating? I didn't bring pizza for you to look at the box." He reached for the pizza box and set it on Quinn's lap, then sank back on the toilet chair.

Quinn ran her hands over the slightly warm box, glad to have a cover for her genitals. "I'm not in the habit of waking up to eat. What time is it, anyway?"

"About two-thirty a.m. Call it breakfast. You won't be getting anything else for a while. Might as well eat."

"What about something to drink? Pizza makes me really thirsty." Maybe she was pushing her luck, but Quinn figured there was a reason she was being kept alive, so she might as well make the best of it.

Blackie stomped out of the room, muttering something like, "Demanding little broad." When he returned, he was carrying two large bottles of water. He tossed one at Quinn, and she caught it one-handed.

She opened the plastic cap and held the bottle for a toast. "Cheers." Doing her best to block from her mind that she was conversing with Dawn's killer, and likely Ana's, too, she opened the box of pizza. Now the aromas of savory sausage and gooey cheese made her mouth water, despite the circumstances. "Share it with me?"

Her captor stared at her through hooded eyes. He took a long slug from his water bottle, and then he reached over to pick up an edge piece. A piece of sausage fell onto the floor, and he picked it up and popped it into his mouth.

Quinn chewed in silence, thinking about what she could do to aid her cause. She didn't think Blackie intended to kill her. Otherwise, why feed her? But what was she being saved for? That was the big question.

She stole a glance at Blackie, as she took a swig of her water. From the side, she recognized the distinctive shape of his pinned-back ear. He slumped in the makeshift chair, and she wondered whether he was about to fall asleep.

"I'd like to thank you properly for the spur-of-the-moment dinner. How about telling me your name?"

Widening and then narrowing his eyes, the man stared at Quinn. She looked away first, picking up a crumb from the mattress. The skin on her wrists and ankles hurt from the shackles, and her muscles were sore from moving with the weight of the chains.

When he spoke, the gruffness in his voice made her flinch. "Don't mess around with me. You know very well who I am. You've been following me around for years, you and that troublemaker, Ana. That good-for-nothing husband of hers, too."

Quinn caught her breath. "Oh, no, you're mistaken. I haven't even spoken to Ana in many years, since—"

"Since when? Since you spied on something that was none of your business in the first place?" He started pacing around the room, like a calculating lion, planning a kill. "Don't act innocent with me. I know all about what you and Ana saw, what you and Ana did. Ana told me, herself."

Quinn gathered all of the courage she could, realizing that anything she said now might cause repercussions. She was entirely at his mercy. "If you're talking about what two curious young girls saw during a sleepover in 2004, you don't have to make it sound like we were the ones doing something wrong. I wish I could go back and un-see that incident." She shut the half-empty pizza box and threw it on the floor for emphasis. "But I truly haven't spoken to Ana or Brad in all these years, and I don't understand why you're coming after me now. I never told a soul about that incident." *Except Becker.*

"Look, it's late, and I don't want to get into a debate. Just tell me where you and Ana buried my ID bracelet—that's all."

Quinn had to think fast. If finding the ID bracelet was her only use to this guy, giving him the location now would hasten her demise. She was sure of that. "What ID bracelet? What are you talking about?"

Blackie replied through gritted teeth. "First you say you don't know my name. Then you play dumb about the bracelet. My name was engraved on the front, so I know you know it. And I know you buried it that night."

Quinn closed her eyes, pretending to concentrate. When she opened them again, she said, "You're asking me to remember something from so long ago. I've blocked out a lot of the details from that night. Maybe it would help me remember if you'd tell me why. Why did you kill Dawn?"

"Don't give me that bull crap. It's not like I'm asking you for the combination to the safe at Fort Knox. I'll tell you what. You think on it, get some sleep, do whatever you have to do to remember. I'll be back tomorrow, and you can tell me then."

Quinn's stomach lurched at the thought of being left alone again. "Maybe it would help me remember if you told me why you want it. Surely you didn't go to all this trouble to recover an old broken piece of jewelry."

Blackie picked up the pizza box, the empty water bottles, and his gun. "Hell, no. I couldn't care less about that ID bracelet. I'm after the stash that was buried in the same spot. So think hard." He flipped the light switch, throwing the room into a cruel darkness. "If you can't tell me, you're gonna end up in the same condition as my niece."

Chapter Sixty-two

Blackie's parting words left Quinn's heart racing. Sitting against the headboard, weighted by heavy chains, her mind dashed over time and space without constraint. Had she heard correctly? Had Blackie referred to Ana, or Dawn, as his niece? Or had Quinn imagined it?

Quinn ran through a list of words besides "niece," words that rhymed or began with the letter "n." She couldn't get around the conclusion that Blackie was claiming to be someone's uncle. The thought of Blackie's being related to Dawn left a bitter taste in Quinn's mouth. She had witnessed the two of them having sex, both in person and on the sex videos. Ana was the more likely candidate, and even that made her gag.

If so, was Blackie a brother to Ana's mother or Ana's father? She had never met him at the Frenches' or heard anyone in the family talk about him. Quinn had spent a lot of time at the French house, some of it with members of the extended family. Come to think of it, most of the family members she'd met were on Mrs. French's side.

Physically, Blackie's tall, slim frame was not unlike Mr. French's. The ears—of course, the ears—Quinn remembered having thought of Mr. French and Ana, even when she saw the man's ears in the porn movies. Though theirs weren't as prominent, the shape was similar.

Had Ana recognized the man at Dawn's as her uncle? Ana had never indicated that, but she had been a girl with secrets. She'd kept her relationship with Brad under wraps, and who knows what else. Was the fact that he was family the reason Ana had insisted on never telling that they'd witnessed Dawn's murder, and then buried the bracelet?

If Blackie was Ana's uncle, his real name must be French. Quinn squeezed her eyes shut in the dark room and revisited the few minutes in which she had held the gold ID bracelet. The streetlight had showered the alley and Ana's backyard with enough light to examine it, and she remembered having turned it over in her hands. The front was engraved with a first name, the back with initials. Was "F" one of the initials?

She willed her brain to remember the shapes of the fancy script letters on the back. "To" and "from" initials. The "from" might have been "D.C."—from Dawn Chrysler. Had Dawn cared enough about her fellow actor to gift him with an expensive, engraved piece of jewelry? Even then, a bracelet like that might have cost hundreds of dollars. Considering the house Dawn lived in, that kind of gift would have meant deep feelings.

Could Dawn have loved the young man whose stage name was Keith Underwood? She was just a teenager. Perhaps he had been her only sexual partner. Quinn compared herself to Dawn. As a teenager, she had fallen so completely in love, too. The depth of her feelings for Brad had made his betrayal that much more devastating—now she could see how her entire life had been marked by Brad's choosing Ana over her. Maybe Dawn had loved Blackie that much. And he had killed her.

What were the initials of the man who wore the bracelet? Was it her imagination, or could Quinn visualize them as "L.F."? She repeated aloud, "L.F., L.F." She turned the bracelet over in her mind and pictured the letter "L," as the first of the six or seven letters. What was an unusual man's first name beginning with an "L"? Leonardo, Lester, Laurence, Lemuel.

Somewhere outside, the faint sounds of a train textured the nighttime quiet, and a cat meowed. Distracted, Quinn tried to imagine where on the mainland she might be, within sounds of train tracks.

Blackie's remark about other girls who had been shackled to this bed made her wonder. Was Blackie and his group part of the sex-trafficking industry? She'd heard rumors that port cities were hot spots for transporting girls in and out of the country on ships. Were trains used, as well? Was that what Blackie had planned for her once she was of no use to him, or was she too old?

Quinn shuddered at the uncertainties. She'd never faced such danger, and she was completely defenseless. The only weapon she had was her mind. The train blew another whistle, and she pictured her brother's toy train set, a Christmas gift when he was a kid. The whistle had sounded exactly the same. Jack played with those trains for years, and the images of the tracks and the cars was fixed in Quinn's brain, as well.

Suddenly, Quinn snapped her fingers and yelled out loud. "That's it. That's the name on the bracelet." Warmth and energy rushed through her body, and she dragged her legs over the side of the bed so she could stand. If it weren't for the chains, she'd do jumping jacks or run around the room.

She was still in danger, standing half-naked, in the dark, but she had a bargaining chip. She'd figured out Blackie's real name—it was Lionel French.

Chapter Sixty-three

Quinn must have dozed off for a few hours, when the grating noise of the garage door opener woke her and caused her to grab the sides of the mattress in fear. She scanned the bare room, wishing she could run and hide. She ran her tongue around the sides of her teeth and gums, thirsty, and disgusted by her own breath. The sun cast a sharp, thin outline around the window's draperies and along the middle. She guessed it was around ten o'clock.

A slammed door and raised voices broke the silence, and Quinn recognized Gravel-voice, shouting. "Where in the fuck is that cell phone? Blackie's gonna kill me if we don't find it."

"Well, it's not here—not in the van, the garage, or the house." The strains of Barbie's voice were melody to the percussion of her compatriot's. Quinn's instincts told her Barbie might be sympathetic.

"Anyway, I don't see why the girl's cell phone is all that important. It's not like she's able to use it."

"That's 'cause you're a stupid bitch. Trust me. We've gotta find that phone." Heavy stomping and the slamming of cabinets punctuated Gravel-voice's rant.

"You keep looking then. I'm going to take this food and water to the prisoner." The slapping of Barbie's flip flops on the floor preceded her appearance in the doorway. This morning her ponytail was down, and bluish shadows showed under her eyes. She leaned against the door frame on one leg, like a flamingo. A plastic bag hung from one arm by the handles, and she held a couple of bottles of water in the other hand. The bag smelled of corned beef. Squinting at Quinn, she could have been an actress, trying to remember her lines, or a teacher, trying to decide how to explain a complicated math problem. Something worried her.

"I brought you something to eat and drink," she said in a louder-than-normal voice. She stepped toward the bed, and Quinn moved her legs over the side, making room to set the items down.

"Thank you," Quinn said. She touched Barbie on the wrist. "What's your name?"

Barbie jumped, as if Quinn's touch was fiery hot. "People call me Nell." She turned to pull the toilet bowl out, wrinkling her nose. Lowering her voice to a whisper, Nell said, "I took your cell phone into Burger King yesterday. I told the cashier I'd found it on a table—maybe the owner would come back for it. Hopefully, it's in their lost and found, and someone's tracking it."

Quinn's heart sang as Nell carried the excrement to the bathroom. *An ally!* The Burger King wasn't far from this house, maybe a minute or two, judging by yesterday's ride in the back of the van. Maybe help was on the way.

Quinn opened a water bottle and guzzled several swallows. Then she took a small sip and swished it around her mouth. Pouring a little into the palm of her hand, like cologne, she wiped it all over her face. She needed a shower and shampoo in the worst way.

When Nell returned with the emptied toilet bowl, Gravel-voice was behind her, pushing. "Did you look around in this room?" He flipped on the light switch and stormed around the room, empty as it was of hiding places. He opened the closet and pulled the string light, pressing his hands along the shelf and into the corners. Picking up Quinn's crumpled jeans from the floor, he shoved his hands in the pockets.

Finally, he made eye contact with Quinn, as though he'd just realized she was there. "Get up." He grabbed her wrist, where it was sorest, and yanked her to her feet. He ran his hands under the thin mattress along all four sides of the bed. When he straightened up, he threw Quinn back down in a sitting position. "You did have a cell phone in that little purse of yours, didn't you?"

Quinn's mind darted from one possible response to another. She didn't want to reply at all—she couldn't afford to make a mistake.

Nell stood in the doorway, staring at a spot on the wall opposite.

The man bent and shook Quinn's shoulders. "Answer me. Did you have a cell phone with you yesterday at the library?" His whiskered face almost brushed Quinn's nose, and his breath stank of hangover.

"I—I th-think so," Quinn said. "I usually have my cell with me."

"Well, it's not in your purse, and it's not in your pockets, so where is it?" His voice roared.

"M-maybe I left it in my car then." Quinn could hardly breathe with this angry man in her face, shouting in her ear, but she needed to think of something. "That's right. I usually leave it in the console when I'm going somewhere I don't want to be disturbed."

She wanted to pummel Gravel-voice in the face with her chained hands, but she'd never act on an impulse like that while she was at his mercy. She glanced at Nell and drew herself up. "I'd be glad to go look for it, if you'd kindly unchain me."

"Very funny. 'Fraid you're gonna have to stay here a little longer." He ruffled the curls on Quinn's head and stared at her bare legs and lap, as if he were a butcher, appraising his stock. Quinn's insides boiled with a rage that started as helplessness and increased to disgust and pure hatred. How dare he play with her this way.

There was no point in popping off at Gravel-voice. Her fate wasn't in his hands anyway. She gripped the edge of the mattress and stared at a spot on the floor, wishing him away.

The man cupped her chin in his paw and lifted her eyes to his. She thought for a moment that he might kiss her, but then he said, "Jesus, you smell bad." He turned to Nell and said, "See what you can do to clean her up before Blackie gets here." He let go and marched out of the room.

Nell muttered something like, "Be right back," and left the room. When she returned, she carried a plastic bin half-filled with water. "You don't smell half as bad as Norm, but maybe you'll enjoy washing up a bit."

Quinn scooped water into her hands and splashed her face and neck. If she got out of this place alive, she would never take a shower for granted again. She repeated the process, each time wiping a larger area of her chest, arms, and thighs. "This feels great. Thanks, Nell."

"Welcome." Nell moved Quinn's sandals out of the way and put the bin of water on the floor by Quinn's feet. "Maybe you'd like to dunk your feet in the water, too."

Quinn followed the direction and wiggled her toes in the water. She washed one foot with the other. She could keep this up forever, but she knew her time with Nell was limited. "Why are you helping me?" she whispered.

Nell pulled the water bin toward her and set it on the closed lid of the toilet. Her eyes grew wet and stared at a spot across the room. So many seconds went by—Quinn wondered whether Nell had heard the question. She started to ask again, but Nell whispered back in a feathery tone, "There was another girl, a friend of mine. I couldn't help her, so I'm helping you."

"What was her name?" Quinn asked.

Nell picked up the bin to carry it out. As she moved toward the door, she replied, under her breath. "Her name was Ana."

Chapter Sixty-four

Quinn had a lot to mull over after Nell and Gravel-voice left. (She couldn't bring herself to think of him as Norm. There was nothing normal about him.) The knowledge that her cell phone might bring help excited her, but she tamped down her expectations. Nell's good deed was a lucky break, but she couldn't count on luck. She needed to concentrate on how she was going to handle Blackie's questions about where the ID bracelet was buried. Otherwise, she might not live long enough to be rescued by anyone. After all, this wasn't the movies.

Once she told Blackie where the bracelet was, he wouldn't need her anymore, and she had no doubt he would kill her. She knew too much and had seen too much. She was a worse threat to him than Ana had been.

Ana had dragged her into this jam, and part of Quinn wanted to hate her for it. But Ana had also helped. She'd sent the tapes and her parents to warn Quinn of the danger. She'd provided a kidney for Jack. And now, she may have inspired Nell's kindness. Anyway, there was no point in hating a dead person.

Blackie's early morning visit, and Norm's later one, had left Quinn disoriented. Her body ached as if she'd been chained to this bed for weeks, although it hadn't even been twenty-four hours. Blackie was probably sleeping off his late night at Heaven's Door, and once he woke up, he'd be back to question her some more. This time, he might even torture her.

Quinn wished she had a weapon, something to protect herself. She gazed around the bare room. She couldn't reach a window, a wall, a closet—someone had made sure of that. She eyed the toilet. If all else failed, she could lift the whole chair and use it as a shield.

She eyed the two bottles of water and the bag of food. She'd already drunk out of the first bottle. Maybe she should keep the other bottle full. It might come in handy somehow. She opened the bag from a local delicatessen.

Inside was a bag of potato chips, a corned beef sandwich, two pickles, a couple of packets of mustard and mayonnaise. At the bottom of the bag her fingers wrapped themselves around a plastic utensil. Her heart leaped as she felt the serrated edge of a knife. Had Nell slipped this into the bag for more than spreading mustard on the sandwich?

Quinn examined the plastic knife, testing its strength against the wood of the bed, where the chains met the headboard. No way could she use it to free herself. As plastic knives went, however, this one was quite sturdy. Quinn had read about how the airlines had removed even plastic silverware from meal service trays, because forks and knives could be used to stab and cut flesh. A plastic knife was no match for a gun, but it was something, especially if used unexpectedly.

Her arms were strong from lifting and pushing bodies, and she had taken karate when she was a kid. She wielded the knife in her right hand and practiced slashing at an imaginary Blackie. The weight of the chains was a burden, but she knew how to turn that into momentum. At least she wasn't completely defenseless.

Quinn secreted the knife under the mattress. Knowing it was there gave her a surge of empowerment and hope.

She turned her attention to the corned beef sandwich. Its spicy aroma made her think of Calvin, who would stand on hind legs to beg for a piece, if he were there. *I wish you were here, buddy. I know you'd protect me.*

The late-night pizza from the night before had left Quinn full enough. She decided not to eat the sandwich now, or maybe at all. The salt would leave her thirsty, and she didn't want to drink that second bottle of water unless she had to.

For now, armed with Blackie's real name, the location of the buried ID bracelet, a bottle of water, and a plastic serrated knife, Quinn was ready to do battle.

Chapter Sixty-five

Quinn had never been much for napping, but she must have dozed off while waiting for Blackie. Curled on her side with knees pulled up as far as the chains would allow, and head resting on the wrist-chains, she jerked when an echoing *ding-dong* pierced her consciousness. Someone was at the front door.

Whoever was there, the fact that potential help was several yards away caused Quinn's heart to beat triple time. She leaped off the bed and lunged as close to the front window as her bonds would allow. Cupping her chained hands as a megaphone, she screamed at top volume over and over again. "Help, help! Please help me!"

Pausing for a breath, she listened. *Please don't go away. I need help.* In the pause, she could discern voices. Had they heard her? "I'm in here. I'm tied up. Please help me." Her throat was already scratchy.

Fully awake now, she gripped the unopened bottle of water and banged it against the headboard with the force of a karate strike. The dull thump wouldn't carry far. "I'm in here. In a bedroom. Help me, please help me." Panic flamed in her throat at the thought that whoever was there might leave.

The light seeping in from the crack where the drawn, west-facing curtains failed to meet was paler than before. The knocking had come from that direction. "Are you still there? Please be there."

Quinn hated to use her water bottle. She'd only have one chance at making it count, but she needed to do something to call attention to the room where she was. Encouraged by the muffled voices outside, she arranged her stance for maximum power, focused her mind on speed and strength, drew back her dominant arm, and with an exhaled, *"Ei,"* she launched the length of the bottle against the lower portion of the window pane.

The bottle hit its mark with a loud *whump*, followed by the sound of cracking and falling glass. The drawn curtains had prevented a clean shot through the window, but Quinn uttered a prayer of thanks for fragile windows and congratulated herself for the success of one blow.

Now she renewed her shouting with full force. "Help! I'm being held captive in here!" She held her breath and listened.

"Over here," a male voice shouted. "This window."

Tears sprung in Quinn's eyes, and she jumped, chains and all.

"Police. State your name. Are you alone in the house?" This time a female voice.

Quinn's heart surged with joy. "Quinn McFarland. I'm alone, chained to a bed. Please help."

"Quinn. It's Mary Hallom. Stay calm. We're calling for backup and we're gonna break out this window."

Mary, oh, Mary. Quinn stepped backward. She climbed over the bed and crouched on the floor behind it. As the melody of smashing glass filled her ears, she used the bed as a shield to protect her from potential flying shards.

Within a minute, the window was cleared of glass, and Mary was parting the curtains and climbing into the bedroom. Never had Quinn seen such a beautiful sight. More tears rolled down her cheeks. "Thank you, thank you."

Mary opened the draperies and bent over the window frame to extend an arm for her partner, a wiry young man with a mustache and wavy, ginger-colored hair. Once in, he straightened his posture and looked around, gun drawn.

Mary picked up Quinn's jeans and underwear from the floor and handed them to her. "Let's tie these around your waist till we can get your ankles free." Mary's expression was inscrutable. "You okay?"

Quinn nodded, but she couldn't hide the whole-body quivering that had taken her over.

Even though warm, muggy air was drifting in through the open window, and the house hadn't been all that cool to begin with, she was freezing. "S-so g-glad you f-found me."

"This is Officer Dendler, from the county sheriff's office," Mary said, over her shoulder. "You can thank him for finding this house. Great instincts. We got a tip from an anonymous caller, and once we tracked your phone to the Burger King, a group of area police and sheriffs partnered up to search. We got lucky. Cameras at the library picked up the actual kidnapping, so we've been looking for the van. Somebody in the next block over recognized it."

Dendler yanked on the chains, one-by-one. "Locked up tight. These ain't comin' loose without bolt cutters."

Quinn wanted to jump out of her skin and run. She wouldn't feel safe until she was unchained and out of there. The light outside was diminishing. "What time is it? We've got to hurry. Blackie could be here any minute now."

Mary had left the room, perhaps to search the house, but she'd been listening. She popped her head in the door and said, "Seven o'clock. Who's Blackie?"

"His real name's Lionel French, I think. Either owns or manages Heaven's Door strip club. Probably a murderer, and probably plans to kill me, too."

"We've got to get you out of here." Mary turned to Dendler and said, "You stay here, and I'll run to the squad car for cutters. It's only a few blocks away. I'll be quick. Backup should be here in no time."

"You'd better wait till the backup gets here," Dendler said, but Mary had already taken off, slamming the front door behind her.

The young officer assumed a lookout post at the window, his gun drawn. He kicked the broken glass into a corner. "I'm going to draw these drapes. Don't want to call any more attention to the window than necessary."

He stood in the corner, peering through the crack where the drapes almost came together. "While I'm looking out, let's talk. Tell me everything you know about how you got here and about this guy Blackie."

Chapter Sixty-six

Quinn had barely started to tell the officer about how she was kidnapped outside of the library, when the mechanical whirring of the garage door opener shocked her into silence. She flinched, and her hands flew to her face. "Blackie," she whispered.

"Shit," the officer said. Dendler looked around, as if trying to find a way to hide himself and Quinn. "I'm going to surprise him as he comes in, keep him from getting back here to you. Hopefully, I can hold him off until Hallom and the others get here." With that, Dendler left the room.

Quinn took several deep breaths. The door from the garage to the kitchen squeaked, and the automatic garage door whirred down. Boots thudded on the tile floor, headed her way with an awful rhythm. Quinn gripped the edges of the mattress on both sides, a bird with clipped wings.

"Drop your weapon. Hands over your head." The deputy's voice sounded stronger and meaner than before. There was an immediate scuffle and a gunshot, what sounded like a body falling to the floor, and Quinn shook with fright.

Seconds later, a wild-eyed, gun-toting beast appeared at the bedroom door, but it wasn't Blackie. Quinn swallowed her surprise—it was Norm, and without Nell, he seemed a million times more sinister. He wore the same get-up as earlier, raggedy black sweat pants and T-shirt, boots and a black leather holster. His eyes scanned one side of the room, then the other. "What the fuck's been going on here? A broken window? Some uniform out there? Guess I showed *him* whose damn house this is." He stormed around the room, his boots crunching on broken glass.

Quinn clutched the bed frame and concentrated on breathing. Obviously, Norm had shot Dendler. Outside the bedroom, all was silent. Was the officer still alive? The bed chains dragged heavier than ever at this moment, and she feared for her own life, as well.

Mary and the other officers should be coming soon, but would they realize that Norm was there? He had closed the garage door behind him. If Dendler had failed to protect her, maybe they couldn't, either.

Norm holstered his gun, stomped over to the bedside, and grabbed Quinn by the neck, spewing bad breath. "You've turned out to be more trouble than you're worth. Tell me now. Where did you bury the money?"

Had she heard his gravelly voice correctly? "What money?"

"I mean the ID bracelet. I know the whole story. Your buddy Ana outed ya. Where did y'all bury it?" Norm's obsidian eyes burned into Quinn's, and a nasty glob of spit appeared at the corner of his mouth. "Make it quick. I gotta get out of here before that goon's buddies come after him."

"Where's your lady friend? I'll tell *her*."

"She begged off. She ain't got the stomach for this stuff."

Quinn's own stomach flipped, but she harnessed her fear and pictured turning it into strength. She was certain he planned to shoot her. "What do you intend to do with me? I think I deserve to know that."

"You? You think you're something special? Maybe you are special to somebody. I ain't never had anybody here worth breaking a window for before. But I ain't got time to find out who you know or who sent this idiot in the next room to rescue you. Just tell me where, and I'm outta here."

Norm's urgency to leave gave Quinn an urgency to keep him talking. "You and Blackie are buddies, so tell me something. Last time Blackie was here, he called Ana his niece. That got me thinking. I thought I'd met all of Ana's aunts and uncles, so how come I never met him?"

"Look, I don't have time to chat." He shoved Quinn flat on the bed. "The ID bracelet. Where is it? I can't dig up the whole damn island."

"I figured out that Blackie must be Mr. French's brother. His name's Lionel, right?" Quinn was multi-tasking. Her ears were focused outside of the room. She listened for Mary and the backup officers, as well as for evidence that Dendler was still alive in the next room. How long had it been? Her mind was rushing ahead, trying to think of how she could delay Norm's next step.

"Nobody calls him that. We've all had a thousand names—everyone just calls him Blackie." He walked to the window and peered out.

Quinn held her breath, hoping he wouldn't see any of the police officers. Where were they? Were they surrounding the house, waiting? Maybe they'd heard the gunshot. "So there's money involved. I should've known. Is that why your guys have been following me around town in a dark sedan?"

Norm's jaw clenched and unclenched. "Listen, I'm not up for a hostage situation, and I'm not gonna stand around jawing. Blackie needs to know. Ana wouldn't tell me. Brad wouldn't tell me. You wanna to end up like them? It's up to you. Where. Is. The. I.D. Bracelet. Buried?"

It was now or never. Quinn gulped oxygen and ripped the jeans from around her waist. "I'm not at all like Ana, and I'm certainly nothing like Brad." Disgust roiled in her brain, but a coquettish smile played on her lips. She arched her back and opened her chained legs. Her hands clutched either side of the mattress. "You mentioned money, and I've gathered that your business has plenty of it. To heck with working for my parents in the funeral home. I want some adventure. Can't you put me to work in your empire? I promise I'll more than earn my keep."

Norm's eyes shifted. "Nah. Girls in my business are a dime a dozen. We got plenty."

"Can't ever have too many." Her voice purred. "Besides, I've watched plenty of videos. I know all the best moves."

Norm slapped her knee, hard. "There's just one move I'm interested in from you. Close your legs and open your mouth. Where's the bracelet?" Norm held the pistol to her head.

"Let me just show you what I've got first." Quinn lifted her hips and rocked them, wishing she were anywhere but here. "I insist."

"I'm losing my patience. Tell me now, or say goodbye."

Quinn pouted. "You really know how to hurt a girl's ego." She lowered her hips and pressed her body into the mattress. "Give me one kiss, and I'll whisper the location in your ear."

"Okay, but let's hurry this up." Norm, the stocky man with a bald head and a disgusting smell, bent over his captive and smeared a cold, wet kiss on Quinn's parted lips. And at that moment, Quinn expelled a harsh breath, saying, "*Gedan-zuki*," as her right hand thrust the sturdy plastic knife into Norm's testicles.

Chapter Sixty-seven

The yowl from Norm's mouth must have originated in his soul. The guttural syllables combined with ear-piercing screams into something like, "*Aichhhhh*," and ended with, "You bitch!" The momentum of Quinn's thrust had sent her captor backwards, and he fell on his butt, grabbing his now-bleeding femoral artery.

Shrieking anew, he pulled the knife out of the jagged hole in his sweat pants, ushering a rapid gush of blood. "I'm gonna kill you, you bitch." Holding his genitals with a bloody hand, he wielded his gun with the other.

Quinn shrunk back into a protective ball, knees bent, face into chest, and chained hands protecting the top and back of her head. With nowhere to hide, she awaited the worst. Her eyes were squeezed shut. All sense of time and place went awry, and various images danced wildly through her mind—Ana and Brad kissing in her bedroom, Dawn's murder, Nell's kindness, her parents' special breakfasts, and Josh playing with her curls. Preparing to meet her death, she tried to block out her surroundings.

So she was shocked when a hand clawed at her thigh, and a gunshot blasted the air around her. Was she hit? She was afraid to look, to find out. Then came scuffling and loud voices. Mary shouted, "You're okay, Quinn. You're fine."

Quinn trembled with cold and fear and pent-up adrenalin. The smells of blood and gunpowder comforted, rather than appalled. She lifted her head. Two uniformed officers bent over Norm, who, apparently would wail no more. Another stood at the door, calling for three ambulances. "Two alive. One dead. Sheriff's officer shot in the shoulder. Looks clean." *So Dendler was still alive, wonderful news.*

By this time, Mary, smelling of gunpowder, was hovering over Quinn, asking questions in a soothing voice.

Quinn shook her head, tears running down her face, unable to put words to the nightmare of the past thirty hours. Her only clear thought—she wanted a very long shower.

After making sure that Norm was dead, the other officers left the room, but their voices traveled, and Quinn could tell more had arrived. A husky man with swarthy complexion and plain clothes stuck his head in the door, looked around, and disappeared. After all the silent, solitary hours she had spent here, this hubbub was jarring, but in a good way.

"EMS is on the way, and they need to check you out before anything else. They may need to take you to the hospital. Meanwhile, I'm gonna take some photos of you, the bed, the room. We might need 'em as evidence later on." Mary snapped pictures with her cell phone. Next, she patted Quinn and smiled. "You just rest there. I'm gonna cut off these chains. Don't let the noise bother you."

Mary's sheer upper body strength, combined with loud grunting, powered the bolt cutters to bite through the hardware chaining Quinn's wrists. "Man, these are some heavy chains. You've been incredibly brave."

Quinn stole a glance at Norm's body, amazed at how threatening it had been moments before, and how pitiful and powerless now. "Th-thank you f-for s-saving m-me." Quinn shivered and hiccupped. "I th-thought I w-was going to die."

"Not on my watch. I promised that handsome brother of yours that I'd find you, and I wasn't about to let him down." She cut the second chain loose and dropped it on the floor. As she started on the ankle chains, Mary took a deep breath. "That was some fancy defense work you did, stabbing that creep in the nuts. I ain't never seen anything like that before. How'd you get the knife?"

Quinn thought of Nell, who had taken a big risk to help her. She wondered if she'd ever see her again to thank her. She pointed to the bag with the corned beef sandwich. It'd been tossed near the broken glass by the window. "Found it in that bag from the deli."

"Smart girl. You proved what my grandmother used to say, 'Find the possible in every impossible.' Mary detached the last cuff holding Quinn's ankle to the chain. "Now let's get those pants on you the right way." Mary patted Quinn's leg, above where the shackles had rubbed her skin raw.

A siren wailed in the distance, growing louder as it approached. Activity in the rest of the house gave Quinn a dose of normalcy. Already, she was trying to distance herself from this trauma.

"Well, the nightmare's over now," Mary said. "Won't be long before you'll be in the arms of a certain doctor you know. I'm sure he'll take good care of you.

Lord knows he's been frantic, trying to find you."

The thought of being in Josh's arms, chains or no chains, wrapped Quinn with an imaginary blanket, warm, soft, and comforting. But was the nightmare over? What about Blackie? "I hope Officer Dendler's going to be okay."

"I think he'll be fine. Many officers have survived clean shots through the shoulder." Mary turned, as footsteps approached the doorway. "Oh, here's EMS now."

Quinn sat up on her elbows as two paramedics entered, one female and one male. The female strode to the side of the bed and knelt on one knee. "My name's Lesley. Okay if my partner and I take your vitals, ask you some questions?"

Quinn nodded. Except for hygiene issues, she felt fine, but she wasn't in charge, and, having never been in this situation before, she'd have to follow whatever protocols were in place. She trusted Mary's judgment, and maybe even Lesley's.

When Quinn said she wasn't hurting anywhere except on her wrists and ankles, where the shackles had chafed her skin, and she hadn't been physically or sexually abused, the paramedics lightened up a little. "Blood pressure's a little high, but mine would be, too, if I'd-a-been through all this." Lesley gestured to include the broken glass, the chains, and the dead body, lying in an ocean of dark blood.

Quinn felt a smile rising from her diaphragm to her lips. "In my line of work, we'd say, 'Business is looking up'."

"What d'ya do for a living?"

"I'm a mortician."

Quinn's profession opened the door for conversation about who knew whom in the business. It turned out Lesley's EMS partner, Henry, was a first cousin once removed of Rory, who worked at McFarland's.

By this time, a team of EMS had loaded Dendler into an ambulance and taken off for the nearest hospital, siren on. Mary, who had stepped out for a few minutes, returned. "What's the deal? Are we going to the hospital, or the station?"

Lesley turned to Quinn. "Usually in a situation like this, even though your vitals are practically normal, we take victims to the hospital. They clean you up, run some tests, observe you for a few hours, make sure there aren't any underlying injuries." Looking at Mary, she said, "'Specially if there's a need to gather evidence."

Quinn had no desire to stretch out the ordeal any longer than necessary. "I'm feeling fine, and I'll be even better when I can get showered and get some ointment on my skin."

"Okay with me," Mary said. "I've got the photographs I need. Let's bag your hands." She pulled two plastic baggies from a pocket and held one out for Quinn's hand. "We'll tie this above where your skin is raw. Now let's get outta here and let these good people deal with the body. You feel strong enough to walk?"

Quinn stood, turning away from Norm's miserable corpse. She stretched her back and legs, taking a few wobbly steps toward the bedroom door. The weight of the chains still dragged on her limbs, even though they had all been removed. She was reminded of being submerged in the Gulf up to her neck, trudging her way to shore.

"I should warn you. We're going to have a lot of questions for you at the station," Mary said, as they walked past the EMS workers and nodded to the other officers.

"As long as my attorney, David Becker, approves, I'll be happy to answer them."

Despite needing food, drink, a long, hot shower, and a good night's sleep, Quinn was filled with a kind of euphoria. She was thankful for so many things—the strength of her muscles, the people who cared enough about her to help, the perfect timing of her rescue, and the end of this ordeal. Most of all, as she plodded out of the house and into the warm, summer night, she felt the exhilaration of freedom. Nothing could spoil this, not even the fact that Blackie was still out there somewhere.

Chapter Sixty-eight

Quinn's jubilation over being free was tempered once she reached the police station. While she hadn't expected a welcoming party, she was disappointed that Josh wasn't there. On the other hand, a whole slew of police officers had gathered, despite the hour on a Sunday night, and Sergeant Schmidt was purportedly on his way. Recovering a live kidnap victim was apparently cause for celebration, with raucous cheers and congratulations raining on Mary as she escorted Quinn to the evidence area. Quinn wanted to enjoy the spirited reception, but the physical memory of the chains and the trauma of her narrow escape hung on. She couldn't even manage a smile.

Once they reached the quiet of the evidence room, Mary sat across from Quinn at a table. "I know you want a shower, and fresh clothes, but we need to do a couple of procedural things first." She took a deep breath and exhaled. "And, being that this is such a big case—multiple murders and a kidnapping—I'm not in charge. Sergeant Schmidt'll be here soon. Since you're technically both a victim and a suspect, he'll need to read you your rights and ask you some questions."

Quinn cringed at the thought of having to face Schmidt again, especially under these new circumstances, but she did a double-take at the word, *suspect*. "What? This is ridiculous." A hot wave of anger surged through her, and her legs twitched with the impulse to run. "After all I've been through, you still suspect me?"

Mary threw her hands in the air. "Hey, don't shoot the messenger. He just needs to clear up a few items, and then we can concentrate on catching the bad guys. Okay?"

"Hmph, I thought we left the bad guy on the floor back there." Quinn inspected her sore wrists, wincing as she flexed them. "Does Chief Ramirez know what's happened to me? Does my father?"

"They do. They've been in touch regularly since you disappeared. Your brother and your boyfriend, too. Anyway, I'll be sticking around to assist, since you'll need a female, and I'm still on duty."

Quinn had a hard time believing she had been locked up in that house for only one day. It had seemed like a year. And now she had to worry about being locked up by the police? "Hold up, Mary. I'm not saying or doing anything without my lawyer, David Becker. Somebody better call him right away."

"That's fine," Mary said, apparently not surprised by the request. "I'm sure he'll tell you this is just routine." She handed her cell phone to Quinn. "Go ahead and call. Remember, it's Sunday night."

The time on the cell phone was 9:03, not a great time to call an attorney, but Quinn had no choice. She started to tap Becker's name into the contacts, but realized she needed her own phone to get his cell number. "You have my cell phone here?"

"Locked up in evidence."

"Well, I'll have to call my dad, then. I don't know Becker's cell phone number by heart." Glad, for once, to be living in a small town where people had each other's numbers, Quinn pressed her parents' home number and hit "send."

Her father answered on the first ring. "Mary, do you have news?"

"Dad, it's Quinn. I'm safe at the police station. I need to call Becker to come right away. You have his private number, don't you?"

"Thank God, you're safe. We've all been so worried. Mom and I wanted to meet you at the station, but the chief told us not to. Do you want us to come now?"

A smile bubbled up in Quinn's chest, in spite of everything. "No, Dad. I need *Mr. Becker* to come. I'll call you when things are a little more settled." *When will that be? I need my phone, my keys, my car, my Josh...*

Her dad promised to call the attorney. "If I don't reach him, or he can't come, I'll call back on this number."

The knot in Quinn's gut loosened. She disconnected and returned the phone to Mary. She was beginning to put together a timeline of events in her mind. "You said you got a tip about my location. Male or female?" It had to've been Nell, but Quinn didn't want to rat on the one person responsible for saving her life.

"Let me do my job right now. Time for questions later." She pointed to a door with an opaque glass panel. "Over there is the shower. There's a locker in there with stacks of clean scrubs for you to choose from. But before you go in there, we need to gather evidence from your person and the clothes you have on."

"What do you mean? What kind of evidence?"

"Hairs, skin, fibers—that kind of thing. I'll be here to assist, if you want, but a female evidence tech will actually work with you." Mary pulled the edge of a roll of white butcher paper from its serrated holder and tore a wide sheet off. She set the paper on the floor under the light canister near the door to the shower room. Then she removed a clear plastic package from one of the cabinets on that wall.

Quinn shuddered at the sight of a comb, brush, plastic gloves, nail scissors, and some test tubes. She had a feeling she was about to be processed, and this was no spa.

Quinn's stomach growled. "This'll have to wait until Becker gets here." As much as she appreciated Mary for rescuing her, this insistence on protocols was getting on her nerves. Why couldn't she shower and get on with her life?

"You must be hungry, girl. I wish I could offer you food and drink, but we can't let you eat until we get the samples. How 'bout a cup of water?"

Now that she thought about food, she'd consider anything a feast, and she said so. Her throat was parched, and her temples throbbed. But left alone, when Mary went to the break room, Quinn freaked out. Even without the chains tying her to the bed, she was still a prisoner, unable to go where she wanted, eat what she wanted. When would this end?

Mary returned a few minutes later with a large cup of iced water. Quinn was thirsty, so she cooperated.

Mary stared at Quinn as she downed the water in big gulps. Tiny red lines streaked the whites of Mary's long-lashed eyes. This shift had been stressful for her, too. After all, a man had died.

"How's my brother?" Quinn asked between swallows.

"Better, now that you're found and safe. He's been a wreck."

That reminded Quinn. "Listen. The key to Jack's house was in my handbag. Probably a good idea to change the locks first thing tomorrow."

"You can tell him, yourself. I'm pretty sure that Calvin, the guard dog, has been keeping him safe, though. That pup's been going crazy, waiting on you to come home."

Mention of Calvin brought tears to Quinn's eyes. She'd imagined his warm, furry body and his frenetic enthusiasm while chained to the bed. She couldn't wait to see the little guy.

After Quinn finished drinking, she leaned back in her chair and closed her eyes. A knock at the door brought her back to the moment, and she smiled as David Becker entered the room, dressed in a flowered sport shirt and khaki slacks, and smelling like summer barbecue. She considered running to give him a bear hug, but that wouldn't be professional. Instead, she gave him her hands as he reached for them and squeezed.

"You have no idea how happy I am to see you, my dear. I've been hopin' and prayin' you were all right, and it seems you are."

He turned to Mary Hallom and introduced himself, extending a suntanned hand to shake.

After all the pleasantries, Mary took the lead. "Appreciate your coming out on a Sunday night. Sergeant Schmidt's in charge of this case. I expect him any minute. We're all set to gather evidence from Quinn's person, but she wouldn't cooperate without you."

"Exactly right." He nodded in Quinn's direction, then turned back to Mary. "Are you gathering evidence from my client as a victim or a suspect?"

"At the moment, both. I tried to explain that I needed to read her her rights, but if her story matches what we already have, we'll be able to eliminate her as a suspect and send her home tonight."

"She wants to strip search me and take samples, too. Do I have to do that?" Quinn hugged herself, as if she were already naked.

Becker turned to Mary. "Can you give me a few minutes alone with my client?" He held a hand up to signal quiet, while Mary left the room and closed the door.

"'Course I understand you might be uncomfortable with the process, Quinn, but I'm sure Officer Hallom and the evidence technician will do everything in their power to respect your dignity and privacy. Technically, they have to get a warrant to search your person, unless you waive and submit to the search. Getting a warrant could take hours, maybe overnight." His eyebrows furrowed, and he scratched his head. "Since you tell me you're innocent of any wrongdoing, and I believe you, it's probably best to help the police do their job. Since you've spent the last thirty hours in the company of criminals, there's a reasonable expectation that there's evidence on your person. I suggest you cooperate."

Quinn sighed. "Okay, but what about the questioning?"

"Same thing. I'll stay out front while you do this first part. I'll see if I can pry loose whatever they have in the way of evidence. After you've showered and changed clothes, I'll come back in for the questions.

Hopefully, we can get through all this and get you home for a good night's sleep."

Quinn hadn't expected Becker to ride in on a white horse and save her from all unpleasantries, but she wasn't looking forward to a single second of "this first part." She took a deep breath and tried to focus on the promised shower and clean clothes. "All right. It's late. Let's get this show on the road."

Chapter Sixty-nine

Quinn wondered out loud how long this evidence-gathering procedure would take. Though it was embarrassing to disrobe on butcher paper in this screened-off area, and have someone probe and brush and scrape each body part, Quinn had to admit that Penny, the technician, had a swift and light touch.

"I try to go as fast as I can without making mistakes." Penny unbagged Quinn's hands and used the scissors to gather particles from around her cuticles and under her fingernails. "Sometimes these are a gold mine for important evidence."

Penny had dismissed Mary to do other tasks. Neither Quinn nor Penny needed an audience, and it was almost better, less personal and more clinical, having a complete stranger "process" her.

"I still wonder whose DNA you're looking for." Quinn thought of the times that Nell had touched her hands or wrist. "The guy who tried to kill me is dead at the scene. You can get all the DNA you want from him."

"I don't know. I'm just a tech, but my experience, bad guys don't work alone." Penny put the tools back in the plastic bag and stood back. "You're all done now. Leave your clothes right here on the paper and go on into the shower. There's towels and fresh scrubs in that first locker." Before Quinn could reply, Penny wrapped up the clothes in the butcher paper, forming a neat package and bagging it to take to the evidence lab.

While showering, Quinn thought about her discarded clothes and sandals. She'd most likely never see them again. Probably a good thing. They would always remind her of the worst time of her life. Her purse and cell phone—those she would miss more. It would be a hassle to replace everything, but she could do that. Right now, she wanted to enjoy the stinging spray of hot water and the astringent scent of the body wash and shampoo. She had earned those luxuries.

Ah, she could stay in this shower forever, letting the tensions melt off her body and swirl down the drain. But Becker was waiting, and Schmidt, and if the grilling she was about to endure didn't carry on too late, maybe Josh. She could always shower again if and when she got home.

After drying off and donning pale blue scrubs and a pair of flimsy slides, Quinn finger-combed through her curls and walked back into the evidence room, where Mary was waiting with a "meal" of peanut butter crackers and a can of Sprite. Quinn tore into the first of five packages and popped an aromatic disk into her mouth, whole. Delicious. Ignoring Mary, she abandoned all table manners as she gobbled and slurped. She was working on the last package when a knock at the door startled her, and Sergeant Schmidt leaned in, with Becker peeking over his shoulder.

Schmidt's gums gleamed brighter and pinker than ever. Whether he smiled because he finally had Quinn where he wanted her, or whether he was genuinely happy she'd been rescued, Quinn wasn't charmed.

"Well, there you are, safe and sound, and we're all grateful." Schmidt crooked his finger, inviting Quinn to follow. "Let's head for the interrogation room—no, I'll tell ya what—since it's Sunday, we can use Chief Ramirez's conference room." He led the way down a green-painted hallway and turned left where it dead-ended.

Behind his back, Becker gave a thumbs-up. For the millionth time, Quinn congratulated herself on hiring Becker. His support sent warm sparks through her veins. Maybe this wouldn't be so bad.

Flicking on the fluorescent lights, Schmidt pointed to a table and six chairs. The room was nice enough, institutional green, with four windows, the blinds of which were drawn closed. On the table were a pitcher of water and six glasses, and a box of tissues. "Have a seat. I understand you've had quite a night."

Quinn gave a tiny nod in Schmidt's direction, then made eye contact with her attorney.

Becker held up a hand. "Before we get started on the questioning, I'd like a few minutes alone with my client."

"Why, sure," Schmidt said, scooting his chair away from the table with a screech. "Ten minutes?"

Becker nodded and leaned in close to Quinn, as Schmidt left the room and closed the door. "It's a good sign that Schmidt's questioning you here, instead of the interrogation room. There, they'd be videotaping you, treating you more like a suspect. You know a woman named Nell Blanchard?"

Quinn straightened and stared at the attorney. Icy prickles traveled down her arms and into her hands, and her nails matched her blue scrubs. Raynaud's kicking in. "I might. What does she look like?"

"I don't know. I haven't seen her. But a friend slipped me information that the police have her locked up here in protective custody. She's talked to them about this case."

"What do you mean, 'protective custody'? Is she in trouble?" Quinn shoved her hands under her thighs to warm them.

"She's giving the police information in return for their protection. They're keeping her safe in jail, but they're not treating her like she's under arrest. So you know who she is?"

Quinn nodded. "She's an exotic dancer who helped kidnap me from the library parking lot. But then she *helped* me. If it hadn't been for her, I'd be dead by now."

"Makes sense. If she's turned on the kidnappers, she needs police protection. Not only from the bad guys, but from prosecution for her own crime in aiding and abetting. What the police will be looking for is your corroboration of what she's told them."

"She helped me, and I want to return the favor, but how do I know what she's told them?"

"Just tell the truth. The truth, as they say, will set you free."

* * *

Ten minutes later, on the dot, Schmidt entered the conference room, smelling of coffee. Maybe he needed the stimulant to stay sharp this late at night, or maybe he planned a long questioning session ahead. Quinn hoped not, but none of this was in her control.

Schmidt ignored the chief's desk and executive chair and sat at the head of the table. "If you're ready, let's get started." Schmidt pulled his cell phone from his pocket. "We're going to run an audiotape of this interview." He looked toward Becker as he punched a button. Then he fixed his gaze on Quinn. "You have the right—"

Becker waved his hand to stifle the sergeant. "No need to read my client her rights. She'll consider herself warned from the last time we met. Let's not waste precious time here."

Schmidt huffed. "Okay, then. Let's start with the kidnapping on Saturday. We know the when and where—in the parking lot of the library at 1:17 p.m.

So tell us about the who and how."

Quinn hated to relive this ordeal, but she'd never get out of here until she did. At least she didn't have to worry about protecting Nell. In a way, she was speaking for Dawn and Ana and Brad, as well as herself. Giving voice to her story might be therapeutic on several levels.

"When I came out of the library, I wasn't paying attention to anything but my growling stomach. I was thinking about what to eat for lunch. A blonde woman suddenly grabbed me by the arm and dragged me to the back of a van, parked next to my car. A man was waiting there, and the two of them took my purse and shoved me into the back compartment."

"Do you know the identities of these two? Had you ever seen them before?"

"I didn't know their names, but I'd seen them at Heartbeat Cabaret a few nights earlier. The man worked the door, and the woman was a dancer."

"Did you learn their names later?"

"I don't think the people in that industry use real names, but I heard the woman call the guy Norm. Later on, the woman told me her name was Nell. She was kind to me."

"Did you know then, or do you know now, why you were being kidnapped?"

"I figured it had to do with the break-in at my house, the threat not to talk. Maybe someone knew I'd received the tapes from Ana, knew I'd been talking to you. There'd been other instances of stalking, as you know, so I was on edge. But that wasn't it—that wasn't the whole reason, anyway."

"Let's back up a minute. Investigators found you chained to a bed, naked from the waist down, in a residence at 5725 Rose Lane, Seaside, Texas. At any time during your captivity, were you physically harmed in any way, sexually or otherwise?"

Quinn gazed at her wrists, raw and oozing. "No permanent damage. Nothing other than my wrists and ankles, and maybe some bruises. Nobody touched me sexually."

"Why were your pants removed?"

"Probably so I could use the portable toilet. Or maybe to intimidate me. I *was* intimidated, for sure."

"Okay, you said there was another reason for the kidnapping. What was it?"

Quinn looked to Becker. He was tilting back in his chair, hands clasped across his middle, apparently not concerned about the questioning at this point. "Well, I told you about the two people who took me away, but they were acting under orders from Blackie. I'm pretty sure he's the mastermind."

"What do you know about this Blackie? Who is he, and why was he after you?"

Thinking about Blackie caused knots to form in her stomach, and peanut butter to rise in her throat. Glancing at Becker, Quinn coughed. "Not sure, but I think Blackie owns or manages Heaven's Door and Heartbeat Cabaret—maybe others, too. He's the same guy from the sex videos Ana sent me. His name was Keith Underwood then. He's older now, and he's had his ears pinned back surgically, but he's the same guy." Quinn reached for one of the glasses and the water pitcher.

Quinn poured a glass and took a few swallows. "Blackie showed up in the wee hours of Sunday morning. He let it slip that Ana was his niece. I thought about that for a while and figured out his real name was French. Lionel French. I thought he kidnapped me because I knew too much about things he'd done in the past, but that wasn't right. Maybe he wanted to ship me away as a sex slave. Other women had been chained to that bed until he could get them on a boat to some foreign country. But, no. Blackie wanted me to tell him the location of a gold identification bracelet."

Schmidt perked up. Apparently, this was new information. "Tell me everything you know about this ID bracelet."

Becker, too, leaned forward, elbows on the table. "Sergeant, I need to halt this interview right now, so I can speak with my client privately."

"Again?" Schmidt stopped the taping, his forehead and eyebrows drawn tight. "At this rate we'll be here all night."

"Sorry, Sergeant. Either you walk through the door now, or my client and I do."

"Okay, okay. I'll be back to check on you in ten minutes." He pocketed his cell phone and left the room, closing the door with a firm *whump*.

Becker huddled with Quinn. "You need to tell me everything about this ID bracelet and why it was so important to Blackie. Before you share information with Schmidt, I need to hear all the gritty details. Otherwise, you might implicate yourself in a crime."

Quinn understood. How could she answer the question of why Blackie had kidnapped her without explaining her role in hiding the bracelet? Once again, she was grateful for Becker.

"I would have told you before, but I'd forgotten all about the bracelet until Blackie asked me."

"That's all right. Tell me now."

Quinn looked into Becker's owlish eyes and revealed everything.

* * *

When Schmidt returned, in addition to the smell of coffee, he wore a look of annoyance. Becker stood and tapped his fingers on the conference table. The clock on the wall read 11:15.

"Sergeant, I'm afraid we're going to have to postpone the rest of your interview. My client has shared information with me that is pertinent to your investigations of the murders of Dawn Chrysler, and Ana and Brad Renfroe. She is willing to share this information with you, but not before she is granted immunity from prosecution for any crimes which she may or may not have committed."

Schmidt's chin dropped. "You know I won't be able to get to the district attorney this late at night. And they're gonna want to know what she has before they issue immunity."

Becker nodded. "Of course. You set up the meeting, and I'll be there with a proffer, describing the nature of the evidence Ms. McFarland will provide. In the meantime, can we arrange to have police protection for her as she gathers clothes and personal items and checks into a hotel for the evening? Among other things, I believe she deserves a good night's sleep."

Quinn had been listening to the volleys between lawman and lawyer, but she struggled to keep her eyes open and her head erect. At this moment she was ready to take a nap on the conference room table. Becker's suggestion about putting her up in a hotel didn't thrill her. She raised her hand, as if in school. "Can I offer an alternative? How about I go to my brother's house, where my clothes are, and I spend the night there? Police can keep an eye on the house, and we save the cost of the hotel."

Becker glanced at Schmidt. "What do you think?"

Schmidt gave the broadest gum-showing smile of the evening. "I think we can manage that. The chief will be all for saving taxpayers' money." He ambled toward the door. "I'll make the arrangements, and I'll be in touch, hopefully early in the morning." Before he left, he turned back. "And, by the way, I think we all deserve a good night's sleep."

Chapter Seventy

Becker escorted Quinn to Officer Hallom's car, waiting to take her to Jack's for the night. Another officer would follow in the squad car.

"Do you need directions to my brother's house?" Quinn asked Mary. The joy of being able to joke about something bubbled up in her like sweet champagne.

"Ha, ha," Mary said. She reached into her pocket for her cell phone. "Here, why don't you call him to tell him you're coming?"

"Good idea. Maybe I should call my parents and Josh, too. They're probably all waiting for news."

"They've all been notified of your rescue by the police. We do that right away, but I'm sure they want to hear your voice."

Missing her own cell phone, she'd started to key in Jack's number when Mary cleared her throat. "Jack's in the contacts."

Quinn yawned and smiled. Evidently the romance had been progressing. She called Jack, and then her parents, who were exuberant but full of questions and concerns, despite the late hour. Quinn promised to talk more the next day. By then they were almost at Jack's, and it was nearly 1:30 in the morning. She decided to wait till she got settled and use Jack's phone to text Josh. Mondays he usually had early shift. He was probably asleep by now. She was practically asleep, herself.

When Mary turned onto Jack's street, welcoming light was pouring out of his open front door, and Jack was sitting on the front stoop with Calvin in his lap. Mary pulled to a stop in the driveway, and Calvin leaped from the stoop and flew to the open passenger door to greet his mistress.

"What a reunion!" Quinn squealed, between licks on her face. She laughed so hard, tears running down her cheeks. "I missed you, too, buddy." After a thousand pets and licks, Quinn set Calvin down on the grass. She darted across the lawn to hug her brother, marveling over how light and free she felt with no chains, no sling bag, no cell phone, nothing to tie her down. She squeezed her brother as if she'd been gone a year, ignoring the soreness of her wrists, and as they hugged, they laughed and cried at the same time.

"Oh, am I pressing on your incision?" She stepped back and inspected Jack's robe-clad body.

"No worries. I'm almost healed." Jack waved to Mary, inviting her into the house. "Thanks for taking care of my sister."

Quinn looked from one to the other of them as they settled into the living room sofa and chairs. "She saved my life, you know."

"I can't stay more than a minute. I've been on duty since noon yesterday, and I've got to get some sleep." She kissed Jack on the lips, then turned to Quinn. "As for saving your life, I can't take all the credit. You did a lot of the hard work to save yourself. I just came in at the finish line."

"For which I'll be eternally grateful," Quinn said.

"Me, too." Jack put his arm around Mary's shoulder. "Do either of you want some chicken and spaghetti? I heated it up once I knew you were on the way."

"Can I take it to go? I'm about to collapse."

Quinn sniffed and peered into the kitchen. "That's what smells so divine. I'm starving, but first, can I borrow your cell phone? I want to text Josh. Then food. Then sleep."

Jack handed a plastic-covered plate to Mary. As she carried it toward the front door, he gave her a playful pat.

As Mary left, Jack tossed his cell phone to Quinn. "Keep it as long as you like. I'm staying close to home, and I've got the landline." He set out the plate of food, silverware, and a glass of ice water for his sister, and yawned. "If you don't mind, I'm going to go to sleep. Calvin's been walked for the night, and you can stay up as late as you want."

"I'll be right behind you," Quinn replied. "I'm exhausted." She sat down at the table and thought about what to say in her text to Josh. How grateful she was to be alive? How much she loved him? How she couldn't wait to see him tomorrow? So many things she had taken for granted.

She looked at the food Jack had set out for her, the first real meal she had seen in more than two days. Though she hadn't been one to say grace before meals, at this moment, Quinn was filled with a need to communicate her gratitude to a Higher Power. Here she was, alive and strong, surrounded by people (and a dog) who loved her, with access to everything in life she needed. She bent her head and prayed, took a bite, and then texted to

Josh: Safe at Jack's. Miss u and luv u. I'm sure you're asleep now, and I'm practically asleep too. Talk tomorrow.

She devoured the plate of food and rinsed the dish and fork. Padding over to the front window, she peered out at the squad car across the street. "C'mon, Calvin," Quinn called, scooping him into her arms and heading for her bedroom, the cell phone in her pocket.

Quinn had no sooner snuggled into the bed with Calvin and the cell phone by her side, than she heard a ping, a text from Josh: Just woke up and saw yr text. Sleep tight, my love. Can't wait to see you.

Quinn couldn't think of a better lullaby. With that thought, she closed her eyes and went off to a deep, though still-troubled dream land.

Chapter Seventy-one

The next morning both Quinn and Calvin slept in. Not until Calvin stirred did the aroma of pancakes and warm maple syrup cause Quinn to open her eyes and check the time on Jack's cell phone—9:58. She jumped out of bed and pulled on a pair of denim shorts and a tie-front top. "Can't believe we slept this long, Calvin. Let's get you outside. Then my turn in the bathroom."

She opened the door to the sight of her brother's back, standing at the stove, wearing cut-off sweatpants and a T-shirt, and flipping a pancake with wild abandon. "Having fun? I didn't know you were the culinary type."

"Don't hurt my feelings. Men can be creative in the kitchen, too. Anyway, I need to pay you back for the smoothies you brought me in the hospital."

"I've got to take Calvin out. Be right back."

Jack slid the cooked pancake to the top of a stack next to the stove and turned off the heat, then moved the stack of pancakes into the oven. "Let me do that. Calvin and I have our routine down pat. You go tend to yourself."

"You sure?" Much as she didn't feel comfortable being waited on and cooked for, she *did* have to use the restroom.

Already out the door, Jack left Quinn to her morning hygiene and getting ready for breakfast. She couldn't get over how much healthier and happier he was since his transplant and new girlfriend. Stars certainly seemed to be aligning for him, and, once this police investigation was over, maybe they would for her, too.

Quinn couldn't resist taking a quick shower before brushing her teeth and blow drying her hair. The hot shower spray stung on her abraded wrists and ankles, but she could tell they had already begun healing. She was starting to feel human again, but more grateful than before, especially for little things. How refreshing to have minty-fresh breath and clean hair, clean clothes, and a pancake breakfast warming in the oven.

"Ready to eat?" On the table, two placemats were set with utensils, two glasses of orange juice, and two mugs. "Didn't know whether you'd want tea, since it's a scorcher outside already."

"I'm never too hot to drink tea, but sit down. I'll get it, myself. In fact, I should be waiting on you." Calvin padded at Quinn's feet, as she fixed her Earl Grey and set it on the table. Then she peered out the front window. "Police are still outside, I see."

"Come sit down and eat. You'll need your strength."

Jack sounded so much like their mother that Quinn laughed out loud. "Yes, Joy McFarland, Junior." She served herself pancakes and topped them with butter and sweet maple syrup, hot from the microwave. "Yum, these are better than Mom's. You'll have to share your recipe." After a few bites, Quinn put down her fork. "I wish I didn't need police protection. The guy who kidnapped me is dead, you know." *Of course, there's still Blackie.*

"Don't let that give you a false sense of security, Quinn. As Mary explained it to me, cases like this, there's usually multiple people responsible. She couldn't tell me details, of course, but I got the impression that the police are looking at a much bigger picture. If they want to protect you, I say you *need* protection."

Sipping her tea, enjoying the way its bite washed away the cloying sweetness of the maple syrup, Quinn thought about Blackie. Who knew how many others had been kidnapped and chained to that bed? Or for what reasons? And while Norm had practically confessed to killing Ana, and maybe even Brad, she was sure Blackie was behind it, and he was still alive. "I guess you're right, but I want to get back to a normal life. What's happened to my car? Is it still at the library? I need to go back home, to work, and, most of all, to see Josh. I need to replace my cell phone and all my identification. Oh, that reminds me, the keys to both of our houses were in my sling bag."

"We should get our locks re-keyed. Maybe we can get a two-for-one deal. I'll call Rudy and see what we can set up."

Quinn cleared her dishes and Jack's. "I'll do the dishes if you make a to-do list."

"What about your wrists? How 'bout I do the dishes?"

Quinn giggled. "Remember how we used to bicker, trying to get *out* of doing the dishes?"

* * *

Thirty minutes later, David Becker sat down at Jack's kitchen table, across from Quinn. Jack had left to meet the locksmith at Quinn's house, giving them privacy to review the proffer Becker was planning to present to the district attorney in a bid for Quinn's immunity.

"As I explained over the phone, this document is a statement of what you will testify to under oath. I'll submit this to the police and district attorney. Hopefully, they'll consider the information of sufficient value, and they'll agree to present a grant of immunity to the district judge. After the judge approves it, you can answer Schmidt's questions."

As Quinn started to review the proffer, Becker instructed her to pay close attention to the factual statements related to her actions on the night of Dawn's murder. "You need to be sure every statement is accurate, and you can testify to each one under oath."

Reading the document caused the pancakes to flip around in her stomach. There was nothing inaccurate, but seeing the events of June 27, 2004, in black and white on the page crossed a new threshold for her in facing the past.

Quinn swallowed hard. "I'm taking a big chance here. That ID bracelet Ana and I buried is what I believe got Ana killed. Maybe Brad, too."

"Yes, but the police are taking a chance, too. What if it turned out that you *were* the killer? They would have given you a 'Get Out of Jail Free' card. In this case, they have as much to lose as you do." Becker's unibrow look was softened by the pat he gave to Quinn's shoulder. "Trust me. They wouldn't be giving you police protection and signing this document unless they needed your help. They aren't about to let the bad guys get to you again."

Quinn jumped up and paced around the small island in the kitchen. "That's what I don't understand. Blackie's the only bad guy I need to worry about. Why don't they arrest him and get him off the street? Maybe then I can go back to living my life. In fact, where's my car?"

Scooting his chair back, but remaining seated, Becker tapped the table. "I know you have a lot of questions, and a lot of energy, too, but please sit down. This is important." Once Quinn took her seat, he continued. "I understand you're impatient for things to return to normal. You've been through a lot. But you can't change the situation with the wave of a magic wand, and sometimes these things take days or even weeks. The police impounded your car to check for evidence. You may get it back today, but that won't mean you can return to your typical activities."

"So, I'm basically in jail, albeit a nice one. Is that what you're saying?"

"Police protection is expensive and rarely provided. Sergeant Schmidt and the officers on duty wouldn't appreciate your going around here or there while they're assigned to watch you. Besides, if you're granted immunity, they're going to want to talk to you pretty quickly. You need to be ready for that."

"So much for getting together with Josh." Quinn muttered the words while, inside, a yearning for Josh's physical presence welled up like a geyser, about to erupt.

Becker patted her shoulder again. "For the next little while, I suggest your young man visit you here in this house. And, as for arresting Blackie, the police need your help to do that. First things first. Let's get the immunity."

Knowing better than to fight against her lawyer's advice, Quinn slumped in her chair, her hopes for a return to normalcy any time soon withering away by the minute. "Okay. You've never steered me wrong, and I'm not going to do anything foolish."

"Hopefully you won't need police protection too much longer. Now let me go present this proffer."

Jack's cell phone rang as Becker slid the document into his briefcase and headed for the door. Quinn's landline number showed on the screen. Swiping, she said, "Jack? What's up?"

"I think you'd better get over here quick. Somebody's broken in, and the house is a wreck."

Chapter Seventy-two

Quinn called Sergeant Schmidt to report the break-in at her house. He arranged to meet her there. Officer Porter, the patrolman on duty at Jack's house, drove Quinn to hers. When they pulled up to the curb, Schmidt was standing on the front lawn in the oven-like mugginess, talking to Jack and Mrs. Tartt, with Duffy barking incessantly at her heels.

Quinn took a deep breath before she left the squad car. Hadn't it been enough trauma to have been kidnapped and assaulted, to have stabbed a man with a knife and watched as he was shot and died, to have been strip-searched and prodded for evidence? Her dreams of going back to a normal existence were evaporating in the summer heat. She feared she was in for another ugly surprise. But, hey, she was alive—and what if she had been staying at her own house when someone broke in? Whatever wreckage she would find inside, she and Calvin were fine.

She thanked Officer Porter for the ride and strode toward the little group. Duffy tugged on his leash, barking, as if relating the whole story to Quinn. When she came close enough, she squatted to pet the burly black pooch, and he licked her hands. "I wish you could talk, Duffy. I'd bet you'd have a lot to say." Quinn addressed the group. "Why are we standing out here in the heat?"

"My fault, I guess," her neighbor replied. "Duffy was barkin' up a storm, and I saw the police car outside. I wanted to tell y'all about last night. Duffy started barking around ten and kept a-goin' for about an hour. I looked through my bedroom curtains. Didn't see nobody in the yard, no cars on the street. I saw lights on in your bathroom and front room, so I figured you was back at home. We hadn't seen you or Calvin for a couple of days."

Before Quinn could frame a reply, Schmidt took over. "Thank you for your vigilance, Mrs. Tartt. The police, and I'm sure Quinn here, are grateful to have observant citizens. We may ask you some more questions, but right now, we need to check out the house."

Mrs. Tartt scooped Duffy up into her arms and moseyed across the yard toward her own front door, muttering something about a safe neighborhood.

Schmidt turned to Officer Porter and said, "You stay out here with Mr. McFarland. Make a list of all the surfaces he touched when he was inside." He nodded in Jack's direction, and then motioned to Quinn to lead the way inside. As she moved toward the porch steps, he stopped her, pulling pairs of gloves and booties out of his pocket. "We both need to wear these. Please don't touch or move anything. I need to remind you, this is a crime scene."

As she put on the protective garments, taking care not to press on the tender flesh of her wrists and ankles, Quinn said, "I thought you'd be at the meeting with the district attorney." She still wasn't comfortable being around Schmidt, but at this moment, she was glad to have police support, even his.

"No, Chief Ramirez went." He sat on the front steps, while he bootied up. "As we walk through, I want you to pay attention to whether or not anything is missing. Your brother says the whole place's been ransacked."

Quinn hugged herself as she tiptoed across the threshold, into the small entry hall. She hadn't planned to speak to Sergeant Schmidt until Becker got immunity. One look, and Quinn gasped at the chaotic destruction that has been her home. Furniture had been overturned, upholstered pillows tossed about. The musty smell of dust-covered corners hung in the air. The contents of the entry hall closet had been scattered onto the floor, blocking the path to the kitchen area. The living area was strewn with pulled-out drawers and magazines dumped from a rack. Quinn wanted to scream at the top of her lungs. Seeing her possessions in such disarray caused her insides to burn with outrage.

"Who could have done this? And how did they get in without setting off the burglar alarm?" She'd been so careful to set the alarm every time she left, and she was sure she had set it the last time. Two days ago? It felt like eons.

Behind her, Schmidt whistled. "Professionals have ways of by-passing even the best alarm systems." He slid past Quinn into the messy interior. "You can't take two steps without bumping into something." Turning back to take Quinn's hand, Schmidt helped her step over a lamp.

In the kitchen, pantry items had been swept to the floor. Even her precious orchid plants had been dumped out of their pots. Dishes and pots and pans were strewn everywhere, but it didn't appear any were broken. The burning inside of Quinn had turned into a full-blown blaze. It would take days of hard work to restore order to her home, and, maybe, years to erase the memory of this violation of her property.

Schmidt had asked her a question. "…looking for?"

Quinn kept moving, stepping over objects, and trying not to jostle anything as she went past. She assumed her bedroom and bathroom had been similarly destroyed, and, as much as she didn't want to see another ugly scene, a strong impulse pushed her in that direction.

"I said, any guesses what these guys were looking for?" Schmidt called from behind her.

Quinn shrugged as she entered her bedroom. As bad as the mess was in the other parts of the house, this room was the worst. Every item from her closet had been tossed on the floor or on her bed—clothes, shoes, accessories, even the scrapbook. The bed itself had been stripped of its coverings, and pillows were jumbled on the floor beside it. Dresser and night table drawers had been yanked from their cases and rifled. The thought of someone's touching her underwear brought a shiver.

A jewelry box, sitting on the dresser, was open, its contents having been dumped on the dresser top. A few necklaces, bracelets, and pairs of earrings covered the maple finish, but nothing stood out as being missing. Still, it was hard to tell since nothing was in its rightful place.

Schmidt followed Quinn like a shadow. "I've called for the evidence team, and they're on the way. Once they've photographed and processed, you can begin cleaning up. You notice anything missing?"

Quinn attempted a laugh, but it came out a whine. "Hah-uh. Right now the only thing missing is my breath being taken away. Somehow I doubt this is a burglary."

The nightmarish scene was causing Quinn's head to pound. If her bed hadn't been covered with items she'd been told not to touch, she would have climbed onto it and curled into a ball. As it was, there was no place to sit, no place to cry without being seen. Her legs moved without her volition, as she entered the bathroom. She half-expected to see another note, wrapped around a golf ball and thrown through a broken window. Instead, she saw every drawer and cabinet door open, the contents emptied onto the floor and counter. Her makeup had been strewn all over, her red lipstick open.

She flipped the light switch with her gloved hand. Perhaps in the light, things might look clearer. But as she raised her eyes to the mirror-covered wall over the counter, her insides clenched, and she thought she might faint. On the mirror in block letters, written in dark red lipstick, were the words, *WHERE IS THE KEY?*

Chapter Seventy-three

After seeing the message on the bathroom mirror, Quinn panicked and high-tailed it through the front door of the house and into the arms of her brother. Sergeant Schmidt lumbered after her like a director chasing a temperamental actor.

"—don't blame you for being upset. Anyone would be." Schmidt stooped to look Quinn in the face.

Quinn was in no mood for platitudes. She turned her head the other way. Schmidt wanted too much from her right now. She pressed herself against her brother, as she had so many times as a child. He had always protected her.

Jack hugged tightly with one arm. "Let's give my sister some time and space, shall we? I'm sure she'll be glad to cooperate with the police once she's had a chance to recover."

"But she's got to—" The screech of tires and the opening and closing of car doors behind them at the curb halted Schmidt's argument. Evidently the crime scene investigators had arrived. "Tell you what," Schmidt said, as though he had planned it all along. "Why don't you two go back to your house? Officer Porter will follow you and continue to watch the house. I'll be in contact once we've had a chance to process the scene."

Quinn didn't respond. Her mind was fixed on the chaotic state of her home. The words on the bathroom mirror flashed in her mind like a strobe light from one of the strip clubs. *Where is the key? Where is the key?*

Blackie had been looking for the burial place of the ID bracelet, and Norm had mentioned money, but no one had mentioned a key, at least not that she remembered. The next thing she knew, Jack was driving her back to his house.

She stared at her brother. A little over a week past major transplant surgery, and here he was, taking care of her, instead of the other way around. "You're not supposed to be driving yet, are you? Maybe you should pull over and switch places with me."

"I'm good. It's just a ten-minute drive." Jack winked, and gave her that sheepish grin that meant, *Don't rat me out. I'm enjoying my freedom.*

Words began to collect inside of Quinn's heart, and swam into her throat. "All I ever wanted was to live a normal life, find someone to love, someone who loves me." She brushed tears from her cheeks. "I thought I might have found happiness with Josh. I wish I could spend quality time with him, like a normal couple. But no, I've got to be stuck in this labyrinth with monsters at every turn and no way out." A sob escaped from her mouth, and she said, "They aren't finished with me."

"*Who* isn't finished with you, Quinn? Isn't the kidnapper dead?"

Quinn's reply rolled out in a syrupy-slow whine. "I th-ough-t so. But, here we are. My house is a shambles, and I'm still being th-reat-en-ed by who-ever. Did you see the lipstick on the mirror in the bathroom?"

Jack pulled over to the curb and took his sister's hand in both of his. "Yes, I saw the mirror. I saw the way your house is trashed. It's horrible. But in perspective, after the worry about what might have happened to you when you were kidnapped, this is no big deal. Lipstick on a mirror is such an amateur stunt. The police are going to catch this idiot. Meanwhile, you can't give in now. One more lap on the track, and that dream of yours will be in sight."

Jack had a point. In the past year, he had been through worse than she'd ever experienced. He'd been sick and weak, and heartsick, too. He'd never given up, and neither would she. "Thanks for the pep talk. I don't know what I'd do without you."

"Heck, Quinn. That's what I kept saying to myself the whole time you were missing. A lot of people care about you—not just me. Josh, Mom and Dad, Marlena and Anise—even Chief Ramirez. And that nosy neighbor of yours, Mrs. Tartt. And all of Dad's coffee buddies. And, of course, Mary. Ana's parents even called McFarland's to offer whatever they could do. The police had contacted them when you went missing. And that doesn't even count your attorney. He kept after Sergeant Schmidt even more than Dad did."

With each name Jack mentioned, a drop of salve soothed Quinn's spirit. Maybe it would take a while not to think of every day as a nightmare, but she could get through this. She had conquered Norm, and she could outsmart whoever had broken into her house. She wasn't sure what key he was looking for, but she had a pretty good idea where it might be located.

"I know I can always count on you to give me a boost. You're the best bro ever." Quinn motioned to start driving again, and, as the car passed the streets between her house and Jack's, she remained silent, thinking about the people who cared about her.

As they pulled into the driveway at Jack's, she said, "I'm grateful to have so many people looking after me. Sometime soon I hope to see all of them to thank them." Quinn unfastened her seat belt and jumped out of the car, and Calvin's barking from inside the house gave her a burst of energy. She wanted to sprint toward the front door, but waited for Jack.

While he climbed the steps and fumbled with the house key, Quinn continued to think about the people she was grateful for. "You know, there's one person on your list I want to see most, and yet another person not on your list."

"Well, the one on my list has got to be Josh. And he's wants to see you, too. He texted my cell phone while you were in the house. Must've thought you still had the phone. His message was hot."

"Hey, let me see it." Quinn play-wrestled with her brother, being careful of his post-surgical midriff.

"Okay, okay." He tossed her the phone, but before she had a chance to check it, he asked, "Who is the person not on the list?"

"What?"

"Who's the person not on the list that you want to see?"

Quinn looked up from the phone's screen. "Her name is Nell."

Chapter Seventy-four

"If you ever want to see how popular you are, get yourself kidnapped," Quinn remarked to her brother, as they scarfed down tomato soup and grilled cheese sandwiches. She was surprised she had such an appetite after seeing her house torn up.

"Or have a kidney transplant. That works, too." Jack pushed the bread crusts to the side of his plate and wiped his mouth with a napkin. "One of the benefits of living on this island. The village is tight."

"Josh wants to come over when he gets off at three. Okay with you?"

"Sure, but I forgot to tell you Mom and Dad are coming over in ten minutes. I made them hold off until we could have lunch, but I can't hold 'em any longer. I'll figure out a way to get them to leave, and I'll take a nap before three, so you and Josh can have a private reunion." He wiggled his eyebrows and grinned.

"That's super-thoughtful, but I don't know how private we'll be with a police officer watching from fifty yards away."

"I'm going to change clothes before the parents invade. Wouldn't want Mom to see these dirt streaks."

Quinn checked her own clothes, deciding they would pass muster. She cleared the dishes and thought about her parents. The last time she'd seen them, they'd wanted to send her to Aunt Virginia's to get her away from the gossip. The kidnapping might have exacerbated their concerns for her reputation. On the other hand, they might be so relieved that she was alive, they'd given up worrying about what other people thought. Meanwhile, she wondered what was happening with Becker and the proffer.

When Joy and John McFarland pulled up in the driveway, after being cleared by Officer Porter, Calvin barked a concerto that ended with a howl. Quinn peered through the sheer living room draperies, holding Calvin like a football, and calling to Jack. "Mom and Dad."

Rushing up the walkway, her mother wore a grim expression. Her father stepped more deliberately, but his face was no less sober. They'd been through the mill in the last few days, and Quinn was stung by the thought that she wouldn't have them forever.

She set the dog down and flung the door open. Hugging her mother, she reached for her dad's hand and squeezed. Buttoning his shirt, Jack joined the group at the door.

"My baby, you have no idea how distraught I've been." Tears ran down her mother's cheeks, unchecked.

"C'mon in, Mom. Let's not air condition the whole neighborhood." Jack exchanged glances with Quinn at the mockery of their mother's fussing the whole time they were growing up.

Joy sniffled and laughed, the combination causing her to choke. "Isn't that what I used to say to you?" She turned back to Quinn. "Are you really as fine as you look?"

Quinn nodded as she hugged her father. "Let's sit down and visit." She led the way to the sofa and perched on one of the two chairs opposite. "I'm glad to see you, too."

The warm greetings and cozy setting could have been a picture of domesticity for Quinn's family, but after a few upbeat comments, Quinn's father cleared his throat. "I hate to change the mood, but your mother and I have something to say."

Quinn's breath caught in her throat. An introduction like that usually preceded trouble, or at least unpleasantness.

"We understood your wanting to meet with Becker on your own, without our interference, and we backed off. We know you didn't like our suggestion to go to Aunt Virginia's, but if you had listened, maybe you wouldn't have been kidnapped. My God, Quinn, you could have been killed—like Ana—and Brad. Not that we want to interfere in your life, but we don't feel it's safe for you here."

This time no angry fires burned inside of Quinn. Her kidnapping had robbed her of the moral high ground. She hadn't realized before what an easy target she had been, how endangered. Her parents didn't know what had happened to her house yet. When they learned of that, they might really freak out. She wanted to reassure them that she'd be okay, but would she really?

"What do you mean, 'Safe for you here'? Here at Jack's? Or here in town?" She was merely buying time. She couldn't leave town right now with the police wanting to question her. And what about Josh? "Did you see the police car outside? I'm being protected around the clock."

Her parents exchanged glances. "Yes, but for how long? Marty won't be able to spare that kind of manpower for more than a few days, and then what?" Her dad scooted forward and leaned his elbows on his knees. "We've been blaming ourselves for not insisting that you leave the state. Consider this from our point of view."

Knots formed in Quinn's stomach. She knew her parents had a point. "I understand how you feel. I didn't before, but I do now. Why don't we do this? I'm expecting to hear from Mr. Becker by the end of the day. Why don't I ask him to meet with the three of us to talk about safety issues?"

Joy let out a noisy exhale and reached across the coffee table to grasp Quinn's hands. "Thank you, honey. That sounds like the best idea. I'm glad you don't resent us."

Quinn shot a look at her brother, who rolled his eyes. "Of course, I don't resent you. I know you love me and care about me, and I'm sorry I worried you so much these last few days."

Jack stood and stretched, yawning. "Hate to kick you out, but this is naptime for me, and I'll bet Quinn could use a little shut-eye, too."

Quinn glanced at the clock on the mantle. It was 1:45. Josh would be here in a little more than an hour. "Tell you what, Mom and Dad. I'll call you as soon as I hear from Mr. Becker." After hugs all around, she escorted her parents to the door. As they walked to the car, Quinn blew kisses their way. Her situation weighed heavily on her, as the words *Where is the key?* thrummed in her head. She waved to Officer Porter in the squad car out front and turned back inside.

Chapter Seventy-five

To get ready for Josh's visit, Quinn jumped into the shower. She couldn't wait to see him, except for the lingering feeling that the black cloud hanging over her would rain on him. Someone less complicated would surely make a better partner for him. The fact that he professed to love her seemed nothing short of a miracle.

As she shampooed her hair, she thought about her ransacked house. Assuming that Blackie, or another of his minions, trashed it, they must have had a strong motive to take that risk, even if they'd done it before Norm was killed. A more logical action would have been to flee. That's what she would have done if she'd killed two people and kidnapped a third, if she knew the police were hot on the trail.

Blackie had asked her for the location of the ID bracelet. When she'd asked what was so valuable about that ID bracelet, he's said something about money. Now he was apparently looking for a key. What kind of key would be so important? A key to a map? A safety deposit box? A storage locker? Or maybe she should think outside of the box. Maybe it was the key to a computer program. There were way too many types of keys.

In his last moments, Norm had talked about the ID bracelet, too. *Your buddy Ana outed ya,* he'd said. Quinn couldn't believe that Ana would have told about their burial of the ID bracelet, but not told where they'd buried it.

Anyway, the secret burial place that rested solely with her at this point, was causing her an incredible amount of danger. Until she could crawl out from under this burden with her life and well-being intact, she would never consider herself worthy of Josh. She dried off, put on a fresh pair of shorts and top, blew her hair dry, and, for the first time in several days, put on mascara and lipstick. That was the closest she could come to putting on a happy face.

When she came out of the bathroom, her brother was waiting in the living room, fresh from a nap and smelling like minty toothpaste. "You look great, sis. Nice of you to get all dolled-up." He winked.

Quinn plumped the pillows flattened by her parents' visit. "Never appreciated the value of makeup so much, until I couldn't use it. Showers, too."

"I'm going to head over to McFarland's for a while. Give you and Josh a little time alone."

"You don't have to do that. Besides, should you really be driving?" She sat, and Calvin curled up at her feet.

"No need to worry. I called my PCP while you were in the shower. I'm good to go for driving now." He dangled the car key, as if it were the world's greatest treasure. "Sorry to strand you here with no wheels, though."

"I can't exactly go anywhere, anyway. Not complaining, but I'll sure be glad to get back to normal." This phrase was starting to become a refrain.

"Well, enjoy your visit with Josh." Jack kissed his sister on the cheek and headed for the front door. "And don't do anything I wouldn't do."

Quinn stood by the window, watching as Jack drove away. Her emotions were jumbled, churning, like a tornado. Every encounter of her life paraded before her, mocking her desire for happiness and peace.

Within a few minutes, Josh turned into the driveway, where he was stopped by Officer Porter. The sight of Josh's car, the shape of his head and arms in the driver's seat, the fact that he was a real-live person, coming to see her—these brought tears to Quinn's eyes. She threw the door open and ran to meet him, with Calvin barking at her heels.

Officer Porter stepped aside, and Quinn threw herself into Josh's arms, hugging as if she hadn't seen him in decades, instead of days. Josh pressed her face into his chest, and she could swear his heart was beating double-time. Laughter and tears sprung forth from them both, and Quinn said, "This is the best I've felt in forever." She stepped back to look at her love. He was still in his long coat, white with his name embroidered over the pocket. He wore khakis and soft leather loafers. Everything about his appearance spoke of normalcy, except for the dark circles under his eyes, and he needed a haircut. He almost looked like he might've lost a few pounds, too.

"Wait a minute." Josh opened his car door and leaned in to retrieve a plastic bag from the passenger seat. "I brought you a present."

The couple walked side-by-side into the house, their legs moving in synchrony. Calvin followed, a spring in his trot. Once inside, Quinn and Josh sat on the couch, and Quinn opened the plastic bag. "A new cell phone, wow! I really need this."

"I figured you might not've had a chance to get a new one yet, and I don't want to keep texting you on Jack's phone. That could be embarrassing."

Quinn leaned over for a quick kiss on the lips. "Thanks so much." She fiddled with the phone. It had all the features of her old one, plus a few new ones. "Did you sign me up for service? I need to pay you back for this."

"No, you don't. As much a gift for me as it is for you." His arm around her shoulder, he drew her in for a kiss. "When you were gone, not answering your phone or returning texts, I couldn't sleep, couldn't eat. You have no idea—"

Quinn buried her head in his chest. First her parents, and now Josh. She had put them through so much. She hadn't meant to, of course, but she still felt guilty for having caused so much pain to the people she loved.

"When you're ready, we should talk about it." Josh stared into her eyes. "We can't let this experience stand between us."

As much as she dreaded revisiting the past few days, she knew he was right. "What do you want to know?"

"Are you hurt? Are you frightened? I want to hear everything that you can tell me from start to finish. And when you're done, I want to help you get past it."

Quinn pulled her feet onto the sofa next to her, bent her knees, and laid her head in Josh's lap, staring at the ceiling. She began talking in a monotone. "I was at the library on Saturday afternoon..." Josh played with her hair and stroked her shoulder as she recited as many of the details of her imprisonment as she could tell him, leaving out the parts she deemed off-limits, according to Becker's admonitions. With each revelation, a knot loosened inside of her, and by the end of her monologue, she found herself breathing easier.

Josh listened without interrupting. If this was an example of his bedside manner, every one of his patients would love him. When she finished speaking, he had only a single question. "Can I ask why a police officer's outside? Is it because this nightmare isn't over?"

Quinn took in a mammoth breath. How would she find the words to explain that after the kidnapping, the stabbing, the rescue, she was still being targeted, her home destroyed in the process? She hadn't told Josh about Blackie and the ID bracelet. She couldn't drag him into that vortex, not yet. She started to form the words that might explain why she still needed police protection, when Jack's landline rang.

Quinn jumped at the sound, and she ran to the extension in the kitchen, hoping Blackie hadn't found her here. "Hello? McFarland residence."

The voice at the other end was hearty and strong. "Quinn? This is David Becker. You've got your immunity."

Chapter Seventy-six

Two days later, Quinn's immunity was signed, sealed, and delivered at the courthouse. As Becker had predicted, the police wanted to interview her immediately. While Becker drove her to the police station, Quinn reflected on her current situation. The police had completed processing of her house, but she hadn't yet put it back in order. The one time she'd been back, accompanied by police escort, all she had done was pick up her uprooted orchids and several more outfits. The rest, like every other part of her life, would have to wait.

Josh had been coming to Jack's for dinner every day after work, and, while there was nothing normal about these days and nights, Quinn was starting to adapt. Getting immunity, Becker had explained, was pretty rare, and also a big step forward.

Visits with Josh had been therapeutic, and between those, the new cell phone, and the immunity, Quinn felt optimistic. Maybe she could put the kidnapping and the murders past her, after all. By the time she and Becker got out of the car at the police station, the afternoon shadows had cut the heat of the day into a more tolerable range, and a soft Gulf breeze stirred hope into Quinn's mood.

Becker led her by the elbow. "You're in good shape to talk about the kidnapping and Dawn's murder. I'll be with you in case I'm needed, but I probably won't say much."

"I'm so thankful for all you've done," Quinn said. Even though she was paying for his services, she couldn't imagine managing this landscape without him. That, too, brought tears to her eyes.

"Don't thank me yet. The police questioning may wring you dry, but now you'll be able to answer their questions without worrying about implicating yourself in Dawn's murder. I'll still intervene if necessary, but at this point, you and Sergeant Schmidt are on the same side. You are a key witness for the police."

At the mention of the word, "key," Quinn remembered two things she wanted to discuss with her attorney before she met with Schmidt. Although they were alone in the lobby, she pulled Becker to the corner of the room and whispered. "Speaking of key, I've been thinking about the message on the mirror in my bathroom."

Becker's eyebrows merged, and he shook his head. "I'm sorry. I should have asked about that. I've been on a one-track rail all day."

"The more I think about it, the more I'm sure that Brad or Ana must have buried a key in the same spot as the ID bracelet. And I'm guessing that key will lead to money—a lot of it." She took a deep breath. "So, I'm still a target. I'm wondering whether I'll ever be safe."

"That's why you need to cooperate with the police. When they apprehend the bad guys—that's when you'll be safe again. But they need your help to accomplish that."

Quinn touched Becker on his forearm and locked eyes with him. Her next request might be over-reaching. "I understand, and I'm more than willing to cooperate with the police, but I'd like to do something before I answer their questions."

Becker's head flicked like that of a horse, shaking off a fly. "Quinn, you can't evade this interview. The police have a lot invested in you now."

"Understood. All I want is to clear up a few things. If I can do that, I'll be able to give the police better information."

Becker looked doubtful. "What are you proposing?"

"I want to talk to Nell."

* * *

Forty-five minutes later, Quinn sat across the table from Sergeant Schmidt in the police interview room. The room smelled stuffy, like worn gym socks left in a locker too long. Before Schmidt would consider allowing her to talk to Nell, Quinn had to submit to an interview. Among other things, Nell's witness protection depended upon Quinn's corroboration of information. Nell would have her own version of the facts, and Quinn didn't want to say anything to jeopardize her captor-turned-helper, but, as Becker had instructed, Quinn's best strategy was to tell the truth.

Schmidt began a digital recording, this time without need for Miranda warnings. The toothy smile on his face seemed no more genuine than before, but Quinn wasn't there to make friends. More than anything, she needed to put this ordeal behind her, and to do that, she needed the police.

After introducing the date, time, and subject of the video, Schmidt took Quinn back to the beginning. He had her recount the breaking of her window with the threatening note, the pornographic movies mailed to her by Ana, the nylon threads she'd submitted from the side of her house. Quinn was impatient to talk about more recent events, but Becker's occasional nods and taps on the table with the palm of his hand kept her steady.

Schmidt was nothing if not thorough, and he was in no apparent hurry. "Were there any other incidents prior to your being kidnapped that aroused your suspicion?"

Recalling the many instances of having been followed, Quinn resisted an impulse to cover her face. "I should have reported the odd noises I heard when walking Calvin in the neighborhood, the sense that I was being followed by a dark gray car, the face that had stared at me at the cemetery. I'd dismissed everything as figments of an overactive imagination, but maybe they formed a pattern leading up to my abduction."

Before long, Schmidt got around to asking about the kidnapping. Quinn's insides tensed as she thought about how easily she was led into the back of the van.

"Please recount whether you'd seen either of the kidnappers before that day in the library parking lot."

Quinn explained how she and Josh had been to the Heartbeat Cabaret, how Norm had worked at the door, and Nell had danced.

"Was there a particular reason you went to the club that night?"

Quinn looked at Becker. Even after watching those porn tapes in his presence, talking about strip clubs in front of the man who had become somewhat of a father figure caused heat to rise into her face, but his expression remained calm. "I'd done some research on the adult entertainment industry, and I had an inkling that the guy in the porn videos might be involved in the local strip venues. I figured the best way to get information was to go there in person."

"So you were doing police work?" Schmidt's tone was light, even if his meaning wasn't.

"I never thought of it that way. Between the note threatening me to keep quiet and the package of videos from Ana, I was between a rock and a hard place. I needed information, and I thought this was the best way to get it."

"Did you find the person you were looking for that night?"

Quinn shook her head. "The next night we went to a club on the mainland, Heaven's Door. That's where we found Blackie." Quinn watched the policeman's face. She could tell by the bland expression that he already knew about Blackie, maybe from Nell. "I later figured out Blackie's real name—Lionel French. He's Ana's uncle."

A fire flickered in Schmidt's blue eyes. Maybe Nell hadn't told him, or maybe she didn't know, but this was new information. Schmidt put a pause on Blackie and led her back to a long and detailed recitation of what happened during the kidnapping and once she arrived at the house. The memories of the chains digging into her wrists and ankles, being half-naked, the hours of being alone and frightened—all were still fresh and painful.

Quinn made sure to include all the ways in which Nell had helped her. As she talked, her throat became parched, and her stomach rumbled.

Becker intervened. "Why don't we take a break?"

Schmidt turned off the camera, and Quinn took her new cell phone into the restroom, where she texted Josh. Being questioned at police station. Dinner might be late. Luv u. Funny how an ordinary thing like texting seemed like an incredible luxury now. It was already past 6:00—no wonder her stomach was growling.

When she returned to the interview room, she poured herself a whole glass of water and drank it. Maybe that would satisfy her stomach.

Schmidt turned the video on again. His first question steered the story into deeper waters. "Now, Quinn, you've done a fine job of telling us about everything that happened to you while you were held captive, but now I'd like you to speculate as to *why* you were kidnapped."

This was the reason Becker had insisted on getting immunity. The *why* required her to talk about the things that she knew, things that she'd taken a blood oath not to tell. A weight sat on her chest, as cold and dense as an anvil, ready to be struck. She refilled her water glass and took a swallow. Her Reynaud's kicked in, turning her fingernails blue.

Stalling wouldn't help, so she shoved her hands beneath her thighs and took a deep breath. "On June 27, 2004, Ana French and I witnessed the murder of Dawn Chrysler..." She explained how they had watched Dawn's nude dancing, how they had sat in the bowed branches of the fig tree, partially obscured by the summer profusion of leaves, and giggled at Dawn's lack of modesty. She explained the events of that particular night in a voice that sounded tinny and far away to her own ears.

When she got to the part about the murderer fleeing down the alley, dropping the gold ID bracelet, a vertical line formed between Schmidt's eyebrows. Quinn explained how Ana had insisted on burying the ID bracelet, and how Quinn had gone along with Ana's demand for secrecy. "I didn't know until recently that the killer was Ana's uncle. Blackie let it slip when I was chained to the bed."

"So, this Blackie arranged to kidnap you, so you wouldn't out him for Dawn's murder? After all these years of silence? Is that what you think?"

"I thought that at first. I even thought he might have plans to sell me as a sex slave, but once Blackie came to talk to me, I realized there's more. Ana was murdered—and then Brad. Blackie probably killed them, too, or had them killed. He had me kidnapped because he wanted to know where we'd buried the ID bracelet."

"How did he know about that?"

"Ana must have told him—or Brad—or both. He was desperate to know the burial spot. I couldn't understand why, but now I think I know."

Schmidt leaned forward, the vertical line in his forehead deepening by the minute. "Well, tell us your theory."

"Something else is buried in the same spot, something important enough to keep Blackie from fleeing. He couldn't get the location out of Ana or Brad, so I'm his last hope. He ransacked my house. Maybe he thought I'd dug it up already, but he didn't find what he was looking for—some kind of key."

"And you know where this key is supposedly buried?"

Quinn exchanged glances with Becker and nodded.

"Then I would say that you, my dear girl," Schmidt said, frowning, "are in a great deal of danger."

Chapter Seventy-seven

After Quinn told Sergeant Schmidt about witnessing Dawn's murder and burying the ID bracelet, Schmidt's whole demeanor changed. Now he agreed to grant permission for a meeting between Quinn and Nell. In fact, he hustled to arrange for Nell to be brought into the interview room immediately. His only requirement was that he moderate the interview, and the meeting be recorded. Becker also insisted on being present.

This might be the one and only time Quinn would ever have with Nell again, and her emotions fizzed like a carbonated drink, shaken before being uncapped. The sisterhood that had developed between them through those few interactions was strong, and though their lives were quite different, Quinn would always consider Nell a friend.

As Nell entered the room, wearing pale blue scrubs like Quinn had worn after showering at the police station, she carried herself with the grace of an eland. As a performer, she was probably used to having all eyes in the room on her, so even after three days in protective custody, she was poised. When she made eye contact with Quinn, her rosebud lips parted and turned up in the corners. Quinn returned the smile. Whatever the future held for either of them, the recent past had created a bond.

Sergeant Schmidt started the video, announcing the date, time, and names of those present. Having interviewed each of the women separately, he was in possession of more information about the case than anyone at the table, and he revealed acres of pink gums with his broad grin. "Well, ladies, we rarely interview two witnesses at the same table at the same time. But each of you has asked to see the other. While Ms. McFarland has corroborated all of Ms. Blanchard's story with regard to the kidnapping, each woman has distinctive information about the man known as Blackie.

"Ms. Blanchard has expressed a desire to tell Ms. McFarland something, and Ms. McFarland has expressed a desire to ask Ms. Blanchard something.

I will give each of you the opportunity to do as you wish. Afterwards, I may have some questions for you both."

Becker sat next to Quinn with his arms folded across his chest. He reminded Quinn of the Muppet, Sam the Eagle. Nothing would get past him, even if he remained quiet.

Called on first, Nell looked directly into Quinn's eyes. "I can't tell you how happy I am that you escaped. Yer the only one I know of who has." A cloud of sadness passed over her eyes, and Quinn wondered how many others Nell had seen chained to the bed in that room.

"I knew you had the best chance. You're strong and fit. Most of the others gave up without a fight, but I knew you wouldn't." Nell leaned forward, elbows on the table, eyes locking on Quinn's. "I wanted to tell you something, though. Don't underestimate Blackie. When he wants something, he usually gets it. He went hard after Ana, but she was tough like you. She wouldn't break. It's not enough that Norm is out of the picture. Norm was Blackie's right hand, but Blackie won't stop. He'll come after you again and again until he gets what he wants." Nell paused, staring at her hands on the table. "I don't know Blackie as well as I knew Norm, but Norm always said that Blackie's heart was as black as his clothes. Norm was what you might call Blackie's best friend, and even *he* didn't trust him.

"Ana and her husband got the best of Blackie. He made them pay, but now he's come after you. You can't let yer guard down for a second. As long as Blackie's free, he'll come after ya like a fiery dragon."

The whole time Nell talked, Quinn had shivers and chills that cramped her hands and feet and made her mouth dry. Nell's words rang true for Quinn. The person Quinn had been even a month ago might have caved in like the other women Blackie had captured, but the experience of being kidnapped had been a crucible for Quinn. She had tapped into resources she wasn't aware she had. She hadn't given up, and she wouldn't give up now. She had come too far. She wanted a normal, happy life, and she intended to get it.

Schmidt turned to Quinn. "Your turn, Ms. McFarland. You have some questions?"

Quinn reached both hands across the table and grasped Nell's. A hug would've been better, but this would have to do—Quinn's cold hands pressing Nell's warm ones. "First, I want to thank you, Nell, from the bottom of my heart. You were kind to me, and smart. What you did with my cell phone, and sneaking the knife in with the corned beef sandwich saved my life. Thanks for worrying about me now, too. I'm not a super-religious person, but I pray the Lord watches over you for the rest of your life. You're an angel."

Nell brushed her hand across her forehead, and Quinn continued. "You told me that you knew Ana, that you tried to help her, too. Yet Ana was killed in her home. She wasn't abducted or chained to the bed like I was. I hadn't talked to Ana in a long time, but we used to be best friends. I wondered how you knew her."

Nell looked at Sergeant Schmidt, one eyebrow raised. Schmidt apparently was to Nell as Becker was to Quinn. Schmidt nodded, and Nell began to talk. "Blackie has no children. Maybe he had a vasectomy when he was young. A lot of the men in the porn business do. Anyway, Norm told me Ana was Blackie's niece. She needed money and came to him. Blackie wasn't the kind to share, but she must've said or done something to shake him up. Or maybe he wanted a family connection. You know, somebody to leave his money to. Anyway, he put Ana to work in the strip clubs."

Quinn gasped. After seeing what had happened to Dawn, she couldn't imagine Ana would become a stripper.

"—not what you think. She didn't dance, like me. She was in charge o' the money. Those clubs—Blackie owns four of them—they're money-laundering empires. People drop cash, not a lot of records—it's a perfect set-up for running drug and prostitution money through.

"Blackie doesn't trust people. The only person he's at all close to is Skye Blue, one of the dancers at Heaven's Door. Norm and I oversaw things at the Heartbeat Cabaret, but we turned the money over to Blackie to deposit. Once Ana was in the picture, we started turning the money over to her. She was friendly, pleasant—non-judgmental, like you—and I got to looking forward to talking to her."

"How long did Ana work with you before—"

"Before she was killed? Maybe eight or nine months. Soon after she started, her husband joined the organization, too. He was involved with illegal drugs, so I didn't see much of him, but Norm and I couldn't believe Blackie had cut those two in. Totally out of character." She shrugged. "We thought he might have some fatal illness, maybe mental."

Quinn could see where this story was going. Ana and Brad got greedy, and if Blackie didn't like it, they had Dawn's murder to hold over his head. These weren't the same people she'd known so well as teenagers. None of them had grown up in upper class households, and money wasn't what drove them back then. "So what happened next?" Quinn dreaded the answer.

"Money went missing, first small amounts, then larger. Blackie is OCD about money, so he confronted Ana. This went on for some weeks, but the money kept coming up short. Finally, Blackie sent Norm and me to meet with Ana. Norm roughed her up, tried to get her to admit to the skimming and return the money. I tried to help Ana, like I did with you. I could tell she was caught in a bad scheme, out of her element."

Quinn remembered Ana's parents' concerns about bruises. They thought Brad had beaten her. "Sounds like once she started stealing, she couldn't stop."

"Or her husband wouldn't let her. I thought all along that Brad was the one who'd concocted the scheme to get out of his own financial problems. Ana may've approached Blackie in an attempt to save her marriage."

Quinn's head pounded. A dizzying nausea made her want to run from the room and never come back. All the years she had nursed the anger of being betrayed by Ana and Brad, feeling bereft because she couldn't have the man she loved. Now she thanked her lucky stars for not having married him. How could she have misread his values—and hers? She might not be rolling in money now, but everything she had, she had earned. She couldn't imagine herself getting involved with blackmail, prostitution, illegal drugs, or theft—not for anyone, not ever.

"Anyway," Nell continued, "you know the end of the story. Neither Ana nor Brad would cough up the money, even though Blackie went after them himself. He probably tortured them. The only thing he got out of them was that they'd put it where he'd never find it. The next thing I heard, Ana was dead, and then Brad."

"Did Blackie ever say how much money went missing?" Quinn tried to imagine how big a storage place would be required. She had no doubt that the key Blackie wanted from her was the key to that location. She recalled the sticky note attached to the videotape Ana had sent her. The word, "ID" referred to the bracelet they had buried together. Ana had trusted Quinn to remember.

"I doubt he knows exactly, but Norm thought it was probably upwards of three million dollars."

Becker's eyebrows jumped to the top of his head, and Quinn shuddered. That was more money raked in over a nine-month period than earned in a lifetime by anyone she knew. Even more astounding and terrifying was the fact that only one person controlled the future of that money, and the person was Quinn, herself.

Chapter Seventy-eight

After meeting with Nell, Quinn's head pounded, and hunger had roiled into nausea. She had a lot to think about. Nell's characterization of Blackie as a relentless persecutor in pursuit of his money had set Quinn's nerves on edge. She hadn't crossed a victory line by escaping from the chains of the bed—far from it. She'd only traded one form of confinement for another. She would continue to be in danger because she knew where the key to Blackie's money was buried.

Becker had dropped her off at Jack's, with the police cruiser following and parking outside. Jack greeted her at the door, with Calvin dancing around Quinn's heels. Quinn picked up the Westie, petting his head and making kissy sounds at his nose.

Jack dangled three new keys, two for her house, and one for his. He had dealt with the changing of the locks while she was at the police station. "No need to thank me," he said, as he bent to buckle a sandal. "Did me good to accomplish something today. I'm about ready to go back to work."

"Right now?" It was past eight, and she couldn't imagine McFarland's had need of Jack's presence at this hour.

"No, silly. Right now I'm going over to Mary's house. It's a quiet night, and she was able to get an hour off for dinner. I wanted to give you and Josh some privacy. He's coming over, isn't he?" He slapped Quinn on the arm and grinned.

"More like *you* wanted privacy. I'm sorry to be such a lingering houseguest." Quinn set Calvin down, put the keys away in her handbag, and took out the cell phone to text Josh. "I don't know when I'll be able to go back home." The plaintive tone in her voice surprised her. She had never been a whiner.

"No worries. Frankly, after the past year of waiting for a kidney, I'm enjoying all the hubbub around here. Not happy for the reason, though." He ruffled the top of his sister's hair and opened the front door. "You can stay as long as your sweet little heart desires, sis. Keep your eye on the clock, though. My coach turns into a pumpkin in one hour."

Quinn closed the door, locking it, and plopped down on the sofa to text Josh. She wanted to see him, but she was so worn out from her activities at the police station, she could curl up in a ball on this sofa and go to sleep for the night. Finally home at Jack's, she texted. Have u eaten? C'mon over.

Frozen dinner. I can stop n pick up hamburger 4 u. On my way.

Don't bother. Not at all hungry. Except 4 u. Quinn texted Officer Porter, who was watching the house, that Josh was on the way. Then she ran to the bathroom to freshen up. She wanted a shower, but Josh would be there in less than ten minutes, so she splashed her face and neck with water and combed her hair. A little concealer, blush, and mascara was all she had time for—oh, and a little spray of cologne. Too bad none of these could remove the haunted look in her eyes. It would take more than makeup and a good night's sleep to remedy that.

A piercing bark from Calvin announced Josh's arrival. Quinn checked through the peephole and opened the door. The sight of Josh's tousled sandy hair, his lop-sided smile and gray eyes, suffused her with a soothing warmth from her toes upward, prompting a smile of her own. Whatever else was wrong in her life, she had a loving and handsome guy, right here, ready to support her.

Pulling him into the living room, Quinn shut the door and threw her arms around his waist, squeezing tightly. "I've been looking forward to this all day," she said, as she lifted her face for a kiss.

Josh pressed his lips to hers, matching her fervor with a passion of his own. When they broke for air, he looked around. "Where's Jack?"

"Next door at Mary's for another forty-five minutes. He said he wanted to give us privacy, but I think he had ulterior motives." Quinn stood on tiptoes and initiated another kiss. Having Josh here with her, alone, was filling up all the ragged spots in her soul, and she couldn't get enough.

Josh touched her cheek with a new tenderness. "Forty-five minutes? What do you think we might do with forty-five minutes?"

"I have a few ideas," Quinn said, pulling him by the hand toward her bedroom. She pointed at Calvin. "Guard the door, Callie." She and Josh went into the bedroom and closed the door, leaving the pup outside.

After they made love, for the first time since her kidnapping, Quinn checked the time. "We have five minutes to spare." She dressed and finger-combed her hair, while Josh smoothed his.

"Before we leave this room," he said, "I need to tell you something important." He pulled her next to him on the edge of the bed. "I've been thinking about this ever since you were kidnapped." His grin was gone, and his gray eyes were shaded by his long, blondish eyelashes. "When you went missing—I was frantic. I couldn't sleep or eat or think straight. I realized how much you mean to me, how little everything else matters besides you."

Quinn stared into Josh's eyes, a little stunned. "I feel the same—"

"No, let me finish. My whole life I've been a book nerd. I studied a lot, and that was it. I was shy around girls. I had a few dates here and there, but I never found anyone who knocked me off my feet. You've got so much gusto. You're funny and independent and adventurous and vivacious in a way that I'm not. Not to mention being beautiful and sexy. And kind."

Quinn wished she could put all of these adjectives into a bottle and store them for the rest of her life. She would uncap it and replay this speech again and again. She had waited a long, long time for someone to love her like this. She wrapped her arms around Josh's middle and nestled her face against him.

"So, what I want to tell you is this—I love you, and I want to spend the rest of my life with you. And I don't want anything bad to happen to you or to us again."

Quinn couldn't remember ever feeling so loved, so comfortable, or so safe with another human being. She pictured herself as the glowing sun, emerging over the horizon at dawn, spreading her radiance over the cool earth. She wanted to stay on this ascending path, warm and happy, but those last words from Josh reminded her of Blackie. She didn't deserve Josh's adoration. She was too much trouble.

Nell's words replayed in her mind, dousing the joy of Josh's. "Don't underestimate Blackie. When he wants something, he usually gets it." As much as she wanted to put Blackie in the past and give herself over to being with Josh, she wasn't in a position to do that—not yet.

Chapter Seventy-nine

The next morning, Calvin made his "take me outside" sounds at six-fifteen. Quinn couldn't believe she'd slept so soundly, the first time since the kidnapping. She had to credit Josh. He really knew how to make her feel good.

She threw on a pair of shorts and a top and padded, bare-footed, to the front door. Jack's bedroom door was closed, so she assumed he was still asleep. She waved to the new officer on watch, as she stood on the front porch, watching Calvin do his thing.

Something had been gnawing at the edges of her mind since Josh mentioned never wanting anything bad to happen again. She had an idea to run past Becker and Schmidt, but for it to work, the timing had to be just right. Too early to call either, she wished two things—that she had her car back, and that she didn't have a police patrolman observing every single move she made. Not that she was ungrateful for the protection, but sometimes she felt more like a suspect than a victim.

She was ready to call Calvin inside, when Mary Hallom turned the corner and parked in her driveway next door. Mary's shift ended at six a.m., so Quinn didn't expect the young officer to pay an early morning visit, but, as soon as she slammed her car door, Mary headed toward Jack's porch.

"G'morning, Mary." Quinn picked up Calvin and waved again to the watching patrolman.

"Hey, Quinn. Aren't you up early today?" Mary looked toward the screen door. "How're things going?"

Quinn contemplated sharing her idea with Mary before she talked to Becker or Schmidt. Mary would know whether she was brilliant or totally off-base, and Quinn could use a sounding board. On the other hand, Mary would probably tell Jack, who would tell their parents, and Quinn wasn't ready to involve the whole world at this point. Also, she didn't want to put

Mary in the awkward position of being part of something that may conflict with her work duties. Better to leave Mary out of it.

Instead, Quinn said, "Okay. Sure wish I could get my car back and get out a little bit. I'm starting to think this is an armed camp, and I'm a prisoner."

"I get it. I would hate to be grounded, too. Hopefully, things will get better soon." Mary yawned and brushed at dirt on the knees of her pants. "Sorry, pretty tired after a busy night on duty. Jack up yet?"

A voice boomed from behind Quinn. "Who's that pretty lady calling my name?"

Quinn turned to see her brother, wearing sweatpants, a T-shirt, flip flops, and a bed-head. Glad she hadn't started that conversation with Mary, she stepped aside to make room for Jack on the porch. Her stomach issued a loud gurgle, reminding her that she hadn't eaten in ages. "I'll let you two talk. I'm going in to fix some breakfast."

In the kitchen, Quinn set out Calvin's food and water, then took ingredients out of the refrigerator for an omelet. The aromas of bacon and cheese and onions, even uncooked, caused her mouth to water. She took four slices of bread from the loaf in the freezer. Might as well make enough for Jack, too.

Cooking occupied Quinn's mind for the next few minutes, and then eating took over. Jack had come back into the house and started the coffee. Neither offered much in the way of chatting. Quinn was too busy eating, and Jack might have been on Planet Mary, for all Quinn could tell.

After they both had cleaned their plates and put down their napkins, Jack asked, "What are you going to do today?"

"Well, let's see. It's seven a.m., and I have a full calendar. I have a house to put back in order, a job I haven't been to in days, bills to pay, including mounting costs for a lawyer." Quinn's voice came out sharper than she intended. "Let's see what else. Oh, and I can't go anywhere or do anything, because I'm under police protection."

"I didn't mean to upset you," Jack said. "If anyone can sympathize, I can. I've spent the past year hanging around, unable to do much more than eat, sleep, and watch TV."

Quinn was ashamed of herself for complaining to Jack, of all people. "You didn't upset me. You've had it much worse than me. Funny how our fortunes have reversed, though. You're now free to roam about the country." She began clearing the table.

"Mary thinks—"

Quinn snapped. "What does Mary think? Why didn't Mary tell *me* if she has a thought about me? Why does everyone have to go around behind my back expressing their opinions?" She turned on the faucet full-force and began rinsing the dishes with a vengeance.

Jack shut off the faucet and pulled Quinn by the hand. "Come sit down for a minute. We need to talk." He sat opposite her, elbows on the table, and an earnest look in his greenish eyes. "No one's talking about you behind your back, not in a bad way, that is. We're trying to help you, Quinn. Maybe being kidnapped automatically makes you paranoid, but I'm waiting for the old Quinn to come back home. Mom and Dad are worried, too. Since you've been back, you haven't given them the time of day. We all understand you've been through a trauma, and being stuck at my house under constant surveillance is a major irritation, but—"

The so-called irritation that had been rolling around with the eggs in Quinn's stomach flared into full-fledged anger. "Thanks for your *concern*, you and Mom and Dad, and whoever the hell else you've been talking to about me. The trouble is, you don't know the half of it. The past few weeks have been a major nightmare, and I'm trying my hardest to crawl out of it, but every time I take one step forward, something happens to pull me back. I feel like I'm doing the cha-cha."

The stricken look on Jack's face caused Quinn to shift her rhetoric into neutral. *Why am I lashing out at the one true friend who's been on my side all of my life?* "Look, Jack. I don't mean to take it out on you. You've done more than enough by letting Calvin and me stay here and getting my house re-keyed. And running interference with Mom and Dad. I'm angry, but I'm not angry with you."

Jack reached across the table to touch Quinn's hand. "I understand how being cooped up is stifling. What I started to tell you is Mary thinks you might be able to get Sergeant Schmidt to approve your spending the day cleaning up your house, with police protection, of course."

Quinn had to admit, it was a good idea. Restoring her house to order would be a big step forward in getting back to normal, even if she wouldn't be safe to live there yet. On the other hand, what she had to talk to Schmidt about was more urgent. "I'll put it on the list. I've got to call Schmidt this morning anyway." She stood and went back to the dishes. After adjusting the water temperature, she turned to look at her brother, who was still sitting at the table. "I'm sorry for venting, Jack. If I didn't have you, I'd have boiled over long ago, just like this water."

Chapter Eighty

As soon as Jack left for McFarland's, Quinn called Becker's office. Ethel answered with her usual friendly, but efficient, voice. "I'm sorry, but Mr. Becker is in court this morning. Is there a message I can give him when he calls in?"

Disappointed, Quinn said, "Please have him call me on the new cell phone. He has the number." She couldn't blame him for being tied up with another case, but an internal time bomb was ticking, and she couldn't wait to take action. The way Becker had explained the immunity to her, she was now on the same side as Sergeant Schmidt. Maybe she could go ahead and call Schmidt without running her idea past Becker. Waiting wasn't an option. After seeing the dirt on Mary's pants, she might already be too late.

Quinn took a deep breath, crossed her fingers, and called the police station. She spoke to three different people, who asked specific questions about why she was calling, but she insisted on talking only to Schmidt, and finally he answered.

"'Morning, Quinn. What can I do for you?" His voice was hearty, but rushed.

"I've been thinking about Blackie. How much he wants the buried treasure. How I'll never be free until he isn't. I want to help you catch him."

Schmidt chuckled. "You've already helped. Between you and Nell, we've got enough to nail this guy good."

"But you don't *have* him, and until you do, I'm going to be in danger. Don't you see? He's going to keep coming after me—for the money, and also to silence me."

A squeaky chair preceded Schmidt's response. "You have a point. So, what are you proposing?"

"Get a message to him. Tell him I'll lead him to the burial place, if he'll leave me alone. When we get there, you'll catch him, and I'll be free."

"Use you as bait? Absolutely not! Have you told Becker about this idea? Or your parents? What you're thinking of is extremely dangerous. You could be killed. Our police department would never take a risk like that. Never." Schmidt's voice screeched like a rusty bassoon. "Besides, our evidence techs already dug up the Frenches' garden. Got the warrant yesterday and turned the dirt in the early evening."

Now Quinn was certain that the soil on Mary's uniform had come from the Frenches' backyard. "You did? Did you find the ID bracelet?"

"Yep. Found a key, too. We're working on figuring out what the key goes to. Probably a storage locker somewhere. That's all I can say about the case, but rest assured, we're working day and night."

Icy sparks shot through Quinn's body to her hands and feet, having nothing to do with the temperature and everything to do with her anxiety. "What about the digging? If someone drove through the alley, would the excavation be obvious?"

Schmidt huffed a syllable that might've been an expletive. "Listen, Quinn. With all due respect, this is an active case, and I probably shouldn't have told you as much as I did. If we need your help, we know where to find you. Meanwhile, you need to sit tight and let us do our job."

Quinn knew a brush-off when she heard one. The problem was, Schmidt was making a big mistake. He might have found the key to Blackie's storage place, and he might actually find the money. But those wouldn't necessarily lead to capturing Blackie. Blackie had evaded suspicion for Dawn's murder for so many years. If he got wind of the fact that the money was gone, he'd be gone, too. Quinn's plan might be their only chance. She started to plead her case again, but before she could utter a syllable, she heard the mumbling of another voice at Schmidt's end.

"Look, I gotta go. Talk later."

"Wait a second," Quinn said. "I had one more thing to ask you. Can I go to my house and start cleaning up?" She held her breath, feeling like a fourth-grader, asking permission to go to the restroom. Resenting it.

Scuffling sounds, like those of a chair being pushed in, came through the phone. Whatever had taken Schmidt's attention must have been important enough to prompt immediate action. *It is a police station,* Quinn reminded herself.

"What?" Schmidt sounded a million miles away. "Oh, clean up your house. Sure. Be sure your protection stays with you every second. Bye now."

The disconnecting click echoed in Quinn's ear, making her feel insignificant. As she put the phone down on the kitchen counter, she had an epiphany. Schmidt may have wanted to solve the murders. He also may have wanted to locate the millions that Brad and maybe Ana had hidden away. He probably wanted to eliminate the crimes associated with the adult entertainment venues in his jurisdiction. But finding Blackie and bringing him to justice for all he, specifically, had done was Quinn's singular goal. Blackie had killed Dawn before Quinn's young eyes. Witnessing that had set her life on a path that crippled her relationships for years. He was responsible for Ana's and Brad's deaths, her kidnapping, and who knows how many other crimes against women. Blackie was an evil that must be stopped now, before he slipped away. If Schmidt wouldn't accept her help in rounding him up, Quinn would find a way to do it alone. She had the calling card that Blackie would respond to. She had his full attention. She just had to figure out how to use it.

Chapter Eighty-one

Quinn took advantage of having Jack's house to herself. After she texted Josh to push back their dinner plans, she showered, played with Calvin, and straightened up her bedroom and the kitchen. All the while, she ruminated over how she could lure Blackie into the arms of the police. Nell's information about Skye Blue made getting a message to him easy. She would give the stripper the message for Blackie, to meet in the alley behind the Frenches' house, where she would direct him to the burial spot.

He'd be suspicious of her motives, so she'd concocted a story. Before she could put everything into action, she would have to check out the digging the police had done the evening before. The flower beds needed to look untouched when Blackie arrived there. She would also need to convince the police to remain out of sight until the perfect moment. Blackie wasn't a fool, and the slightest misstep could cause him to flee, maybe even taking Quinn with him as a hostage. As a backup, Quinn might involve the Frenches. She hadn't spoken with them since that day at the funeral home, but Sergeant Schmidt had mentioned a warrant, so they must be aware of the burial spot.

As she folded a load of laundry, someone knocked at the door, and Calvin launched into a doggie sonata. She checked through the curtains to make sure her patrolman was watching, then through the peephole. It was Mary.

"Just the person I wanted to see," Quinn said, flinging the door wide. "C'mon in. Jack's gone to the funeral home, and I'm getting ready to head over to my house to start cleaning up. I wanted to ask you something important, though." Quinn patted the sofa. Quinn took the chair kitty-corner to Mary.

Mary rubbed her eyes, but she seemed attentive. "What's up? Did you get permission to clean up?"

"Yes. Sergeant Schmidt said it's okay, as long as I take my babysitter along with me." She tilted her head in the direction of the front door. "Listen, Mary, I don't want to take advantage of our relationship, but Schmidt told me the police had dug up the flower bed behind the Frenches' house yesterday, and I saw you brushing dirt off your pants."

Mary's dark eyes squinted, and her nostrils flared. "You know I can't talk—"

"I don't expect you to disclose confidential police business. We are on the same side, though, and I only have one simple question." Quinn took a deep breath and talked fast, afraid Mary might walk away at any moment. "After you found what you were looking for, how did you 'clean up' the site? If I went there today, would I be able to tell someone had dug in that flower bed recently?"

Mary exhaled and made a swiping motion with her hand against her knees. "Everything's back to the way it was before. We even planted new geraniums on top of where we dug." She stood and paced in the living room. "Why are you—don't tell me you're thinking of doing something stupid back there. And if you are, don't tell me about it, because I'll have to report it."

"I've got to. I'm okay with your reporting it to the department. I'm going to tell them anyway. Blackie's never going to stop coming after me until he's captured. Don't worry. I've got a plan."

Mary knelt next to Quinn, grabbing her by the shoulders. "You've gotta be out of your mind. You could get yourself kidnapped again—or shot. Does Sergeant Schmidt know about this? Does Chief Ramirez?" Mary's loud voice and laying hands on Quinn's shoulders aroused Calvin's ire, and his bark added to the diatribe.

Quinn picked up Calvin and paced. "I told you I have a plan." She walked back and forth to the couch, petting Calvin, who was panting in the crook of her elbow. "I mentioned it to Sergeant Schmidt this morning."

"I know he didn't approve. We don't operate that way. You need to take care of your own self and let the police do their job. We'll get the perp on our own."

Quinn didn't want to insult Mary. She needed the police for her plan to work. Quinn wasn't critical of the police—well, maybe a little bit—but she felt the bureaucracy kept things moving too slowly, and Blackie was shrewd enough, once he cut the losses of the money Brad had hidden, to run away to some far-flung reaches of his porn empire. She couldn't bear the thought of his getting away with murder again. Nor could she live her life with the threat of his ultimate return.

"Don't worry. I have no intention of interfering with your own personal work or that of the police department. You may think I'm crazy, but let me tell you something about the recently-murdered Ana Renfroe."

Quinn sat on the edge of the chair and reached for Mary's hand. "Ana and I were best friends for a long time. We called ourselves blood sisters. I was the timid one. Ana taught me that nobody wins anything by sitting on the sidelines, waiting for things to happen."

Mary clicked her tongue and said, "But—"

Quinn kept talking, a train on a schedule, not to be delayed. "Ana did something years ago to hurt me and push me back into my cocoon, afraid to take a chance on living. But since her death, I've felt a stirring from her spirit. Ana's the one responsible for getting me into this mess from the very beginning, but now I see Ana as guiding me out of it. I know this is the right thing to do, and I'm going to do it."

Mary's hands were gripped in a tight ball. "I can't support this. At least promise me you won't do anything until you discuss this with Schmidt. That's all I ask." She sat for a minute, arms folded. "Oh, and don't put me in the middle between you and Jack, either."

Quinn set Calvin down and gave Mary a hug. "Thanks for understanding. I wouldn't dare move forward without Schmidt, or my attorney, David Becker, either." Quinn moved back to the laundry basket and picked up one of Jack's T-shirts. As she shook it out and folded it, she said, "I guess I'll have to tell Jack. I hate to put him in the position of keeping secrets from our parents, but they would never understand."

"If you have doubts, Quinn, don't do this. You don't have to risk your life, and you don't owe Ana Renfroe anything."

"That may be true," Quinn said, as she smoothed the wrinkles out of her brother's shirt. "The person I have to do this for isn't Ana—it's me."

Chapter Eighty-two

That afternoon, after sharing her plan with Mary, Quinn worked in her house, while Officer Porter stood guard outside. Every room of the house had been turned inside out and upside down. More than a few hours' work lay ahead, but Quinn attacked the job methodically, taking one room at a time. She wouldn't finish in one day, but there was one thing she wanted to accomplish while she was alone in the house, and it involved the letters from Ana in her scrapbook.

The first room to receive a make-over was the kitchen. Quinn started with her precious orchids, which had been unpotted. Soil was scattered all over. Quinn had taken the plants to Jack's house, where she'd repotted them into empty jars, using dirt from his backyard garden. Now she opened a new bag of bark and perlite and transplanted the orchids into their original containers. She mixed plant food with water and gave the flowers their regular nourishment, setting them back into the kitchen window. She smiled at the hope that they would survive and re-bloom. She wished the same for herself.

Next, she tackled silverware, dishes, and glassware. These had been strewn about on the counters, kitchen table, and floor. The thought of Blackie or his cohorts having touched her dinnerware made her stomach flip over. She couldn't put them back in their places without running them all through the dishwasher.

Wearing gloves and using rags and anti-bacterial cleaning products, she proceeded to wipe down the kitchen and breakfast area, while listening to a YouTube playlist through her ear buds. From the kitchen, she moved to the bathroom. These were the two hardest-hit areas of the house. She was on her hands and knees, scrubbing the inside of the cabinet under the sink, when her cell phone rang.

It was Becker. Quinn pulled off her gloves and wiped her forehead and upper lip before accepting the call.

"Sorry it's taken me so long to get back to you. Everything okay?"

She could picture him sitting at his desk, tapping his pen against the edge. The twinge in her stomach had become a stab, and the deep breath she took did nothing to make it better. "I want to run something past you, but before I do, I want to clarify. Having immunity from prosecution in Dawn's murder means I'm able to cooperate with the police, correct?"

"Y-e-s-s-s," Becker said. "In fact, you're *expected* to cooperate with the police. Where is this leading?"

"Well, if I'm expected to cooperate with the police, are *they* expected to cooperate with *me*?"

Becker grunted. "Quinn, why don't you tell me what's going on?"

Quinn had planned a personal and passionate explanation of why she needed to lure Blackie to the burial spot so the police could capture him, but she could tell by Becker's curtness that she'd better cut to the chase. She told him her plan as concisely as possible. "I wanted to share this with you before I talk to Sergeant Schmidt."

"What?" Something slammed at Becker's end. "You've got to be out of your mind! I can't let you offer yourself as bait to the police. That's out of the question."

"Don't you see? I have to do this. If I don't, Blackie will walk—no, run—away, and I'll spend the rest of my life worrying about when he'll be coming after me again."

"What makes you think the police won't catch this Blackie without you? They have better resources, better training. This is ridiculous."

"Please—" Quinn wanted to hang up and run away, not so much from her lawyer's words, as from his tone of voice. Becker's criticism stung like a million hornets. If only she could make him understand.

"I'm sorry, Quinn. I can't stop you from carrying out what I consider to be a reckless and foolish plan, but I can't continue to advise or represent you under these circumstances. If you're hell-bent on doing this, I'll have Ethel draft a letter of termination."

The word slashed her in the solar plexus, as if it were a sword. She hadn't anticipated this much resistance. The easy thing to do would be to give in, let the police go after Blackie in their own way. But she had been sitting on this egg for a while, now, warming and nurturing it. She wanted it to hatch, even if it meant losing Becker's support.

Quinn took in a deep breath and let it out slowly. "That makes me sadder than I can put into words, but my mind is made up. I've got to put my whole effort where it will make a difference. Blackie has gotten away with crimes against women for too long. He has to be stopped."

After she disconnected from the call with Becker, Quinn sat cross-legged on the floor of her bathroom, reviewing the plusses and minuses of her plan. She wasn't naïve about the inherent dangers, but she was convinced she had them covered.

The kitchen and bathroom were tidy, and Quinn's energy was flagging. The rest of the house could wait. Right now, she had two important things to do. First, she gathered the pieces of the disguise she had worn to Heaven's Door. Then she found her high school scrapbook lying on the floor of her closet next to a pile of opened shoe boxes. She carried it to the small desk where her laptop and printer were set up. Fortunately, these had been undisturbed by Blackie's vandals. *Of course, they weren't looking for online info. They were looking for a key.*

Quinn opened a new word document and started typing:

> Dear Quinn,
>
> I know I've hurt you, and I'm truly sorry. You were the best friend I ever had. I didn't appreciate that until I lost you. Things are bad with me and Brad, and you're the only one I can tell. It's a long story, but Brad was desperate for money, and I made the mistake of telling him about Dawn's murder. He knows everything, including where we buried the ID bracelet. And something I never told you—that Dawn's killer was my uncle. Brad has gone off the deep end, and our marriage is finished. I have reason to believe my life might be in danger, and yours, too. If something happens to me, please find my uncle and show him where we buried the ID bracelet. He goes by "Blackie" and runs the strip club, Heaven's Door. If Blackie gets his bracelet back, there won't be anything to tie him to Dawn's murder. I promise you'll be safe then. And don't tell anyone—especially Brad. Blackie isn't the worst guy—Brad is.

While she printed out the letter, Quinn opened her scrapbook and located the letters Ana had written her. She studied Ana's fat, calligraphy lettering, the way she formed capital A's that looked like the outlines of long flipped hairdos with a broad tilde across the middle. Using a medium felt tip pen, she practiced signing "Ana" until she matched the original signature. Then she signed the letter and set it down to dry.

Next, she removed a plain envelope from the desk drawer. Ana had written, "Quinn," with the same wide, rounded letters. Quinn practiced making the 'Q' with the same precision as she had before. When she was satisfied that her forgery was perfect, she wrote her own name on the front of the envelope. She folded the note and inserted it into the envelope. She left it unsealed.

Finally, she used the felt tip pen to print two sentences in block letters on the top of the flap. "DO NOT OPEN. GIVE TO QUINN." Setting the envelope down to dry, Quinn marveled at the fiction she'd created. She hated having to slam Brad that way, but she was confident that Ana would have approved of the lie if it meant bringing her killer to justice. In this small way, Quinn felt the support of Ana, and even Brad. Everyone else might have abandoned her for undertaking such a risky plot, but her best friend and her first love were right there with her.

Chapter Eighty-three

Having had Mary Hallom and Mr. Becker shut her down for her plan to capture Blackie, Quinn knew what she had to do to persuade Sergeant Schmidt—she'd tell him she was going to carry out her plan, with or without police backup. Her resolve was stronger than the chains that had bound her wrists and ankles. Blackie's desire for the money Brad had stolen and hidden had driven him to take big risks in kidnapping Quinn and searching her home. She had to strike now, while she held the Queen of Spades.

There were two big hurdles. The first was to convince Schmidt. Quinn wanted to get this over with as soon as possible.

When she returned to Jack's house, she was relieved to find her brother gone. Taking advantage of the privacy, Quinn called Schmidt and told him what she intended to do. "Don't try to talk me out of it. My mind is made up."

Schmidt pitched a fit, as predicted, but once Quinn explained her reasoning, he acquiesced. "Well, if you're going to go rogue on us, I suppose we'll have to back you up. When can you come in for a planning session?"

"How about eight o'clock tomorrow morning? We can put the plan into action right away, and by tomorrow night, you should have your killer in custody."

"That soon? Why don't you come in tonight, then? That will give us more time to strategize."

"Don't worry," Quinn said. "I already have everything planned out. Besides, I have something important to do tonight." She clicked off the call and punched the air with a fist. That had been easier than expected.

Now if she could just clear the next hurdle so well. Quinn had promised Josh that she would communicate more openly with him, and she owed it to him and to their relationship to let him know what she was about to do. She didn't expect him to approve, but she wanted him to understand.

Hoping her brother would give them alone-time again tonight, she planned what to say and how to say it. In an earlier text, Josh had mentioned bringing dinner from The Spot. Quinn looked forward to the large, juicy hamburgers, loaded with toppings. Maybe the hearty meal would make the lump in her throat disappear.

That lump was all about Josh, not about Blackie. Ever since she had made up her mind to help capture Blackie, Quinn had relaxed into a peaceful state of mind, certain she was doing the right thing. An aura of calm surrounded her, and her hands were warmer than they'd been in days. To fill the time before getting ready for Josh's arrival, she played with Calvin while doing push-ups, sit-ups, deep knee bends, and jogging in place. Her regular jogging routine had been hampered by the police protection, and she needed to be fit for tomorrow night.

* * *

Conversation over the hamburgers had strayed from clean-up efforts at Quinn's house and new antibacterial procedures being put in place in the surgical areas of the hospital to plans for Thanksgiving at the Bradys' house. "Do you think your parents will mind your not being here with *them* this year?"

Quinn pleated her paper napkin into narrow folds and used it to fan herself, geisha-style. "I don't know, honestly. I've never spent a Thanksgiving away from them. There were a couple of holidays when Ana ate with my family, but never vice versa." Quinn's parents would probably be so thrilled that she and Josh were becoming more serious, they'd push her out the door without a twinge. "Maybe Jack will invite Mary. That will take their minds away from missing me."

Josh took one of Quinn's hands in both of his. "Our first major holiday together. Means a lot."

"Maybe we could spend Christmas together with *my* family. Do you think your parents would like to come here?" Quinn eased her hand from between Josh's and picked up her napkin again, twisting it into a corkscrew shape. Planning ahead beyond tomorrow night felt frivolous and dishonest. Her tasty dinner sat in a clump, lodged in her stomach.

"What's wrong?" Josh's lopsided smile disappeared, and his grayish eyes bored holes into hers.

"Let's go into the bedroom. There's something I need to share with you, and I don't want Jack to walk in while we're talking." Quinn led the way, her heart in her throat.

The futon in Jack's guest room had been pulled away from the wall and converted into a bed and had remained that way since Quinn had been staying there. There was no other place to sit in the crowded room, and the futon was more comfortable for reclining than for sitting. "Have a seat," Quinn said, as she turned on the goose-neck lamp on the dresser. The room's only window faced east, so the natural light seeping through the blinds was evaporating.

When she and Josh had entered this room before, it was with a playful and passionate spirit, but this time was different. Josh sat, ramrod-straight on the edge of the futon, waiting. Quinn sat next to her love and brought his hand to her lips.

"I have something important to tell you, but I need to look you in the eye to say it."

"You're scaring me, Quinn. Just say it."

"No, let's lie down, so I can look at you."

Josh stretched out on his side, facing the door, his usual spot. Quinn positioned herself opposite, her head propped on her bent arm. She may never have seen a more handsome face, staring at her with anticipation, or perhaps fear. Had those faint lines at the outer corners of Josh's eyes been there before, or was she causing his face to be marked with worry?

Taking a deep breath, she launched into her prepared speech. "Those hours when I was kidnapped—I had a lot of time to think. I thought about you, about us, how much our relationship means to me—"

"Same for me. I was frantic that I would lose you."

"Let me finish." Quinn touched his arm. "I thought of how frustrated you'd been, how I'd kept secrets from you, not wanting to, but having to. I swore if I got out of that horrible place, I would never leave your side again."

Josh propped himself on an elbow and touched Quinn's cheek.

"And I never want to. I'm happy for our time together, but, let's face it, this isn't ideal." She waved her arm to indicate the futon and the sparse quarters. "Our privacy depends on Jack's inconvenience, and the police watch every time I breathe. I hate being under so much scrutiny, but I know it's a privilege, and a temporary one, at that. What will happen when the police are no longer there? Will Blackie or his cohorts come after me again?" Quinn's voice rose with the angry fear that filled every space of her brain, and she paused to tone it down.

"I can't go out to run, I can't work, and I feel like I'm caught in a trap. True, it's not as bad as being chained to a bed somewhere, but it's not a *real* life. I've put my home at risk, you, Calvin—everyone I love. I've got to change this, or I'll lose my mind."

"But how—"

"I'm going to work with the police. Tomorrow night. We're going to lure Blackie to a place where he thinks he'll find the money he's been looking for. We're going to get him there and then they'll arrest him."

In the dim, indirect light, Josh's face went pale. "Why can't the police do this without you?"

"The police haven't caught him in over fifteen years. He's not dumb. He wants what I have, but he's not going to take any more chances." For all Quinn's bravado, she wasn't positive that Blackie would take her bait, either. But she had to try. "If everything goes according to plan, tomorrow night we can go back to living our normal lives." She pasted a smile on her face and squeezed Josh's hand.

"And if it doesn't?" His voice was a whisper.

"I refuse to go there. Blackie may have gotten away with murder, and sex trafficking, and heaven knows what else, but this is the end of the line for him. Trust me."

Josh wrapped his free arm around her waist and drew her closer. "I do trust you. I admire your courage, but I'm also afraid. I worry that you're taking such a big—risk."

Quinn's eyes were even with his Adam's apple, which bobbed as he spoke. She leaned her head back until their eyes met. "What if something really dangerous happened at the hospital—like a toxic spill, or a pandemic? Wouldn't you want to face it head-on, do what you believed was best?"

He hesitated. "Yes, but—that's different. That's my profession."

"It's still a choice you would have to make, to risk your health and well-being." She wrapped her arm around his side and pressed him to her. "And if you did, I would be worried, too. But I would support you, because I would know that you were doing what you believed was right."

Josh rolled Quinn over on top of him, so they were gazing into each other's eyes. "Okay, my love. You've got my support. I'll be a wreck until you tell me it's over, but I appreciate your trusting me with this."

Quinn couldn't ask for more. As her lips moved in for a long kiss, she closed her eyes and let what happened next force thoughts of Blackie and policemen and buried treasure far, far away.

Chapter Eighty-four

Early on the morning of Quinn's planned trap for Blackie, Quinn sat at the table in Chief Ramirez's conference room with Sergeant Schmidt. The chief wasn't due in for another hour, and, considering his friendship with her father, Quinn was glad. It'd been hard enough to get Schmidt and Josh on board, but she doubted anything she could say or do would convince her father to support her plan.

Armed with the forged letter from 'Ana', a diagram of the Frenches' backyard and alley, and a tepid cup of tea, Quinn was ready for her part of the battle. How and when the police would handle the arrest would be up to Schmidt.

For his part, Schmidt's eyes were shaded by crumpled brows, and his head tilt reminded her of Calvin's, though less endearing. "I don't know about this. We've got to weigh your protection against Blackie's ability to see through this set-up. For example, I'd like you to wear a bullet-proof vest under your clothes, but that bulk would be an instant tip-off." He picked up the diagram and taped it to the white board across from the table. Using a pointer, he showed how little cover there was for police units. "The garage has no opening, except to the alley. Not a good spot for surveillance or reaction time. One solution is for us to be inside the house. Right here." He pointed to the window overlooking the back porch.

"That would mean involving Mr. and Mrs. French. And Blackie is Mr. French's brother."

"Yes, but estranged, and he also probably killed Mr. French's only daughter. The Frenches will be supportive. Besides, we'd get them out of the house anyway. They wouldn't be safe if there was a shoot-out, and we don't want any lights on in the house to spook Blackie."

It felt like a rock was lodged in Quinn's throat. Her risk was multiplying by the minute. "We need to put something in the ground for Blackie to find, since you've taken the ID bracelet and key."

"Way ahead of you. One of our officers has already planted some fakes and covered over them. You'll find them under the eighth geranium plant from the concrete steps." He pointed to the spot on the diagram. "By the way, we located the storage unit where Brad hid the money. Close to three million, cash."

"What happens to that money? Do the police get to keep it?"

"Yes. It goes into a fund for equipment and training. We can't use it for personnel." Schmidt shifted in his chair. "Let's go back to the plan. My guess is Blackie will have you do the digging." He brushed the sides of his crew cut with both hands. "How are you planning to get this guy to the scene?"

Quinn showed him the letter and held her breath while he read it.

"Ana wrote this? How did you get it?"

"*I* wrote it. My plan is to show it to the stripper, Skye Blue. Remember, Nell said that Skye Blue and Ana were close."

Schmidt's mouth stretched into a gum-revealing expression that could've been a smile under other circumstances. "No guarantee that Blackie's gonna fall for this. He's probably seen our patrol cars protecting you. He's too smart to walk into a trap like this. Unless he has a plan of his own. That's what worries me. This could turn into a hostage situation in a hot minute." He rolled his chair back and stood, propping both arms on the table. "No offense, but this plan smacks of amateur thinking. I'm asking you one more time to back out."

Quinn had expected this, but she had come too far now. Retreating was not an option. "I've planned for that, too. I'm going to tell Skye that I'm acting on my own. I don't trust the police because they suspect me in Ana's murder."

"Let's do a little mental practice." He spent the next few minutes reviewing potential movements Quinn might make under specific circumstances. "You need to have an exit strategy, so you can duck out of the way when we try to take him down. Here or here," Schmidt said, pointing to the diagram, "whichever is fastest, based on your proximity to danger. Whichever route you choose, you must get out of the way fast."

Quinn nodded, as Schmidt blocked out her possible movements on the chart. She would be an actor on a stage, William Tell's son with the apple on her head. "We will have officers poised to act from various sight lines. You don't need to know where. The trick is not to have anything in the environment look unusual or out of place." He stared at the drawing of the Frenches' backyard for a long while, running his fingers back and forth, as if measuring the distances from the garden to the alley to the garage. "What we need is an ordinary spot for an officer to hide—like right here." He pointed to an empty spot in the yard near the garage.

"Like a dumpster?" Quinn asked.

Schmidt's eyes lit up. "Something like that." he exhaled, hissing through his teeth. "You're a resourceful young lady. Resourceful and courageous."

At the moment, Quinn didn't feel resourceful *or* courageous. She felt like a powerful, whirring machine—a buzz saw or a bulldozer—fueled, charged, and ready.

Chapter Eighty-five

Getting hold of Skye Blue's contact information was easy. Explaining how she'd gotten it was not. Even if Skye and Blackie didn't know that Nell was in protective custody, no one would have seen Nell at the club since Norm's death.

Calling Skye's cell phone was out of the question. Quinn would have to go to Heaven's Door in person. This first step in the plan provided Quinn with the first bit of risk, but also the first bit of freedom in days. Schmidt had provided her with an unmarked police car. She dressed in the same outfit she'd worn when she and Josh had gone to Heaven's Door, including the blonde wig. She waited until 6:00 p.m., a time when she hoped Skye would be working.

The sun was still adding heat to the thick, humid air. Five other cars occupied spots in the parking lot. Pounding music and the distinct aroma of garlic assailed Quinn's senses as she approached the vermillion-painted door.

Inside, it was nighttime. The same loud music and flashing lights, the same lighted stages and performers, though the audience was sparse. Quinn paid the cover charge and strolled past the Alpine-costumed, semi-dressed waitresses, past the buffet tables already loaded with entrees. She moved slowly, taking in the shows on the first and second stages, trying not to call attention to herself, a single woman in a strip club. Neither of the dancers looked like Skye, who, as Quinn recalled, had huge breasts, a tiny waist, and a mane of thick, shoulder-length, dark hair.

A stocky man wearing a business suit and a plastic grin accosted Quinn. "Welcome to Heaven's Door. Can I help you find your heart's delight?"

Quinn's heart beat a little faster. Her heart's delight was cloaked in secrecy and subterfuge. "Thank you," she said. "Right now, I'm looking for the nearest ladies' room."

She looked around, keeping her face angled away from his, her eyes half-covered by the blonde bangs.

"Right behind you." He pointed to the door she had just passed, clearly marked 'WOMEN'.

"Well, if it had teeth, it would've bitten me." Quinn pivoted and headed for the restroom, calling thanks over her shoulder. Once inside, she went to the row of sinks, ignoring the posters of naked men on the walls. Resting her palms against one of the sinks, she gathered her energy. She hadn't imagined how exposed she would feel without Josh. *Better get used to it. The next several hours will be a one-woman show, and this is the part that you auditioned for.*

Quinn wondered what to do next. She looked in the mirror and found a tiny glob of mascara to remove from under one eye. She fluffed the wig's layers, marveling at the fiery calm of the face staring back at her, more like daring Ana than timid Quinn.

She opened her slingbag to check on the forged letter in its envelope. A tube of lip gloss sat next to it. As she drew the stick over her top lip, the door opened with a whoosh, admitting notes of Amtrac's "Between the Lines," and a slim, dark-haired beauty, saying, "Shit. Of all the times for the dressing room toilet to back up."

Dressed in a silk shirt with rhinestone buttons, unbuttoned to the waist, and pale blue, ripped-knee jeans with rhinestone studs down the outer seams, the girl carried a fur-trimmed see-through jacket over her arm and a vinyl makeup kit in her hand. Humming to the music, she strode to the sink next to Quinn and peered at herself in the mirror. Leaving the makeup kit on the edge of the sink, she set the jacket on the purple love seat in the corner of the room.

Quinn forced herself not to stare. She couldn't believe her luck. This was definitely Skye, and a faulty toilet had thrown the stripper smack-dab into Quinn's path. She continued to primp, as if her insides weren't screaming.

"Hey," Skye said, as she unzipped her makeup kit and rummaged through it. Pulling out a tube of mascara, she turned to appraise Quinn. "Hey, haven't I seen you here before?"

Quinn sucked in a breath. This was the perfect opening. "Actually, yes. I was here with my boyfriend, looking for Blackie. You told me about him, remember?"

Skye nodded, giving Quinn a head-to-toe once-over. Quinn returned the favor, wondering what this pretty young woman saw in someone like Blackie, who was almost twice her age and probably abusive.

"In fact, I was hoping to find *you*. I've got an important message for Blackie. I need you to tell him right away." She smiled as she spoke, a sprinkling of sugar on the ground glass.

Skye's eyes met Quinn's and then shifted, as if to make sure they were alone in the room. "What makes you think I can get a message to Blackie?"

"You're my best hope." Quinn continued to smile. "It's a long story, but Blackie's looking for something, and I know where it is. I got this letter from a friend of mine who died. Her parents gave it to me." She pulled the letter from her purse and showed it to Skye.

The dancer skimmed the letter and stared at Quinn, who grabbed it and stuffed it back into her purse. Before Skye could comment, Quinn rushed ahead. "I'm planning to leave town tomorrow. If Blackie wants his money, now is the time. Tell him to meet me in the alley behind DeeDee Young's house at ten o'clock tonight. No weapons, no funny business. And tell him I'm not doing this for him. I'm doing it for Ana."

Quinn closed her purse, mission accomplished. She was especially gratified when Skye repeated, "DeeDee Young's at ten o'clock." It had been a stroke of genius to use Dawn's stage name from the videos—something Blackie would surely remember, but Skye likely wouldn't. As Quinn walked past the skimpy jacket lying on the loveseat, she called out, "Thanks."

The die was cast—there'd be no turning back now. Her internal motor whirring, Quinn walked out of Heaven's Door. She hoped never to be back.

Chapter Eighty-six

Quinn drove back to Jack's, pretending that she wasn't being tailed, that she no longer needed to be. If all went well tonight, she'd finally be free. The taste of freedom swirled in her mouth like cotton candy, airy, sweet, and elusive.

On the way, she passed through the alley behind the Frenches', rolling down the window. Their yard was the picture of ordinary, except for the green metal dumpster that stood next to the garage. Quinn smiled to herself. Hopefully, Blackie would accept the dumpster as part of the landscape. In the few seconds it took to roll past the small yard, Quinn smelled over-ripe figs on the gnarly old tree, and the pungency of garbage, peeking through the cracked lids of plastic cans. The raucous-red geraniums decorated the otherwise-plain backyard. The ordinary sights and smells provided only a little reassurance to Quinn, whose adrenalin had already started to build. In a few short hours, this modest backyard would be the scene of a major police sting—*if* Blackie showed up.

Meanwhile, Quinn needed to prepare herself, mentally and physically. In karate class, she had learned about the Okinawan diet, low in calories, but high in nutrition. Her master had stressed never to eat past being eighty percent full, especially before fighting. "A full belly makes for a weak stance," was his saying. As she pulled to a stop in front of Jack's house, she visualized the food stored in her brother's cabinets and refrigerator. Maybe some seared tuna, edamame, and green tea would fit the bill. She could fix enough for Jack, too.

She would have to confide in him. He would have too many questions about where she was going at night, by herself, without police protection. Tumbleweeds rolled about in her belly. Becker and Schmidt, and even Josh, were easy audiences compared to her brother, who knew her longest. Jack would want to protect her. He always had.

Calvin met her at the door, wagging and yipping. Jack was standing at the stove, wearing an apron over his shorts and polo shirt, putting something in the oven. The smell of teriyaki sauce wafted in the air, as Quinn picked up Calvin and strode to greet the chef. "What're you cooking?"

"Searing some ahi tuna. Sound good?"

"Perfect." Shaking her head at the culinary coincidence, Quinn stroked Calvin between the eyes and gathered her nerve to tell Jack what she was about to do. Before she could utter the first word, he turned on the microwave, and the mild aroma of edamame filled her nostrils. "Exactly the meal I was planning to cook," she said.

Jack's eyes met hers. "I know."

"You know what I was planning to cook?"

"No, I know what you're planning to do tonight. Mary told me. Don't be mad at her. She knows how important you are to me, and she couldn't stand to see me left out in the cold, not knowing. I remembered what you used to eat on karate nights, so I figured you'd want something light." He smiled, straight teeth that shone more than the dull light of his eyes.

"You don't approve?"

"No, but I know I can't stop you. You're a grown woman, and I trust you've weighed the risks and benefits."

Quinn set the dog down and hugged her brother. "I was going to tell you myself. I needed for you to know."

The microwave *dinged*, and Jack dumped the edamame from the package into a bowl. He removed the tuna from the broiler and sliced it thinly. "Let's eat," he said in a husky voice.

As long as it's not 'The Last Supper,' Quinn thought.

Chapter Eighty-seven

At nine-thirty, Quinn left Jack's house on foot. She had only five blocks to walk to get to the alley between Dawn's house and the Frenches'. She'd dressed in a pair of light green leggings, an eggshell-colored tank top, and a matching nylon jacket, tied around her waist—the outfit she had described in detail to Schmidt. The heat from the July sun still hadn't dissipated, and an oleander-scented mugginess hung in the air around her. Whether from the thick air, her heightened senses, or the gnawing tugs inside, Quinn struggled to breathe normally.

With each step, she pictured the diagram of the scene, reviewing the strategic points of exit Schmidt had suggested. Blackie, as she'd last seen him, hovering over her chained body, was taller, thinner, and older than Norm. He should be less overpowering if things got physical. On the other hand, she had used the element of surprise on Norm, and Blackie might be prepared for her karate moves. And, despite her "no weapons" instructions, he might have a gun.

She strode through the neighborhood, chin up, chest raised, shoulders relaxed. Here and there a dog barked, or lights from a television punctuated the landscape.

She *could* chicken out. Nobody would blame her. Nobody had asked her to risk her life, but getting rid of the threat of Blackie overrode every self-doubt. The old Quinn hadn't disappeared entirely, but the new, strong Quinn shook her by the shoulders and said, *You have to do this. Your whole life has been a path to this moment. You have everything it takes to conquer Blackie and all the evil he represents. Don't think—just do. And you'll never be safe until he's caught.*

The police were supposedly ahead of her, already in place. Some were probably behind her, as well. The invisible protection bolstered her as she slowed pace, her steps making soft, shuffling sounds in the gravel. The alley was dimly lit by the same corner streetlight that had illuminated Blackie's retreat from Dawn's house, the falling ID bracelet, all those years ago. Everything had come full circle, and that same streetlight stood as a sentinel.

By contrast, a rectangular patch of light, emanating from the back porch, illuminated the Frenches' backyard. Neighboring yards on both sides remained dark. All of this had been choreographed by Sergeant Schmidt, but it looked random and natural, like other yards Quinn had passed to get here. Quinn moved to the gnarled old fig tree. In fifteen years, it had increased its spread, but the U-shaped curve where she and Ana had secreted themselves was still there. She removed the light jacket from her waist and put it on, possible protection for her arms and shoulders if she needed it. Lowering herself into the fig tree's makeshift chair, pulling the broad, pungent leaves around her, she was as ready as she'd ever be.

A few minutes later, crunching sounds announced someone's approach. Quinn's view from the fig tree encompassed the back of Dawn's old house, that portion of the alley, and the front and side of the Frenches' garage. The footsteps came from the east, though, and the person was out of view. Quinn wanted to swing her body from the tree and run to the alley to see who was there, but she knew better. Right now, she had the advantage.

Several more seconds passed without a sound or a glimpse of the person in the alley. Maybe it wasn't even a person. Maybe it was a dog, scouting for food from the garbage cans. Quinn considered easing herself from her hiding place, moving along the edge of the garage, and peeking into the alley.

Before she could do that, a shadowy figure, tall and thin, appeared at the edge of the dumpster. He moved about the back of the yard, stepping slowly and keeping to the darkness. As he came closer to the fig tree, Quinn saw him clearly in the moonlight, the pinned-back ears, the black clothes—pants, shirt, cowboy boots, and raincoat. He carried a revolver, and as he moved, he waved it in front of him, like a flashlight. *Good, he's on edge, probably even more than I am.*

Blackie turned toward the alley and started to walk away, when Quinn emerged from the fig tree, behind him, whispering. "Hello, Mr. Lionel French. Shall we go digging?"

Blackie swung around, pointing the weapon directly at Quinn's midriff even as he looked around the yard. His mouth contorted into a teeth-baring, joyless smile. His breath was sour. "Glad you decided to do the right thing. Too bad Ana didn't step up sooner. I only want what's rightfully mine." He pulled a six-inch gardening spade from the pocket of the raincoat. His face shone with sweat.

"Glad to see you brought equipment," Quinn said. "It's going to take you a while with that small spade."

"Take *you* a while, not me." He pushed the tool toward Quinn and used his gun to nudge her away from the tree. "Let's get this done."

Quinn grasped the spade, wondering how effective it would be as a weapon, combined with a karate punch. Compared to the power of a firearm, probably not at all. "If I'd known you wanted me to dig, I wouldn't have worn my best workout outfit."

"Shut up and get moving. Where's this burial spot?" He gave a rough shove to Quinn's shoulder.

Quinn rolled her shoulder back. "No need to be gruff. Since we're on the same side now, how about telling me why you killed Dawn?"

"Not that it's any of your business, but she got too big for her britches. She wanted too much from too many people. That makes you very unpopular in this business."

Quinn thought of the millions of women who were unpopular and dispensable in the adult entertainment business—Dawn, Ana, Nell, and even herself. She walked into the lighted portion of the yard. When she reached the flower bed on the east side, she stared at the area, pretending to measure the distance from the steps to the digging spot. She was actually counting.

Trying to forget that a loaded revolver was held to the back of her head, Quinn crouched in front of the flower bed. She used the tip of the shovel to draw a big rectangle around the seventh, eighth, and ninth geraniums. Their earthy smell filled her nostrils with memories of the night of Dawn's death. She had hated that smell ever since.

"How long's it gonna take to dig out that spot? I haven't got all night."

"If you'd brought a real shovel, it wouldn't take long at all," Quinn said, over her shoulder. Unlike her inquisitor, she wasn't in any hurry. As long as she didn't find the bracelet and the key, Blackie would have reason to keep her alive.

Blackie squatted close behind her, peering over her shoulder. "Nothing's perfect. We all just have to deal." His breath on her back was hot—perhaps the devil's own.

Quinn scraped away at the dirt. The police had done such a good job of making the garden look untouched—the dirt had been compacted tightly. Her energy was concentrated, not on soil, but on Blackie. She pictured herself as a coiled snake, ready to go into action.

Blackie paced behind her, the rhythm of his steps staccato. Now and again the tip of a cowboy boot poked her in the back, a reminder of who was in charge.

Quinn had removed the seventh, eighth, and ninth tall geraniums, leaning them against the outer wall of the house, where an open space elevated the house by about two feet. All the houses in the neighborhood, including Jack's, had been built up to prevent flooding from hurricanes. Perspiration dripped from her forehead and stung her eyes as she dug in the dirt. When one hand cramped, she switched. So far, the hole was broad and shallow, only about three inches deep.

"This is taking too long," Blackie said. A black cowboy boot came over her shoulder, and kicked at the dirt and spade, where Quinn's hand had been. "Now, see what you can do, and hurry."

Quinn struggled in the dim light to plunge deep enough and angle the handle to pull it out with a dirt-load. She began working harder and faster, her hands moving apart from her thinking. Her efforts in the oppressive heat reminded her of gravedigging, and she shuddered.

Finally, the hole was substantially deeper, about six inches, and the shovel hit against something solid. The sound was just a thump, but enough to draw Blackie's attention.

"Faster," he said, as Quinn shoveled around the square aluminum lock box. When she and Ana had buried the ID bracelet, they hadn't housed it in any such fancy container, so this was new. Either Brad had brought the six-inch square box to the site, or the police had. Blackie crouched next to her so he could gaze into the hole while he jabbed her in the back with his gun.

"Open it," he said, breathing onto the back of her neck.

Quinn pulled the metal box out of the hole, dusting off the clinging dirt. She opened the box, revealing a broken glinting ID bracelet and a thick industrial-sized key. The originals were locked up at the police station, but these were good imitations. "These what you're looking for?" She rose from the ground, clutching the open box against her chest.

"I'll take that," Blackie said, reaching in and snatching the bracelet and the key from the box. He shoved them into a coat pocket.

Quinn turned to see the gun pointed at her temple, Blackie's finger on the trigger, and she flew into action. A karate block knocked Blackie's aim off, and she punched with the spade, aiming for the area beneath his belt. The tool connected with flesh, and Blackie uttered a howl, but Quinn didn't stick around to assess the damage.

Quinn drew herself into a compact cylinder and rolled into the open space beneath the Frenches' house, the place where she and Ana had hidden so many years ago. Dirt and debris stuck to her skin and clothes as she moved, but she kept rolling, until she was several feet under the house.

Blackie, who had fallen to the ground from the shovel-punch, had picked himself up and fired off a shot. Under the house, Quinn was protected like a turtle, but anyone could fire a shot beneath the house. She couldn't stay there. She scooted on her back, moving toward the front of the house, but keeping her eye on the backyard, as much as she could see from that perspective.

Without warning, a mega-watt flash of light and a loud cracking noise filled the space. The wood frame house couldn't protect her from the explosion, and Quinn trembled, wondering whether she would be blinded, deafened, or crushed. A plaintive yowl came from the backyard, and thumping boots surrounded the shrieking Blackie.

As much as she wanted to stay to make sure Blackie was taken down, Quinn had promised Sergeant Schmidt that she would exit. She rolled to the front edge of the house, got up from her knees and sprinted, faster than her dirt-caked running shoes had ever run, her arms pumping a breeze in the air where there was none.

Sirens pierced the night behind her, but she kept running. Her breath was coming in gasps, but she kept sprinting. By the time she reached Jack's block, she had an escort behind her—the headlights of a patrol car. Forgetting about how she must look, filthy and bedraggled, Quinn dashed up the driveway, and Mary Hallom parked the squad car and jumped out to climb the steps behind Quinn.

Standing at the front door was the happiest, handsomest, and heartiest welcoming committee Quinn had ever seen—Josh, Jack, and a barking, pointy-eared Westie.

Chapter Eighty-eight

"We did it!" Quinn's smile radiated through her whole body, as Josh held her aloft in a victory twirl. "No more Blackie, no more threats. Woohoo!" She glanced at Mary to be sure what she was celebrating was true.

"*You* did it, Quinn. Blackie's been captured. You led a successful sting operation, and you're not even a trained policewoman. My hat's off to you." She removed her hat and waved it.

Josh set Quinn down, and the four of them adjourned to the living room. Quinn sat on Josh's lap, thinking she never wanted to move. She closed her eyes and leaned into his chest. "That was some strong flash of light, and my ears are still ringing. How long is that going to last?"

Mary peered into Quinn's face. "Let me get you a glass of water. Flash bang images stun, but usually last just a few seconds. The ringing of the ears can last a couple of hours, though."

Josh nodded. "Water would be good." He asked Quinn some questions about what she was seeing and hearing presently, then said, "Let's see if we can make it go away this way." He kissed her as if he'd never let go, and Quinn was sure she'd found Nirvana. If all the difficult experiences of her life had led her to this moment, with this man, they were worth it.

Quinn guzzled the water, amazed by how parched she was. As she held the glass to her mouth, her dirty hand and sleeve—in fact, her entire body—screamed for attention. "OMG, I need to take a shower right this minute." She gave Josh another kiss, before jumping off his lap. "I don't know how you could stand me, looking like this. I must stink, too."

Josh laughed. "You could be covered in the slimiest muck of all time, and I would still love you."

Quinn looked at Jack, and the two of them said in unison in Mr. Rogers' voice, "I love you just the way you are."

"Mind if I take a shower? I'll be right back."

Jack said, "Go ahead. And I'm going to call Mom and Dad to come over. They need to see you and know you're okay before this hits the internet in the morning."

"You want me to stay or go? Technically, I'm still on duty. Just happens that my assigned duty is tending to our SWAT team hero." Mary moved to give a high five to Quinn, but Quinn hugged her instead.

Jack crossed the room to put his arm around Mary's shoulders and kiss her on the lips. "I want you to stay. I can't think of a better time for my parents to meet my special woman, can you?"

Quinn chuckled, thinking of how surprised her parents would be to learn what both of their children had been up to behind their backs. *We may not be living our lives exactly the way they would have wanted, but we are both, finally, healthy and happy.*

* * *

After Quinn's shower, Joy and John McFarland stopped by for a brief visit. By all accounts, they appeared to be delighted with Jack's girlfriend, especially after hearing what a significant role Mary had played in helping Quinn.

By this time, it was almost 1:30 a.m. Mary told the story of how Quinn had brought down a serial killer, drug dealer, and reputed porn industry and sex-trafficking leader.

Quinn marveled at how Mary exaggerated the heroic parts and minimized the dangerous parts. Her parents hugged her, said how proud they were, and expressed their hopes that everything could return to normal now that the crisis was over.

"By the way," Mary said, "I just heard from headquarters that Blackie's been charged and taken to the hospital. Quinn, you really know how to hit a guy in the private parts."

Jack crouched over, crossing his arms over his middle. "Ouch."

"Quinn, darling," Joy McFarland said. "Dad and I would like to give a little party in your honor. Tomorrow night." She looked from one to another of her children. "The four of you are invited, of course. And Marty Ramirez and Ed Schmidt and their wives."

Leave it to her mother to turn this into a social occasion. "Don't forget David Becker. He's been wonderful." *And Nell. Though she had probably already gone to another city under witness protection by now.*

"Do you think it would be appropriate to invite the Frenches?" Quinn's mother was on a roll.

Quinn thought about all the losses Mr. and Mrs. French had suffered, all that Ana had meant to them—and to her. "I think it would be lovely to include them. Jack can thank them again for his new kidney, and maybe we can cheer them with a few stories from better days."

"Wonderful. I'm sure everyone will have a good time." She stood and reached for her husband's hand. "We'd better go home now. We've got a funeral in a few hours, and a party in its wake."

"Sheesh! Another funeral joke," Quinn said. As much as she hated to admit it, she had missed the joking around these past few weeks.

After their parents departed, Mary said her goodbyes and went back to her patrol duties. Jack yawned and excused himself.

Quinn and Josh walked Calvin for the night. Not having a policeman watching her every move was a particular treat. "Are you tired?" Quinn asked Josh. Thanks to adrenalin, she was still full of energy.

"Not too. I was thinking we might celebrate your heroic victory by spending the night at my apartment. I've got the day off tomorrow, so we can sleep in, and then I can help you get your house back in order."

"Great idea. Jack won't mind taking care of Calvin. He did a great job of it while I was gone."

* * *

Thirty minutes later, Josh popped a cork on a bottle of champagne, and he and Quinn snuggled in his queen-sized bed with their drinks and a 2:00 a.m. snack of pistachios and strawberries. "I'm starving," Quinn said, as she stuffed a handful of nuts into her mouth.

"That's my girl. Glad to see your appetite is intact."

"The Okinawan diet is great for karate, but I couldn't live on edamame for long."

"Have I mentioned that edamame is my favorite food? When we get married, I want to have it at every meal."

Quinn shook her head. The ringing in her ears had subsided, but she didn't believe what she'd just heard. "Say that again."

"That I love edamame more than life itself?" Josh's gray eyes sparkled in the dim light spilling in from the doorway to the kitchen.

"You do not! You love thick steaks, cooked rare, and barbecue, and potato salad. You love seafood and stir-fry and Grand Marnier souffles and—"

Josh laughed, and Quinn giggled, too, both of them more bubbly than the champagne. "That's right," Josh said. "What I *meant* to say was that I love *you* more than life itself. You are the prettiest, cleverest, kindest, and definitely the bravest woman I've ever met. And I want you to be my wife."

Quinn burst into tears. She wasn't sure where the tears came from, but emotions rolled inside as she thought of all she'd been through, all she'd yearned for, and all she wanted for the future. She looked into the eyes of the person she wanted to share the rest of her life with, and she knew for certain, this was the happiest she had ever, ever been.

Author's Note

When Quinn McFarland started whispering in my ear, I became fascinated with her situation, and I couldn't wait to tell her story. To do so, I needed advice from funeral directors Jay Carnes of Carnes Funeral Home in Galveston, Texas, Lee Walasavage of Terry Funeral Home in Downington, Pennsylvania, and Shari Schwartz, who filled me in on certain important ways for caring for the recently departed. Information about Jack's kidney transplant and various medical details related to Josh's fifth year of residency came from Dr. Lora Silverman Durling, Hal and Dr. Jessica Rochkind, and Concetta Maceo Sims. Lauren Martino, Kevin Kinney, and Jay Sims, of the Rosenberg Library in Galveston, Texas, helped me with portraying Quinn's library research on the adult entertainment industry. John Norton assisted me in describing Heartbeat Cabaret and Heaven's Door. I drew inspiration from my own long-ago blood sister ceremony with Cheryl Schraub Gardner and a childhood experience with Rozanne Halfant Rubin.

Many are the questions I put to Lieutenant Destin Sims of the Galveston Police Department. I also consulted with Mike Guarino and Harvey Bazaman regarding Becker's legal maneuverings to protect Quinn.

I am indebted to fellow writers, Susan P. Baker, Phyllis H. Moore, and Gary Hoffman, for their thorough feedback and their invaluable encouragement.

I'm grateful to Eddie Vincent, Cynthia Brackett-Vincent, and Deirdre Wait at Encircle Publications for having faith in *Bad Blood Sisters*, as well as for "dressing up" and improving it.

Last, but not least, a special thanks goes to my husband Ed, whose alpha reading and suggestions throughout the writing process are an invaluable part of this, and every book.

About the Author

Award-winning and bestselling author, **Saralyn Richard** was born with a pen in her hand and ink in her veins. A former educator, she loves connecting with readers. Her humor- and romance-tinged mysteries and children's book pull back the curtain on people in settings as diverse as elite country manor houses and disadvantaged urban high schools. She is also the author of *A Murder of Principal* (Encircle Publications, January 2021), and the Detective Parrott Mysteries. Visit Saralyn's website at http://saralynrichard.com, and sign up for her monthly newsletter to receive special notices, surveys, and other fun content.

If you enjoyed reading this book,
please consider writing your honest review
and sharing it with other readers.

Many of our Authors are happy to participate in
Book Club and Reader Group discussions.
For more information, contact us at info@encirclepub.com.

Thank you,
Encircle Publications

For news about more exciting new fiction, join us at:

Facebook: www.facebook.com/encirclepub

Twitter: twitter.com/encirclepub

Instagram: www.instagram.com/encirclepublications

Sign up for Encircle Publications newsletter and specials:
eepurl.com/cs8taP

CPSIA information can be obtained
at www.ICGtesting.com
Printed in the USA
LVHW041343120322
713311LV00004B/96

9 781645 993209